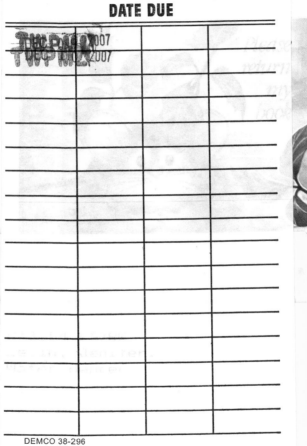

DATE DUE

007			
2007			

GAYLORD S

WATER

JENIFER LEVIN

DANCER

POSEIDON PRESS ⚓ NEW YORK

Copyright © 1982 by Jenifer Levin
All rights reserved
including the right of reproduction
in whole or in part in any form
Published by Pocket Books,
a Simon & Schuster Division
of Gulf & Western Corporation
Simon & Schuster Building
Rockefeller Center
1230 Avenue of the Americas
New York, New York 10020
POSEIDON PRESS is a trademark
of Simon & Schuster
Designed by Edith Fowler
Manufactured in the United States of America

10 9 8 7 6 5 4 3 2 1

Library of Congress Cataloging in Publication Data

Levin, Jenifer.
  Water dancer.

  I. Title.
PS3562.E8896W3   813'.54   82-479
ISBN 0-671-44764-5   AACR2

1

SARGE

S ARGE WOKE UP the way he did every morning, thinking about the kid. It was that half-dream crawling from his intestines up, a black and white image of the way he'd looked out there with capped head bobbing between waves while Sarge leaned over starboard to see. The kid's lips were blue-gray. Daddy Daddy! he screamed, Daddy Daddy Daddy! He was puking up the hot glucose Sarge had passed him on a feeding stick minutes before. He was treading weakly, fingers shriveled to bird's feet by the salt. Stone-gray waves slammed against his shoulders, broke over his face. Daddy help! he screamed, and the wind bent it to a whisper. Daddy! Even in black and white his lips were blue.

Sarge flicked off the alarm before it buzzed 4:30. The water should be cold today, fifty-eight, maybe fifty-nine degrees. He pulled on an extra suit and reached in the drawer for a few caps. Leaving sheets crumpled he walked barefoot through the hallway past his wife's bedroom, past the empty bedroom, past the two dorm rooms with their rows of naked cots and blank shelves. The gym door swung open on squeaking hinges. He ignored the Universal and stepped over some free weights to a mat, bent down, trailing fingers against his toes to the count of thirty. He went through his stretching routine. Reaching inside to turn out the yard light he let the screen click shut behind. Breeze rushed across his chest. He squinted towards the pines and lake. Time to swim. Sarge swam every morning.

White pebbles glowed bas-relief from the lake bottom. When he slipped in water glided around and, after a few seconds, rippled to stillness. Sarge dipped his face into it. He spread his hands on top and in slow circles caressed, moved them gently underneath. He could feel that dense power pushing back like frosty calm tentacles, brushing his wrists and elbows, waiting. He floated face down. Against him the tentacles softly rubbed.

Rolling on his back to breathe, Sarge gasped with cold and remembered that time years ago, said to himself it didn't matter how many. That time after the Dardanelles when he shipped over to Haifa and on down to Dahav because the water there was warm and still, purple-green, alive along the coral reef, and the swimming was good. The swimming was easy. What he wanted after fighting the long gut-busting stretch of cold was some easy swimming, some warm water, some R and R. No Americans placed at the Dardanelles except him, and what he'd won by placing third was enough to pay for hospital costs and plane fare back to the States, but coming to his senses on an I.V. in Izmir he decided the hell with it, he'd blow some extra to visit what one of the Egyptian swimmers had described as a tropical pool of epic size.

The Egyptian was right. There was the Red Sea's desert coast, directly west of Mecca, north of Cairo, south of Jerusalem, and if shark fins were spotted daily farther down near Sharm-el-Sheikh—if that Swedish distance swimmer whose name kept slipping his mind had been mangled to death the month before—Sarge was strong. He'd put in his lats and his laps all those countries away, put in his sprints, his long slow distance. Enough of that and, as with no other physical pursuit you can name, the body becomes tireless. It can breathe endlessly. Kick gracefully. Reach forever, breathe flutter-kicking and reach some more. He felt just about invincible. And danger seemed unreal in the palm-filtered twilight, water lapping rhythm, sucking sand, gentle, deep, gliding darkness lit only sporadically near the surface by darting schools of night fish signaling eerie glows, as if the Milky Way's stars were reflected off and on by the dark lapping mirror of tide. He rented a palm-branch hut from the Bedouins, at the beach's north end, for thirty cents a day.

After Turkey he was tired, he'd lost fifteen pounds. By his tropical pool thoughts of violence seemed laughable. All there could be was the glow-speckled gliding darkness that was darkness to the bottom and darkness at the core, a core from which no blood would ever spurt. He ate plenty of figs and fresh hot flapping slabs of pita bread that the Bedouins sold. He bargained with them for the oil-saturated fish that came in cans with red Spanish labels.

"Y-allah!" the boys sing-songed, selling bread among the huts. "Y'allah! Pita, pita, allo. Pita, salos lira, salos lira mister." Afternoons, he swam across the bay from reef to reef to reef to reef, chuckled to himself and wrote in his diary that he'd initiated a solo version of something called the Red Sea Relay. The boys shrilled along the beach, their thin curved torsos shrouded in black.

One afternoon at the height of heat he stroked easily halfway across the bay, breathing to his right every four strokes, and turning for breath saw the barracuda sliding silently alongside, keeping perfect pace. Sarge went on stroking in rhythm. He figured twenty minutes to the other reef. He stroked, stroked, stroked, breathed, stroked, stroked, stroked. The fish's staring eye froze on him as they swam smoothly parallel. It was a tiny eye. Sarge stroked, counted strokes until he lost count in the static blanketing his thoughts, then started again with one, two, three, four, and the barracuda kept pace. Five, six, seven, eight, Sarge breathed. Its jaw hung perpetually open. Turning in unbroken rhythm for air, he wondered how long the pin-tipped teeth were, razoring out of the relaxed, ready mouth. He got to fifty, fifty-one the next time and scarlet coral signaled his reaching the reef so he slowly shifted ninety degrees towards shore, and when he breathed again there was no sign of any barracuda, just schools of silver-glowing small fish passing across the bright coral like a cloud's moving shadow. He kept going and kept counting, didn't stop until his feet touched sand. He pulled goggles off and sat roasting on the beach for a while, let the sun lick droplets from his skin.

That night after moondown Sarge dug a small sandpit, made a fire. Into it he carefully dropped the shredded pages of his diary as sacrifice to the God of Barracudas. Flames hopped over the pit's edge. They flashed briefly on the water like reaching golden fingers. The following afternoon he did a

9

Red Sea Relay again, with not a fish in sight. A few days later he left.

Now he was floating in lake water. It always waited, let you make the first move. He rolled over again. Stroked stroked stroked stroked and breathed to the right and again again and again and again. Bubbles spilled from his lips. He could tell it wasn't much more than fifty-six, fifty-seven degrees this morning, and between that cold and him was memory, his mind working like a pair of runner's legs during hill training, burning precious calories as fuel for every motion of every thought.

The Reef to Reef Roughwater Annual out off the West Coast—he didn't care how long ago that had been either—the water was about this cold, and rough too, and it was saltwater. He could still see them hanging over the gunwales to shout, each voice hoarse as if the vocal cords had been rack-stretched and grated raw. The wind blew every word out long, vibrating, unrecognizable, like something screamed from the other end of a tin barrel. Keep the pace keep the pace keep the pace the pace the pace! they howled. Come on killer come on kiddo come on champ come on keep the pace the pace come on, we ain't reached heaven yet. Repeat repeat repeat repeat, one of the two of the three of the four reaching reaching reaching and on. Waves washed into his mouth, salt scraped skin off both lips while under goggles his eyes swelled half-shut, and he heard a whistle signal feeding time but kept reaching, reaching into the twelfth mile. Ice crawled under his skin so he no longer felt toes or thumbs, just the chattering ache of water and shoulders screaming soreness, battering in rhythm at advancing needles of ice. In the twentieth mile he wanted to curl into the green-blue and sleep. His eyes shut the rest of the way to the reaching again and again, and someone beat the waves with a feeding stick to keep him awake. In the twenty-sixth mile, they told him later, he barely moved at all. Took him a good hour and a half to cover two thirds of it, even though by then the wind had calmed and the waves gentled, and when he touched that sand he was the only one who'd lasted to finish so they said he'd won.

This morning Sarge cut a direct line along shore. He waited

for the rhythm to lull him, numb him, ice blades scraping away at clutter so that finally, five hundred strokes along, his insides were pitch-dark and empty, and he was aware of what glowed gradually to a cold-defying light. His son stood before him and he witnessed a transformation by degrees as the naked young body arched upward in a sprinting dive's strong grace, triceps cording hill-and-valley indentations on his upper arms' smooth water-beaded flesh, latisimus dorsi rippled and fanned taut with expectation. The only part of his torso not displaying contours of muscle was that area from his pink-brown nipples to the smooth boy's belly. The kid looked like him.

Hauling himself to shoreline Sarge sat blindly for minutes in the morning's breeze. Hands shuddered on knees. He sat until ice melted to the stomach's center, streamed wet-hot to free his feet and fingers. It spouted up to pry his lids open. It boiled there, just behind the eyes, like tears that never spilled.

Sarge stepped to firmer ground. He turned towards the pines and home. Peeled off caps, swung his goggles around. A touch between the thighs let him know that in the lake's cold his cock had shrunk, shriveled to baby size. There was still a little time before sunrise.

Daddy!

That was in the fourteenth hour. The fourteenth hour and close to dusk.

Daddy Daddy!

Corrosive power it had, all that salt in all that water in all that cold, force of those elements meeting the force of reaching and stroking, causing a friction that did more than rust and did it a lot faster. A twenty-three-year-old, babbling Daddy as if he'd gone back through time to become a baby again. Well in a way he had, the mind got unhinged. It happened a lot. On these long swims more often than not, hallucinations, regression, disorientation, terror. Daddy help. Help. And Sarge had shouted over the side in wind and spray and growing darkness, keep it up Matt, keep it up, don't worry, you're doing fine. Just fine. Daddy help. Hey Sarge, they'd tugged his elbow, he ought to come out now, call it off he's sounding bad. Temperature just dropped. Forty-eight degrees, for Christ's sake. That's cold water. Let's call this all off for now. Keep it up Matt, stay strong now, stay strong keep that pace. Everything's fine. Trust me.

But how much longer? Much longer? How far?

Not much, he lied.

Daddy! the kid screamed, Daddy! The way he'd sounded with those lips of his all puffed and blue. Daddy! Christ, the way he'd looked. Sarge would never forget it.

Sarge had made some nice money on the swims—he was one of the lucky ones. After a while he just refused if the purse wasn't big enough. But the refusing came later. Early on he'd swim anywhere, he remembered, do just about anything to get to where the water was so he'd be greased up and ready by the ten-count. And he'd made himself outstanding in the field. Kind of a legend. David "Sarge" Olssen. He could swim twenty miles of rough water at thirteen. Could speak and write five languages at eighteen. Had been thrown out of three Ivy League colleges by twenty-one.

An adventure—that's what he'd said. All of it, an adventure. So he swam solo and he swam against the world's finest professionals. Set some kind of a record by finishing every event he started, set another record by winning more of them than anyone before or since. Not just for the money. Adventurous, he'd described himself to Ilana later, that's what it is, not frivolous, but adventurous. The swims? No, they're not for the hell of it either, the swims are serious business, love them. Understand. Love them more than just about anything. Not while they're happening—it's the feeling afterward—that's why you do them in the first place.

Meeting her. Walking up through the pines now, Sarge remembered how it had been. It was Hawaii, Hawaii recovered from war fatigue. He even forgot why the hell he'd been there. But he remembered her—it was the name that first interested him when he heard it: Ilana de Luna. A good cliff diver—higher up she got, they told him, the better she

12

got—but for some peculiar reason she'd often do poorly on the lower ledges, attain the high, spectacular ones only rarely but then, ah then, there was a diver worth looking at. Great form. Grace. It was a dark, tropical-flower grace almost Oriental in its delicacy. The spring, jackknife, turn, the clear, clean arrow-straight fall to pierce water. So he'd gone up to her after some competition and introduced himself. She had a ripe kind of darkness found in that tropical part of the world —by blood an extravagant mixture. He knew what it was like, that half-breed feeling—his own father was Danish, his mother a dusky-skinned Arab Jew from Palestine. So he was two unmixed things—Oriental and Teutonic—and Ilana was many things more. She had a good smile. Sarge knew when things were serious. Adventure had taught him that. He tossed off the reputation of bon vivant with ease. He'd play classical things on his guitar for her—Segovia, Villalobos. And explain the swimming, what it was like. Ah, she said, I think I understand. But I don't feel that way about diving. For me it's not that. Sometimes I do want the feeling you get— that sensation of leaping, just bolting right out into nowhere and then you're free somehow and you weigh nothing, nothing at all for just that flash of a second. But I don't want it all the time. Not even most of the time. You see, I'm not like you that way, always wanting to feel it. Or needing, I think you must need, more than want, to do what you do. I think you are remarkable. And she'd leaned over then, quite solemnly, taken his face between her long hands and kissed his mouth. He was surprised. The dives? she said, smiling. No, no. I don't need to feel that. At least I don't think so. The hot air thick with tropical scent, heavy petal perfume, rotting greenery, mixed with salt spray. Something brushed the center of him like a feather.

Swims and the money. He'd made enough. Sarge wasn't frivolous. He made it make more. Now, he kicked at a pine cone. All this wood, it was representative of his land, his house. His camp. Because he'd wanted to coach—that's what he decided on when most of the good swims had been done and most of the money made. And the lake country, upstate

13

New York, was a good setting for a competitive camp. Just across from the Canadian border, right smack in the middle of a hell of lot of cold water that froze your joints to a creak and separated the ones who had it from the ones who did not. All right men, he'd howl, in there and not out for another two hours. He showed them what he did best and what they could do. Twelve young men a season—no more, no less—and Sarge was selective and expensive. Because he'd survived the ice-cold of the Irish Sea and the sharks of the Farallons and the man-o'-war stings of the Gulf Stream, and he'd run seven marathons to say he could do it even though it wasn't his main sport, so he figured he'd be one of the best teachers around for this kind of stuff. He was.

Now, dripping water in sunlight, he faced his house. Ilana would be getting up soon. All the wood of his house and the camp gaped back at him, surviving on investments now, the pool shut down, camp shut down, the lake open only to him these days. Never reopened after Matt's death. Sarge remembered the San Antonio Strait, State of Washington. It was cold that water, and gray. No one had ever made it across. But the kid was in great shape—hell, he'd trained him. Trained him lovingly, with everything he had, trained him to be one of the best. Want to go for it, kid? he'd said. He'd grinned. Want to go for it?

Ilana's face hinted age around the eyes' corners, around the smooth-lipped mouth. The rest of her was still slender, hips curving gently, flowing into legs where muscles were long and lean. A perfect diver's coordination had stayed with her through the years. On ground she seemed to glide.

She watered her plants carefully, the morning routine. This morning she felt a need to cling to routine because she'd had another falling dream last night that left her rattled. What remained when all the sleeping had gone was that nauseous spinning sense of falling uncontrollably. She'd just stepped off a cliff and started to back-flip, then realized that instead of diving she was falling very, very slowly, and whatever there was at the bottom wasn't water. The air was bright blue. It smelled like magnolia. She'd woken up. Of course.

She watered the cacti and then the jade, decided to move it for better exposure. She could feel that suggestion of a cold autumn come breezing through open windows. She cradled the potted plant in one arm and headed down the hallway. Paper rustled faintly through the half-open door to Sarge's study. He'd finished swimming earlier than usual.

Ilana set her plant on the kitchen table, then noticed someone standing just outside the screen door. The body pressed dark against the screen and she couldn't tell at first if it was male or female. But Ilana was used to being around men, big, definite men, and something in the posture told her—before she made out features or silhouette—that this was a woman, and not a large or in any way particularly imposing one either. Seeing that, Ilana felt a rush of relief, felt somehow secure. Puzzled, she raised a hand in greeting, saying hello, who are you.

She went to open the door. From out there bird wings beat signaling breakfast, there were rustlings and baby-pitched squeaks from the pines. Once in a while the lake slapped on shore.

"Hello?" Ilana repeated. She opened the screen and it was a young woman nodding greeting at her. Ilana looked for lines. She did that, her way of sizing someone up—by age. Young, she guessed, twenty-five. No. Ilana reevaluated. Older than the looks, that's what the eyes told her. Twenty-seven, she guessed, a young twenty-seven. Certain, she smiled. The woman carried a canvas athletic bag. She looked tired but made no move to enter.

"Hi," she said, "hi there. My name's Dorey Thomas. I'm looking for Sarge."

Why don't you come in? Ilana invited. So she stepped in then, back nearly brushing the kitchen wall and bag held in front of her across the legs like a wearily lowered shield.

"I'm really sorry to bother you," she blurted.   15

Oh, Ilana found herself saying, oh, no bother, and wondered why she was so quick to give that reassurance. Something was familiar here. Maybe she'd seen the face before. Then she realized it was not the face that tugged at her memory but the general physique—all the strength apparent waist up, hips less significant, legs slender. A swimmer.

Ilana introduced herself. If Sarge was the coach, she was the coach's wife. It had always been that way, she joked. She repeatedly offered a seat until Dorey Thomas seemed to relax a little and sat on the edge of one with the beaten old bag set just so between her feet. Nice to meet you, she told Ilana, voice flat and polite, slightly hoarse with fatigue. She offered a hand. Surprised, Ilana took it.

"Is Sarge here?" She cleared her throat. "Excuse me. It was a long trip. Well pretty long."

Ilana made tea automatically and waited for an explanation. She realized how taken off guard she'd been by such a simple thing—the sight of another person, a young person, at the door.

"Where did you drive in from?"

She told Ilana where—it was a northeastern location, sounded like a town or suburb in Connecticut maybe, maybe Massachusetts. Later, Ilana wouldn't remember. She offered tea but Dorey Thomas sat there shaking her head quietly, smiling a polite thank you. Was it possible to see Sarge? she wanted to know. She had to talk to him.

"About a swim. I need some advice."

"A swim?"

She nodded. A hinted grin spread around the eyes and mouth. Then Ilana had it, knew she'd seen her before, the name familiar. It had been in Quebec one year—swimmers standing there at the lake's edge before the count, arms raised, trainers swathing them with various kinds of insulating grease and her son, Matt, among them—all those hulking men, and a few women. "Oh," she said, "a swim. Yes you're a swimmer, I think I might have seen you before. Five years ago?"

"Well sure," said Dorey, "sure. You could have."

"Sarge. Someone here to see you." Ilana poked around the doorway. "She says she's been traveling all night."

Eyes meeting his wife's Sarge shrugged, brushed invisible journalists away from the air in front of him, told himself he thought he'd licked that problem for good. Ilana's eyes were unusually dark, almost black, and the memory of admiring their darkness and that slight hint of Oriental curvature made him smile briefly. He heard himself ask with a touch of the old bullhorn sound, well who the hell is she and what does she want.

"Dorey Thomas, and she wants to talk to you about a swim."

Sarge's pencil tip drew cartoon goggles on the blotter's forest green. Tell her to get lost, he wanted to say. What whispered instead were words he'd later swear weren't his idea at all.

"I'll see her in a few minutes."

"Do you want some tea, Sarge?" He shook his head, looked up from a sketch of Niagara Falls he'd drawn.

"I'll tell her to wait."

Glaub nicht, dass ich werbe. Engel, und wurb ich dich auch! Sarge fiddled with the pencil while a couple of leaves drifted through the window, settled alongside his chair. *Du kommst nicht.* He marked the passage with brackets. He'd never seen a translation that suited him.

On the opposite wall was an Aztec sun clock, its lacquered sky-blue clay geometrically sectioned by dim lines of yellow into patterns that dissolved and resolidified in front of your eyes if you stared long enough. He often did. It was a perfect mandala. He turned to the Eighth Elegy but his pencil tip slid along the page in disgust. He remembered when his concentration had been better.

Sarge stared at the clock. His son had swam against Dorey Thomas about five years ago in Quebec, and she'd just missed placing because of him, missed out on even a taste of the prize money. Still, he remembered thinking that she was damned good and damned persistent, give them both another few years, they'd be first and second instead of third and nothing. Sarge had seen her looking like a fetal Martian, body dripping globs of lanolin and features strapped away behind blue-tinted goggles, but he remembered she'd worn a cap with a red lightning streak down the middle and the kid had admired it, commenting on how small she looked that day, small next to the men.

He'd kept up with things in his own way, Sarge had, sure. He knew what was going on, who'd done what crossing and when. He could quote distances, times to the second, the frequency of flood tides, the neap tide cycles. Three years ago the women of the Professional Marathon Swimmers Association said Dorey Thomas was their best. And she'd been training at Seal Beach for a double crossing of the Catalina Channel when, midway through the eighth mile of an easily paced workout, swimming strongly, she rolled onto her back and refused to continue. When they hauled her from the water she refused to talk too, and after more than a week of watching her huddled silently by a window looking out at sand, waves, and fluttering gulls, her trainer threw up her hands, announced to the crew that the crossing was off indefinitely, and Dorey Thomas, so far as Sarge knew, dropped out of sight.

"Hi there."

She stayed in the doorway, canvas athletic bag swaying against her knees. Deep gray shadows spread in semicircles below her eyes gave her a slightly sullen appearance, and her face wasn't pretty so much as well-formed, large-lipped, with a childlike kind of slackness around the jaw so that only the eyes' dull glitter saved her from looking perpetually in awe. Sarge nodded her towards a seat.

"Hello. What's the world like these days?"

"Depends." She sat. "Depends on what you're comparing it to. I don't know, the same I guess."

"Too bad."

"I would have called first. Or written." The tone was uneasy, a little apologetic. "But your number's a secret. Well, no. No. Anyway, I'm here."

18   She looked pale from lack of sleep, that thin-worn traveler's pallor. He nodded. Here she was, unoiled, without goggles, wearing land clothes. Hard to believe this person sitting tiredly

on the other side of the desk had spooked his son's heels every
bone-chilling yard of the way. Still, here she was. He waited.

"Well. Well everybody's time is limited. I won't waste
yours." She blinked at him wearily, leaned forward. "I want
to swim the San Antonio. Will you train me?"

After a moment he walked barefoot to the window. Sarge
never wore shoes if he could help it. Who the hell did she
think she was. Look you little snot, he wanted to say, leave
me alone, beat it, but didn't.

"Why the San Antonio? There are other swims."

He sensed her head shake firmly behind his back. When the
early October cool had calmed his face he turned to look
down at her. "Listen, nobody can do that swim. I should
know. And anyway I'm not in the market for a swimmer, not
for solo or relay or anything, understand?"

"How come?"

When his fists inched from the pockets and his shoulders
jerked, her eyes glittered a dull, sudden warning. He leaned
against the wall, hands swinging stupidly by his sides. She
fixed that tired stare on him directly, so he would have felt
challenged if not for the vulnerability in her voice.

"I've been looking over the charts. The tidals and nauticals.
I've studied it, believe me. It's possible. It's possible and you
know it. Or you'd never have tried."

Sarge sat again. His hands imitated hers and made a steeple,
remembering making steeples with endless fascination as a
child, remembered trying to make steeples while floating on
his back in a pool and that sudden drenched whiff of chlorine
up the nostrils when his face went under. Heard himself ask
her with a calm point-blank certainty how she knew she could
swim at all anymore.

"You mean Seal Beach?" He noticed how broad her shoulders were. "Well I'll tell you what that was, I got lonely. Look.
We all make a bad mistake at least once, right? I mean, you
ought to know."

He didn't want to hit her anymore, just wanted to be left
alone. The words slipped out before he caught them. "What
kind of shape you in?"

She said good. Five- to seven-mile runs at around a 7:30

pace four times a week, no great shakes on the track but she was steady. Weights three times a week. She'd put in plenty of pool time and plenty of sets of sprints, long slow distance in rough water when it was available.

"Cold water?"

"Not much. Not lately."

He sized her up the way he might a blue-ribbon calf he'd had vague thoughts of buying. It was difficult with her clothed and seated. She definitely wasn't underweight, but she was still too thin for real cold water. "You'd have to load on another fifteen, twenty pounds, maybe more. Hell." He shook his head. "You get up here by car?"

She nodded. He could see her jaw tense.

"Well, stay on overnight. Wherever you came up from it's too long a trip back there on no sleep. But tomorrow morning I want you out of here. Understand?"

The arms went limp then, mouth slackened, and for a second her eyes closed. "Sure," she said softly. "Too bad." Her lips seemed to shiver briefly with exhaustion. He looked for tears about to start but saw none. "Well mind if I try out the lake?"

"Feel free. I don't own that water." He rearranged his papers without seeing them or noticing what order they'd been in, and held on to the desk's edge so she wouldn't spot his fingers shivering. Ridiculous that those fingers of his, which were long and thick, could betray a sensitivity. From the back he saw her outlined inside jeans and a formless blue T-shirt. Broad shoulders, long husky torso and long arms, tiny ass. He yelled after her that she was welcome to dinner.

Sarge paced. He was a big man, bull-chested. He pulled open a drawer and his hand hovered over a pile of nautical charts. He slammed it shut and stalked outside.

From the lake came splashes. She'd just jumped in figuring on a warm welcome. He grinned. There was silence before the next sound, the slow definite entry of a hand and arm, a stroke, then another, and another, and he listened to the increasing rhythm of it, expecting it to stop any second now, listening with more and more interest as she continued without missing a beat. He counted the sounds, could tell she was going back and forth within a particular area, sticking close to shore, and he thought of her tired eyes. Maybe she was crazy. The ripples cut four-four time through the air, each one the same. Sure could swim.

He headed down to the lake before realizing that he wanted to. How often he'd imagined watching a film of himself when he was going strong, and the closest he'd ever really come was watching his son. Especially in still, clear water on a summer afternoon, or indoors when the kid put in some long slow pool distance. "Well, what do you think Sarge?" he'd ask, and Sarge would visualize the perfect rhythm, the nearly soundless way his hand entered the water and that tenacious mule kick of his that beat relentlessly just below its surface, and he'd toss a hot towel around him. "Not bad Matt," he'd grin. "Damn good." He'd rub him down on the way to a steaming bath. Sarge was a couple of inches taller and he'd rest an arm casually across Matt's shoulders. "You've got the guts for it, kid."

Goddamned beautiful son he'd been, the best. That last morning he'd weighed in at one-ninety-five before breakfast and joked that he was catching up to the old man. Twenty-five of those pounds were gone by nightfall.

Sarge stepped out of the trees, went to the end of the small dock and let his feet hang over the edge when he sat. His toes were numb in no time.

She was a few hundred feet out, heading back in his direction. Let her show her stuff then, it couldn't be finer than what he'd seen before. But he wanted to watch.

He watched for half an hour. Her goggles were dark and she never saw him. He wondered if she closed her eyes now and then. He wondered did she dare bend her fingers once in a while, only to realize that she felt nothing at all. Her breaths made more sound than her kick. Rising, turning, arm following hand into the water, everything fit. She hadn't been joking. She'd put in plenty of work, and on her own this time. For a second his eyes stung.

·

"Well what do you think?"

"I think you're pretty strange." He draped a long towel, fresh from the oven, around her. The heat singed his fingers slightly. He ignored it and draped her with another. Superman. Supergirl. Only comic strip heroes didn't shiver like this. He reached for the third towel and, kneeling briefly, wrapped her from the waist down, rubbed the backs of her thighs roughly through the hot material. "Probably crazy."

"So what," she said.

He laughed.

A hot bath and she'd loosen up easily. Some heat, some food, then she'd be ready to go again.

"Take your time," he called. "Take it easy."

Maybe she'd need help. That lake could numb you. Once he'd spent fifteen minutes trying to pull his suit off with fingers practically paralyzed by cold. But at the closed bathroom door Sarge stopped. Then he turned and went looking for Ilana.

Ilana shut the bathroom door behind her, offered Dorey a mug of hot chocolate.

"Well thank you. Thanks a lot." Dorey held the mug with a hand gloved in bubbles. One elbow rested on the soapy side of the tub, the other she'd hooked casually over a wall faucet so her arm hung like a teenager's swinging out a car window, the fingers vanishing in white froth. From the shoulders down she'd disappeared.

Ilana watched her sip. "Sarge thought you might need help, but I see you're fine."

"I appreciate it."

Ilana figured she'd learned her manners from a very good book, probably some coach's. In between the daily regimen of intervals, distance, weights, time trials, homework due, carefully planned meals, strict curfews and alarm clocks buzzing, these niceties had been ingrained as another drill in a routine where drills layered the road to triumph. Eat enough apple pie consistently over a long period of time as one part of a program that worked in its entirety, and without a doubt you'd

22

start to believe apple pie was an integral aspect of success. Matt hadn't swallowed that. There'd been Sarge as the antidote all along.

"I heard there was a pool here."

Halfway out the door Ilana turned. "There is. But no water in it now. It didn't make sense, not after Sarge decided to close things down." She couldn't meet Dorey's eyes, a kind of embarrassment. No, that wasn't quite it. Shame. It was a gut-deep sense of shame and it blackened all clarity of thought, it was the color of her son's hair. She'd managed to avoid this feeling for years, wondered why it tackled her now. "Would you like some more hot chocolate?" Motherliness was the cure. She decided she'd digested her own share of niceties long ago. The shame lifted and she looked up again.

Dorey's smile surprised her. It was expansive, wide-lipped, slicing across the face's well-formed blandness in an almost Oriental way. Her eyes slanted. For the smile's duration she appeared foreign, and Ilana had the vague sense that she'd seen someone different, well-hidden, surfacing momentarily.

"Sure. That would be great."

Dorey blew bubbles from her palm before blowing them from the mug and, blushing suddenly, handed it to Ilana. She mumbled something about being sorry for the mess, and Ilana laughed softly. When Dorey stopped blushing she glanced up open-mouthed, eyes questioning.

"I hope," Ilana teased, "that's the worst mess you've ever had to apologize for."

Dorey made a mountain of bubbles. Her thumb scaled it and she scattered it all in one breath. "Well it's not," she said.

Ilana went for more cocoa.

It was noon. When she offered breakfast Dorey thanked her, accepted an egg, whipped it with a fork in one of the long-stemmed wine glasses Ilana never used. She downed it quickly, washed the glass and fork meticulously with another thank you. From her bag she took a white package wrapped in plastic that contained melting ice and asked for refrigerator

23

space. Through the white seeped dark stains. "Raw," Dorey said, half apologetically, "everything raw. Thanks a lot." She asked was it true they had a track. Ilana pointed the way.

Ilana felt sun streaking the day's breeze with occasional warmth. She was knees-and-palms on the earth checking defunct furrows. In the summer her garden was fabulous. Everything got equal attention, but she'd have to admit that the blood-red roses, set slightly apart, were the snobs and champs of the lot. They'd grow twisted with thorns. One or two buds always bloomed savagely into a spike that pierced their core like a bull's-eye. The velvet petals were tongues. Come and get me, sucker. Her hands had never been soft, not for as long as she could remember. First they'd been callused from wrist to fingertip by gripping the rocks she'd climbed repeatedly, each dive that scored enough qualifying her to climb one ledge higher. Sometimes she welcomed the thorns. If they'd been animal's teeth, that animal would be surprised at how difficult her hands were to cut. Other times she wore gloves. She liked to sprinkle a little fertilizer evenly in the furrows every autumn, close them up, let the food gestate for a season. This noon she used her bare hands for the job. Her fingers were unusually long, tight and thin, young-looking. They gave an illusion of delicacy.

"She asked me to train her!"

Squinting against the sky at her husband, Ilana noticed approvingly the firm mass of him outlined there and something tiptoed up to her chest, beat in secret extravagance for a moment with her heart's rhythm. "Are you going to?"

"No." There was hesitation in his voice. He crouched, handled the earth absentmindedly, stuck an index finger deep in. "She's gunning for the San Antonio Strait. I don't know. Things I've heard. She's too damned unstable if you ask me." On his heels Sarge rocked. "You think she's crazy?"

"I don't know her very well. I think she's tired." Ilana chuckled. "And very polite."

24   She reached out to lay her hand on his thigh. After a moment of surprise his hand covered hers, and to both of them the feeling was strange, almost new. When she looked she saw

wires of white stringing through his hair, how remarkably young his face was underneath it. A kind of heaviness lifted then so she met his eyes, for the first time in years, without the weight of fear. A short distance away on the half-mile dirt track that tough, ample young male bodies had pounded around, lanes blurred with rain and disrepair, a fatigued young woman neither of them knew was pushing into her second or third 7:30-paced mile. Covered by colorless old sweats her body ran across the imaginary field of vision between them, like an unexpected afterthought.

"She went to the track, Sarge."

Ilana watched him go. He moved on ground as if it were water. His shoulders and chest did the work, blazing through invisible waves like the broad end of a bullet. He kept his arms swinging by his side with difficulty. They wanted to reach. She'd seen him break through rough water many times like that, massive chest and shoulders battering away and head lowered in a frozen kind of fury so she'd half expected him to sprout horns. If she squinted she could see his shape change slightly in the water's dark until he'd become a serpent, or a bull in the sea.

Dorey didn't like running much, it felt unnatural to her. It was a duty, a task to be completed as well as possible. Like all such tasks she went at it with icy steadiness, established a visible meter, a beat, so that to anyone watching she seemed to flow easily. Sarge scanned her face when she trotted past the second time. It was blank as a thumb-sucking baby's. The mouth hung open and the eyes were shut off.

He nodded now and then to the pound of her heels on the hard, untrod earth. To himself he grinned. She was too much arms and not quite enough legs. The torso, in its flapping faded T-shirt folds, thrust forward futilely expecting the calves to flutter rather than stride. But despite all that she looked okay. What nature lacked, discipline made up for. Another few minutes and she slowed to a finishing walk at the track's opposite side. When he waved she headed towards him.

25

Her forehead, the slope of her shoulders, betrayed exhaustion. But the flush of damp bright sweat gave her an enormously healthy look, and despite those dull shadows her eyes were awake, watching him. He noted with appreciation that her breaths came quicker but were even, steady as that lovelessly performed pace.

"First college I went to I ran a lousy 220." Sarge's laugh bellowed. When he recounted anything it was usually in a monotone, a clipped speedy barrage punctuated by those bellows that kept everyone's attention peaked. "I had the muscle for it. Track coach was a mean, skinny bastard who shaved off his hair and didn't like mine being wet when I showed up for practice straight from the pool. He gave me a shove once and I gave him a broken jaw, and that was that. I was released from academic responsibilities, they told me."

"The 220?" she sounded surprised.

"Sure. Didn't much care for it, though, I'll tell you. It doesn't give you a chance to care. Pound away full speed ahead and as soon as you can form a thought you've finished, and there you are rolling on the track in stitches trying to remember what it felt like to breathe. The hell with that. If I'm going to give a damn, personally, I need the time. Plenty of it! And time means distance as far as I can tell. Plenty of that too."

They walked back along the road. She kept her eyes cast slightly down. Still, he got the feeling she was watching him somehow and, exposed, he stayed silent now.

The air was all pines mingled with occasional drafts of that fresh, cool lake smell mingled with the sweat dampening her hair and neck and the sweat he'd worked up walking that made his shirt-back cling. He glanced up so sun seared his face.

"Well why won't you train me?" For a second her voice pleaded. "Isn't it a long enough swim?"

They both stopped. She kept his stare with the clear-as-ice question in her eyes. What he felt boil up his throat then were words he hadn't known he'd been saving. They left him quietly. "Listen. That swim was my son's. You stay away from it."

When the color returned to her cheeks she smiled, whispered she'd thought maybe that was it. "You're pretty crazy yourself, mister. Someone's going to do it sooner or later. Right? Ten to one I'm the first. A hundred to one." He laughed and her jaw jutted nastily. "The way I see it, it's water. Not some shrine to your son. It's a great swim and that means whoever intends to swim it had better be great, I mean the best, and he just wasn't. You know he wasn't."

Sarge checked his thrust partway, so when the intended slap reached her cheek it was only a cuff, not even enough to sting. She was damned strong though. He realized suddenly how much his nose and mouth hurt before he realized she'd taken off at a run. He touched his lips. There was blood.

She'd left her stuff in one of the old dorm rooms, and when she reached the house that's where she went.

The cot mattress was striped dull blue. Springs whimpered a little when Dorey sat, bounced getting cross-legged and comfortable. She'd flicked off the overhead and bruised both sets of knuckles wrenching the dust-caked window open. Afternoon cool floated in with fading yellow light. Along the wall were five other cots. It was one of two dorm rooms. Sarge was selective. Twelve young men he'd trained a season, if they qualified. She thought of Ilana gliding quietly through the small complex, the only woman, and when Dorey smiled it was with appreciation. Her bag was packed and she'd take off soon. Cut out of a doomed situation before it got worse, that's what common sense told her. She ate the meat raw out of its package with her fingers. She wiped fingers on a napkin after each bite, patted another napkin against her lips after each swallow.

When she finished the meat she shook two carrots out of plastic, crunched into one and with thorough chews whittled it down to a greenish-brown stub which she dropped back into the bag. The second carrot she held tip up. When she was a girl, the bulletin board in her bedroom hung to one side of the trophy shelf. Her schedule of morning workouts, team practice, meets, homework assignments due, spread across its entire bottom half like a neatly drawn checkerboard with most of the squares inked nearly black by dates.

Above it she'd tacked two pictures.

One was a Kodacolor of her at twelve. Her mother Carol had taken it. In it she wore a plain black tank suit, held up the blue ribbon she'd won in the 100 at the Divisionals that year. She was grinning for Carol, for the camera, for herself. As always, the smile helped her pass for pretty.

The other was one she'd cut out of some long-ago *National Geographic*. This picture was of a cave's insides. Stalagmites sprouted. Stalactites dripped. It was a crystal cavern, and the formations were mostly opaque frosted white, with here and there a spot of clear see-through matter towards the needle tip of each long spike.

On her dresser were lotions. Vaseline. Baby oil. "Hey Carol," she'd say, "got a cure for chlorine on the brain?" Carol would laugh. She'd wink.

Dorey held the carrot point down, snapped off the end between her teeth. Like everyone else she'd started out in pools and even now the smell of chlorine was what she expected from a body of water. She expected it, sometimes, from the food she ate too. She dropped the carrot back in the bag. Well it wasn't the first mistake she'd ever made, coming up here. She guessed she'd find other options. Had to. Eyes shut, she smiled for bravado. Go team, go. I'm tired, she said. The smile stuck. She'd been tired before too. Come on, she said, there are other ways, remember who you are.

She shut the window. Picked up her bag and wondered where to find Ilana. She wanted to say goodbye and one last thanks before Sarge showed up. If he showed before she could make an exit she'd have to go through some ritual or other—what, she didn't quite know—after all, what did you say? She didn't mind pain so much as long as it was quantifiable and qualifiable. As long as she had some idea of when it would begin and how long it would last and how deep it would go. Then she could take whatever it was in spades. Still, if he showed she'd have to go through with whatever it was because she'd quit only once before in her life, and that would never happen again.

She sat suddenly, eyes shut. Vague hints of images had been spinning around inside all day and now, quietly, she concentrated, let the images clarify.

She was thinking pool bottoms. Baby blue tile. She was thinking that in the blue she'd seen Carol's face like one of those faces you see sculpted in clouds sometimes, passing, changing, so when her shoulders rested in the water they floated on the image of that face. Well she'd thought of Carol today, and wondered why.

She was thinking sprints. She'd been the 200-meter freestyle whiz kid that year. Coach yelling go go go go go. Chlorine drying on the eyelashes. She'd churned up a perfect line of wake flutter-kicking or butterflying and in the locker rooms, the many locker rooms, twirled 22-8-26 on the combination with fingertips pinched white by water. Sure she'd thought of Carol but how come today? Showers spat into all that soggy air from one locker room to the next in dozens of towns throughout the state. Lots of dripping locker rooms on lots of sopping benches in front of mirrors fogged by steam the girls giggled, and they posed for each other, whispered things and touched their new breasts, and sometimes the blurred images of their faces in the blurred mirrors shaded slightly red while they blushed. She'd twirl her lock. She'd hum to herself and the mindless sing-song brought back lullabies, then images she held inside from the past. The earliest ones were little more than sensations really. Carol dangling her by the wrists at the water's edge. Here darling, feel that—fun! isn't it fun! The dip, the sudden cool surge of a wave, the quick lift up free and breathing into air. Or she'd go back to very young and see herself: little girl standing in the kitchen doorway looking far, far up. A man there with Carol. Her father she thought. That's what she always thought, anyway, when she remembered, but maybe it was not him, only one of the others who came later. Dark, he circled arms around Carol and kissed the back of her neck. She'd watched for a while. Then gone to eat a sandwich. And always what came back to her,

29

when she twirled locks or sat and thought and dripped water, was this sense she had of other water, long-ago water, her mother Carol dipping her and always reclaiming her for free air at the last possible moment, the recovery inevitable, both of them laughing. Feel that darling. It's fun. It is free, do you see that? Dip. Lift. The breath and reach for open air, reach back down for the water.

Carol who was so very female and delicate. Fragile, she'd said, I am fragile darling but don't you be. You won't. Strong. I know, I can tell, strong, that's how you'll be, how you are. Remember. Remember how at the beach? All the waves. They're hungry, the water's hungry, that's why it makes waves because it's reaching up with hands for food, and when you see the waves fall apart into white that is the water's teeth. See how white? It's chewing. Ah. Here's another. Remember?

In locker rooms she hummed sitting there on the bench, songs Carol'd hummed to her the time she got that eye infection. From the pool, they said, that's how. And the eyes swelled shut. Carol stayed next to the bed with ice packs. She'd go to practice that morning anyway. Sure. And afternoon. Strong, Carol murmured, hummed in between words, you do what you want to do.

Well she wanted to swim. That was it, nothing else.

She was thinking shoulders. Because she'd been swimming freestyle for Carol. The broader her shoulders grew the better she'd figured she could carry her because Carol was so beautiful, somebody had to. She was thinking rules and the rules she'd eaten lock stock and barrel. She'd hummed 22-8-26 to herself and sat slightly apart.

The room's air had deadened again with a smell like laundry locked in a closet too long. She swung the bag over one shoulder and, in the hallway, figured he'd be back any minute. Outside, metal scraped pebbles in the earth. Ilana was fertilizing her garden.

The sight made Dorey stop, feel her shoulders wilt. For a second it had been all right. Now the taste of what she'd consumed that day rolled over inside, sour with fatigue. Too long, she told herself, too long since the last good sleep.

"That's nice, you know." It came out a little hoarse. When Ilana stood, Dorey paled, stammered slightly. "I mean that you looked very, I don't know, picturesque there. What's the word? Pastoral?"

"Something like that. Thank you, that's kind."

"Uh-uh, no, it's not. Look. I'm leaving now and I'd like to say thanks for everything."

"Where are you rushing to? You can—"

"I really am going."

"Okay, champ." Ilana was sorry as soon as the words were out. Dorey's expression didn't change but she could sense an inner recoiling, a hidden flush of embarrassment. "Excuse me! I shouldn't have said that, it was flippant."

"It's okay."

Maybe, maybe not. She wondered if Dorey carried a grudge and then wondered why she wondered, she'd be gone soon. She realized the flippancy came from long ago. It had crept up and out like a badly timed motion picture flashback.

Well *were* you? Matt would tease, and she would tease back, well was I *what*? Hot as hell! came the answer. She threw sagging strands of weed at him, called him rotten to the core, and they both laughed. How dare you assume, she'd ask, that I'm *not* anymore.

When Ilana spoke it was gently. "Listen, dear. I don't know you but I can see you're tired. Why don't you stay for dinner and leave in the morning? Or if you need to go today at least sleep for an hour or so."

"Well I don't sleep very easily. Thanks anyway. Really. Thanks." She turned. Where was he? Then she knew that much as she wanted to avoid him she also wanted to wait because everything was flapping tattered and unfinished between them, and not finishing a thing made her insides desolate. So she turned slowly back to Ilana. Saying well, if it was okay to change her mind she'd stay, for a little while, after all.

"Good," said Ilana. "Would you like some tea?"

In the kitchen Ilana kept all windows wide so the air chilled slightly. She washed her hands while water boiled. Dorey traced imaginary faces on the table's knotty-pine surface, saw flower petals in the wood.

"That garden, is it your obsession?"

"That's a funny way to put it! Do you know much about plants?"

"Uh-uh, no. Only seaweed."

Ilana grinned. "Maybe. I suppose you could call it that sometimes, yes. Only sometimes."

"Well if it's just sometimes it doesn't count. Obsessions are all-the-time things, aren't they?"

"Obsession"—Ilana poured the tea—"is a way of going about things. Any thing. It doesn't so much matter what it happens to be at the moment, the frame of mind creates obsession."

"You mean you're the one controlling it? You're the one with the foot on the gas all the time?"

"Yes, why not?" The perforated silver ball holding tea leaves swung from one cup to the next. Foot on the gas? Sure. What did you say, though, when your foot slipped, and what did you call accidents? Were accidents, too, in your control? "Sometimes," she smiled at Dorey. "Sometimes."

"No, wait. Not fair!"

Ilana handed her a steam-rimmed mug. "How did we get around to this? We were talking about the garden."

"Right. Well. Is it your obsession?"

They both laughed. Sitting, Ilana dangled a white napkin. "Truce," she said, "truce."

Dorey accepted that with a nod and a lift of the mug. Ilana was suddenly grateful. She'd found herself treading foreign territory. Summers ago, all kitchen camaraderie had been with young men. Bulky, gleaming, rippling, and always somewhat damp with lake water or sweat or a slight unacknowledged embarrassment, they'd sat tipping chairs back, thighs spread wide, flirting with open clumsiness and all due respect to Sarge, banging the table in applause at a particularly quick sequence of repartee. Sometimes Matt stood in the doorway, a mixture of pride and confusions to which he lent his own noise, but more often than not he'd seemed to her physically set apart from the rest and not just because he was her son. It was something about his way of standing, arms folded across the chest and eyes waiting. Always waiting, alertly. To those who didn't know him he'd seemed to have Sarge's sureness, a total confidence of roots firmly planted. In reality he'd been much less sure, but this he'd camouflaged magnificently with a sharp cutting edge of defiance so there was something steely about him. Except for the question mark around the eyes, anticipation, bravado, wondering. And there was absolutely nothing about this woman across the table that reminded Ilana of him or of those summers or of those brisk, gleaming young men. Perhaps it was only the contrast. She gave a nod of her own, lifted her mug and sipped.

"One more question. Different subject."

"Go ahead."

"What's it like"—Dorey blew into the tea—"diving off a cliff?"

Ilana spoke with careful seriousness. "Like nothing else. It's like diving off a cliff." She watched something spread over Dorey's face. The mouth's corners curved gently. Ah. She nodded again but to herself this time, sure, I see. Then maybe she was smiling a little, Ilana couldn't tell. Dorey saluted her briefly, and the gesture was only semi-mock.

"Touché."

It was getting close to sundown. Outside the lake was blue-tinged, in its still period before the increasing motion of evening breeze tickled its surface to wrinkles. It was that time of day when if you walked through the pines you'd hear every crackle, and squint to see where sounds were coming from in the shadows.

Ilana had the sense that if they just kept talking, the afternoon would stay a while longer. Inside, it was that period of indecision between remaining loyal to receding pools of natural light and flicking on a lamp. While they waited they talked.

"Well if it's not an obsession," Dorey challenged, "then what do you call it?" and Ilana noted with curiosity how, aside from those well-rehearsed niceties she'd spotted before, Dorey seemed utterly incapable of really easygoing conversation. It was as if an entire shade of experience—the dimension of getting accustomed by degrees—had been totally lacking. But the question stood, and Ilana went to meet it.

"A meditation," she said.

"Is that how you spend your time?"

Ilana gave her a questioning look.

"Meditating, I mean." Dorey blushed slightly. "I don't know. I was wondering what you did."

Ah, Ilana nodded, I see. Now she had to ask herself questions. She'd been feeling this since Matt died, this need—when her focus turned inward—to justify her own existence. So she took some time now, clicked over the things that would qualify as justification. Gardening, she might say. Or, euphemistically, meditating. Or show her things she'd done. Things. A little pottery here and there. All the books she'd read. Or run through an exercise routine for her now, display the remnants of a diver's discipline that had in many ways never left her. The stretching, long minutes of it, the routine bends she'd taught to a camp full of young male swimmers, curls. What she did.

But she realized that the question of how she filled a day would not be answered to this woman's satisfaction no matter what the reply. Because she'd come to see Sarge, and so was like him in some way—in some way obsessed, or wholly preoccupied with the constant doing of one particular thing. Swimming. And Ilana could offer nothing to compare. She'd spent her life without an obsession. Never having had one, she could not feel any lack. Still, she supposed that the times she felt most free of sadness were active times, bending and stretching or leaning over earth maybe, digging in hands. Rhythmic motion took her mind somewhere else, above the incessant weight of things.

"Living," she said out loud. "Living each day. That's enough sometimes, you know—"

"I know!"

Her emphasis took Ilana by surprise. She hadn't expected any confirmation at all. And now Dorey paled, fingers curled around the teacup.

"I mean," she said clumsily, "I know. Sometimes that's hard."

Sarge left the road, and when he got to the pines he took his old Marathon trainers off. He kept walking. At the waterline he cupped a handful to splash across his face. He stretched out a few feet from the lake with shoes for a pillow.

He grabbed another pine cone, held it to his mouth as a microphone. Well how does it feel Sarge? They were always asking you how did it feel. The *it* was probably victory. They never asked how did *you* feel, otherwise they'd get answers they couldn't print.

He'd taken pride in a strong finish. Whenever possible, when just enough inside was left over, the end clearly in sight and all foreseeable dangers behind, use up that reserve in the tank. Put on a sprint if you still could. If not, maintain form. His trademark. They'd rarely dragged him from the water— most of the time he'd managed to walk out. Except at the Channel when he'd busted his toes on offshore rocks, or Ontario that year when after twenty hours his legs were dead weight so he crawled onto shore. A strong finish his trademark, weather permitting. Sarge called it style. How does it feel, Sarge? It feels like dying, he said. Then he threw the cone, heard it splash. His upper lip's inside swelled against the teeth.

Wind riled the lake. He heard its lapping syncopation on shore quicken and deepen. Sitting, he jammed a foot into each old shoe. Maybe she'd gone and maybe she hadn't. Either way he'd be damned if he couldn't head straight towards whatever waited. Even if it was nothing. He got to the road humming Sor's Estudio 12. It was sundown.

The punching bag made that dull popping sound when his knuckles slammed in and he worked up some nice sweat, felt good, easy. He'd stalked past the open kitchen without a glance, heard Ilana's voice, and when he heard Dorey's voice too what settled in his belly was a sizable calm slice of satisfaction. The voices stopped when he went past. He just kept going through the swinging gym doors.

Pop. It dangled helplessly. Bam. The sounds scribbled themselves across a screen in his head like some old Batman strip. He shifted feet. Work out the other arm.

This pursuit, it is an insanity. That's what Bachmann had said the night before the Río Paraná. They'd been put up in chilly prison-style military bunks on the outskirts of Buenos Aires, a cot and one lousy blanket apiece. Already there'd been grumblings from some of the swimmers about the rotten accommodations and the stinginess of the purse. Winner took all. Someone mumbled Arabic in his sleep and turned over. In the cool dark he heard a cot squeak and then sensed bare feet across the stone floor. Three hours after bedding down, two before dawn and breakfast. Large flying roaches buzzed past Sarge's ear when he sat. He listened, figured it was none of his business, but something made him stand quietly and trot across to the doorway where he felt along the wall, brushed insects off so they whirred angrily around his groping fingers. Outside there was some light, the moon the kind the cow jumped over. Someone retched noisily in the bushes. He waited. Vomiting was a damned personal thing and you never wanted to have anyone else around when it happened. So out of respect he stayed where he was, and when the sounds stopped Bachmann moved from the bushes and stood, a little dazed, before noticing Sarge. What he said next Sarge always figured he'd never have said except at that vulnerable moment. Only fear, he smiled at Sarge. This pursuit, it is an insanity.

Sarge remembered saying in his schoolbook Spanish that the most important thing was sleep, so they both returned to the cots and when he caught Bachmann's first snore drifting with insects' buzz through the air he played some music in his thoughts and fell out too. He'd gotten up with everyone else a short time later, chowed down on his usual pre-race meal— ten raw eggs, a stack of toast, steak, some cereal—good old iron stomach going strong for him. He'd noticed Bachmann at the table's other end looking pallid and exhausted, shoving some tomatoes around a piece of soggy bread crust, staring at the plate's rim. Only fear.

Damned if he hadn't given him a run for the money that day, though. Sarge felt him biting at his heels just about the entire time, riding his wake, pulling up on the side to pass so in the river current Sarge was forced to sprint ahead, and then Bachmann would fall back but only slightly, ease onto the line of wake again, gliding through water Sarge had already broken. They cat-and-moused it like that for a good nine, ten miles. Until Sarge said to himself the hell with this, he'd break Bachmann and break him good. So he put on a sprint, kept it on for more than half an hour, and that pain wringing through the backs of his arms was simply a price he'd agreed to pay for leaving the feel of someone riding his wake behind.

Lungs boiling, shoulders numb, he slowed then and felt the first stab of winner-take-all confidence he'd felt that day. He stopped to tread for a feeding. It was a cup of honey which he ripped off the stick's end and sucked down quickly. Air tingled warmly against his skin, his trainer asked how he was doing and Sarge shouted better than ever and shook a victory fist, flapped a steadying butterfly kick into the current and went on head first. Only his pace had faltered, he'd made himself more tired than he thought.

Bachmann never caught up but some woman did. When she pulled to one side he sprinted ahead and then she burned a streak right past him in the second-to-last mile which he couldn't match. He rolled over and over in the water like a speared dolphin, mile and a half to go. Then he stopped for more honey, couldn't raise his arm at all this time, and though it was warm in both water and air his teeth chattered uncontrollably. He pawed around. A numb grin spread across his face when he realized they were shouting at him from the boat because he'd started off in the wrong direction. He stopped again. Couldn't really see them and couldn't really hear. So he plucked off his goggles and blinked blindly in the agonizing sunlight, treading. He pulled one cap off, then the other. He watched caps and goggles disappear downriver. They still shouted from the boat and he still couldn't hear, 37 but now if he squinted he could see them pointing the way. Looking to where they pointed, his eyes hurt. He thought of Bachmann and guessed he'd still have to put on some speed to beat him, so he closed his eyes for a second and when he opened them he was stroking ahead again. It seemed to him that he was going at a pretty good clip. Later they'd say how achingly slow it had been in the last mile and a half. The current went into his eyes through the reddened membrane and spilled out again from his ears, and every inch of him was swollen, about to burst into all that rushing river. When he finished second he staggered out twenty steps on shore and crumpled like a depleted sack of grain tossed onto the heap in a pickup truck. That woman was wrapped in baked towels, shivering and grinning and talking Dutch. Five minutes later Bachmann crawled to shore.

The bag swung dully. Sarge slammed it so hard his wrist bones ached. That night in Buenos Aires sitting on the edge of Bachmann's hospital bed, his own legs still shaking and whole sections of torso spasming so he had to lean over head between knees occasionally to make the nausea go away. Always he was reminded at the end of what his own fear was. Only fear. *Miedo. Temor.* It was fear of hurting so bad you'd lose control.

You speak Spanish as if from a book, Bachmann said, and Sarge had grinned then with pale lips, told him, of course from a book, hello Juan, how are you, I am going now to my class of Spanish, the pleasure is mine. Between grimaces they'd shared some chuckles. Refined, Bachmann was, from a wealthy family of half-German merchant lineage. He was nearly Sarge's height, had a wry snapped-shut mouth and large eyes that looked as if they might once have belonged to a deer, or a woman. They talked a lot. Interesting how much you could say with a sparsity of vocabulary. Shook hands that night and kept the palms pressed together, fingers gripping, a little longer than usual.

"Are you hitting that instead of me?"

She'd walked in without his noticing but he didn't break rhythm. Bam. Thud. When he paused it was more to give the bag a rest than himself.

"Matter of fact I wasn't even thinking about you."

"How come?" She moved to the other side and leaned against the bag, steadying it, and peeked around at him. Despite himself he grinned back. His mouth hurt.

"Crazy day today." He gave it a half-hearted slug. "I've been remembering things, all sorts of things. I'll tell you, I think it's the change in season. I think it's the change in season and growing older. Sorry I took a swing at you."

"Some lip you've got there." Her grin wasn't just embarrassment, it was distinctly mixed with a kind of pleasure, or maybe pride, and Sarge realized he was working up another good sweat, this one wasn't from exercise. When he slugged the bag full force she let out a grunt but hung on.

"Ever hear of a swimmer named Carlos Bachmann? He retired early I guess, a little before your time."

"Argentina."

"Right. He was a good friend of mine. Funny guy. A gentleman. Told me once he swam because he was afraid of the water." Slam. She held it firmly this time. "We wrote to each other, pretty frequently, for years. Never forgot what he said in one of those letters. 'My fear is without limit, so to pretend that it doesn't exist I do things which only the fearless should do.' " Body blows. Sarge pounded two, three, four to the middle like machine-gun rounds. "I write Spanish better than I speak it, we had a damned good correspondence going there. Eventually the letters just stopped coming from him—I sent three, four more, over a period of a few months. Turns out he'd gotten political at a bad time. His body showed up the next year way the hell out in the sticks there, stashed in some bushes. What was left of it anyway. They I.D.'d it I don't know how, his arms were gone at the shoulders." Thud. Pop! went the lightning-streaked words in his head's cartoon. "Sliced right off."

He thought he saw her wince. "Anyway, accept my apologies. I don't go around slapping women."

"Well I'm sorry too. Not sorry that I hit you"—she reddened momentarily—"I don't know, just sorry about everything."

"Yes." Sarge had the urge suddenly to slip to his knees on the floor. Or open his arms to her with that supplicant palms-up gesture and ask for something. What, he didn't know. The hell with it. He didn't want to know.

Only there was the sore prodding in his mind like a faintly heard far-off drum beat, and there was something he'd have liked to tell her. Maybe just sensations—or the memory of them—that couldn't be said or told. The feeling of Bachmann's fingers crushing around his for those few seconds in the hospital's dimmed lights where rows of beds rustled with pain, his elementary Spanish forcing him to use the same words over and over again like the same stroke endlessly repeated in the same nasty river, insistence of repetition reminding him after a while of some rugged form of poetry and, eventually, of music. Music bringing its cart loaded with many items, one of which was nostalgia, and with nostalgia an inevitable sense of loss. Sure. Loss was what he wanted to tell her about. Yes, he said instead, yes, I'm sorry too.

She sat facing him. When her mouth fell open wider it was with a kind of delight, and he got the feeling she was a kid about to ask him to tell her a bedtime story. He was getting hungry and didn't have much more energy for this. She bothered him. Maybe it was the silence that bothered him.

He leaned forward. What the hell. "I'll tell you a story."

"A true one?"

"A true one. It's about third or fourth hand now, though, so that's pretty much the same as if I'd made it up, right?" She nodded, dead serious. Balanced on the old bench she drew her legs up and crossed them, made him feel her attention was total because in that pose she looked very young. "You know about the Warsaw Ghetto, Second World War? There was a pretty extensive sewer system underground there. You could stand up in it, some parts were only ankle-deep—that's what they say, anyway—wide enough and deep enough to hide out in for a while. Imagine this." His hands flattened a stage in the air. "Six people down there when the uprising was just about crushed. Five men and a woman. And this woman is pregnant. Matter of fact, she goes into labor. They delivered the child the best way they could. Figure that somebody had a knife. Somebody held her down there in some shallow part of the sewer and put a hand over her mouth because one sound too loud and that was it, they'd all have had it." He glanced at her. She was focused on the invisible stage he'd set, features blank and intent. "You know how babies cry. This woman had gone hungry for months, for many months, and she didn't have any milk. Figure that a hungry baby cries a hell of a lot more than even a normal newborn. There they are down in the sewer. A couple of them had candles. One box of matches. Know how precious matches must have been to them? This woman just gave birth and the kid is screaming. Screaming. What do you suppose went through their minds? I ask myself that a lot. What goes through a man's mind when things are impossible and still you're alive! For some reason here the six of them were"—his hands made a tunnel spreading away from each other—"and for that same reason, whatever the hell it was, they were still alive. They'd survived. So here was a baby screaming, and this baby was going to be the death of them because up there on the ground were a lot of rotting bodies and the place was crawling with the SS and the German army. In a way they didn't really have a choice, did they? They drowned the kid. They were down there for days. Every single one of them made it, too, which is pretty damned amazing when you think of the odds." He shrugged. "I heard that one from my mother. I guess none of my true stories have happy endings."

"I don't know."

"What?"

"Well. Well they made it, didn't they? That's the point."

"How do you know? How do you know what the point is?"

"Look. I just know what the point is for me. For you I can't say. I mean, that's your business." She stood, stretched, and he noticed the momentary perfect slight curve of her from the hips up as her arms swung above her head, then back to her sides. When she faced him her eyes were cool. "For me it's a happy ending."

His own eyes measured. They always measured—heights, weights, muscle-to-fat ratios and lengths of reach and lengths of stride. She was so small compared to him. Still his lip was split inside and swollen enough to see, and she was the one responsible. For a moment he completely understood that pride she'd shown over drawing his blood. But it was enough to make him stop feeling sorry for everything, enough to stop him from trying somehow to make it all up. He wasn't going to fight anymore but he wasn't going to try, either.

"Have it your way," he said.

Her sigh was less pain than exasperation. She told him she'd be leaving tomorrow.

Even though the gym light was eternally fluorescent you could sense darkness around its edges, as if outside would creep through the walls and mellow all that pale hard illumination with the suggestion of shadows. Dorey wished he liked her but he didn't, that was plain. It came as a sort of shock. She stood her ground because it didn't feel right to move just yet. Oh come on, she wanted to say, why not? She wasn't used to dislike, not really, and when she had trouble absorbing anything her initial instinct was to fight it tooth and nail. Especially now because Sarge was for her a kind of hero.

Let it go, she told herself. Let it go. So she did, and what flooded in to take its place was a vast, quiet sadness she couldn't support. Didn't have the muscle for it yet. She lowered her inner temperature, felt it freeze. No more sadness. It was being shoved out as if by the frontal edge of a surely growing, slowly shifting glacier. No more. When she spoke, there was in her voice a mechanical precision.

"Look. I don't want to argue. I'm still sorry about everything."

"Okay," he said. It wasn't. He couldn't stop himself from asking her. "What do you plan on doing?"

"Swimming."

He'd worked up another sweat. "That's not what I meant."

"Well I'll get someone else. Somebody will want to train me, somebody good."

"You think so? Then what?"

"I'll swim," she said. "Just swim."

•

Along the ledge of her bedroom window Ilana had a couple of baby cacti coming along. Between them she'd potted an African violet. This ledge was sufficient to remind her of tropical climates, which she sometimes missed. Gorges they'd dived into as children. The rocks that snaked up and up, ledges twisting out sharply and footholds tenuous, slippery with their toes' water and slippery with plant stems that clung far better than fingers. Everything saturated by color, heat, dampness, mingling smells. This saturation of foliage green, of warm water rushing illusory clear blue or stagnant moss-dank and dark, smells of blooming mixed with those of rotting, the heat and hot cloud-rimmed aqua tint of the sky through leaves—this was the tropics to her and it was a temperature she regulated herself to all the time. Sarge could take the cold, he'd been reared in it and for it. She'd never wanted to.

Ilana ran a fingertip very lightly over one of the cacti. Its thorns were still tender, like the first pricklings of fuzzy stubble on boys' cheeks.

He'd wanted more children. Her hands overflowed with Matt, who was all difficult energy, bullying, testing, never really sleeping until a comparatively late age and so neither did she. No energy for another. In the long run Sarge didn't protest, he'd thrown himself into Matt just about as much. Hell, he said after a while, I was an only child and I was always glad, got a hell of a lot more out if it, why not spoil the kid rotten? In a way they had.

Ilana watered the left cactus just a little. She whistled something that went flat.

When Sarge knocked she said come in.

He closed the door and leaned back against it. "Strange day it's been."

She set the jug down. She was noticing him today in a way she hadn't for quite a while. Things were jumping restlessly inside, tappings below her left breast that made the nipples change size and texture slightly, impatiently. An odd mixture, his face. Too young for his age. Hers was too old so somewhere things balanced. He was an unexpected mingling of Nordic and Mediterranean. Thick, gently curling brush-black hair wired with gray, dark eyes, skin always giving that impression of being a little bronzed even in the dead of winter. Throw in the big-boned, long-boned, broad-chested Viking build, rigid chin, wide forehead and well-shaped, straight bridge of the nose. He'd taken her by surprise today, after all this time. Only she'd thought his capacity to surprise like that was gone and this feeling, this noticing him again, upset her. Butterfly wings brushing the insides of her thighs. She recognized the feeling. It made her angry.

Ilana was glad she'd set down the watering jug or she'd have spilled it. Her arms were quivering as she crossed them over her chest.

"Damn it, Sarge, just leave me alone."

He blinked.

"I don't want any part of this one, can you understand that? I don't care what you decide to do, I just don't care. Leave me out of it."

What, he breathed after a pause. Her cheeks were red, she could feel it.

"I'm not contributing to this! Not a thing, do you understand? Don't think for a minute that you're going to get a hint of my opinion without asking for it, not this time. You don't want it anyway."

"Listen, Ilana. Don't tell me what I want."

"You bastard!" If she'd let herself listen she'd have had another surprise, this one at herself. These words were all news to her, and because of that she simply let them flow. "You walk around as if no one's here except you. Anybody else exists only when you need them to, when it's convenient. Or when they force themselves onto your territory. And I don't want any part of this, Sarge." The tears were anger and they were in her voice, not her eyes. "You don't know the effect you have. Maybe you don't care."

He couldn't remember her like this ever. For some reason, though, a smile was curling across his face slowly, curiously.

"You're wrong," he said quietly.

Sarge wondered if she could see the swelling around his mouth. Something was about to crumble in the air between them. He sensed it start to avalanche and somehow this avalanche was all right, as it should be. On his face the smile stayed.

She told him to leave now. She was about to cry and didn't want him to watch. It was the kind of crying where comforting would be a mistake, holding forbidden. What pushed up into his chest was hot and moving, like lava. So for a minute he wanted to yell, or open his arms to her. But he shut the door very softly behind. He'd always respected her wishes.

Sarge reached down and wrenched a drawer out and off its runners, onto the floor with a heavy rustling thud of wood and metal and closely pressed sheets of paper. It tipped over so the contents spilled.

The only light was the desk lamp. It was getting late. Sarge knelt and ran a hand through the mass of paper, looking for that map. He was looking for that nautical chart and he'd know which it was just by the feel, the curl of those grayish well-used edges, the way it frayed at the folds. Because he'd carried it everywhere that year, the many months of training that spanned each season. He'd carried it in hip pockets, back pockets, shirt pockets. Carried it in his belt, caressed it against the lining of his jacket pockets as if the information displayed would transmit through to his fingertips. That map folded a million times, stuffed into a million places. It smelled like him. It smelled like Matt and like saltwater, like the insides of boat engines and the damp wood odor of boat cabins, gull feathers, deck rails sprayed with froth. His fingers touched a folded corner, pulled it from the mounds of papers, maps, charts, news clippings, scribblings, and then just as he was about to hold it to the light he dropped it as if it had emitted a burning acid substance.

Sarge sat. In the solitary light he looked like some darkpallet painting of a tired, sweaty monarch. From wood and leather throne he surveyed his kingdom of paper.

Daddy!

Where is he? There. Hold on he's going under, I'll have him

out in a second. Dove in. Felt the bitter salt-drenched freeze smash back against him. A couple other bodies flailed around him now too, dove down with him and they got a hold. Here. Got him. That's it head first and up you go kid. Up you go. Sarge tread water. The waves tossed him south and west, flogged him against the side of the boat. He waited for the others to board. Matt. Better see to the kid. Matt. Then rode the next wave right to the ladder, crawled up and spilled over on deck.

Matt. Hey kid. Hey there.

That's it, bring him around. Matt.

Daddy.

The eyes rolled.

Daddy.

Something wrong. That blue tinge, the blood. Circulation, something wrong. Matt. Hey Matt. Towels, where the hell are the towels. Hey you, get me some, get us some towels will you. Eyes closed. Rolled open again.

I'm cold, he said.

Sarge held him.

Sarge stood. He left paper mounded on the floor, turned off the light, and without having to see stepped into the hall. It was past his usual hour for turning in, for double-checking to make sure the alarm he never needed was set for that same, unchanging hour. The hell with schedules tonight. Things were falling apart in a way he couldn't qualify, and Sarge had never been a man to sit by and watch that happen without taking some action. Action. It was moving, it was the rhythm of moving that was important. In the hallway he froze for a second with the thought that perhaps this movement, like the friction of movement in water, quickened whatever disintegration was occurring. But thought was an enemy too tonight. So he stopped once more in front of Ilana's door. There was no light on in there and if he went in he'd probably wake her. Tonight that would be all right. He knocked softly.

46   She was sitting up, awake. He sensed that before his eyes adjusted to the dark. "Want some light?"

"Let's wait a while."

Something warm snaked down his spine. Funny how he remembered every step by heart, even though he hadn't been here in the dark for quite some time. He could tell by the pale bare shining of her shoulders that she was naked. Had she always slept naked? Couldn't for the life of him remember. He couldn't remember anything she'd worn to bed, either. He shook his head, chuckled softly.

"Ilana, I'm getting old."

"Maybe that's why your face keeps getting younger." She sounded relaxed. Peering, he could make out her features, gentled around the eyes and mouth. She didn't look angry anymore.

"Younger? You're kidding."

"No, I'm not. I noticed for the first time today—it's true."

"So by ninety I'll have the face of a choirboy."

"Something like that."

When they laughed he placed a casual arm around her. "Strange goddamn day," he muttered. She curved right into his lap. Her fingers twined around each other against the back of his neck. He leaned down slightly towards her. If her legs had wrapped around his waist it would be a near-perfect demonstration of a life-saving carry. He remembered all those moves by instinct. Take a deep breath and submerge, while underwater place a hand on either of the victim's hips so when you hit the surface again you could tilt the panicked body backwards, them holding on to your shoulders so you as rescuer assume top position and push forward through the water.

She detached one hand to move it under his shirt, softly, moving upward from his belly, pushing through the hair that spread in a V over his chest as if her fingers were a comb. He picked her up easily and then lay her down. Either he'd gotten stronger or she'd gotten lighter with the years.

He stretched out next to her. They kept their faces close, watchful. He was feeling the texture of her skin, which changed from place to place. It was tougher across the back, the forearms, the calves, than along her rib cage. Softest of all were her breasts, and though he felt the spots where this skin of hers seemed to have come a little loose with age, over-

47

all she was still firm and simultaneously soft. She was strong, he knew it. He'd seen her lift things. Seen her stretch those arms up cliffsides, legs reach for toeholds and every inch of her cling with a physical determination that might have eluded most men. What surprised him over and over again down through the years, especially tonight, was this combination of gut strength blended so smoothly with her slender sort of softness. It was to him a mystery. He eased one knee between her thighs. Felt them close around the denim and warm through to his own skin. In the lack of light her body seemed all one color, but he knew differently. It was a subtle collage of tints and shades, pinker on the face, browner along the shoulders, darker down the back and forearms, paleness ringing around both breasts and expanding like a cloud across the stomach. Her thighs lighter than her lower legs which were lighter than her feet. How could they call her white? He kissed her neck.

Ilana sent her hands searching. There was always something about contrast that amazed her, the ease he had in making an impression on her body. But what she found her fingers looking for was a vulnerability, a softness, some core to him that could really be penetrated.

She gave up and let herself appreciate his solidity.

"All the mistakes," he said, "I want to take them all back."

She was saying how she'd missed him.

He picked up from a long, long time ago. Picked up surely, with little hesitation. For now he just wanted, felt for the first time in who knew how long that he had a right to this wanting.

Where are you? he was saying, half serious, ah. Here. Here. He touched her thighs, her belly, teasing. She smiled. No hurry. Hadn't lived this long to hurry now. Only she could change things, Ilana, change the pace of things with just a word, a certain way of using her tongue. He cupped her chin in his hands, moved her head back up along his body, wanted to look at her. Something wet there in her eyes, water about to spill. Still she smiled.

"I wish."

"Tell me," he said.

She just spread fingers on his back, palms gently pressuring. Moved her hips up under him and he was in more of a hurry.

I wish. What? You'd come inside. He went into her deep and just stayed there a moment. Her legs wrapped around to keep him there. For a second he wanted to cry. But she was moving slightly, almost in circles, little ledge like an echoing voice inside her saying find me, find me if you can. He started to pull back and then moved in deeper, matching her circling motion. No time to lose. Not now. He looked for her where she was warm and wet. Sometimes what he wanted was nothing more than to keep going, going and going until she made that sound he'd hear in his dreams, like a primitive kind of singing chant.

The pattern of Dorey's sleep had been what she called regular for several years. Regularly disturbed, she'd add, then grin. It left circles beneath her eyes but didn't seem to affect her level of awareness or capacity for exertion. Made the eyes look bigger anyway. Tonight was as usual—she dozed and then slept for two or three hours. It was dream-packed, crazy, busy sleep, filled with colors and things she never recalled upon waking but that left her panting.

She sat stiff and sweaty and when the cot squeaked knew where she was. Dorey gave herself the task of regulating her breathing, relaxed the only way she knew how. She had a name for that too, restless relaxation.

While she'd been asleep a nasty drizzle had started up out there. It dribbled against the panes, a soft, nagging sound. After a while she swung off the cot to stand. One of the blankets Ilana'd given her looked like the Andes. Thunderbird knitted gray and brown and blue and white by some Peruvian hand, some leather-fingered Inca grandmother peering while the wool transformed in front of her faded eyes to landscapes symbolized by the sewn body of an imaginary eagle. Here some mountain snow, here the earth, white light of the sun, blue for the water from which it all had emerged way, way back before the grandmother's beginning. Dorey wrapped it around. The drizzle's tempo never changed. Essence of monotony. She took a rhythm from it and began to pace: cot to window, nose against window to feel the cool, pace back from window to cot. Again. Again. Reps. She counted eight steps between window and cot. At the window she pressed her forehead to the dusty chill, shut her eyes.

She stripped the cot of blankets and sheets, folded everything neatly, stacked it on the stripped mattress. She slipped into her jeans and another T-shirt, tugged on her training shoes and laced them by certain methodical touch in the dark. Dorey left the door to the room open and wide. Step by step she was feeling a little lighter, more revived.

The air outside was denser, cooler. It misted her face and hands. It made the sparse, colorless hair on her forearms curl up, beaded dark drops around the top of her head, and when she turned her face up to catch it more fully it dribbled faintly down her neck. She didn't like that yard light, too public. She half expected the pines to start applauding. Dorey felt along the inside wall where she knew the switch would be—enough suburban patio lights had taught her that, enough indoor buttons that made garage doors sidle open or roar shut. Buttons and light switches she'd imagined all those high school kids pressing at all those too-late hours during summers that smelled like tanning lotion, chewing gum furiously to cover up smoky breath or the scent of Schlitz or somebody else's Chablis. She found the switch and pressed down. Maybe she'd breached some rule by doing this. In that case he had something else to hate her for, she'd be leaving in a few hours. In the dark's quiet drizzle she felt thankful.

Sarge listened to the dull timid patter of mistlike rain on pine needles. It was two, two thirty by Ilana's clock. He'd woken and eased out of bed careful not to break the rhythm of her breathing because she looked damn good sleeping like that and he wanted her to rest a while. He slipped on his pants and roamed into the hall. Felt rested, calm in a way he hadn't felt for years. It wasn't dreaming that had woken him tonight, but he'd woken suddenly nevertheless. So now he stood at the screen door watching.

When he'd seen the light out he'd figured on a short. Or maybe a bird. There was that time a few years back some crow had flown head-first into the bulb, shattered it, flopped dead to the ground so singed feathers mixed with shards of glass. Then he made out the figure moving back and forth near the pines, and when he'd made out it was her he wasn't at all surprised.

His initial instinct had been to flood the area with light again. Either that or give a call, make his presence known. But he stayed silent and still. She turned her face up. Supposed to be good for the skin, rainwater. Some woman had told him, some swimmer, long ago.

She quickly pulled off her shirt, and that sudden illumination of skin in the wet night bounced back towards him. With each movement something rolled smoothly underneath. Good muscles, clearly defined for a woman, no excess. She turned halfway, folded the shirt to a bundle and rolled her face in it. In profile he saw her breasts. They were full, nicely molded, very pale. She turned face up for the full force of the water again, ran hands over her forehead and down her neck and ran them down across her breasts, circled the nipples, fingers spreading half-moon shapes below the breasts and passing over her entire torso again. She held hands out, palms up, to catch the water.

Sarge turned away. There were rituals everyone had, everyone, personal actions that with any witness other than yourself lost all significance. When someone else acknowledged them, these rituals were no longer in your power and could thus make you a victim. So Sarge walked away quickly, silently. He was a private man. He respected that in others.

With papers slapdashed across the floor, his study looked as if it had been burglarized. He turned on a lamp and surveyed the damage, picked up handfuls of sheets of his scribbles, his clippings. He stacked them on the desk. Then he reached among all the rest for the neatly folded little chart. Section by section he opened it. Where it had been folded the markings were blurred, the paper frayed. He followed faded red lines to a midway point. The blue colorings of water still looked strong, hadn't faded much. Why'd they make it blue? The water wasn't blue, it was gray, gray and white and you could smell the salt stick a freezing tongue out at you. In September it had to be, had to be then if you were going to do it at all. Because of the winds. Temperature close to optimal early in the month, as optimal as it ever got. Midway point there had been the end-point. Markings, measurements, key scales, blurred a second and he rubbed his eyes.

He spread it across semi-ordered heaps on the desk, then folded it diagonally. He gave it another couple of folds and it was an airplane. Sarge sent his paper airplane spiraling towards the sun clock on the wall.

Its point touched a circular rim and did a weary tail dive to the floor. So long, he said, goodbye charlie.

Back in Ilana's room he lay next to her for a few minutes. Her eyebrows arched when he traced them but she didn't wake up. They were lightly speckled with gray like her hair. He recalled running his hands through long ago like a rake in thick black silky hay, and that sense he'd gotten of how easy it might be to get lost there. The way Ted May'd been lost between Cape Gris-Nez and Dover back in '54, his body washed ashore months later with a broken compass strapped to the wrist. Her eyelids quivered and her mouth opened to ask something. It's okay, he said, go back to sleep.

Sarge stopped in his own room, pulled on shoes and a sweatshirt. He checked the clock. Nearly four. Another short while and the sky would start to lighten a little even if the rain continued. He figured she'd be getting ready to leave soon. The clock's minute hand glowed green at him, its clicks silent. For a second he thought of how she'd looked there half-naked, spreading hands out to the rain. It reminded him of something—what, he didn't know. Something like a long-ago dream maybe, because it felt like he'd seen it before even though that was impossible. He checked to make sure the alarm was off. He left and went out the back way.

Her car was parked there. It was third or fourth hand, hubcaps dented and the body covered by many coats of paint, this top one a dirt-spattered light blue that couldn't hide rust at the edges. Drizzle was turning its veneer of road dust into thin trickling mud that ran down the sides. The dark vinyl inside looked old, clean, impersonal. Sarge stood in the chill.

Sometimes you didn't know what you were going to do until the time was there and the options limited. Sometimes all you had to do was a simple thing. You'd spend days, maybe years, deciding and still never know exactly what you'd do, and then suddenly the moment was there and all cards laid bare on the table, all hands open to choice, and because of whoever you happened to be at that moment you made one choice or another. The more limited the options, the more weighty the decision. The more limited the options, the better you had to know yourself. Sarge pressed the car door open. He moved inside, rested arms easily on the wheel. Then he just waited.

"Morning." He slid over. Outside she hesitated a second. He'd noticed that first jump of panic but now she seemed cooler, just a little anxious and grim. She threw her bag over into the back seat. She got in shoulders-and-head first as if diving.

Dorey's eyes examined his. Well what now, they asked. She turned to look ahead. The windshield was a mess, streaked dirty wet on the outside, wipers pasted to its bottom with mud.

"Trouble sleeping?"

She shrugged.

She'd changed clothes, new jeans, maroon sweater that made her look awake and compact at the same time that it accentuated her paleness. Awake the better part of a few days and still she looked steady, still capable. Trained to endure and exert continuously for long, long periods of time. That's what I like to see! he wanted to say, but held it inside. Then he wanted to tell her more and ask about a hundred questions. He didn't know how to start.

"The trouble's that temperature and the currents." It slipped from her casually. She wasn't talking to him so much as talking out loud. Watching, he felt her exhaustion deeply. "Around midway is when you hit that south-flowing stream, 53 right? The fifteen-mile point, straight-distance miles. If it's worst around late July, I figure take off at an easy tide sometime late in August. Island to the mainland. With the right timing and a good tide you can clear the rocks. Late August."

Sarge frowned. "September. First week in September."

"How come?"

"You're forgetting the weather factor. You can peak for August and then spend weeks waiting while the gale warnings keep coming. They won't even send tugs through there most days in August. No, it's got to be September."

Her jaw tightened, voice came out bitter. "What else do you know?"

He was silent because he knew he was still waiting, and the best way to wait was in silence. That way he could feel words form clearly, cleanly. The longer you waited, the more decision became inevitable. He'd have liked to tell her that. He'd have liked to ask her to be patient. Then they met each other's eyes fully, and he recognized her expression to be not anger but something different, one he'd seen before.

It had been some child's face, probably a boy's, peering around the folds of a tent flap. Along the Mediterranean, south of El Bureij maybe. Just a small, dark face glimpsed in passing, and he remembered it clearly because he'd known, seeing it, that the child was in pain and had been for quite some time. It was a face prematurely lined with strain, mouth and forehead compressed, eyes wide, dark and sad. The look was of patience and waiting. Recognizing it now, he saw that requesting patience of her would be an insult. She'd already practiced the art of it, had been patiently waiting a long time.

Sarge flipped through things he'd heard, her reputation, news clippings, whatever sparse history had been presented as official. All brief, all impersonal. A series of swims, some competitive, some solo. Progressions. Maybe a record broken here or there. Impressive statistics. Then Seal Beach, then nothing, not a sign of her. He tried to make all the file notes count for something and none of them, separately or together, accounted for the person sitting next to him. Not her presence or her affect.

He thought of what his own history on paper might look like and he laughed. Told her that according to the institutions he'd been expelled from he knew very little indeed.

Then he got serious, and examining her face, he was cautious. "I know a lot about that swim, though. More than anyone else. More than you."

Water streaked trails over the windshield's dirty rivulets. Their breath clouded. Outside it was gray, just about morning. If he'd had all the words ready he'd have told her that without his blessing and aid she'd never stand a chance because it was his water, his swim, everything he was etched into the dizzying drift of its currents. That if she thought he'd let her touch it without both his hands in the deal she really was crazy, totally nuts. And there were other reasons only he wasn't clear on them. They were confused, bound up somehow with that slug she'd taken at him and the way she'd looked going back and forth, back and forth in the lake's cold and the way she looked now. How it felt pressing his lips against Ilana's neck after who knew how long, the texture of her skin, sounds she made there in the dark, the whole strange day of remembering. He shook his head to free it. He could feel her watching him now.

"Listen, don't take this the wrong way. Hell, I don't even know if there's an answer. Do you consider yourself to be emotionally stable?"

She grinned. It was a funny look, a tired kind of smile, almost triumphant.

"No," she said. "What about you?"

"I wasn't joking."

"Me neither." She sighed. "Look. What do you want to hear? No. Yes. Maybe. I don't know. I don't know what that means." She looked ahead through the glass. Her hands toyed with the steering, gave up and fell to her lap. "This is the way I see it, Sarge." It was the first time she'd addressed him like that, and for a second it unnerved him. "If I give the answer you want to hear then that's the right answer and you'll like me for it. I'll leave with you liking me. It's nice if you like me, I'd like you to like me. Only it doesn't do me a bit of good next

August, right? If I'm out there on the eighteenth mile or so. Say it takes twenty hours. Say longer. I don't know. It doesn't matter so much then if I said the right thing."

For the first time, he liked her.

"Okay," he said. "Let's talk."

"What?"

"This swim. Let's talk. Tell me about yourself." His voice sounded strange to him, harsh and monotonous. He thought of Ilana, her neck's soft jugular warmth leaping beneath the skin when he kissed. For a second it felt like some substantial weight inside him would break in half. "And it's September, not August," he said firmly, "first week of September."

II

BENEFICIAL PAIN

A THOROUGH EXAMINATION, Sarge had insisted. Recovery rate, all that stuff, he knew just the man. There was no beginning things without it. She agreed. He'd made a phone call. Then they drove down together, a trip of many hours. Sarge talked a lot of the way and she sat in nearly comfortable silence. She was glad for his presence, especially when they hit the city—traffic, crowds, the noise. Glancing over, he thought she looked a little dazed by it all. At Tycho's office Sarge stayed in the waiting room.

"Chest pains, shortness of breath, et cetera et cetera?"
She shook her head.
"Have you ever been pregnant? Abortions?"
"No."
"Allergies?"
"No."
"What do you think of astrology?"
She stopped, then laughed, delighted. "Well. Get more specific and I'll tell you."
"Wheels of fortune. Matters of luck. Mere coincidence—do you believe in any or all of the above?"
Dorey gazed across the desk, and after a pause she smiled. "One percent."
"What?"
"Sure I do. One percent of everything is probably chance or luck or something, you know."
"The other ninety-nine percent being?"
"Ah. Work, I guess. Yes, sure. Just a lot of work. You have the will and then you do the work."
Tycho adjusted his glasses, eased back in his chair and returned her gaze. Not quite the answer he'd had in mind but it made him ask questions he hadn't planned on asking, so he liked it. "You're a firm believer in willpower, then."

She nodded.

"And not in destiny."

"Well I didn't say that." She frowned. "I didn't say that at all, that's something different, right? I mean, it's different from luck and chance. That's the way I see it." Then she grinned, almost teasing. "But so is astrology."

His chuckles punctuated the room's sunlit stillness. "Okay. Just testing."

"How'd I do?"

He winked. Gave her the A-okay sign, forefinger circling over to meet his thumb. Dorey leaned into the chair's cushioned backing. In a lot of ways he had probably the oddest face she'd ever seen. His hair had been rusty brown and was now half gray, balding smoothly away from a wide forehead, making it wider. Heavy jaw, large mouth with smile wrinkles at the corners. He had thin eyebrows that looked perpetually raised in surprise. The eyes were small, dark, and behind extraordinarily thick glasses they seemed even smaller. They twinkled, like a continually surging laugh. The glasses were metal-framed, looked like part of a mask that would normally be attached by bolts and screws.

His nose created the real oddity, though. The tip of it was flattened. The bridge crooked, curving to the left. From both sides, thin white scars sprayed out partway across his cheeks. Seemed like the nose had been crushed and spliced right off and then haphazardly replaced. In fact, it had.

He hauled himself easily from the chair with long, loose arms, strolled to the stereo embedded in bookshelves. "Music?"

"That would be great."

"Bach? African Mass? Brubeck? What's your pleasure?"

"Do you wear headphones to bed too?"

Tycho laughed, long, loud, and dry. "Not me. That's Sarge's domain, he likes to inundate his senses in stimuli. I prefer a lighter touch—it's a matter of choice, of course, no judgment intended." He decided on something simple. Sephardic romances, the vocals in Ladino. Sarge would approve. "Here. Unless you've any objections, something lovely coming up. Press the buzzer to the left of the door in the examination room when you're ready. Let's check everything out, okay?"

Okay, she told him. On her way she glanced up. Noticed thin, night-blue outlines on the ceiling. Outlines of constellations. They strung a circle on the white surface in twelve concisely cut pie pieces. A zodiac. She turned to him, pointed up. "Will you tell me about that later?"

"Sure. In the meantime think of it as a macrocosm of your own body, there's food for thought. Ring when you're ready."

In the examination room she stripped quickly, neatly, and hung her clothes. She ticked off these familiar items in her mind: the scale, the sink, metallic tools wrapped in sterile plastic on white shelves, table in the middle that looked even more ominous when those stirrups were attached, reminded you for a second—even when you were used to it as routine —of some primal fear you had of being impaled.

She ignored the paper-thin, sacklike pullover robe. False modesty. He'd touch everything anyway. Naked, she searched the small white shelves until she located broad folded sheets of tissue paper. She spread some herself on the table's dark cushioning, then realized she'd been listening to music that filtered faintly, pleasantly, into the room. A woman's voice, solitary except for an occasional guitar bridge in A minor, E major, and the rattle of maracas, the background brush of leather-skinned drums. It was a high, melodic chant that repeated. One verse, chorus in chant. Two verse, the chant again. Sounded like Spanish but not quite. Dorey caught the word for "beautiful." *Hermosa*, the "s" pronounced with a shhh, as in Arabic. Drums were tapped lightly. Always a predictable syncopation. She pressed the buzzer. Then swung herself onto the table, cross-legged, waiting.

White jacket, stethoscope, he'd donned the works. When he entered the room he paused. "Be with you in a minute." He moved swiftly to the sink, washed his hands with routine thoroughness. He'd been surprised to see her totally uncovered. Sitting there easily, impassive, arms resting along crossed thighs, hair swept in dark contrast back from her fore-

61

head and cheeks, she'd struck him for a moment as a watchful lioness at rest. Used as he was to bodies both common and extraordinary, in accordance as he was with the written and unwritten rules of his discipline, Tycho's appreciation—which he acknowledged silently, and to himself alone—was professional rather than sexual.

"The music. It's not Spanish, right?"

"Right. Ladino." He admired the honesty of that gesture, her simple intentional neglect in donning any covering. Direct, for sure. Sometimes he'd found himself wondering what it was about these coverings, these tissue-thin sheets spread between one body and another, that seemed so necessary to the maintenance of what passed for human civility. Boundary lines. Standardized set of limitations. The covering was only allowed off in specific circumstances, those circumstances clearly delineated. Or in conditions of unimaginable extremity —sure, there the stripping took place as well in unforeseen, unsought-for ways. Ways that might or might not be condoned in retrospect. He turned off the water.

"Ladino."

"The Spanish Jews spoke and wrote it." He dried his hands. "An old form of Castillian with a lot of Hebrew and some Arabic mixed in. That's where you get the soft 's' and the glottal stop—listen."

"I like this. What's she saying?"

"Singing to the moon. 'When the moon goes high in the sky, always before dawn, I also rise, and my eyes are dizzy from so much looking at the sea.'"

Dorey nodded approval. "A swimmer."

Tycho grinned. When he turned to her, she was offering out her right arm. Asking did he want to check the carotid or radial or both. He held her wrist gently, placed her other hand's fingertips along the pulse of her neck. "Both. Let's see what we come up with, then double-check with this thing." His chin jutted towards the stethoscope. They timed her pulse. He told her the count and she smiled proudly in agreement.

Pressing the rounded shape against her left breast, then just under it, he listened. The loud pulsation beat drums, a direct line to his head. Always made him shiver a little inside. It was slow, this heart of hers, clear, steady. A nice slow large heart. "Fifty beats to the minute right now. That's nice, very nice. We'll do a little treadmill later, check out the recovery rate."

"Okay. This Ladino. Do you speak it?"

"No. But Sarge studied it for a while, I remember. He told me at the time it was part of Ilana's background, Sephardic on her paternal grandfather's side by one sixteenth or something like that. Cough, that's right."

Boom thump thump, boom thump thump. Heart of the matter. That was a phrase he'd always liked. It was such a simple thing really, elongated kind of globe suspended in the mediastinum, pulsating at liberty. Core of the body's universe. Without it, everything was no go. Even with all his years of familiarity, of business as usual, Tycho'd never lost that edge of awe he felt for the organ. He never operated unless the stars were with him.

"Breathe in. Out. Nice." He glanced at her face and the impression occurred to him by instinct. "Experienced any insomnia?"

"Why?" It was a challenge.

"You're aware that sometimes in training you're putting out so much maximum effort that you're marginally ill. That's when sleep keeps you going, deep sleep, lots of it."

"I can do straight sets at a hundred percent"—she emphasized the *percent* proudly "—on no sleep."

"Oh," he spoke gently, "I don't doubt it."

She relaxed.

"Say ah. Good." He beamed the tiny bluish ray into her throat. "Tonsils intact, bravo. What's Sarge starting you out with? Distance?"

She turned an ear to him and he flashed the light again. "Sure. A couple of months at least." Offered the other ear. "It's not like starting from scratch, you know. I've been putting in a lot of work myself. For a long time."

His eyes smiled. "I don't doubt that, either."

"That last song. The one in minor key, I liked it."

"Another breath. Thanks. Want a translation?"

"Uh-huh." The cold pressed circles against her back. Left side. Right side. It stepped up, then down, and she breathed deeply.

" 'This mountain I see before me is on fire, burning, there I lost my soul and I sit here and weep, I want the sky for paper, I want the sea for ink, the trees I want for pens, to write my tears.' Translation courtesy of Mr. Olssen himself. Let's do the height and weight, okay?"

"You memorize things." The scale's rubbery tread was clammy against her feet. "That's good."

"I agree. It means you don't have to haul books around all the time, you just internalize the text. Tell me about your training. What you've done on your own."

The metal stick leveled with the top of her head. She ran down facts for him: hours here, hours there, how many a day, how she'd paced herself. He whistled during a lull in the music.

"That's a lot of calories on the funeral pyre."

"I eat a lot. Everything raw."

He wrote things down and took one more listen at her chest. "Stamina," he whistled, "stamina. Interval work. That heart of yours, that's a blue ribbon heart."

"I know."

She sat again, dangled legs over the table's edge, tapped a fist lightly above her left breast in a simulated series of pulsations. He stepped to the sink, and before turning on the water again glanced back to see she'd crossed her legs on crinkling tissue paper and was facing him, waiting. He caught her shoot a quick look at the footholds now attached to the table's end, neat metal place for heels to dig in, two prongs striking out from the edge there like bulbous-headed antennae. For an instant her expression was sullen. Then it changed, a bright flash of resentment that just as swiftly vanished. Tycho washed his hands.

64   He took the speculum in its plastic wrapping, along with a packet of gloves, and approached her. She waited, a compact self-contained world of lungs sighing, axions, dendrites, joints

and tendons all greased and popping in extraordinarily well-coordinated fashion. Sure the heart kept all that ticking but what kept the heart ticking. Sometimes, he'd wonder. Amid the flurry of bodies passing his way with an array of complaints ranging from shin splints to thrombosis, there were one or two who'd stand out from time to time and—for any or for no apparent reason—touch off a spark of fundamental wondering in him. His professional veneer was several walls thick. No one ever knew that he wondered. Those cases Schweitzer'd reported from the gold mines of Africa—workers dying there of no obvious pathology, nothing traceable, the heart just stopped. Broken heart, Schweitzer called it. These men are dying of broken hearts. The chemistry created by the choice between resignation and despair too stressful, that's what it must have been. So the constant torment of hoping, or of waiting—because waiting indicated expectation—would constitute a more favorable homeostasis for some, whereas adaptation of the organism to an ostensibly less stressful state of quiet resignation proved, for others, impossible, morbidity the result. How many beats per minute would break it? What was the average pulse rate for an anxious heart in waiting? Ninety-six? Eighty-four? If you gave it an attainable goal towards which it might carefully, methodically expand, would you bring it down to sixty-five? Add intelligent, often repeated doses of near-maximal activity, soaked in desire. Would you get it down to fifty then? Maybe. Sitting there, intentionally blank-faced, she touched off a few question marks inside him and something poked its probing metallic head through his own layers of covering. Emotionally honest thing to do in this situation, he guessed, would be at the very least to blush. All professionalism aside, he looked at the unsheathed head of the instrument he held, smeared in sterile jelly, and for just a second wanted to apologize to her, or ask her forgiveness for what would under any and all circumstances be a violation. Her movements were precise and deliberate, fitting her feet into the stirrups.

"Can you move down a little? Thank you."

Sometimes violation was necessary, part and parcel of a

healthful process. He liked to think that, anyway. So he did, obscured the twinklings of doubt between his natural layers of certainty, like something buried in a wall. What was that one of Poe's? *Tell-Tale Heart*. The music drifted to silence. For a minute he felt he'd understood something but then it was gone.

"Okay," he said, "thank you. When you're ready come on into the office again and let's talk. We'll run the treadmill and a few other tests later, you know the routine."

She'd swung her legs back to dangle loosely over the table's edge, rubbed the tops of her thighs as if just completing a few sets of leg presses. He saw her face nod in profile. It was a cool, blank, well-molded profile, lips held slightly apart, the eyes directed somewhere else altogether.

That bypass Tycho had performed the day before was just about the last operation, at least for a while. He'd gotten to the point where the only way he could avoid being available was to die. Or close things up mostly and drop out of sight—that's what Tycho was in the process of doing. He'd just awoken one morning to realize that, in some unconscious way, he'd been planning this for years. The money saved and invested. Paperwork all up to date. Accountants paid, taxes in order, the file cabinets neatly arranged. He'd gone uptown and started with some arm curls, bench presses, some pulling. Written off the marathon for this year. Telling himself all right Tycho Brahe, it's time now, it's time. Time was important. And then Sarge had called after more than two years. Sure time was important but still their friendship had spanned it. Not that anything could or would span the death of a man's son, but then friendship wasn't meant to compensate for anything, Tycho knew. Friendship was just there and—in the ideal sense—enduring.

That day Sarge sounded urgent. This swimmer, he was training a swimmer and would Tycho take a look at her. They'd kept in touch through letters, but the man's voice broke through something inside of him. Then Tycho knew where the excitement came from: they were going to see each other again. There was something in the physical presence of one another that had a strange effect on him and, he guessed, on Sarge, calming and exciting at the same time. It was a trade-off of ideas. They'd click in on the same things and expand the same kernels of thought in different directions. Brought out the best in each. This was friendship, he guessed, in the ideal.

Sarge was flipping through the sketches in Tycho's manuscript. They were deceptively similar in appearance. All hexagons drawn with the length vertical, large circles protruding from the tip of each corner. Some were drawn with circles bisecting each vertex too. Some had additional circles inside. Within some circles were symbols. These symbols were letters and, in Hebrew, also words. He had to sound them out silently, to himself.

"Smack in the middle of heritage. How does it feel, captain?"

Sarge snapped the manuscript binder shut and left it on the couch when he stood. He grabbed both of Tycho's shoulders. They looked at each other full-face before bear-hugging.

"Johnny. You look good."

"You too. For your age."

Sarge told him to go to hell. Tycho adjusted his glasses, grinning.

"What do you think of the Tree of Life, maestro? See, they knew it all back then. We're just beginning to understand what we've lost—take those shapes there"—he motioned towards the black binder—"and manipulate them into pyramids, into circles, triangles, anything and everything. Like the Philosopher's Stone."

Sarge squeezed his shoulder roughly, happily. Saying the difference between them had always been that Tycho kept searching for some intrinsic key that bound things together, whereas he himself figured if he spouted off loud enough and long enough, carried his own ideas to their ultimate conclusions, he'd learn plenty in the process and realize by the end that there was no single key. Aspects of life appearing to be at variance with one another were actually bound together—not by a single originating principle, but by certain elements different in application only, the same in the abstract. Dedication. Same thing anywhere. Be it a dedicated guitarist or a dedicated marathoner. Could you say that the same seed inspired both? Maybe. Maybe not. For Sarge, that wasn't the point. You could say, for sure, that both employed dedication in pursuit of widely different goals. So that after a while the goal—like the key—became an utterly secondary consideration.

Tycho wasn't so sure. Part of his style, never to say he disagreed unless he'd proven fallacy to his own satisfaction. Not that he was overly cautious. He was simply a thorough thinker. Sarge allowed him room for this style's peculiarities, always had. Vice versa. So they'd been friends a long time.

Tycho sat loosely on the couch. He'd taken off the white jacket but forgotten the stethoscope, swinging crookedly against his high-necked sweater. Sarge paced, hands in pockets. Tycho observed him. Hands in pockets were, with Sarge, an indication of tension. He'd stuff them in, arms half-bent and rigid. At least the old dark-toned coloring had returned, tingeing his face, the backs of his hands. Several years ago had been a different story. What he remembered most about those days that were still not speakable was Sarge's sudden lack of color. He'd been blanched, less than white, less than gray.

"She's a beauty, Sarge. Great condition, I'm sure the tests will bear it out." He watched Sarge pace. "What's the story?"

An insanity, Sarge chuckled. Tycho gave him a raised-eyebrow questioning look. Sarge sat again. He noticed subtle differences in the way they were built. Tycho had a more balanced center of gravity, so he seemed planted firmly on the cushions from his waist down, whereas Sarge leaned over, elbows on knees, torso nearly displacing the rest of him. "I don't know, Johnny. Maybe I'm out of my mind."

"I wouldn't say that. You look healthy. Lucid, no paranoia, in control."

"Hell. I'm always in control."

"Does that bother you?"

Sarge had to think a minute. He shrugged. "Sometimes. Anyway, that's not important. It's good to see you again. It's been too long."

"For me, too." He considered carefully before speaking again. "I guess I ought to tell you, when you called I was a lot more than surprised. Then I got a feeling right here"—he patted his stomach—"that was familiar. It was excitement! That's when I realized it was more than just looking forward to seeing you again, bastard." Bastard this and bastard that. They'd thrown it at each other ever since day one, a derogation born of affection. Tycho leaned forward too, so his knee almost touched Sarge's. "It was a feeling that what you're doing is right. You know what I mean? So no, I don't think it's crazy." He lounged back again. "Frightening. Exciting. But be selectively careful and just go with the best, it's a good process to latch on to."

"And leave the rest to fate?" It was a dig Sarge couldn't help. Looking up, he saw Tycho accept it, mull it over, saw that it would be all right anyway. Tycho grinned.

"Exactly."

One of his hands rested firmly on Sarge's knee. They were quiet, sinking for a minute into comfortable insulated stillness offered by the room's pleasant lights. Outside car horns bleated, bleats multiplied at each stop. Noon. Midtown was nearly unwalkable for all the bodies walking. And it was fall's last slap of heat before the real cold set in, so haze filtered westward from the East River, broke over the snarling currents at Hell's Gate, blew down southward from the Harlem, eastward from the Hudson's docks. It was an island. Twenty-eight miles of surrounding waterway, a surprisingly small island.

Things outside there swirled, rasped. Inside where they sat you'd never have known it. Tycho'd done a lot of soundproofing. He was particular about the tonal quality of the music he listened to, didn't like exterior static of any sort to interfere. He knew that from curb-level it all seemed to be a lot of shrieking chaos. But from, say, tenth-floor, or twenty-second-floor level, you looked down and saw the geometric delineations. Armies advancing with uniformity of pace and form and style, the squares apparent, triangles becoming clear after a brief search, the lines and bisections and angles of moving people, vehicles, static formations of buildings. Even the noise followed discernible patterns and rhythms, like tides. All contained by a circling of water. He'd realize, time and again, that it was usually only from bird's-eye view—or in retrospect —that patterns became clear.

He slapped Sarge's knee lightly, removed his hand. "Look, let's get the business over and done with first. As soon as she comes down we'll test, okay? In the meantime tell me what your plans are."

"For her?"

"Training."

"You know I'm a mean bastard."

"Drill sergeant." Tycho chuckled. "Maybe she's upstaged you on that count. I think she's been over-training."

"Right! So I'm planning on just switching gears to begin with. Minimize the intensity for a little while, cut down on sprints. Maximize distance. Pound it down solid, good solid base there. Then build."

"Training suggestion."

Sarge nodded, listening.

"What kind of running is she doing? Seven, seven-thirty pace?"

"Right."

"Have her stick to seven-thirty for now and increase the distance to nine, ten miles a day, say six days a week. That's a lot of leg work. So while you're laying down the pool distance you're building up kind of an additional storehouse."

Tycho told him what he had in mind. After a while she could step up the pace for those nine-to-ten miles. Bring them down to seven minutes each, then again as close as possible to six-thirty. So by the time they began the heavier intensity training this winter, she should be coming in after ten miles at better than seventy minutes and—although they'd rapidly cut down on mileage at that point to make way for the increasing length of swimming time—she'd maintain that quicker pace until Sarge said no more running. And have successfully tacked on another basic layer of endurance.

They talked nutrition, supplements. Weight training. She'd been working with weights three times a week, doing a circuit that emphasized the upper body. Disciplined. She'd created her own schedule and stuck to it without deviation for many months. Her tendency, they both noted, was to overdo it rather than slack off. While Tycho spoke Sarge listened carefully, once in a while smiled agreement.

Sarge's hands swabbed an invisible canvas in the air in front of him. Slapped down the repeats. Dabbed in the intervals. Painted with great care the distance work he'd planned.

"Easy." There was a note of satisfaction in his voice that made Tycho lean back, relax. "I'll just go easy on her for a while. Relatively speaking that is. Easier than she expects. Do her good."

"What about sleep?"

Sarge paused and his mouth opened wordlessly, troubled. "I thought music," he said finally. "Or meditation. Or both." He ran his shoes against the carpet, soft scuff like brushing velvet in the moment of silence. "The question's sanity."

Tycho frowned. It made his nose curve in an even odder way, flatten more across the breadth of his face. "Maybe not. She doesn't seem psychotic."

"Stable?"

"Disciplined. Isolated." No, that wasn't quite it even though it was true. Then he had it. "Sort of in a—I don't know, just a sense I have—a self-imposed exile. You know what I mean."

Sarge did. Their eyes met briefly. Tell me, Tycho was saying, tell me about Ilana. So Sarge told him. Sleeping better these nights, he said, she didn't seem bothered by nightmares much anymore. About the rest of it, well, he didn't exactly have a handle on that. He just knew that, for him, a chink was made in whatever wall had existed between them for so long, something opened up now and he felt freer touching her, being with her. Beautiful, he told Tycho, sure, that's what she was. You had to admit it. His voice lit with a touch   71 of pride.

While he spoke his shoulders let loose, he seemed to be

actually, fully sitting for the first time that day. Sometimes his lips curved, on the brink of smiling or the verge of something else, some gentle kind of glow, that Tycho couldn't pinpoint but didn't need to, either.

When Sarge glanced up he noticed Tycho watching, kept the gaze longer and said, hell Johnny, looks like you've been working out yourself these days. Tycho nodded.

"Rowing?"

"Rowing."

"How's it feel?"

"Good," Tycho said finally. "After all this time."

That's good, Sarge told him. "Ever feel like being around other kinds of boats? Using some of that expertise of yours?"

"What do you mean?"

"Navigating," said Sarge. "Just navigating."

Then Tycho understood what he meant, and they sat in silence for a while still looking at each other. There was a weight on Sarge now, something almost visible, perching firmly atop his shoulders. Tycho felt himself perspire a little. After a while he nodded. Okay Sarge, he said. Okay. Then the weight jumped through the air between them, landed in Tycho's lap. He felt it crawl up, swing around to the back of his neck. It hung there heavily. Still he managed a quiet smile and told Sarge all right then. They'd talk about the details later.

When they glanced up Dorey was waiting in the doorway. She'd dressed and looked that unique combination of slim and solid.

Ready? said Tycho. She nodded.

"Treadmill then," he grinned, "let's go. You wait here, Sarge. We'll run that machine down."

"Okay," Tycho warned, "okay."

The treadmill slowed swiftly to a stop. She was bent just about in half, hanging on to the side rail. Between gasps and lightly formed sweat her eyes rolled up to his.

"There's a danger signal," he grinned, "right in the center

of your forehead. A little dent shows. That's where the highest form of spirit's centered—yours was experiencing stress."

The pressure subsided, gasps slowed, so did the drum in her chest. She straightened. She was wired into a machine, the meter of which had shot up past 190 and was now rapidly needling back down. He watched the speed with which it dropped in surprise, and then he wanted to gloat for one happy second. Physical health of this paradigmatic sort was something that pleased him unutterably.

She leaned on a rail, gave him a quizzical look. "Where's the lowest form of spirit?"

He pointed directly between her breasts and thought that for a split second she stiffened, or paled even more beneath the sweaty flush. He asked was anything wrong but she shook her head.

"Great recovery," he nodded. She knew, smiled slightly with assurance. Outside through the window, it was early afternoon. Shadows had already begun to stretch along the eastern faces of taller buildings. Tycho handed her a towel.

Sarge dialed the number and waited out four rings. A male voice answered. There was that initial second of wondering on both ends, then he asked was Anne in and the answer came back just a sec.

"Hey Anne," Sarge heard, "phone."

"No way!" a voice boomed back. "No! Tell them I'm not home. Who is it?"

"She says she's not home."

Sarge gave his name. The message was relayed and there were seconds of silence, then some banging, paper rustling and a dog's high-pitched yapping came through distinctly.

"Sarge! Hey where are you? How are you? Just a second, okay? Hey calm down will you! Rick. Rick, can you take him with you, I can't hear a thing. Thanks. Whew. Mr. Olssen!"

"You belong by open water, Anne." Sarge's voice teased. He smiled as if they could see each other. "City's sent you over the edge."

"What edge? Who says? How are you? Wait. Is this business? Because I want you to know Sarge, I'm not swimming for you or against you."

"What have you been doing?"

Her laugh rolled tangibly in his ear, like the trilling crest of a larger undefined shape. "Up to my elbows in archery. Studying the viola. Did you know I'm going to be a doctor soon?"

"No kidding."

"No kidding, well not really. Doctor of philosophy, Spanish Lit. Don't ask why, my father always said I'd be a great internist. So it's P H instead of an M before the D. *Pues que tal, muchacho?* I mean really."

"Alive," he said, "I'm in town. Let's have dinner."

"Rick! Hey, is that concert tonight or tomorrow? No? Good. I'm free at six, Sarge. Around then anyway, make it six fifteen because I've got practice this afternoon and I'm going to do well. Then at eight thirty I've got class. That okay? Six fifteen to eight ten, say, it's all yours." She named the place.

"Six fifteen," he pretended he was writing it laboriously, "to eight ten. Yes, doctor, yes."

"Hey. It's good to hear your voice, I want you to know that. You were my main hero for a long time."

"And I'm not anymore?"

They laughed.

In the moment of silence he heard puppy barks in the background, a man's voice growling back playfully. Then she took a breath. "So how bad, Sarge," she said, "how bad has it been?"

He didn't respond immediately. When he did it felt as though someone else were speaking. "Difficult to say." The hell with it. "Like hitting the wall, Anne, only it doesn't stop. Just about the worst. The worst ever."

Now he wanted badly to hang up. Couldn't stand the faceless, presenceless silence much longer. She must have sensed it, through the wires, in that way she had. You'd think her focus was shot, scattered impossibly in countless directions, and all of the sudden she'd zoom in with a sudden concentrated sharklike aim that took you totally off guard, left you

74

frightened and exposed and sometimes delighted, always a little breathless.

"It's okay," she said, "it's a good time to hang up anyway, really. Six fifteen."

"Right," he said.

Sarge set the phone quietly in its cradle. The buttons blinked, then went dark. He rested his head against the back of Tycho's chair, closed his eyes, and when he opened them felt very clearly something he hadn't felt in years. It was fatigue. Out of habit, he fought back by moving. Stood, ambled to the shelves, the racks of records, looked for Beethoven's Ninth.

Your first impression of Anne Norton was always that of a perfect all-American cross between tomboy and cheerleader. The features were in good proportion, bluntly pretty, and she'd let her hair grow out so it brushed the tops of her shoulders. The entire effect was of wholesome, sporty openness that bordered on gullibility, face and lengthy gestures signaling unfeigned goodwill. So after that first impression you'd step in closer. Then notice that her deep purple blouse was pure silk, jeans custom-made, and what dripped in delicate glittering curves from her ears and neck was at least eighteen carat. When the lips moved, they were fuller than apple pie style and sometimes came together in a firm intentional line that bordered on cruel. Or the eyes—on those rare occasions when they focused for any length of time at all—shone with something altogether different from good-natured ease. Whoosh, she'd go, with one of those deceptively lazy, graceful gestures, and by that time you'd stepped very close indeed and a piece of you was vacuum-swept into her processing machine. She'd churn it well, inspecting, civilly talking and laughing and joking the whole time, then either spit it back out and turn away suddenly, or decide there was some nourishment there after all and then she'd stay because you had her interest, offered something she didn't already know and, thus, earned her respect. And you could be proud. Anne always made you feel a part of some great moment in history. At first it was embarrassing. Then you had to admire her capacity for heightening the moment's impact. And since by then you were also a part of her process, in admiring her you'd admire yourself. By holding her interest, your own self-esteem was, somehow, expanded. To many, that was both the least tangible and most precious fringe benefit of knowing her. To Sarge, it was that she reminded him, in some elemental way, of himself.

"Hey Sarge!" she waved from the door, interrupted the maitre d'. Heads turned. Noticing them, she broadened the wave to include everyone. Sarge stood. He grinned, rose to the occasion by waving back.

Books bulged up under the flap of her shoulder bag. In one hand she held a cased viola, in the other a waterproofed athletic bag from the outside loop of which dangled her shooting tassel. Her jacket was velvet. Walking towards him, she glimmered gold, flashed a lightning grin. Her hair was every color, red and blonde and many shades of brown in the low-slung light. From custom-made cuffs peeked a pair of track shoes. She looked terrific. He told her so.

When her arms swung around him, so did everything else. Books slammed his ribs. He heard a fine-tuned string complain. "I know," she pressed against his chest, "you haven't changed your looks much either." Then she was stacking things under the table. The maitre d' was suggesting strongly that he hold them for her in the coat room. No, she told him, no, those books were rare, the tassel had just been party to one hell of an illustrious practice session and nobody, but nobody, touched the viola except her. He could take the jacket for her though, thanks so much, and while he was at it some mineral water for the gentleman. Did he know that this gentleman was just about the greatest athlete in history? Well, one of them, anyway.

Sarge sat. The maitre d' left in a sort of daze, and she called after him that he'd forgotten her jacket. Then she draped it over the back of her chair and sat too, facing him. The blouse flowed a gentle V to her breasts. She crossed her legs, leaned towards him. "You missed a great set of bull's-eyes. Down to the *wire* Sarge, let me tell you. It's my concentration that did it, though. Tournament next weekend, will you be around?" Her eyes stopped meandering, jumped directly to his face. She reached across the table for his hands, curled her own around them. "Hey! How are you?"

"Heading for Sherwood Forest?" he teased. "Still swimming?"

"No. Never. I've done my bit, amen."

"Miss it?"

Now her eyes were sliding away again, to the salt, the couple walking by. "Uh-oh. Sarge, you're scheming."

The mineral water came bubbling around twists of lime in thinly frosted glasses. He raised his to her, saying it takes one to know one. Then he shrugged, told himself change tactics, don't let this one get away. He asked had she gone and gotten married while everyone's back was turned.

"No way!" Her eyes slid back rapidly. "Rick's got a brain and a half. Sometimes I think it's almost a fair match, Sarge, I tell you, but no thanks to bondage, no way. No screaming bambinos for yours truly. This is strictly off the books."

They ordered. She wanted swordfish steak, broiled but very, very slightly. Tender, she said, winking at the waiter, almost alive.

Smiling, Sarge let his guard down for a second. That was when she sprang. It was casual, though, so much so that he nearly missed the intent. "What brings you," she said, "to this time and place?" Her grin lit the dull-glowing air.

"Medical exam, I'm training a swimmer. Remember Dorey Thomas?" Their eyes clicked together like swords meeting. For her, the question would be rhetorical. He knew that but took the risk, knowing also that on some level it would appeal.

She inched her hands away. He could see her back arch proudly, bristle just a little. Then she laughed, nodded acknowledgment, squeezed his hands again, and the unexpected gallantry of her gesture took him slightly by surprise. "Ah-hah! I placed first over her in Australia, Sarge, didn't I. You know I like to remember my triumphs." They laughed.

77

She a little ruefully, because that had been the one time she'd pulled off such a coup. Every other race they'd both entered had been the other way around, and it wasn't until Thomas dropped from sight that she'd attained number one ranking. Sarge figured that, all fair play aside, it rankled. He knew her history, knew that before turning pro the only time she'd had to swallow number two status was the year when, at sixteen, she'd breaststroked to an Olympic silver medal. Now her hands flashed over the candle holder. Her bracelet glowed, he noticed the stone inset. Topaz. She was setting a stage for him, voice gone a little far away and dreamy. "Whew! That was the toughest thing I ever did, let me tell you. After the first six hours I was throwing up everything right smack on the half hour! You could have told time by it." She giggled almost merrily, shook her head. "After that, things took a turn for the worse. And by thirty miles the going really got rough."

"That was a tough swim that year, I remember."

"It was the best! When they held up the board that last time I could make out NUMBER 1 and I said to myself, Norton, Norton, you'd rather drop dead than not finish this one and you know, that was true, Sarge, it was absolutely true. Then at night—the sharks. They just kept showing up by the dozens and they'd do a kind of slow circle around and around. I was hardly moving by that time, I'd hit a real low, I remember thinking that if this ever ended I'd never do it again, no more swims, not ever, this was it. They weren't just cute little sand sharks. You could see white flashing everywhere. And the circle would get smaller and smaller, then every spot would glare from the boat and flood things with light that I couldn't much make out anyway at that point—to me it was some other great white belly. They had three marksmen from Melbourne riding shotgun on the bow. I was pretty hysterical. I thought they were out to get me, not the sharks. I kept stopping and treading in the general direction of the boat and screaming 'What time is it? What time is it?' " She'd raised her voice. Heads were turning again. Neither of them cared. "Only of course I was a blubbering idiot by then so they couldn't even make out what I was trying to say. My trainer was talking to me, I couldn't understand a word. And these sharks kept coming, the marksmen would fire into the water and scare them off and I'd nearly faint with fear, and once in a while they'd actually pick one off, way to the side there, and then I began to imagine that I *myself*"—she placed a hand over her heart solemnly—"had become a shark. I had visions of blood gushing past my head in the water, I started congratulating myself and feeling very crafty indeed, to have evaded being blown to smithereens by all those humans on the boat." She sat back, spoke to the top of the pepper grinder. "Do you know what I think pulled me through the last eight hours? Chocolate bars. I told myself if I would only finish I'd be able to eat a chocolate bar. I'll tell you, a Cadbury wrapper never looked so good as the picture I had in my head. It was an epic chocolate bar, the Moby Dick of all chocolate bars, Sarge. It was dripping coconut too, I could taste it oozing down my throat and my only fear was that when I finished I wouldn't be able to find one anywhere. I'd forgotten what country I was in and kept wondering if they sold this chocolate bar I'd promised myself in the stores, and the more I wondered the more frantic I got that maybe they didn't. That's how I kept swimming swimming swimming. It took me until just before sunrise, remember? See? My finest hour, Sarge, and I owe it to Almond Joy."

He grabbed for her hand across the table. She pressed his back, half smiling with satisfaction, and dinner was served. Amazing, she told him, pretty amazing how hungry she was now, and she guessed it was because recounting something like that couldn't help but bring you in touch with the basics, like eating. He speared into his chicken, pretty ravenous himself. So, he commented, she was through with all that stuff for good.

"Yes sir, good assumption. It's over." She crossed fork and knife over her plate in an X, the cloth napkin arched with a smooth flourish towards her lips for a second, then dove out of sight. She noticed the steaming bread basket, noticed the waiter passing by with bobbing tray of sirloin strips, noticed the wall carpeting and then zoomed in on Sarge. "Do you know why it's over?"

"Tell me."

"Because I have sucked it *dry*, Sarge. After all, I realized pretty quickly I sure wasn't in it for the money." She grimaced. "That meant I had to be getting something out of it, right? So I was. I guess I was learning. Then the lessons started to repeat and I realized, well, maybe this is it and I said to myself okay Norton, okay, it's time now. It's time. Terminado. So I got out."

Sarge crunched into some string beans. The heat in here was a little uncomfortable. He'd grown used to lots of air and plenty of windows open for the cool breeze. He liked cities sometimes and especially this one, but right now the sooner they pulled out the better. Had to get cracking. Only she'd given him a clue unwittingly, handed him part of the key, and he took his time now figuring the fit, the correct angle of approach.

He gave her a big smile. She'd grown a little wary and gave one back. Something similar in the set of each face.

"Tell me," he said gently, "what the future looks like. Good things planned?"

"As soon as I'm Dr. Norton I'll teach. Why not? I can spout off all my great ideas about *La Vida es Sueña* a few hours a week to captive audiences, just think, and then I can publish all these great ideas too. This archery, Sarge, let me tell you. I intend to *dominate* in the area, just give me another year. Shame you're missing out on next weekend but that's how it goes. Hey! Did I tell you? You would have been proud of me, I did the Marathon last fall."

"No kidding."

"No kidding. In three-nineteen, and I cried the last four miles. These legs were made for kicking." Her eyes gleamed. They focused in on his. "Okay Sarge. What is it?"

"I need a great pacer."

"You're asking me."

"Right." He took the risk. Outrage her enough and at least you had her interest. He kept his voice calm, almost gentle. "Maybe you can learn something from it, a brand new experience, Anne. Just think."

Pride stung, the hurt streaked instantaneously across her

face, replaced immediately by anger. No ordinary rage. This was royal wrath. He leaned into it full speed ahead and she let it loose. Oddly enough, her voice was quieter than it had been all evening.

She smiled. "You swim straight to hell Sarge, and stay there." She was standing. She disappeared around a corner. He drank from his glass, carved into the rest of his meat. His appetite had increased these last few days, no question about it. Year he'd trained Matt for the English Channel she'd been there too with her trainer and crew, waiting her turn, and they'd all gotten acquainted by force of circumstance, sitting around in the same bed-and-breakfast inn playing endless rounds of chess, checkers, and cards while a week and a half of unexpected gales stopped all plans dead. They'd glare blearily out the window, she and Matt, watch the silver-rimmed, storm-bashed cliff edges immobile under pelting rain, and she'd joked with everyone, complained for everyone, made half-hearted attempts to seduce everyone, ate bowls of oatmeal and gulped frantic cups of some protein-carbohydrate glue in a last-ditch attempt to throw on more weight before the weather cleared. And the rain kept whipping down until one afternoon Matt grabbed a sugar bowl and heaved it at the wall, porcelain shattering, white grains flying like wind-raised snow drifts on the carpet. By one a.m. the sky had cleared, and they went out at morning with a beautiful neap tide. Good swim it had been, the kid came close to a record. She hadn't been so lucky, caught a two-day stomach virus at the last minute and had to wait through some more rotten weather, finally decided to take a spring tide. Matt convinced him to go along with her crew. Saying come on Sarge, hell of a lot of heart she's got don't you think? Sarge agreed. He didn't need much convincing anyway, but the extra attraction for him had been that she'd found favor in his son's eyes, and the reason she had—her hell of a lot of heart—pleased him no end. So they'd gone along. It was a night crossing, spanned the last few hours of August and went through September's first dawn. Rough water, not everything in her favor to say the least, a little before midchannel they knew a record was out of the question and so did she but she kept going. Hot damn! Matt yelled when they hit Calais, hot damn hot damn hot damn Sarge what do you think of that! Jumping from port to starboard with arms winging heavy-muscled circles above his head. He was moving more than she by then. He was more excited than Sarge had seen him before. Hot damn she did it, Sarge. As if she'd topped the record. As if it had been he who'd made it through this time.

Sarge's shoe tapped the bags and viola case under the table. She'd left her stuff. She'd be back. Anne never left things behind, not even in rage. And the longer she was gone the better. He could just about feel her brain wheels spinning, spinning. Sarge finished eating.

"On your way to hell, tell me." She sat, looking grim. "What's the swim, it's got to be a big one if you want pacers. Michigan? Ontario? No? The Farallons? Tell me, I haven't got all night."

"The San Antonio Strait."

He was surprised at how simple it sounded. He blocked all images from his mind, concentrated on the ease of the words, those six quiet syllables. So far so good, he told himself, it's all right this way. To himself, he said the words again.

She'd settled back limply in the chair and her eyes stopped moving. Oh, she seemed to say, I get it. For a minute they were silent. Then, "Hey Sarge," she said, "hey. I miss him sometimes, you know. He was my friend." She toed the viola case, tapping dully. "Do you want to talk about it?"

He told her no, not yet.

"Will you talk about it someday? To me?"

He lifted his eyes to hers. Would that be the bargain then? Maybe she wanted to know for the sake of the brand-new information it afforded. Something not yet experienced. But a deal was a deal and he'd asked for her seal of approval on a pretty hard-driven bargain himself just now. "Someday," he said, "yes."

"Dorey Thomas. You know, we've never even met. I always saw her just before the count and sometimes after a race. I guess we avoided speaking and maybe it was some kind of mutual instinct, I don't exactly know."

"Want to meet her?"

"What's supposed to be in this for me, Sarge, all the thanks I can eat?"

"You might even get money."

"Wait. I'm still telling you no, really, no way. When does all this come to pass? I'm not familiar with that water, just things I've heard. It's cold, right? Second on the list to the Irish Sea or something like that, right? You know me, Sarge, you know I hate cold worse than anything, I'd rather go for rough water and puke my guts out and that's the truth."

He grinned and the grin was a dare. "Right. You'll be glad to know it's rough as well as cold. Two out of two's not bad, huh?"

The half-finished slab of swordfish cooled on her plate, a dull off-white. She stared at it, shook her head sadly. "Oh that's great. That's just terrific."

Sarge sat back. Tense, but he'd done his best. He could say no more without it bordering on a plea, and pleading was something he never did. He'd have liked to talk about stroke mechanics, the way her style was so close to Dorey's at times their arms spinning from the water might appear identical, some essential similarities in physique that made them a nearly perfect match. But these were things he guessed she knew. However impulsive she might appear to be, he knew her approach had always been painstakingly methodical. She simply absorbed the necessary matter from each step along the way very quickly, giving an illusory impression that she was flying wildly towards adventure at full speed and to hell with the consequences.

Now she was laughing. It compressed her features to a pretty, pink-toned mask of smiles, and he cocked his head looking at her. Humility! she was chuckling. Humility, Norton, humility. Then the smiles went away, the laugh died down. She asked with an odd edge to her voice was he trying to steal her thunder.

"Anne, I want the best help in the world. No one could steal your thunder."

Well it was true.

"I'm not in that kind of shape."

"I'll get you there," he said calmly. "Come up for a visit."

"Now wait. How much of my life do you want for this, how many months? Because I've got tournaments this winter and I'm going out of my mind trying to keep my committee together, without them I don't get to be a doctor, Sarge, not to mention Rick, and there's the puppy now too. A Boston Bull. You're talking about closing up shop for a while. I don't know. I don't like it. I don't even know the details and I already hate it." Then she paused. Something was spinning in there, something new. He saw the wheels stop, knew that she had it. Her expression was strange, as if she'd smiled in her sleep. "That means maybe I love it, doesn't it. If I hate it. Opposites, opposites." She was chuckling again. "Let me tell you Sarge, I have the right to reserve final judgment. You call when you're ready and I'll meet her. Then if we hit it off I'll consider it and if I hate her guts I just won't."

The waiter was there. Sarge didn't remember asking for the check, didn't remember when the thin perspiring film of relief had first layered his forehead. But he nodded, took the check, tucked it under the rim of his plate. "Okay. Okay. When the time comes I'll want a commitment."

"Do I ever give anything else? Hey! It's almost ten after, I've got to run. By the way—is she out of her mind? Dorey Thomas I mean. Ah-hah! Look who's talking. Who cares anyway. Know what I thought of just now?" She reached around for her jacket, eyes careening, then suddenly still again, and he was taken totally by surprise to see tears glittering there. He reminded himself that, with Anne, tears were no more a sign of real vulnerability than a softly exclaimed ouch. They were merely a mode of proclamation, a formal way of staking out claims to some well-justified grief. "I thought of my father, that bastard. I hated his guts, Sarge, still do, let me tell you. Also I loved him more than anyone. *Anyone.* You know what that bastard did to me when I was five years old? We went out on his yacht—he and all my brothers and I—and in the middle of nowhere he picked me up by the arms. I was giggling. I had high expectations of being swung around. You know how kids love that. Then he held me over the side rail and dangled me, Sarge, and I started to scream because I thought he was going to let go. Know what he said to me? 'Honey,' he said, 'honey, let it be a *challenge* to you.'" She leaned forward towards the yellow-glowing candlelight. Her lips curled at the edges in a kind of snarl, tears streaked steadily down the smooth-hewn, blue-blooded line of her nose, and for a second he wanted her because she looked so much like what she was, raw, revealed, and unashamed. Wanted to reach for the unmasked face but, out of respect, kept his distance. "And then, whoosh, he let go." She held a wrist to her cheek, let one tear soak into the silk and she stared at it a moment. When she glanced back at Sarge tears still ran freely but she was smiling. "So I learned to swim!"

He stood. Leaned over candle and plates and kissed her.

Once in a while, particularly when shaving, Dr. John Aaron Gallagher would look at his face in the mirror. He made it a point to stare fully every time he thought of it—that way he knew he wasn't avoiding the truth. And it wasn't really awful anymore or even jarring. He'd grown accustomed to his appearance over the years, even attached to it. So took it for granted, in fact, that he often had to remind himself of what the effect might be on others who didn't know him. So whenever someone previously unknown made any kind of impact at all in his life, he was bound to be reminded of his face and then give it another thorough glance-over or two while shaving.

Early on, the question had always been whether to bring it up himself and offer explanation, or to wait uncomfortably until the other—just as uncomfortably—asked. With years, though, this need to explain had disappeared as had the awkwardness of waiting. So that morning, while shaving, he'd merely looked carefully. A little lather clung to the nose's crushed tip. He smoothed it away with a thumb. His glasses fogged in the bathroom steam. One inspection to make sure that he didn't hate his face. One look to make sure for the umpteenth time that, even as it was, he could find something there to appreciate. He did. Figured Dorey Thomas would ask later or maybe turn out to be that rare kind of bird who never asked at all. Of course he'd noticed her noticing the day before. Still, he hadn't recognized any distaste, and whatever questions had flashed through her brain had seemed to him something other than curiosity.

Tycho Brahe! Tycho Brahe! they'd called him in lab, half jest, half a pervertedly friendly way of coming to terms with him once they knew the story. Tycho Brahe. Because he was their substitute shaman—he and his fascination with astrology, with the history of alchemy, with ancient Hebrew mystical rites—legendary among them. That and his busted-up face. Tycho Brahe! Tycho Brahe! Maybe they pictured him back in the sixteenth century like his namesake, measuring interstellar motion with the crudest glass, spending long predawn hours plotting out the future by what those same stars told him. Setting quill to oily paper while he discovered the strange course of his own destiny. Tycho Brahe! Tycho you should have watched the stars that day. When he'd gotten used to it he'd laugh, and so everyone became a little more comfortable. Tools poised over the jigsawed cadaver, he'd grab a dessicated coil of intestine and toss it haphazardly over his shoulder so it landed on some unlucky head, crack that he guessed the stars weren't with everyone all the time, were they. Med school, sleepless nights, napping between three and five a.m. Then jogging down to the crew house by five thirty for practice. He'd kept up with the rowing as much as possible for quite a while. After the accident he'd changed from double to single sculls.

One dazed September sunrise there was Sarge hanging around the place, asking questions. Wanted to know the sport. Because it was one of the heavy sports in his book, he'd said, hands proudly on hips, he ought to know after all. He stood there, dark, bronzed, bull-muscled, young. Checking out equipment. Watching them warm up. Who? Tycho'd asked casually, not really caring about the answer. Somebody Olssen, one of the men on crew told him, new on campus and I heard crazy stories, he just got back from swimming the Nile, they have a race every year where they do about a thousand figure-eights around a couple of islands there and whoever lasts through or croaks last wins, something like that.

Then Tycho got interested. He approached him, offered a hand. John Gallagher here, tell me about the pyramids. The hand was shaken vigorously, eyes met and locked into something good. The pyramids? Sure I'll tell you what I saw, makes a great story. Tell me about that face of yours too. Looks like another hell of a story to me. And it was so direct, clean and harsh in a way that felt completely honest, therefore kind. They had a good talk that morning.

Tycho snapped off the bathroom light and stepped into the bedroom. His bed was in a low oak frame, less than three feet from the carpet.

On the hard mattress, legs stretched easily among cushions soft in contrast, he relaxed and removed his glasses, closed his eyes without sleeping. Tycho concentrated his sightless focus on a circular area in the center of his chest. To its left beat his heart. He traced the flow, followed sensation to his groin. Another invisible circle there. He focused, felt what circulated back and forth between chest and groin, pulsings, rhythms. There was in her something missing. Something missing that he couldn't place or name, and it wasn't that she lacked affect and it wasn't even related to the disciplined brand of politeness with which she seemed to face everything. It was bound up with the emotions, but this curious lack in her didn't spell psychosis either. No, it came from another tonal range altogether. He tried to track it down, the missing piece. The blankness there. Images of her faded as he gave it up, passed to images of Sarge. Sarge now, Sarge before, Sarge before the before. Tycho's blood ran a long course. He traced his heart beat and the waves it sent flooding arteries, keeping predestined time to an orbital cycle all its own like mollusks in land-locked laboratories keeping time to tides thousands of miles away. His relaxation slowed the beat, deepened the swell. Slowly, slowly, he plodded the course from chest to groin and back again. Little by little, day by day, he was inching his focus higher. By now he'd gotten to the base of the neck. Beyond that he wouldn't go because then it became difficult. Each advance would be minuscule for now, stopping at the point of pain. This slow advance was aimed for a circular area in the center of his forehead. It would take many more years, he knew.

On the bed Tycho opened his eyes.

Sometimes when he opened them like this he'd still see it happening. He was sure it had to do with that split second of disorientation before his glasses were slipped back on—the sudden blurred images surrounding him, the sudden blinking, gave way to an instantly vanishing image, a semihallucination. Whatever the cause, he'd see it clearly as if it were repeating. He'd feel himself on the crew house floor, legs soaked and chilled with river water, arms battered and too sore to move. He'd see the head of the oar swinging down towards him. Direct line to the face.

Sometimes he'd see it happening all over again the way it had then. It seemed to be arcing through the air in slow motion, flat of the paddle approaching inch by inch until he could no longer focus and it blurred in front of him. Could he have moved a hand or two in front of his face for protection? It seemed not, then, but often he'd wondered. Felt as if he were meeting the force of the oar for the first time ever, and seeing it come down towards him he'd also felt that— though still—he was somehow rushing towards making its acquaintance, arms flung wide. Understanding this tool he himself had been using daily, year in, year out, finally understanding something essential about it and the motion of it, the rolling pulling striking motion of which his own body had been a part. Its power revealed. When it came close enough to blur, he hadn't breathed for an instant. Then an explosion of white silence. Inside a shard of shattering glass with the sound turned off. It was pure blinding light.

88   Nadav Ha-Kareesh was older than Tycho, but even so his close-clipped hair was jet black, face nearly wrinkle-free. He'd been lounging shirtless on a deck chair to catch the last rays

of autumn heat, puffed a Gauloise sans filtre down to where it nearly burned his fingers, dropped it in a cold cup of coffee by the chair's side and listened to it sizzle. When he heard Tycho's feet boom along the dock he blinked. His sole movement was lifting a hand to shade his eyes.

Shalom, he'd said.

Hello, said Tycho. He'd stepped on deck in old tennis shoes, jeans and a sweater, neat thick packet of charts under one arm.

Ha-Kareesh half sat then, and his head nodded greeting. It was an oval-shaped head in the classical Egyptian style, broad-browed, blunt-nosed, full-lipped. Mostly there was no discernible expression other than a rock-worn smoothness there. On rare occasions, though, he would smile. There were two reasons for which he smiled. One was to get his way—it was the least time-consuming method of persuasion he knew. The other was to show his pleasure. Sitting, he'd smiled. Tycho couldn't tell what kind of smile it was. Then he'd swung himself easily from the chair to stand. He was a medium-sized man, a good deal shorter than Tycho. His arms were quite long, though, and when he walked it was swiftly, in a deceptively clumsy-seeming, short-stepped sidle. Like the face, the body was younger than its years. It was the body of a tumbler, maybe, or a wrestler.

Come, he'd said in Hebrew, motioning and blinking in the sun. Held open the cabin door. Please to enter. Tycho kissed the noon light goodbye. He had to stoop going through the upward-swinging hatch, straighten slightly on the rung-steps that led down.

Light sprayed through the circle-shaped windows. Even so it wasn't enough, and Ha-Kareesh switched on a lamp bolted to the cabin's center table. They sat across from each other. They were mostly silent, both inspecting the chart spread on top of other charts in the packet Tycho had brought. Ha-Kareesh lit another cigarette. As the thick blue-tinged smoke drifted under Tycho's nose he waved it awkwardly away.

It was a dark cabin, expensively paneled, lacquered and stained, walls oddly bare of ornaments. Just the wood, the table, the equipment necessary. Ashtrays. Fold-out bunk. Storage closet. Rope coiled and hung on a plain steel wall clamp. It smelled of French cigarettes, stale coffee, varnish and damp salt. Once in a while he'd hear the dock water lapping and rocking many feet below his own. It was cold water this time of year, he knew, temperature dropping daily by degrees. He coughed in the smoke-laden silence.

Ha-Kareesh puffed out another cloud, crushed the cigarette into a metal tray. He flipped through the charts quickly. Once in a while he'd stop, make a notation. He was watching for patterns, comparing lines and measurements and prevailing conditions from year to year. After a while he reached for a knob in the wall to his left, pulled a compartment open to take from it measuring tools and marking pens. He glanced at Tycho, lit another cigarette.

"It's possible to open the windows."

"I'll do that now," said Tycho. "You will die of smoking."

An almost-grin flicked across his face like a stray ash. He shrugged, went back to the charts.

Tycho unlatched every circle, pushed them open as far as possible. He imagined each emitting spumes of smoke like teapots hissing steam. He wanted to crash up and out through the lowered hatch and bounce on deck, breathe deeply a polluted air that just now seemed preferable to this quiet cloud of stale tobacco. But he held himself back, nearly against his will. Patience, he told himself, just wait.

"There are three things important." Ha-Kareesh turned off the table lamp. Sun splashed stripes vertically down the length of his chest, bleached the glimmering sweat and the darkness of his hair. "The thing first, weather."

Tycho turned to him, nodded intently.

"The thing second, this current. In the middle just to spite you, you're acquainted?"

"I'm acquainted with it."

"The pattern of it changes." His thumb stabbed the chart here, bounced from it there. "Here more wide. Here narrow but here also there is to it a flow that goes in the opposite direction with much force. These things don't remain the same. You need to follow it a long time. You need to travel the length and you hunt like that for its weakest point. When you discover it then you pass through there."

Tycho shook his head. "That's fifteen miles out. I mean statute miles and from bird's-eye view—understand? From above. Not counting this"—his hand zigzagged like a fish piloting its way through an obstacle course—"and that means by then it's a good ten hours if she's lucky. Right? So you're saying that's when we make a grand detour?"

Ha-Kareesh nodded, unblinking.

"How far? How many more hours? Give me miles."

Lighting up again, he let the match burn itself out in the ashtray and held Tycho's gaze through the smoke. He shrugged.

"Can you please estimate?" Tycho's voice was urgent.

Ha-Kareesh flipped through the packet again. He took several minutes that seemed longer, forgot his Gauloise while he figured things, scribbled in ink and then crossed it out. Alone, the cigarette smouldered black, orange glaring through at the tip in eye-like specks. Ha-Kareesh finished his estimating and looked up again.

"If all things will be perfect, three miles. But perhaps ten. This current does not remain the same. To predict it exactly now, that's a foolish thing."

Tycho wiped his upper lip, breathed deep and coughed. "All right. Okay. What else?"

"The thing third."

"The thing third."

"Cold water." Ha-Kareesh leaned back. He spread both hands on the unfolded paper. They were enormous hands, Tycho noticed, fingers thick and bluntly strong. "The cold. You are acquainted."

Tycho felt sweat on his forehead. "I know it."

"Very good," he smiled. "For this, it's good to know these things intimately."

Smoke was spinning in Tycho's head now. He felt a little nauseous and wanted to leave but made himself stay still. The feeling passed and he was running a sleeve across his forehead, frowning at the charts. Then he raised his eyes to the pair across the table. There was no way to read those eyes that looked back at him—he got the feeling they'd have looked the same way at a tree, or a monkey. Somehow that thought was reassuring. Nadav Ha-Kareesh was probably one of the world's best navigators. Largely unknown. Totally unsung. No one knew how he'd made his money but he had plenty. Some deal he'd struck back in the forties. Tycho had heard things. In Bremen, maybe, maybe that was it. He didn't know the details. He guessed he didn't want to know. "Thank you," Tycho breathed. "I'm grateful for your help."

Ha-Kareesh shrugged again, easily. He'd seen a lot of faces in darkness and remembered well what they looked like. That time in Brindisi they'd attached a wire stretching from ship's bow into the harbor, fastened at its other end to the dock. As many as possible crowded into a leaky rowboat that had no oars, one stood at the rowboat's bow and one at its stern, clinging to the wire, pulling hand over hand in laborious progress from dock to waiting ship. The faces he'd seen approaching had been skeletal. Eyes gaping, burning fever, the arms sinewy bone. He'd stretched out his own arms when they got close, held hands down over shipside as they clutched and writhed their way up rope ladders, arms barely covered by colorless flesh and still insistently reaching so he'd thought each reach would be the last but it never was. Then they'd sent the rowboat back for more.

The last run of the night he'd gone himself, his baboon arms pulling easily along the knife-line of wire. At stern huddled one of the refugees, volunteering as translator should that be needed. This was a young man whose hair had fallen out. He hugged his knees to him in the stern as if they were lover's breasts. Once in a while he'd kiss them. He babbled to himself in several languages, and although Ha-Kareesh didn't stop to look back he began to understand bits and pieces of French mixed in with the other tongues.

92   A gentleman in the water, the lunatic laughed. A gentleman in the water with a knife. He carves the boat for supper.

Ha-Kareesh glanced down then and noticed a flash of disappearing flesh to starboard. He stopped for a second and heard unmistakably the sounds of a sharp instrument piercing the rowboat's bottom. He proceeded slowly another few feet. Then silently let go of the wire and jumped to the water off port with a knife between his teeth. They are feeding, laughed the lunatic. Kissing both knees again he huddled tighter and waited. There were sounds he didn't hear, water sounds and human sounds and a combination of the two that, had he listened, would have seemed like powerful tails thrashing. When Ha-Kareesh surfaced, blood had been washed from his knife and from his teeth by the water.

Back then it was his profession. He'd made a habit of smuggling these half-living bodies from a variety of unofficial European embarkation points into Palestine, past British gunboats. Now he looked at Tycho, and his look was strictly observational. Once in a while a swimmer's navigator or trainer would ask him. If the event smacked of an urgency that appealed to him, he'd lend his help. Sometimes for money. Sometimes not. To him, it was all merely interesting. Always the thought of these swims filled him with a rushing swell of recognition. The skin bleached, features so deeply lined they appeared scarred, eyes enormous in gaunt skulls and shining delirium. When their legs stopped working they clutched with their hands and reached with their arms, and every remaining fiber was caught in the breathless motion of reaching towards a place that at first they could only imagine, each reach bringing them closer to touching it. So examining the strange face of the man who sat meeting his gaze, Ha-Kareesh shrugged again and then nodded.

"Of course," he said, "I'm pleased to help." If there was a place you needed to reach more than you needed to sleep and more than you needed to love, this was to him worthwhile.

He smiled, then offered his hand. "Good luck," he said. Tycho shook it.

Rhapsody in Blue was over. A radio voice announced four a.m. The Boston Bull whimpered awake, baby tail thumping.

Some Pilot Razor Points at the edge of Rick's drafting table took a plunge to the carpet. Static whined over the vital statistics of the morning's next selection. Someone's something of something by Delius. Anne rolled the covers off, stretched up and out of bed with a sudden arching motion.

"Come on pal." One arm reached down for the puppy and hoisted him up to cradle against her shoulder. The other hand fiddled dutifully with the alarm. She reset it for Rick, quickly turned off the sound before it disturbed him.

The dog whimpered softly again, then was quiet. She guessed it was a little early for him, knelt and placed him back on the big tooth-mauled floor cushion and, tail flapping tiredly, his pinkish eyes watched her. One was circled black. She pulled on a pair of old sweatpants and twisted her torso gently in semicircles from right to left then back again. Did some reaching, some stretching. Stretch. Deltoids. She groaned almost under her breath, groaned repeatedly and the groan became a sort of hum. Then before she knew it she was singing to herself not quite below the breath. That's when Rick opened both eyes and time beamed back at him in blood-red from the clock's face, seconds visibly rocketing by. He shrugged one shoulder out from under, swallowed, cleared his throat. Said it was kind of early for her to go running already, wasn't it? Yes, she said, oh no, she'd woken him up, she'd go into the living room and let him sleep some more.

"You're not running this early, are you?"

"No." Her arms macheted through dark air, slow motion. He saw her, from the waist up, twist and weave. In the dark her torso glimmered white. She looked like a wonderfully graceful marionette beginning the steps to some crudely choreographed pantomime.

"But you're up," he said.

"I'm up."

"Without so much as a kiss."

"Without a kiss," she agreed sadly, but never stopped moving. "I'm swimming today."

"Oh. This is serious."

"Serious."

He waited for the usual burst of words from her but none came. Her silence confirmed that whatever was going on was not only serious but out of the ordinary. They were always there, her words, rambling, spinning arguments and resolving them, theorizing, wondering, questioning, and sometimes maddening, but he'd found that for him her talk had become a kind of ongoing source of sustenance from which, at will, he could swallow inspiration. The Millrose Games at the Garden in January, they had to go. Running. Had to put in at least a hundred miles this week, *had* to, for the Marathon. And target practice. Maybe next step would be crossbow, and they couldn't forget that concert, that dinner, the book she'd sent out searches for in every decent store in the state had finally arrived after half a year but was well worth it because everything worthwhile took time didn't he agree? Breathlessly, in seeming chaos, things got done. She got them done. On time, too. And, looking back, he'd see that the steps taken had all been simple and methodical to a tee. They had just been taken at a gold-medal clip. Yes things were in order, and it was no miracle but rather her dogmatic sense of order beneath the mirage of freneticism.

"Can I ask why you have to swim?"

"I *want* to swim," she corrected. "I decided to."

That was that, he knew.

The puppy nibbled some more pillow. Rick told himself get back to sleep. There were water sounds from the bathroom, then in the kitchen a light snapped on. Best to leave her alone. He got out of bed. On his way through the door stepped on pens, picked them from the carpet, lined them neatly on his drafting table's indented edge. Rick was a graphic designer and illustrator. He designed jackets for books other people had written, and covers for records other people had cut. His initial success, though, had been in the magazine field. He'd made somewhat of a mark for himself as chief designer in an ad campaign for waterproof wristwatches.

"Anne."

She was measuring cupfuls and spoonfuls of stuff into the blender basin. Pineapple juice. Banana slices. Soy bean powder. Egg yolks. Chocolate-flavored protein powder. She plugged it in and set it on high. She'd taken a two-minute shower and her hair still dripped onto the shoulders of her favorite T-shirt. It had on both back and front the same rippled blue line of water, some ominous fin protruding.

"Anne, what's the story?"

She didn't answer immediately. She unplugged the blender, shook it by hand vigorously a few times and then poured the sun-colored goo into a waiting glass. He knew she'd heard him and knew she wasn't ignoring him. Ask her point-blank what the story was and you'd get an honest answer. For a moment he was a little afraid—of what, he didn't know. Glass in hand, she turned to face him.

"I may or may not help a friend out with some swimming. I haven't decided yet. If I decide yes then I want to be in shape."

His eyes asked for more and hers half apologized. The tired thought yawned through him that what he was really asking for was some kind of reassurance. Then he felt foolish.

She drank it in three gulps. Her nostrils flared at the barrage of flavors. It was offensive, like mismatched colors, in bad taste. She reminded herself that sometimes unpleasantness was necessary. Already she was running down the plan. Feel out the water. Then a few 200's. Then a few 50's, just a taste. Then some 400's. Then kicking work and a couple of hours of distance, say sixty-seventy percent effort today. Not too much. Start out slow. She'd be out in time for her first class and after that to midtown for target practice, downtown for the week's viola lesson, uptown to catch that lecture and then back down for dinner and maybe there'd be time to hit the library on her way. Had to cut out the running today. No way. Just no way. Well something always got sacrificed. She reminded herself that this was nothing, this was really starting slow. Just a spatter in the bucket. Inside she complained and then told herself hey cut it out Norton, no more of that, understand? She did.

She looked at Rick.

He appeared boyish for a minute, standing there rumpled. A nice, proportionate body, muscles in the right places, strong but not pretentious, just enough hair curling here and there, chin firm but not jutting, nose well-molded but not classical, eyes large enough but not whimsical. He'd grown up picking cherries and fishing stream trout in Hemingway country. He was one of the very nicest looking men she'd ever seen. That was the word for it, nice—there was little striking about him except for the long-fingered nervous sensitivity of his hands and, of course, his mind. His own words hadn't yet bored her. He'd take what she spilled out and mold it finer, carry it further. When she looked, that was what she saw.

"I'll walk the mutt," he offered.

"Hey great! That's great. Will you be around for dinner? Want to eat in?"

He nodded, relieved. This was okay now, at least for the moment. This concentration on schedule, the details. Walk the mutt. Get going on the mechanicals for *Adventure* magazine. He was illustrating a fictional piece about moose-tracking in Minnesota. One of those hunting survival stories where bit by bit each member of the original party fell to the wayside in some awful way until only one was left. Rick's illustration work was his meal ticket. It was a good meal ticket. Illustrating these adventure tales, his trademark a photolike realism bleached by light tints, a pale pallet that nevertheless didn't obscure those strong, bold lines of figures brawling, sprawling. Masculine stratifications. A marked style that had a nice lucrative market. He'd gotten into it after the wristwatch campaign. Lots of illustration work and lots of bucks, lots of corporate parties where word was out on who'd done what with the latest television campaign, the latest campaign for this peanut butter or that brand of scotch, the latest big job for the latest selection of such-and-such's latest thriller appearing in this or that monthly. He'd stand in corners and drink too much, once in a while take some woman home. Once in a while buy a pack of Marlboros and smoke them all in one evening. Once in a while smile, or say things he'd later forget. The work kept going out on time and by now he was freelance. The bucks kept coming in.

97

Then an oddity had fallen his way. From the *SportsYear*

account. The new art director wanted to do some experimental stuff and thought that being a Michigan boy he might be interested in the assignment. Anne Norton was going from Chicago to Benton Harbor the hard way, by water. It was sixty miles and it was cold water and she was after the record which meant she'd have to beat thirty-four-some hours. And it was good press because she always made good press. If he was interested *SportsYear* would send him along on the press boat to illustrate it. He'd accepted the assignment on his fourth Wild Turkey and the next day flew to Chicago.

He'd expected excitement. This was an obscure sport, had a reputation as one of the very toughest. Where was the blood and guts, he'd wanted to know, where? He stepped onto the press boat without meeting her and, aside from the initial rush of *they're off!* excitement when she dropped almost casually into the water from the nearby escort boat, he'd figured after a short while that this was the most boring goddamn thing imaginable. All you saw was an arm stroking, arm stroking, head turning. Hell of a spectator sport, elbow-watching. He snarled to himself and wondered how he'd manage to wrest a few halfway interesting drawings from the experience, turned away from the sight of that white-topped head rolling, arms churning at a constant and monotonous pace. He looked back half an hour later and they were still churning, same pace. He cussed it all out and, wishing he'd brought a flask of something, talked lacrosse with one of the Canadian boys. When he looked back six hours later she was still going, same pace. He opened his waterproofed jacket and let the spray cool his neck. It was cold, gave him an instant of frozen shock. He watched her, saw the tiny crew hanging close by that side of the escort boat. Felt the freeze on his neck again and he started to understand something.

He kept watching. It wasn't daylight anymore and soon it wasn't sundown but darkness. On the rail his hands were numb. He shoved them inside gloves and still couldn't feel the fingers, a cold day for summer. Somewhere there was land, but the whole big cold lake might as well have been a sea. The wind made waves. The escort boat turned on its floodlights and so did the press boat, shimmering on the opaque wind-chopped surface of water and highlighting that methodically rolling head, the arms that lifted perpetually in rhythm. He was cold and his legs shivered. They were feeding her on the hour. Someone offered him sandwiches and a beer but he said no, he'd wait for her next feeding. Didn't feel right somehow to eat without her. He wasn't hungry anyway.

The unrelieved glare of lights on water hurt his eyes. He turned away, wandered in small circles from stern to bow and blinked at the dark night air, blinked at the stars that shone back coolly. The wind sprayed his face and left a feeling of ice. It dampened his hair. He was tired but felt as if he'd downed a gallon of strong coffee. Jumpy, not at all hungry, wrenched with a kind of anticipation he failed to place. He refused food and forgot about the beer, refused blankets offered. He stayed out on deck all night, clung to the port side and watched. Around three thirty, four o'clock in the morning she'd slowed drastically, noticeably weaker. That was the twenty-hour mark. His legs shook now constantly, and when he cleared his throat it was sore. Despite the cold he sensed himself perspiring. His numb fingers wrapped tightly around the side rail. Wind had died and so had the choppiness, and across the brilliantly lit surface between boats he watched as she stopped, tread in the direction of her escort boat while they poked out a feeding stick. He leaned over farther because he thought he heard someone speaking but couldn't make out the words. If he stopped breathing he could hear just barely. Her trainer was talking to her, voice loud but coaxing. He was spending a long time on each word, trying to sound it out as distinctly as possible and still hold on to an edge of gentleness. You're going strong. You're going strong, believe me. You look beautiful, just beautiful, don't cry sweetheart don't cry. It's all right. It's all right, believe me. We're all damned pleased and proud right now, you're going strong. Keep it up, we're all damned proud to be here with you. Don't cry sweetheart, you're looking beautiful. Keep it up. Just keep it up.

Another body dropped from the escort boat then, a woman suited up, capped, and goggled, covered from neck to toe with

99

a thick layer of black grease that glimmered the same silver as water surface in the floodlights. She paddled calmly over to face Anne. She was treading there, saying something he couldn't hear. He saw her lift a black arm from the water repeatedly, motion towards the tip of the feeding stick. She'd motion, once in a while laugh, and the comfort of the sound, the reassurance of it, cracked lightly through the dead weight of that tar-dark time of night. After a few minutes he thought he heard Anne laugh too. Faintly. Then she reached up for the cup offered. She drank whatever was there bit by bit, dropped the cup so it sank from sight and still tread, facing this other woman who by now he guessed was perceivable to her only as a vague dark form. Then they started to swim again, both of them. He'd never seen anything like it. Without touching at all—that would have disqualified her—they were swimming close together and breathing face to face. The other woman settled immediately into a comfortable pace that matched Anne's, and after a while picked it up just a little, almost imperceptibly, so that Anne naturally matched hers. The boats moved. This woman stayed in the water a little over half an hour, and when she climbed shivering back over the side of the escort boat the body she'd left behind was still going at the pace she'd established.

His throat was closed by now, lips cracked, eyes red from rubbing and wind-whipping and no sleep. Most of the others on the press boat had caught at least a nap during the night. He figured no one on the escort had. When dawn rolled around they looked like phantoms, pale arms and heads hanging once in a while overboard, watching. In the east the water became gray instead of black. Then the skyline streaked gray, then white, touched with an icy yellow. Cold, cold for summer. He wondered why he'd always remembered dawns as glorious dashes of scarlet flame and gold smothering the sky —this dawn was a quietly spreading pallor, its gray turning by degrees to a brutal strawlike color. She was still swimming.

100

An hour into morning she stopped. There was discussion on board the escort. The pacer went in again, different suit and caps, new layer of black. He'd begun to feel some sun on his neck, his shoulders, a little warmth creeping through the night's chill. Maybe she did too, because she even stepped up her speed after the pacer'd left the water this second time. The glow of warmth didn't last. Soon she'd fallen back to turtle speed and that pacer went in again, swam twenty minutes, got out. Forty-five minutes later she went in again. Swam half an hour, face to face. Out. Then again. Rick gnawed his underlip and got blood. Ten a.m., twenty-six hours. Pacer out. Eleven a.m., feeding. Twenty-seven hours. His toes were numb, soles of his feet throbbing dully from standing all night on the gently swaying deck. And on the escort boat now was some commotion. The trainer was throwing his arms up, jamming hands angrily on hips and leaning forward to glare at the water. The pacer was ready to drop into the water again. She poised there in the bow, her head moving side to side to ease soreness, he could tell by the weary curve to her shoulders that her job was no piece of cake either. He wondered who she was. Then stared back at the exhausted head rolling in painfully slow rhythm through the water, and forgot about the pacer. His nose ran freely. The wind had started again, got heavier, the water surface chopped up. He made a grab for the shoulder of a reporter from one of the Chicago sports monthlies, asked what was going on. Across the expanse between both boats blew wind, and now her trainer was motioning towards the pacer. Hand slashed through the air. It's off, the hand said, don't go in. What? Rick asked, voice hoarse. You could see Benton Harbor. Maybe four hours away, maybe five. How many miles. Sun glared coolly in a nearly cloudless sky, shining heat between drifts of rushing wind.

The reporter turned to him. "The water," he grinned in a twisted way, shook his head. "Water temperature just dropped almost two degrees."

"So?"

The reporter rubbed his stubble, sighed. "So that's a big difference when you're in there without your long johns, pal."

She took half of one more feeding. Her trainer was leaning far over, hanging down towards the water, and he was yelling things to her, gesturing, but the winds made it impossible to hear what he said. She went on again. Her arms slapped feebly against the chop. She rolled over on her back. Twenty-eight hours, forty minutes and they hadn't moved much lately. Rolled over, rolled back, and again. She started to breast-stroke.

Inside the gloves he'd forgotten to remove, his fingers perspired now and hung to the railing like they'd been nailed there. When he saw her go under he lurched forward, ready to jump in himself. Someone grabbed him from behind, chuckling.

Her crew had gone in after her and she was being hoisted up and over the side, into the boat. Twenty-nine hours, eleven minutes. She'd lost consciousness eight miles short of Benton Harbor. Watching them lift the limp body easily, swiftly, Rick realized his jaw ached, realized he'd been grinding his teeth all night and all day.

That evening in a hotel room in Benton Harbor he rocked back and forth on the edge of his bed. He switched on the TV and turned the sound off. Watched a young Laurence Olivier chase a young Merle Oberon over the MGM moors in black and white. Watched a commercial for Timex watches. This watch was a real survivor. You ran a truck over it and then tossed it off a cliff into the lashing waves of the Pacific, fished it out and sure enough it was still ticking. Sitting on the edge of the hotel room bed he rocked back and forth and then he cried. He cried a good long time. His heart pounded him to sleep with a frantic kind of beat, driving anxious blood-tides through the crazy splotches of that night's dreams.

He'd woken to find a lot of the press still hanging around. It seemed a subtle change had occurred overnight, a shift in the emphasis of reportage. What had first been wired home to offices in Chicago, Detroit, and New York as a heartbreaking failure had become, instead, a magnificent attempt. She'd been hospitalized, of course. But remarkably, by evening of the day after she was sitting up in bed and by that night over-riding doctors' orders and holding court with a few reporters in her room. Saying things like that water was one of the meanest coldest bastards on earth and she'd certainly given it a run for the money hadn't she. Sure had given just about as good as she got. Yes, yes, and if swimmers were boxers she guessed she'd be one of the world-class heavyweights, wouldn't she. Sitting there propped up by pillows, she'd grinned and flexed a muscle. The men wrote things down. They kidded with her and she kidded back, asked her questions and she answered the ones she wanted to and spouted off some more philosophy and they agreed with everything she said, ate it all whole loving every minute, and when she said she was tired, time to call it quits for the night, they spontaneously cheered her.

There'd been a victory party that week. What the victory was, no one seemed to know exactly. Surely, though, it centered around her. The sense of triumph caught on. Some of the press people left, but others came in to Benton Harbor working on stories with different angles. Psychological angle, character-study angle. He hadn't spent a second on any sketches. Hadn't cracked open a pad, hadn't unlatched his supply case. At the party he stood in one corner and watched her circulate. She'd suffered severe muscle spasms immediately afterward and still limped a little, still wasn't free and easy lifting arms or moving her shoulders or turning her head, but her sunlit grin obscured all that. She wore silk, designer's scarf. She looked pretty. He drank too much and wondered if she was stupid. There was that jocky cheerleader quality to her. Well maybe she was. He had another seven-and-seven and figured he'd test it out. He approached her while she was standing back from it all in a corner of her own. As he did with all women he might admire, Rick gave his best imitation of a drunken swine. He swaggered up without introducing himself and asked did she read much. She'd grinned then openly, almost gullibly, saying no, no, unfortunately that was one of the things she hadn't seemed to have much time for of late although she had in the past and certainly hoped to again in the future, it was the kind of question most people didn't ask her and she wondered why he had. Because, he told her, crunching on an ice cube, he'd been standing around wishing

Joseph Conrad were here but before he mentioned that to her he'd wanted to make sure she knew who Joseph Conrad was. She gave him a sweet smile. Why Conrad? she wanted to know. He was taken off guard by the lack of rancor in her voice, her face. Why Conrad and not, say, Unamuno? So he thought a minute then finished his drink, saying because he'd been wondering if redemption were possible, and she considered that before staring him straight in the eye with the same good-natured smile on her face saying of course it was possible, as long as it was absolutely necessary it was also possible, and she guessed that was true not only of redemption but of anything and everything in life. You could look at every painfully difficult process kind of as an adventure, couldn't you, or a challenge that brought out the best in you, didn't he agree, it wasn't only to be viewed as a dreary task you had to endure for the sake of some abstract moral attainment, and had he noticed the ceiling in this place? The lights on the chandelier there. Had he noticed the way they were set up, in perfect radiating circles so shadow patterns spread across the ceiling like a whirlpool, or a tornado. Good job of design there. Stylistically innovative despite the intended traditionalism of the chandelier itself.

He followed her everywhere that evening. He listened.

The series of illustrations for *SportsYear* were stylistically like nothing he'd done before. There were no traditional figures, but plenty of brilliant colors. He mixed oils: crimsons, violets. It came out swirls of circles and half-circles and impressions of hands meeting arms meeting ovals against a sea of boiling waves, sun-streaked winds. Dimly defined shapes of two androgynous bodies, naked, face to face in water, mirroring each other's outstretched arms. He stayed in Michigan after everyone else had left, putting on the final touches. Flew back to New York with a week and a half's worth of beard scruffing his face, delivered the job in person and then went home, stripped totally, crawled into bed with a brain-searing headache and slept twenty hours. Woke up answering a call from the art director at *SportsYear*. Those illustrations, they weren't quite what he'd had in mind, he knew that damned well. Rick told him to go take it up the ass. He drank some water and went back to sleep. Woke, cleaned, shaved, stalked naked around his apartment dabbling at the drafting table, dabbling in sketch books, gessoing some canvas. When the originals came back from *SportsYear* by messenger he mounted and framed them, had them delivered to her with a note enclosed asking would she please be his friend.

"What about the laundry?" She was running tap water over the blender's plastic cone-top, glancing at the clock.

"I'll pick it up tomorrow." Four thirty a.m. Time to get back to bed.

Now he stood in the bedroom doorway and watched her. She'd rinsed out the glass, changed clothes, thrown three tank suits and a towel into her bag, tossed in a tube of skin cream and a neat stack of heavy-bound books and her gloves, her pens, her change purse, her Master lock. She slipped on a jacket. Bag slung over her shoulder. One hand for the viola, one free for hailing cabs, for fishing bills and change and slips of paper with addresses on them out of the portable whirlwind of things she carried. She approached to kiss goodbye, stopped because there was an odd look in his eyes. He wanted to tell her he'd heard her on the phone the night before. Heard her talking with people, conniving here, convincing there, calling up the clubs with pools, rounding up lane time for herself for the next morning and the next and more. He wanted to tell her he'd known then that she'd leave early this morning. Wanted to tell her that it was all right and that he was afraid.

The kiss turned into a hug. She hugged him close a second time, then was out the door.

"Who did that to his face?"

"Tycho?" Sarge stepped on the gas a little and they passed a moving van. The White Mountains poked skyward ahead, north and west, only sign of human society yellow-lined pavement, telephone wires, cars whistling by occasionally. Dorey had opened her window all the way so air blew the hair across her forehead and cheeks. Her hand grasped at it out the window like a kid's, playing that old car-traveling game of trying to catch the breeze. He found himself wondering at her phrasing of the question—*who* did that to his face—as if the damage told a tale of uninvited aggression. Then he wondered how she'd picked up on it. "Long story."

"That's okay. Long ones suit you."

Her voice was teasing. Recognizing that with surprise, he shot an approving grin sideways.

"Right. Before I met him he'd been rowing double sculls. Did damned well at it too, he and his partner. Bob something. Hell! I've forgotten the guy's last name, funny how that happens, huh? Bob something. They were a team. Won every college title in sight a couple of years running, double sculls, always double sculls. One day the man just went berserk. Ran around the crew house smashing anything in his way to pieces with an oar. Tycho was there."

"Just him?"

"What do you mean?"

"He was the only one hurt? Tycho?"

"Right. Got his face split wide open. Know what he told me? He told me his nose was hanging somewhere over his lips by threads when they found him. They had to sew his damn nose back on."

Dorey sucked in air that tasted different from city air, the dampness cleaner. She asked were they alone in the crew house when it happened, and Sarge got them past another truck saying he didn't know, he thought so. Well why, she said, why did it happen.

"The man just went berserk."

"Uh-huh. But why?"

"That's it. That's all anyone knows."

"Just like that?"

"Just like that." Sarge shrugged. "Crazy, huh? I guess it happens sometimes."

He sensed her about to say something, but whatever it was she stopped herself and was silent. To the west now hillsides were spotted with sparse pine groves. These dark patches grew larger, thicker, as they drove north.

"Well." Her voice bordered on disappointed. There was that childlike quality, something very young about her. "Well it wasn't a long story, not really." Then he felt her formulating what she'd say next and for some reason his shoulders tightened nervously. "You left out most of it."

"Did I."

"Uh-huh. Look. When something like that happens it changes your life. I mean, it makes you different."

"Maybe. Don't you think that's his business, though?"

"Well sure. But you're his best friend."

"I met him after all that happened."

She rolled up the window a little. He heard what she said next as if overhearing something barely spoken. "You only know half of him then."

Maybe she was right. The John Gallagher before and the John Gallagher after, well, they had to be different. So perhaps he knew only the afterward part, had missed out on the twenty-some years before. Sarge wondered if they'd even have known each other, were it not for the accident. *Accident.* That's how Tycho'd always referred to it, when in fact it had been an outright attack, premeditated or no, an act of violence and not much accident to it at all. But Tycho knew better than anyone. If he wanted to call it an accident, let him.

"Right," he said. "You're right about that."

They passed a dairy, stench blowing from the big, blank-eyed brown and white grazers near the road. He thought maybe she'd pop a few more questions out at him and—without knowing why—he wanted to avoid them. So he maneuvered away from it all. "Been doing your homework?"

Yes, she said, sure.

She reached for the black looseleaf binder on the dashboard. He'd thrown it together with her in mind, stuff he'd searched out in his desk files. There were clippings. Some cold water swims, open water, successes and attempts. Newspaper reports as well as the official statistics, temperature of water and temperature droppage, the distance covered with each and the time it took. North Channel of the Irish Sea. The

Strait of Juan de Fuca. The Farallons to San Francisco. Ontario south to north. Ontario north to south. Michigan. Et cetera. Then an up-to-date nautical chart, three-hole-punched and neatly in place on binder rings at the very end. This was the San Antonio Strait, misnamed stretch of water between San Antonio Island and the Washington mainland.

"Interesting stuff?"

"Some," she said. "Some of it I knew already."

It wasn't really a strait. The distance between island and mainland was a little over thirty-two miles. More than a strait, it was a kind of channel, but not really that either. It was a rough, cold stretch of open water. A snarling stream of south-flowing current snaked, in approximate parallel to the mainland's coast, about midway between both bodies of land. Running up against it in gale-darkened weather, nineteenth-century boatmen had surmised that the current's savageness was a channeling effect caused by the island. Their visibility had been about zero, they'd figured land was close, and when they capsized swam west straight into that current. The one who survived dubbed it a strait. The name stuck. Sarge rolled his window down as far as it would go. Chill rippled his hair.

"Punta Provechosa. That's where I guessed, too. To start." She shut her eyes, leaned back onto the headrest. "What's it like?"

He drew a miniature peninsula-type shape in air and when the car began to swerve placed his hands back on the wheel again. "Hell, just a point of land. You've seen it a million times, right? Sticks out from that eastern coast of the island like this"—again his hands came together, returned to grip the wheel—"so it's the point closest to the mainland. Take off from the northern side of that tip there, get a nice tide, you have to push out a ways and then ride around towards the southern side, then head due east. Only way to avoid these rocks." Because the island had been clamped in its own particular sort of chastity belt, coastal granite cliffs and offshore rocks that with the water's suck and pull would kill, no questions asked or exceptions made. That tiny almost-peninsula of land jutting out from island towards mainland was, on any

108

map, dotted at the tip, the dot named Punta Provechosa. And the tip's north side was nearly rock-free. This—along with the dot—was its sole distinction. "That's why you don't go in August. No one fights rain and seven-footers and makes it clear of the coast, especially not starting from an unprotected point like that. Good weather and you have the best chance."

She nodded, saying sure, she knew, but what was it like? To be there, she meant.

Blue pines lined the road on either side now. They made its concrete surface darker and the air a tangy perfume. Sarge's hands tightened on the wheel. He didn't want to answer her, didn't want to talk at all anymore. He'd been afraid of this and, recognizing his fear, he understood it, then did something for her he hadn't done for anyone else. Because she was the one who'd be in that water hour by hour, all five feet, five and three-quarter inches of her. And he'd be the one watching continually for the duration, watching as weight dropped off her by degrees, holding out the feeding stick at consistent intervals. Sure. Well maybe for himself, too.

So he started talking. The words came out quietly. He told her about the color of water blending gray into the sky's texture when you stood on that beach before dawn. How things chilled at night in September, wind slapping your skin. Told her about the underlying rocks meandering out from the tip's south side, how water swirled vanishing free-form designs over them, images that reappeared with the next wave breaking and the cool summer's-end scent of air laden heavily with salt. It was a barren, rock-strewn oval of an island, spattered here and there by clumps of pale trees, streaks of rope-tough grass lining the freshwater trickles that rolled down a couple of the interior hillsides. Gulls used it, fish bred near it, and flying along its cliffs were winged multicolored insects that sailors had long ago mistaken for some strange kind of butterfly. The Coast Guard had a small station there. Near Punta Provechosa was a lighthouse. Caught in sudden July squalls, fishing boats or ill-directed weekend yachts or equipment scows might try to anchor in near the lighthouse. Nineteenth-century fishermen, forerunners of the one who'd dubbed the water a strait, had landed there, abandoned it, left only names behind. San Antonio Island. Punta Provechosa. Costa de Piedra, coast of stone. Pretty much good for nothing except to leave it. Go back to the mainland, eastward towards rising light and a multitude of promises. To get there you had to cross over, by way of the San Antonio Strait. Just cross over, that was all.

"Are you Anne Norton?"

"Yes! Which lane am I in, did he leave word?" Ah-hah. It was number one of course, special courtesy of an old acquaintance, kind of an inside joke. Anne was feeling good. She moved past the security guard, past the desk attendant and cut a left down the hall, then a right, swung through the locker room door and dumped everything on a bench except the viola. Its case she wrapped tenderly in a couple of towels from her bag, stood it upright against the back of the locker she'd opened. Number 18. *Dieciocho*. Sarge was always saying it was a lucky number. Chlorine permeated the fluorescent-lit air. She sucked it in, throat acclimating to that heavy damp. It had been a long time.

She took out one suit, frowned, and pulled a second out slowly. Then two caps as well. Goggles—gold-tinted, custom-fit.

She stripped and every movement had nice form to it, audience or no. She locked things up and carried suits, caps, towel, goggles to the shower. Anne wet herself down, shoved her hair under the first cap—which was black rubber—and then pulled another over that. The second was Lycra. It was also black, but shimmered. She stepped into one black suit, pulled it up firmly, grimaced at the second and then stepped into it straight-faced. This suit had wild gold-colored swirls spread across it from every angle. Never wear drab on the outside. In tropical waters the bright-colored fish were the ones you stayed away from—only dangerous fish needed no camouflage. Then there were the bright-colored ones that weren't dangerous at all—their camouflage was in successfully passing for dangerous. Anne reasoned that what this second type had going for it was a gloriously stylish spirit and cleverness to be reckoned with. You had sharp teeth or you had sharp wits. Either stood you some kind of chance, best was to have both. She pulled it on and felt the double drag already pressing down on her shoulders, gave herself a full-length look in the mirror, smiled. Go Norton, go. Looking good there. She slunk towards herself and swiveled to profile, turned full-face and flashed a seductive look. She tossed her head back imagining the hair shaking out. Then she laughed and flexed a muscle, grabbed her towel—which was golden yellow, her initials darkly scripted at one corner—and headed for the entrance to the pool. Dampness got even more pervasive, chlorine smell so strong she'd stopped smelling it. In front of the door she paused a moment, then lifted her shoulders, relaxed them and breathed deep. She pushed on through the door.

The water caught ceiling lights. It sparkled back at her. Clear, bottom sky-blue at the shallow end and darker at the other. Even this early a couple of bodies were in there doing slow laps but most of the lanes were empty, lifeguard lounging barefooted and T-shirted at the deep end.

Anne looked like the real thing and the lifeguard glanced up, then fixed his gaze on her from an Olympic-sized stretch away. She draped her towel smoothly over the wall rail. Stepped over a couple of stacks of kickboards and went right to lane one. He watched her crouch at the gutter, dangle goggles into the crystal sky-blue and spit into them once, twice, before fitting them on. She kept the strap edged slightly above where he knew the tops of her ears would be. The goggles rendered her bug-eyed, golden-eyed, made every feature insignificant. She stood and balanced there, legs slightly apart, gold-swirled vision against a background of black. Perfect form. She was about to dive. He waited. He held his breath.

Only she didn't dive. She straightened, stepped back from the edge and turned. Anne stalked to the wall, clutched for her towel to rub each hand on, then her lips, then draped it again, just so, over the rail. She was examining patterns in wall tile. Same as the pool-bottom patterns. Rectangles, rectangles. She split them into fours. She split them into eights, twos, twelves, sixes, focused on indentations between each tile. She'd been thinking too much. Had to cut down on all the external stimuli, clear the mind. No, she wasn't ready yet. Not quite.

The lifeguard was disappointed. He slipped ankle onto bare knee and settled back in his chair. Come on lady, come on. Looked like she knew what she was doing. Looked like it, anyway. He watched the other bodies swimming evenly in other lanes, blinked drowsily at the blue-tinted sparkle.

Anne was talking and once in a while words slipped out aloud. She was asking herself some questions this morning. This was what facing the water you were about to jump into did. She'd forgotten how it always did that. You had to be sure, to jump in. Had to be. To know exactly what you wanted out of it and how much that was worth to you. How much of a price you were willing to pay for what you wanted. If what you wanted was a lot you could bet the price would be high and it would come from your own flesh. Yes, yes, you could bet on it. And she wasn't so certain right now because, before, the goal had always been clear. Now the goal had changed. Change fogged it somehow in her mind's sight, and because it hadn't yet become clear she wasn't really sure what she'd be willing to give. For Sarge, how many 200's this morning? What percentage of effort. Was he worth seventy percent? Fifty percent mingled with some ninety percent intervals? Worth a few miles at sixty percent? She wasn't certain. Always brought you back to how much you had to give. Then you understood something fundamental about yourself, risked knowing through and through the value you placed on your own effort. Risked finding out what was the carrot that led you on and what was the yearning that kept you going and what was the music that made you dance. Sometimes it masqueraded as a chocolate bar. Sometimes.

112

No, Norton, no. She was shaking her head. No, it couldn't be for Sarge. Not for friendship, nor grief, nor money. All were lovely visions that appealed but none touched her core. So she wondered, asked herself discomforting questions until as escape she became aware of only one thing clearly, one desire, the desire to swim now. Throw all this questioning junk to the winds because it would never be sorted out now and maybe it would never be sorted out ever and there was really just one thing clear and that was to swim now.

The lifeguard had shut his eyes and yawned again. He missed her dive.

It was silence that sparkled gold-stained blue and white at goggle level while she breaststroked. It was silence and she'd remembered again what the phrase blessed silence meant. All the babble and clutter. All the books, languages, words spoken, ideas important or trifling, bombardment of sights and of sounds. All cut away with a whoosh! and splash and then the gliding in continual rhythm, this her favorite stroke, her silver medal stroke, the one she'd first survived on. Nothing else mattered here. In that first rush of silence she knew how much it was worth to her. At the deep end she rolled onto her back, reached behind to brush the wall and flip-turned, breathed to the left, stroked freestyle. High elbow recovery, arm arching in a strong curve down, hand the arrow-tip that broke surface in measured repetition while her legs kicked a strong two-beat, creating domes of water around the feet without actually spinning up wake. From poolside it looked effortless. She'd become an extension of what she was moving in, some hand of the water clad in a black, gold-speckled glove. Anne stepped up her pace. Then again.

An hour later her shoulders hurt and she was humming some of Haydn's 49th. It had occurred to her that she'd done this more than any other thing. Had spent more time on it. More miles. More distance. More years. She was realizing that, of all the things she did so well, this particular series of motions, repeated to the point of idiocy and beyond, was the one she did best of all. That Anne Norton, doctor-to-be, was at her most excellent when stroking monotonously through water. She found that amusing. Flip-turned again. An hour and fifteen minutes. Blue blank space swelled around her, halo, bubble, and blessing. Her shoulders were hurting plenty now and she just kept going, crowded the empty blue with her favorite tunes. Stillness encased her. She filled it at liberty.

She was stopping at the shallow end and that lifeguard was leaning over saying something she couldn't hear. Anne stood without feeling the tiles against her feet and gazed at a fogged-over image of him. Gently, she lifted the black layers up above both ears.

"Excuse me," he said, "time's up. Someone else scheduled now."

She wished he wouldn't speak so softly, hard to hear.

Anne held up two fingers. "Two more. Laps."

Oh well, he mumbled, okay, go ahead.

She backstroked easily, at the deep end flipped into a last-lap breaststroke. Easy now, easy on the glide. When she bobbed up for breath one final time he was still crouched over the edge, watching. Slowly she pulled the goggles up to rest against her forehead and, in the sudden fogless night, blinked at him. His smile was young, a little nervous, muted with respect.

"Excuse me. Do I know who you are?"

"Well if you don't," Anne grinned, "you should." Her grin was mildly teasing, and when she pulled her goggles all the way off and tossed them gently to him, the gesture was easygoing mixed with a kind of defiance. She rolled the caps back over both ears, winked at him and spun around, focused on that other end. She ducked in, arched up, breathed and her arms spanned batlike over the water. She butterflied.

Eighth day of November it rained. You could hear it muted by the pines. Once in a while sounds like a bullwhip lashed through the air. The trees swayed in wind freezing north off the lake. By late afternoon Dorey'd eased into a bath. It was so hot steam rose visibly, and she breathed in with relief, tilted her head back against the wall, closed both eyes.

"So. This is where you really sleep."

She opened them to see Ilana standing there, towels draped

over one arm and in her other hand a pan of steaming water which she set carefully on the tub's edge.

Dorey smiled. "I went somewhere else for a while."

"To the tropics?"

"Well maybe. Maybe, I don't know." She thought a minute. "Uh-uh. No, it wasn't the tropics."

Ilana pulled a stool up to the side of the tub and sat. "What did it look like? Here, breathe in deeply, that's right. Were there colors? Images?"

No, she told her, just a feeling. Some feeling she couldn't really describe. She'd gone to the place where this feeling was and to get there shut her eyes so it looked like she was asleep. Leaning slightly over the pan she let steam wash her face, her eyelids. Through thick walls she could hear that rain.

Sometimes at two, three a.m. Ilana'd wake up. When her eyes began to perceive things in the dark she'd also start to differentiate sounds, separate the beating of her own heart from the rise and sink of her husband's body breathing against hers. They slept together most nights now. She'd started depending on that again, the feel of him against her, texture of his skin and hair and his smell, the rhythm of his breathing and familiar thump of his pulse. Then she'd hear it dimly through the walls. Faint ring of footsteps. Pacing. Same dully-sounding back and forth pace. Several times she'd wanted to get up, throw on a robe or some clothes and step into the hall herself, go knock on that other door. Say listen, would you like to talk now? If we talk do you think you'll be able to sleep? But something always pushed her back flat on the bed and told her to keep hands off, stay out of it. Sarge, she'd said, do you think she's getting enough sleep? No he didn't and he didn't know what to do. Still she was functioning at top level. Goddamned gold-medal level there, get a look at that style and that persistence, she didn't let up for a second, not a second. Today she'd have stayed in another six hours without a complaint if he'd said to. She'd do anything, go through anything, he'd rarely seen that kind of ability to absorb punishment and still come back for more. Well this insomnia pattern bothered him too. But he'd known a few world-class types in his life who'd gone on four or five hours' sleep a night. Didn't know personally what made them tick but he knew it must be possible. Maybe she was one of them. Maybe.

Ilana didn't think so. She sensed that, bottom line, neither did Sarge. Somewhere up the road waited a point of limit. Beyond that she wouldn't be able to go without solid layers beneath her composed of many things, one of which was months of conditioning and one of which was food and one of which was self-assuredness and one of which was sleep.

Dorey's hand reappeared from the bubbles. She rubbed her shoulder.

"Sore?"

"Uh-huh. A little."

"These towels are warm. Here." Ilana folded one lengthwise and placed it across the back of her neck and around over the shoulders, ends dangling into tub water. Dorey leaned forward slightly and Ilana folded the second towel, laid it on top of the first. She reached over to run both hands firmly over both, pressing down slightly. Dorey sat back again and Ilana's hands returned to rest on her own knees. "Hungry?"

Dorey relaxed. She smiled. "Always."

"All that food, it's remarkable. Where does it go?"

"It burns away. You didn't know water could burn, did you?"

"I never thought of it that way. You're like the earth around my cacti, you know. Water it and turn around and you wonder where all the water went because it looks dry again."

They grinned at each other. Dorey blushed but not without pleasure. "Well. Carol used to say I consumed more per day than a Sumo wrestler."

"Who?"

"Carol. My mother. That was the year"—both hands rose from the water, fanned delicately in front of her for a moment before disappearing again—"I won everything there was to win. Well almost. The 100. The 200. Then the 800—that was a surprise at the Regional, they had me pegged for shorter distances. Freestyle."

"Always freestyle?"

"Yes." She bunched the towels' warmth around both ears, felt it flood through into her head. Seemed the real gut-level pain always came down to one thing—chill. Stay long enough even in pool water and there it was, cold that crept into your muscles and remained. Took quite a while to root it all out.

"And in college?"

"By then it was the 1500 freestyle. I was all right, nothing spectacular. Pools. They get, I don't know, tiring after a while."

"Here. More steam." Ilana watched her breathe in, last of the steam dampening her face. "And after the 1500 there was only open water?"

"Well yes. But I didn't know that. See." Her hands reappeared to flutter again, prettily. For some reason the movement surprised Ilana. "To me all water was chlorinated. Except for these ugly beaches where you didn't want to swim anyway. I mean, I knew that once in a while someone crossed the English Channel, but it seemed like something different. Not swimming at all, I don't know. My last year at school they changed coaches. The new one was Jensen Burns." She smiled. Ilana nodded, connecting the name with the man and harboring memories of her own. Sarge had swum against him a few times, mostly in Canada, the year before Burns retired. She remembered him as a tough, stocky, grizzled sort of character who sounded surly when he spoke—which was rarely— and showed up everywhere trailed by a prematurely gray wife and plenty of children. Dorey soaped her hands. She rubbed soap smoothly over her upper arms. "Well the second week of practice he called me into his office. He ordered me to sit down and pounded his fists on the desk all of a sudden. Then he sort of barked at me, 'What are your goals in swimming?' I told him something about what I was studying in school and what I'd do when I got out—I don't even remember what I said exactly, it wasn't important I guess. He gave me this disgusted look"—she twisted her mouth, squinted—"and said he didn't understand how I could work so hard at such a demanding sport and come off sounding so—well, so bland." She'd blushed again.

117

Ilana tilted her chin in surprise. "Really."

"I told him to go to hell." Her eyes were bright, a little ashamed and more than a little proud. "He liked that! He said then that as far as speed went for the standard indoor distances I'd never really have the necessary edge for national-class competition. Well I knew that already. But he said that with my stroke and endurance I could be doing more. 'Like what?' I said." Her face brightened. "So he told me."

Ilana listened. It had been as simple as a weekend trip up north. Dip in the lake while that surly old bastard and his boatload of family looked on. She'd torpedoed right in with a poolside dive. Then surfaced, tread frantically between half-frozen gasps. Finally she'd gotten the words out: It's cold! It's so cold! Too much for you? he'd barked, grinning. She stared back while treading. Then, teeth chattering, shifted to turn away from the boat and started to swim.

"Sumo wrestler." Dorey laughed.

"Did she swim too? Your mother?"

"What?" The look on Dorey's face was a kind of mild shock, or profound discomfort that—making its appearance once—faded immediately. "Carol? No, no. Not really."

Ilana grinned. Not *really*, she teased, just *sort of*?

"Yes, sort of. No. Well I don't know. I mean, she liked the water a lot. She liked the beach, getting a tan. That kind of thing. She used to go down"—her fingers spread on invisible sand, imaginary shoreline—"just to sit in the water and feel it. I remember that."

"But you were the swimmer in the family."

She hesitated. Ilana watched carefully. Something seemed to drop away from Dorey now and she became motionless, face and voice softened to a quiet husky tone bordering on tender. "She encouraged me a lot. She didn't push me into anything. A lot of the kids, their parents forced them into it. Carol just encouraged me to be strong. Then she let me go ahead and do it."

Ilana couldn't remember her speaking this much before. She realized something inside her had wanted Dorey to— maybe just the sound of her voice, which was pleasant, steady, young—she felt hungry for more words, to know more, somehow come closer. She wasn't sure what she wanted. But now she found herself leaning forward with interest, waiting.

"That year," Dorey said softly, "the year I told you about. When I won nearly everything. The 800. She was so happy, Ilana! That meet, I remember, she jumped down out of the bleachers just about to the pool gutters. She was proud. Her arms—she had these very frail arms, sort of slender—she was waving her arms all around."

Ilana watched the young face, slightly vulnerable now around the mouth. She knew that any questions asked would be risking something, but she decided to anyway.

"Are you very close?"

"What?"

"Your mother and you." Ilana spoke carefully.

"No," said Dorey, "uh-uh." She smiled pleasantly, her schoolgirl smile. "Thanks a lot for the towels, Ilana. They're not so sore now—my shoulders."

"You're welcome."

She stood. She'd been detoured and knew it. Puzzled, she nevertheless respected it. "When you're finished in here, there's a full refrigerator. I keep it stocked especially for Sumo wrestlers."

It was well-taken, her grin returned.

Dorey sank further down. Now even the towel-draped shoulders were immersed, sunk under warm mounds of bubble. These bubble baths were a daily habit of hers, which, like that delicate fluttering motion of hands, seemed to Ilana somehow at odds with the single-minded simplicity of the rest of her style of being. At the same time she found both oddities pleasing.

It was November eighth. It was Matt Olssen's birthday. Ilana felt inside a vast gaping pit over which she'd dropped a lid. Extending herself outside the realm of private pain seemed the only solution for getting through the day. Thus, her questioning of Dorey.

And she'd been missing something, she realized, missing something for years, that had now poked its way irretrievably into her conscious thoughts. It was just this—the observing of a singular gesture, the speaking to a person who was young. The presence of youth, that's what she'd missed. It brought about a certain kind of tenderness in her. And it was this tenderness in herself, too, which Ilana found pleasing.

The tape had been sent up by Tycho. Headphones tight, she listened. It was her favorite, the one sung to the moon. When the moon goes high in the sky always before dawn I also rise and my eyes are dizzy from so much looking at the sea. *Cuando a tan alta va la luna.* Dorey stretched out on the carpet. Her elbows were supported by intricately embroidered cushions from some village in northern Greece. Sarge had brought them back. Ilana'd told her the women of this particular village spent their entire days embroidering. Young girls embroidered from the time they were twelve years old. Aprons, pillows, pillows and blankets. *Y mis ojos me se sashayan de tanto mirar la mar.* Well, Dorey'd replied, no wonder. No wonder what? Ilana asked. No wonder the Greek women don't rank internationally as swimmers, they're too busy embroidering, they forgot what it was like. Forgot? Forgot what?

What it was like to be gods. *A la luna.*

"I'll convert you yet."

Sarge was grinning, stepping barefoot across cushions, hassock, spread maps, containers of electrolyte replacement fluid that—lining the base of the north wall's floor-to-ceiling bookshelves—looked like overgrown baby bottles. He sat on an arm of the sofa. Looking up, Dorey noticed his hair was still wet. He'd been putting in some pool time too. She plucked off the headphones, reached to turn power down. Outside the rain rattled. Once in a while wind slammed full-force against the windows, and sometimes a drenched leaf stuck flat on the outside like the spread palm of a hand.

"She's here," said Sarge. "Wants to meet you."

120   Dorey stayed where she was. Great, she told him. Her elbows dented the cushions, waiting.

Anne had stacked a couple of small bags near the back door,

hung her slicker and jacket and sweater, taken off her boots. They were leather, hand-plied, custom fit, and she'd have to oil them later. Expensive things meant time. She'd slipped into her track shoes. She stopped in for a talk with Ilana and soon Sarge was there, telling her she looked better than ever. Anne felt that good, too. Walking down the hallway towards the front room, she wasn't aware of harboring any expectations. But rounding a corner she realized she'd been expecting to come smack face to face with her, expected her to be there just at the entranceway, standing and waiting. Instead Anne had to look around. Dorey was stretched out in a tumble of cushions and headphones near the sofa where Sarge sat, and Anne stood a second with eyes roving here and there, taking in the furniture, taking in Sarge, and this woman she'd competed against who knew how many times without ever seeing her this close on land. Only in water had they nearly brushed skin, those occasional neck-and-neck miles. Anne evaluated. She withheld all judgment for now.

"Hi there." Dorey slid from her elbows to sit cross-legged in one plain, easy motion. Her face was unguarded, pleasant and without malice.

Sarge watched. Anne dug up one of those smiles that illuminated rooms. She nodded at Dorey and approached calmly, arm outstretched, hand angled down. "I'm pleased," she said, "to meet you."

Dorey smiled back. "Good." She didn't hesitate to reach up, offer her own hand openly. "That's good."

Over a baked potato and tall glass of blended eggs, grains, powders, extracts, and assorted secret ingredients, Anne sliced her knife through the air pretending it was an épée. She'd challenged Sarge to a duel.

"But I'm warning you, you're outnumbered. When's the last time you were surrounded by so many women? The Río Paraná?"

Sarge had to laugh. He thumped his chest in mock pain. "Hah! You won't let me forget that one, will you?"

"No way, not on your life."

"Hell, all right. Give us the famous speech."

A white lump of potato steamed on the prongs of her fork. She waved it casually around the table at Ilana, at Dorey, the motion inviting them in on things. "Mr. Olssen here ran into a streak of bad luck several years in a row when it came to the Rió Paraná. It seems that when he boasted no man would beat him"—she rested utensils against the plate's side and her voice assumed a tone of satisfaction—"the women weren't impressed. He was right about one thing. No man did beat him. He was firmly trounced, not once, not twice, but three times *in a row* by women." Her smile sparkled at Sarge. Again, he had to laugh. "Whose names I'm sure he's forgotten."

"You're wrong!"

"I dare you!"

He said their names.

"Bravo," Anne grinned, "you're in a generous mood tonight."

Ilana laughed along with him this time. She reached quickly for his hand and he caught hers, trapped it down warmly on the table surface. Come on now, he was teasing Anne, come on and give us the rest of the speech. Get it over with once and for all. Between bites she did just that. Saying she herself had beaten men twice her size under circumstances requiring the utmost in raw strength, and what was the reason? What? Well what could it be but her capacity for endurance, which must have far exceeded that of these muscle-graced brutes. This power to endure was a quality, she'd since surmised, inherent to a superior extent in the so-called weaker sex. Yes, yes. She'd rest her case.

"What about solo swims?"

Dorey's potato was uncooked. She ate it salt-free, washed down with bananas and mineral water. While Anne was speaking she'd nodded once in a while, come close to laughing.

"Solos? Even more so."

"Uh-huh. But it's a different consideration. Solos. I mean, the nature of the competition's different."

Anne met her gaze. "I agree."

"Because you're just with yourself, right? There's no one else to beat."

"Agreed! That's where the endurance comes in—I don't have to tell you."

"Well." Dorey'd stopped eating. They were all listening, made her a little nervous. "Well this is the way I see it. For solos what you think about is the water. Your concern is how to train to a peak for that particular body of water. So you do. That way you're at your best, really, your very best."

"Right!" Sarge nodded.

"Well if you trained—I don't know, if you just trained for all the races too, as if they were solo crossings, you'd enter each one with the best frame of mind, right? You could say to yourself: this is the competition now, just this, to make the best time possible across this particular body of water." She half shut her eyes, placed an index finger on each temple so it looked for a moment as if she were meditating. "And you block everyone else out."

Anne chuckled. Her voice, laced with humility, had sharp teeth around the edges. "I could *never* block you out." Some-- how Sarge was proud of her.

"That's not true. You did in Australia." Dorey's words rang across the table with a quiet urgency. Detached from her, they were calmly telling the truth. "You were the best swimmer there. You were better than me that day."

Anne rarely blushed. She did so now, and Sarge noted the date and time for future reference. He pressed gently on Ilana's hand, kept his face immobile.

Anne didn't know whether to say thank you or not. It hadn't sounded like an intentional compliment, more a simple statement of fact. She was silent while her potato cooled on the plate. Then she sent eyes straight to Dorey's.

"Okay. What about all the other times?"

"Maybe," Dorey said quietly, "maybe you should have been thinking more about the water."

Ilana watched the two women. Very different faces on bodies that were in many ways strikingly similar, faces younger than their age, for—she guessed—totally different reasons. When Anne had first challenged Sarge in that way, commenting on how unusual it was for him to be surrounded by women, Ilana thought to herself that it was just as unusual

for her. She'd always thought of herself as sociable. That so-
ciability—the summers, the full camp—had been with men.
So Ilana was something of a treasure to them all. Queen Bee,
that's what Matt said. As queen, and the only female, she'd
moved with a lithe kind of confidence. It was a confidence she
seemed to lack around women. And she realized, now, how
much of her silence this evening had been due to awkwardness. Silent, she could be graceful. Gracefully, she listened.
She heard Anne ask pointedly, well, and had Dorey ever concentrated on beating *her?*

No, said Dorey, uh-uh, just the water.

"Alas," said Anne.

Then they both laughed.

"Two hours," Sarge pointed, "and back in the pool you go."
He turned to Anne. "Want to watch?"

"To swim!" she exploded. "I'm swimming tonight, Sarge,
who wants to *watch?* What do you think I am, anyway?"

"God knows," he teased.

"Ah-hah! That's debatable."

"Take a six, seven-minute warmup. Go easy. Do a quarter."

He thought he saw Dorey's neck arch expectantly. She
sensed some speed work in the offing, just a taste. A little
variation would do her good right now. And give Anne an
inkling of what he had in mind for later.

They stood at the pool's edge, admiring. It was the size you
dreamed of and it was empty, waiting for them. Sarge examined their bodies, both double-suited. Anne was an inch taller,
a pound lighter. Aside from that they had the same general
lines. A lot of the weight centered high—shoulders, arms,
upper torso. Legs strong but thin-looking in relation to the
rest. Hips there, all right, but not so prominent. Perfect, he
said to himself, just about perfect.

"Hell's freezing over and so am I. Waiting to take the boat?"

"The hovercraft," Anne cracked.

124   "Get in!" he roared.

Anne dove, a perfect flat-out missile of a racing dive. Dorey
waited a second more, then reached down, kept one hand on

the edge and swung in feet-first. Anne was flipping at the other
end, heading back. Dorey paused. Then she pushed off the
wall and her first stroke curved up, around, down, and the
second, the third, breath following naturally with her body's
roll. She and Anne passed each other halfway down the length
of the pool. Sarge saw them in profile. For an instant they
appeared to be meeting face to face, heads blending together
so the bodies seemed to grow into each other, opposing arms
raised in nearly identical motion. He was reminded of Tycho
and that zodiac stuff. One of the standard symbols, two fish
meeting head on, blending head first, sharing the same eye.
He wished Tycho were here now so he could show him that.
How good they looked. Outside it rained. Then he remembered. November eighth. Matt, he said, Matt. Hey kid, happy
birthday. Inside him something busted.

Long-distance, Rick's voice was occasionally obscured by
static. Happy anniversary, he was telling her, and Anne said
you've got to be kidding, not already?

"Well no," he admitted. "Not quite. It will be on Saturday."

"Hey." Anne swung a leg over the sofa's arm. She'd dragged
a phone in and now the extension cord was tangled up with
headphones, books, cushions, the base of a lamp. "We've
known each other a lot longer, haven't we? I recall—"

"Sí, sí, señorita. But Saturday marks the big night."

"Stud. Is that all you think about?"

"Constantly."

"Really."

"Really. What I want right now—"

"Hey! Don't. No, no, don't Rick—"

From far away he laughed. There was something comforting in the sound, and she was surprised at herself. She hadn't
known she'd been seeking that.

He was teasing. Telling her what he'd do if. When. She told
him hey, cut it out, two could play at this, but there wasn't
much conviction in her reprimand. Still, even when she felt   125
herself begin to squirm slightly and press her thighs together,
what rippled under everything was this bedrock layer of com-

fort, almost relief, at the sound of his voice. It made Anne a little ill at ease. She was glad when a few high-pitched yaps broke through from the other end.

"Hey! How's my pal?"

"He tore up one of your old Adidas."

"That's the spirit. Tough shoe to crack."

"So I told him. Okay, okay, down you go buster. Anne. I'm working on another goddamned hunting tale. I'm running close to the limit on this crap."

"Deer hunting?"

"No."

"Wolves?"

"Try again."

"Ah-hah! I've got it. Canadian mounties hunt maniac loose in the north woods, right?" She giggled loudly and, from the kitchen, Dorey heard. " 'Somewhere in those woods a madman lurked. He was armed and dangerous. One would have to go in after him. Before he killed again. When they drew the straws, it was Big Rick Barton.' "

"Love it, but no. Trout fishing in Colorado."

"Close!"

He said something she didn't hear clearly. Then he was asking did she plan on coming home tomorrow, and she said yes. Good, he told her. Had she decided what she'd do. She hesitated.

"We'll talk about it when I get back, okay?"

"Sure." He sounded a little glum. She stage-whispered something into the phone that got him laughing.

Recradling the receiver, Anne felt her eyelids creeping down. Shoulders sore. Old man was a drill sergeant for sure. But she'd surprised him, hadn't she. Yes somebody'd been working quite a bit this past month, whipped herself into a good semblance of minimal condition. Well, she'd have been damned if she'd show up here looking like a fool. She hated that thought, hated it, worse than just about anything—and she'd always figured if she did her best there was no way she'd ever put in a bad appearance. No way. Her best was pretty much the best there was.

"Tired?"

Dorey stood in the entranceway, barefoot, smiling pleasantly. Anne yanked a drawstring and her lids rolled back up like window shades.

"Fried to a crisp. What about you?"

"Tired." She sat on some floor cushions.

"He's tough! He's a tough old son of a bitch, Sarge." Anne chuckled. "Matt used to tell me things. Whew! But I wish I'd known him in his prime—Sarge, I mean. I'd have liked to race him, just to see how I stacked up. Has he told you about any of his swims?"

"Some."

"When he talks, listen well. You can always get a few helpful hints."

"I hope you decide yes," said Dorey.

"Okay," Ann grinned. The remaining word stuck in her throat, but she didn't want to let on what havoc it was creating. Like those bright-skinned fish, make the danger zone seem easy. So her grin appeared casual. "Yes," she said.

"I'm glad! Thank you."

"I swam with pacers a couple of years ago." Talking, Anne started to feel better. She'd talk the throat-jam away. "That was the Catalina Channel." She glanced at Dorey, wondering, but there was no flicker of anything on her face other than open listening. Anne picked cloudlike designs from the disconnected ovals of shadow up on the ceiling. "Special technique to it—those women were so tuned to my pace—there were a couple of them—I couldn't tell after a while which one was in the water. That was a crazy time, let me tell you. A month before I was set to go, I had to fly back east, my father was in the hospital. This was all of the sudden—that bastard had never been sick an hour of his life before, he was always yachting or banging tennis balls around or going a few rounds of golf, or else he was off closing some deal, trading in copper futures. Something like that anyway, I never really understood what exactly he did because whatever it was was a family tradition and he was William Randall Norton the Fourth, you know, so daughters weren't usually in on any of it. I got to the hospital straight off the plane. I hadn't slept all night but I must have looked like a million bucks—I was *bronzed* and spectacularly strong and my brothers were milling around everywhere looking very pale. Very frightened. Nobody was saying anything much except that he'd been waiting to see me, I had to see him immediately. *Had* to, they said, he'd want me to tell him. Finally I cornered my brother Bill and asked, what? Tell him what? Cancer, he was crying, it's cancer. Cancer of the what? Of the everything, he said." Anne propped herself on an elbow. Outside the rain had slowed some, the wind diminished. "I went and talked to a doctor, and I drank about a quart of ice water for lunch. I remember I was incredibly thirsty. Then I went in to visit my father. He was sitting up, he'd lost weight and looked pretty tired. You know what surprised me most, though—his hair had turned white. Just like that"—her arm swept the air—"the first thing he said was 'I'm glad you're here Anne, the rest of them are all a bunch of sissies.' He asked how the swim was shaping up and would I go for the record and I told him he could bet on it. I sat next to him on the bed. He smelled awful. Everything did, this rotting smell. 'I think I'm dying,' he said. 'Yes Dad, that's true,' I said. He asked how long it would take and I told him what the doctor'd told me, which was that without surgery and without chemotherapy it wouldn't be long at all. 'That stinks,' he said. He cried some. Then we held hands. Let me tell you, that cancer just ripped right through him. It took three weeks. He weighed"—she turned to Dorey, a kind of awe spreading across her face—"my father weighed eighty-five pounds when he died!"

Dorey reached to softly press the sofa edge near Anne's elbow. Catalina to the mainland, she was saying, that had been a good swim hadn't it? Neck-and-neck with the record even though she hadn't broken it, a much-admired crossing.

"It *was* a good swim." Anne nodded, satisfied. "We wound up postponing it to October, I lost my peak somewhere in there. Still, it was good."

•

Rick walked the dog once more that night. In the city drizzle came and went. When they both got puddle-splashed by a passing cab Rick thought about a drink, then was proud when he decided against it. On the way upstairs he lifted the mutt to one shoulder, patted his wagging behind, and mumbled some baby talk. He got a few slobbers on the neck.

"Tomorrow. Hear that?"

The drafting table was a clutter. He switched on the fluorescent, watched it whitewash the bleakly colored forms he'd painted. Kidded himself with the thought that Big Rick Barton had succeeded in doing the impossible: rendering both Colorado and rainbow trout oddly colorless. It was what the account wanted, he knew. Assholes.

Methodically he recapped each pen, lifted the illustration board from the table and stashed it away with his inks and watercolors. He sat at the high stool, ignored whines ringing shrilly behind him until they became tiny snores, panting growls and paw-twitchings in sleep. Rick thought a minute. Then he took out some papier d'arche, pencils numbered through eleven, and a box of crayons.

I only sleep with my friends, she'd said. When we sleep together we have to be friends, otherwise it's a waste of time, don't you think? Good. That's really kind of a relief that you agree, let me tell you. Those colors of yours. First I thought they reminded me of something of Van Gogh's but then I realized I was way, way off. It was Edvard Munch, after all. *Cri*. No, no, maybe not that exactly but one of his others, I don't know which. Not anything like *The Kiss* or *Vampire*— what do you think of that progression, anyway? Which could it be.

"*Encounter in Space*," said Rick. "I'm relieved too."

Sitting there, he'd spoken out loud. It brought him back to the drafting table. He'd been doodling with crayons.

Okay, he whispered months later, now. We're friends now. Pressed against her on her water bed, so hard he was almost hurting and he had that feeling of wanting to rip both their clothes off in one swift motion so he stopped a second, pulled back from her and told himself calm down, it's okay. He did.

129

They relaxed side by side on the gently warm, undulating surface and she smiled. Her face and neck and the revealed chest area above where her shirt began were flushed. He started to talk but she touched a finger to her lips for hush and then with the same finger traced his lips and his chin, bobbed over his Adam's apple, tapped his breastbone. Her hand traveled down slowly. She undid all his buttons.

That's pretty.

Pretty? he chuckled. Her fingers played with the hair curving around his nipples. Sure, she said, why not, some places you're pretty. He shook his head, just smiled back at her. He'd never thought of it that way. She was tugging at her shirt. Then she stopped, accepted his hands. Want the job? Let me, he said. He made sure to go slow. He peeled things off her by inches. Well she said everything worthwhile meant time, plenty of it. She liked that. Tilted her head back.

Lie still. On your back, lie still, like that. Please, will you hold. Hold on. My hips, like that, yes. Feel it? Do you feel what it does underneath the way we're moving? The bed. Like oceans. Don't you think. No, no, lie still, lie still, otherwise I can't wait, don't want it to stop. Do you feel it. The moving.

That's you, he said, that's me fucking you.

When he pushed up into her he held her firmly at the hips. Above she swayed. Again and her back arched, shoulders rose, face flushed darker and tightened in a kind of pain. He felt her thighs go stiff. Twelfth night of November.

Tonight was the eighth. Rick peeled some more waxy wrapping off the navy blue. A few more strokes, nice melt with the violet. He'd drawn a ship. It was a small ship with high-carried prow and old-fashioned plank deck. Around it swept water. This was plainly ocean water, green-tinged, gray-shadowed purples and blues circling together in sharp-edged wave patterns. He'd made the whitecaps red. Stick figures bent over prow and stern watching a figure in the water. It was a full-bodied figure with no facial features and no sexual organs. On its chest was a jagged streak of scarlet, like a wound. Above everything the sun glowed hot yellows. Two hands stretched out from the sun to clutch a bowlike sliver of moon that aimed down towards the boat, the sea. The moon was arrowless. The sun smiled. It had Anne's face.

"Johnny Walker Black."

What? she'd said, eyes opening while the bed rippled loosely beneath them. Johnny Walker Black, he repeated. Lifted a hand to his lips. See I smell you now on me, and I taste you, it's as if my mouth were inside you too. So what came to mind was Johnny Walker Black. On the rocks? she teased. No, straight up. Double shot. Come here.

Rick switched off the light. Crayon stubs mingled at random with pencils, messing up the table. He left everything that way, undressed and stepped over the sleeping dog to bed. It was a king-sized bed with firm mattress. When they moved in together, he'd said absolutely not to the water bed. Told her sometimes it was wonderful but he was basically a land creature, after a while the thing made him seasick. She'd kicked up quite a fuss, then pouted, then come around to the bargaining stage. No surrender of hers was ever unconditional. The conditions were that the bed be the largest available. Its frame, chestnut, finished to her specifications. One set of sheets must be silk, the color of her choice. It was a serious thing, a bed, you had to choose where you would sleep and make love with as much care as you chose what water to swim in. He saw her point, was quick to agree. Matter settled, decision made, she became immediately gracious again, got on the phone and began researching this question of mattresses. Sizes, compositions, textures and varieties of firmness. She was keeping an alphabetical list. Days later he'd be given a rundown on the history of the bed from pre-medieval times to the present. She was ordering wood.

Rick set the clock. Wasn't even midnight but he felt exhausted. He stretched comfortably under the quilt, against silk, reached over the mattress edge to caress the bedframe for which she had driven three carpenters nearly mad. There were no sharp corners or edges—everything was finished smooth, appearing to curve rather than angle. From the floor came snores, an occasional growl. He dragged a pillow against him and ran fingers down its back as if it were her, wanted the

131

time to go by so on Saturday he'd wake up smelling himself on her, smiling good morning and proudly sober. His fingers felt sticky with crayon.

"Matt."

Ilana sat up reaching for Sarge but he wasn't there. When the dark was familiar again, she tried to relax. She'd woken clutching at the sides of the bed to keep herself from falling. For a moment the motion of tumbling was real, as was the terror, mixed with a sliding sense of vertigo.

She glanced at the clock as it ticked past midnight. Day officially over and she felt relief. The feeling didn't last. She slipped out of bed and pulled on a robe. A couple of hours before, she'd realized he wasn't coming to bed, then heard through the wall between their rooms his guitar strumming "Romance Anonimo." When it stopped there was another sound. Some combination of frantic breaths and strangled noises that came from the chest. It was frightening to hear. It was repulsive.

At the door she listened. Nothing. Ilana knew what she'd see if she looked into his room: him stretched on floor cushions next to the guitar. He'd have left a soft lamp on, and the polished wooden surface of the instrument would reflect that in a solid dark shine. The tapes on the machine would rotate once in a while, click automatically off and on. While he slept, a headphone perched over each ear, feeding him Vivaldi.

In the kitchen she turned some light on. She made tea, waited for it to steep and cool. Pulling back a curtain she could see a reflection of herself in the window. Getting older. Even dimly reflected, the facial lines were apparent. Using the window as a mirror she ran a hand through her hair, patted it into some semblance of shape. Keep the hair together. Lips still. Keep the mouth from twitching, there, that was it. Control was a simple enough thing if you clung to external details—

rules of behavior, of appearance. She poured a glass of water and drank it standing at the sink. She was thirsty.

"It's all there," Matt pointed down deeper than the floor. He'd just come from the pool and was waist-up naked, semi-dry, towel slung over one shoulder while sunlight splashed through the window across his face. "All down there off the coast of Bimini. They found these ruins—buildings, lots of structures, and there's a whole lot more underneath they think."

"A city?"

"Hell no, a *continent*. Those ruins, they're just the tip of the iceberg." When he got excited his jaw tightened, eyes took on a strident brightness. "It's all tied in I'll bet. The flood myths, the Big Bang theory, the pyramids, everything." Had she known that the Atlantic was called in ancient times the Murky Ocean? Filled with silt and debris that apparently hadn't yet settled, leftover matter from some comparatively recent terrestrial disaster. And how could the Pacific be called the Pacific when it was anything but that? He figured only if you compared it with something far more turbulent. Like the Atlantic back then. Sure. So what he'd concluded was this: he was carrying on the world's finest and maybe most ancient tradition.

"What's that?" she teased. "Sinking?"

They both laughed.

"*Swimming*. Just imagine all of North America suddenly going under water! Who'd survive? If anyone at all? The distance swimmers, of course—who else could last in that kind of water for as long as it'd take to get to the nearest stable land mass? And once we got there, well"—he posed for her, winked, flexed muscles—"guess who'd be acclaimed as gods?"

"You've got it all figured out."

"Sure do. All that old Mediterranean blood in me—from you and from Sarge. All the ancient peoples, like the Egyptians. No wonder it's one of the big sports there. I'm descended from the first of the great survivors. Marathon swimmers are the original heroes."

133

Ilana drank some tea.

What was that? That gash? Matt? They tried heart massage.
They had to cut his chest. What? Why? She was hitting someone, some man, some doctor. She was hitting Sarge, hard,
pounding away at the arms he'd crossed dully over his own
chest for protection. What? Because his heart stopped. It just
stopped. Hearts get too cold they'll stop working, like an engine you leave outside overnight in the winter. No, it had been
Tycho. Tycho she'd been hitting.

They had to cut his chest with a knife, it was the closest
knife on hand, the kind you scale fish with.

How? she'd asked. How could it just stop?

"Ilana?"

"Go away, please," she said.

"Can I help?" Dorey sat across the table. Ilana told her to
go away. Told her she was sorry.

"No, don't, it's all right."

"I'm sorry."

"It's okay. Let me make you some more tea."

The thought of drinking anything seemed suddenly horrible. She tiredly met the dark eyes that stared at her from
across the table. Dorey was fully dressed, jeans, sweater, barefoot. Had she picked up the habit of bare feet from Sarge?
Ilana couldn't remember. "Listen dear. Don't try to help me
right now. You can't."

"No," said Dorey, "no, I won't go away."

"People don't listen to me around here."

Dorey was at the sink, then the stove. Ilana watched her
move, legs mostly stationary, back and shoulders and arms
orchestrating the making of tea.

"I can do that."

"Sit down, Ilana." The firmness of tone surprised them
both. Ilana obeyed. "Here. It's ready."

She paused, at a loss. Then accepted the fresh cup. "Thank
you."

"You're welcome."

"I had a frightening dream tonight."

"Do you remember it?"

It was a sensation of falling, she told her, just falling endlessly. She'd woken up trying to stop.

That was all she told her. Ilana felt the pause, empty space filled with words unspoken. Well what could she say. Say somewhere tangled in the air through which she'd been falling was the body of her son, naked, moving towards her. That somehow, mid-journey, the body she'd thought was his had transformed and was no longer male but still moving towards her, arms flung wide. Or that she'd begun this dream chasing a brown furry creature with vicious slits for eyes and sharp saberlike teeth. What was clear to her was that this creature could kill. What was also clear was that, of all people, she alone could safely hold it. She'd climbed a cliff. The granite scraped her hands, cut deep. She left tiny spots of blood on each hold. Jaw open, fur bristled, it was cornered and crouched there waiting for her. She reached. Then began to fall.

"What am I doing sitting here crying."

In Dorey's chest the thumping increased. She saw Ilana's hand shiver, open, on the table. She hesitated, then reached over to cover it with her own.

"I'm sorry, Ilana. I'm sorry about Matt."

How? How could it just stop? Like that? Just stop?

He'd lied to her. Gods were not engines that broke down in the cold. And there it was, neither god nor hero but only her son's gashed, blue-tinged body, heart at a permanent standstill. It had lied to him too, that heart, lied to them all.

The hand covering hers was a cool, firm one. For some reason it had a calming effect so Ilana let her own hand remain there, thinking in that manner to invite the calm through her fingertips to every part of her body. "My son," she began softly, and paused, surprised to hear herself speaking. But it felt better this way, talking, so she continued. "My son told me once that he came from a long line of heroes. Gods, actually, that's what he said." She kept talking, told Dorey about Matt's theory, myth of the deluge, ancient peoples and lost continents. "He believed"—she smiled sadly— "that the survivors were crowned as gods when they finally reached land. And all survivors would have had to be swimmers, of course."

"Well," said Dorey seriously, "maybe he was right."

They sat there in silence, hands touching, for a long time.

"Here's the plan." Sarge leaned over the meticulously drawn schedule spread on his desk. It had dates, times, boxes for each. Boxes within boxes that would give workout results, record predictable progressions, monitor sudden improvements, best efforts on a daily—sometimes hourly—basis. Next to him, Tycho examined it, ticked the figures off quickly in his head and visualized some rough graphs, estimated curves.

"You've got her peaking twice?"

Sarge nodded emphatically. "Early June. That's the first. See what kind of peak we can count on later—she's agreed, we've discussed it."

"You have a race in mind."

"Right! Big Mouth Bay to Laughing River."

"Quebec?"

"Right."

"Cold water."

"They don't make it much colder."

Tycho drifted to the window in that way he had of wandering at will. You'd think he wasn't hearing or seeing you. Actually he was, he'd just focused somewhere else for the time being. Outside it was snowing again, new flakes gently rewhitening the hardened layer already there. "I don't know, maestro. Aside from a test run, what's the point?"

"Victory. No better food, Johnny. Makes you sleep at night, too."

"Granted. That's a tough race, isn't it?"

"Sure. She picked it."

Tycho turned to look at him, shoulders rising momentarily as if to embrace, an affectionate grin twisting his features. "You're a crazy bastard. Maybe you've met your match, captain. She likes these risks, doesn't she?"

"She does!"

Sarge's voice was all pleasure and pride. Made Tycho's grin stay longer. He asked how well, realistically speaking, Sarge thought she'd do. In a field of sixty with, say, forty finishing, Sarge told him, maybe she'd pull in eleventh or twelfth overall with a lot of guts and a lot of luck. First among the women if everything went their way—no matter what, he doubted she'd place lower than third among the women. This guaranteed her at least a piece of whatever pie there was, guaranteed her some kind of mention and a respectable reclamation of status. All of which, he believed, she needed. "Come September," he tipped back with both feet on the desk, "I want her to walk into that water feeling like a champion. Like one of the very best. Has to, Johnny, I don't need to tell you. Has to be that way."

Tycho saw his point. He didn't argue, asked instead how was the running working out.

Sarge shook his head, smiled dryly. "All right. She hates it!" He chuckled. "Sometimes when she thinks I'm not looking— I get a glance at her face on, say, the fourth or fifth mile. Pure distaste, Johnny, purest expression of distaste I've ever seen. Consistent, too. Matter of fact, she's up at the track now."

"Alone?"

"Ilana's there." That proud pleasure had crept into his voice again, this time with a softer tone. When he looked up, Tycho stared because he'd never seen quite that expression on the man's face before. It was as if some covering had been ripped completely away, and what showed beneath was awe-filled vulnerability. Then it was gone. "She's good with a stop-watch."

"Good," Tycho said gently, "I'm glad. I'm glad."

Sarge was saying maybe he'd want to go on out with her one of these mornings. Pace her a few laps around the track, see if he could brighten up the prospect for her. Tycho told him sure, why not.

"Weight training?"

Sarge flexed his arms. "Some."

"You've been swimming hard."

"Right."

Tycho didn't pursue it. He posed with his own arms instead, rolling up the sleeves, smiling. "Get a good look at this, you bastard. You swimmers think you're so solid, try a little single sculls on for size. Soon I'll be too top-heavy for the road."

"Hell, you've been working."

"*Right.*" Tycho grinned.

Hands clasped behind his head, Sarge gave him one of those rare bronzed smiles. "I hear they row a lot of the way across Big Mouth Bay. The escorts. Ever been to Quebec, Johnny?"

"Not even in my dreams."

"Think about it." His legs swung from the desktop as he stood, chin motioning beyond the window. "There's the kid."

Turning, Tycho saw her pause with surprise and give a wave. Face flushed, ski cap snow-topped and sweatsuited shoulders covered with white, at first she seemed to him to have grown taller. Then he realized that was illusory. It was the white out there that visually enlarged everything, including her.

Stepping closer to the window, she removed a glove, pecked her palm with a kiss and planted it flat on the pane directly in front of his face. He pulled back a second, eyebrows raised. Then grinned with delight. He touched fingertips to his lips, touched them to her through the glass in return. Behind him Sarge laughed.

Behind Dorey stood Ilana. Her hair tumbled thickly here and there from her wool cap, stark rich black salted with definite white more permanent than snow. She wore one of those Peruvian capes. Tycho glanced from her face to the knitted form of the thunderbird and back. He hadn't seen her in he didn't know how long and, standing there, she was more striking than he'd remembered, like a willowy-strong tropical plant acclimating to northern weather. Hello dear, he saw her lips form silently through the glass barrier. One gloved hand fluttered greeting to him. The other gripped a stopwatch and, curled around the snapped-shut compasslike case, rested a minute on Dorey's shoulder. The two of them stood a little longer, looking at Tycho and Sarge. Then Ilana held up a finger, saying just a minute. She and Dorey turned, headed out of sight for the doorway.

"Sarge. Guess what day it is."

She was drinking raw eggs in between bites of toast and gulps of the sustagen milkshake. She was patting lips carefully with the napkin after each bite and swallow. Very neat eater, even when consuming enormous amounts. Was it his imagination, or did her voice shake just a little in anticipation? He never could tell with her. Still, he grinned and played along.

"Tell me what day it is."

"December *tenth*."

"No kidding."

"No kidding."

Tycho finished some juice and tea. Oh, he remarked, step-up-in-intensity day, right? Uh-huh, she told him. Right. Following the schedule to the hour, this morning they'd start to mix a lot more maximum intensity work with the long slow distance. That would take them through to the end of February.

Tycho sprawled easily in his chair. "After that?"

"February twenty-fifth. That's when we start the spring work."

"And?"

April twenty-third through May twenty-sixth, she told him, one pool workout a day, and daily lake workouts of four to eight hours each. On the twenty-seventh a hard all-out lake swim for the better part of a day. Then a week lay-off to taper. Up to Quebec on the third of June. Into Big Mouth Bay at six o'clock a.m. on the fourth. Out of Laughing River between three and three thirty p.m. that same day. This was the plan.

"You've got quite a memory," Tycho teased.

"Uh-huh. There's more."

"Like?"

Like a two- to three-day recovery period following Quebec. On June eighth Anne Norton would join them for the duration. They'd spend the rest of June with one pool workout a day and the daily lake workouts, mixed up here and there with shortened outdoor swims and some double sessions of intervals or sprints in the pool.

"July fifth we go to Washington."

"Ocean workouts, I take it."

"Through until the third week in August." There was no specific date on that yet. Depended on how the weather seemed to be shaping up.

"And?" Despite his teasing tone he was excited, felt himself lean forward, thighs tighten anxiously in his seat.

"Then," she grinned, "I get as fat as possible."

"How fat is that?"

"Twenty pounds more. I'll just eat my guts out."

"You're shooting for the first week of September some time."

"Uh-huh." For the same reason there was no specific date on that, either. But what spread across her face now was a lovely, smoothly illuminated glow. All signs of worry, strain, and maturity vanished from her features—the face was a child's face, contemplating some wonderful toy. Tycho watched her and his heart picked up pace a little. He felt Sarge stiffen in the seat next to his, also silent, waiting. "Well," she said softly, "well guess what happens then."

What?

She straightened regally, announced it with quiet pride. "The Dorey Thomas crossing of the San Antonio Strait." She was looking to him, to Sarge. "You can come too, Tycho. On the boat I mean. Well. Well if you want. I invite you to be there."

In Sarge's absence, Tycho had usurped his swiveling leather desk chair. Between them was an unspoken understanding that, of all men on earth, he alone was welcome to do so.

"Knock knock."

Ilana curved into a chair and he looked up smiling.

"How *are* you?"

"I'm well," Tycho said. "Tell me."

"What?"

"I don't know. Anything. Just talk and I'll listen."

She clucked her tongue. "Ah, no fair. There's too much safety in your listening. That way you pretend to be what doesn't exist—an impartial witness. Listen dear, at some point"—her hands twisted on the chair arms and he watched them struggle—"at some point you stop just listening and you become involved." She smiled, there was a kind of sadness in the expression. "Up to your neck."

"That's okay," he said gently. "As long as it's not over."

"Who knows? Sometimes you can't know until it's too late."

He felt chill against his back and wanted to reach across the room, caress her hands between his own to calm them, but didn't dare. His voice soothed instead. "How are you feeling? Sleeping enough? Eating well?" She nodded the questions away. "You know, you look fabulous, Ilana. That's the truth."

She thanked him. Told him the truth of the matter was that she *did* feel better now. She didn't know what to attribute it to. The passing of time, perhaps. Yes, that was it. And Sarge of course. There was Sarge. "He's gotten better looking, I think." She laughed. He thought he saw her blush slightly. "Don't you?"

Now he was blushing. "I don't notice those things."

"Why not?"

"Okay," Tycho nodded. "Yes, he looks well too."

Just above her head was the sun mandala. She reached up to touch its rim lightly. "He's the most remarkable man I know, Tycho."

"He's in love with you."

"You're strange sometimes. Was that a response? Or is there something implied?"

"Just a statement of fact! And as far as meaning goes, well" —he winked—"it means he's got good taste."

She went to the window. Swiveling in Sarge's chair, he turned to her when she balanced on the ledge, body framed darkly against the thick flaking white outside. He was asking her any more bad dreams these days?

"Some. Sometimes. A strange thing happened the other night. It was actually just a feeling I had—and listen, dear, this is in strict confidence. It was awkward—it's awkward to explain."

"Take your time."

"I woke up terrified. Then what I had was an overwhelming feeling that she, that Dorey, was there in the room with us. I even looked around to make sure. It wasn't true of course. Only Sarge and I, and he was sleeping so soundly. He's really wonderful to watch, you know, when he sleeps. There's an extraordinary balance to his breathing and he looks quite beautiful." She stopped, confused. Without the color-blurring background of white, he guessed he'd have seen her blush again. "Anyway, that's when I experienced a strange sort of urge, it just dropped on me from nowhere. I wanted very much to go out into the hall and find her. And I wanted to offer her my breast. I believed so strongly that if I went ahead and did that she'd accept! And then, I thought, *then* every-thing will be all right somehow, if only I could realize this image I had in my mind of holding her very gently against me while she fed. I don't know what she would have fed on now, it wasn't milk, that I know." She looked at him, unblinking. "On a scale of one to ten, Doctor. How perverse is all this?"

Tycho thought a minute. "I guess," he said carefully, "I'd say perversity has nothing to do with it. Neither does a scale of one to ten. It seems—well, that you're reaching out to her somehow." He spoke slowly, calmly. "That you see yourself in a capable and nourishing role where she's concerned—does that make sense?"

Her laugh was almost a giggle, girlish, hinting tears around its fragile edge. The laugh maintained, though, tears never came. "Everything you say makes sense. Tell me why is it I still want to be dead some days? Some days food tastes too awful to eat, it hurts me to touch anything some days, still. Why is that?"

"You're in pain—"

"Bravo, Doctor."

"—And alive. You've survived."

"Why?" she said. "Why have *I?*"

When she stumbled a little he was right there to lift her in both arms. She soaked into his sweatshirt. He felt her body stiffen in some sort of protest, then relax, arms curled over her breasts shuddering with fatigue.

"Not bad," Sarge muttered.

It was evening. End of the day's third workout.

"I can walk, Sarge."

"Glad to hear it. So can I. Bath now, I think. Get some food into you, what do you say."

"Uh-huh."

Standing, her legs quivered and she dripped onto the bathroom mat. She did as she was told and held on to his shoulders while he peeled the suit from her, lifted each arm alternately while he stripped it off, draped it over wall rungs. Rushing into the tub, water steamed. It hissed around the mirror. It clouded the image of them reflected there.

He plucked at the second suit without thinking, one strap, other strap, hauled it down so her breasts poked gently free. He paused, then knelt in front of her, tapped the backs of her legs signaling her to lift each one in turn. She stepped out of it. He rose along her body's length without touching her. Noticed that where her hips had rested on the pool's edge were two small bruises, perfectly parallel. Her abdomen was tight beneath the skin, rolling musculature obvious only on second glance. Hurt plenty now, he knew. From there she sprouted up, paused at the breasts, leveled off and out at the shoulders. Her body was changing subtly now by the week. No, not changing exactly, maybe just becoming more like itself, being chiseled by degrees into its most natural form. They looked at each other.

"Up we go."

Sarge lifted her over the tub edge.

143

Bubbles, she was saying, almost petulantly, you forgot the bubbles. Those goggle indentations under her eyes made her face appear slightly bruised, or swollen. The tone of her voice surprised him. Then he wanted to pick her up again and hold her to him naked in the steam-clouded heat, both of them dripping water.

"Sorry." He handed her the vase-shaped bottle, caught a delicate musky perfume from it. "Here."

"No, it's no good now. You have to pour some in while the water's running. Well. Well okay. Okay."

"How do you feel?"

"Like I just threw up."

He laughed. While he did she gave a pale grin. Then she was looking at him intently, eyes asking. He got serious. He smiled.

"All right," he said, "you know it. You're good."

"I felt it today, here"—she pointed to her abdomen—"I was good."

"You are!"

"I felt it."

She leaned back, exhausted, and he soaped a body sponge to squeeze over her shoulders. He rubbed the lather gently around her neck, down her upper arms.

"I'm going to make you"—he lifted her chin with one hand, soaped smoothly across her chest—"a very strong lady. Much, much stronger than you are now. A thousand times stronger, that's a lot. Better than any man or woman in that water. Lift more than two hundred pounds. You'll be able to run thirty miles and swim a hundred. I promise you. You'll be"—he fished for her wrist and held it, rubbed the sponge along her arm—"the strongest lady on earth."

"Work," she mumbled, eyes half shut. "Just work."

"Tear things down a little, they grow back stronger."

"Ah," she said, "I know. Sarge."

"Yes?"

"You think I'll be?"

"What?"

"That strong. I mean the strongest. I think—"

"What?"

She'd slipped from his grip, hand submerged to point to her belly again, and half closed, her eyes had an uncharacteristically shrewd appearance. "I am. Now. Just needs work." She smiled. "Training."

He supported her head and neck with the flat of his palm. She'd fallen asleep.

Off and on that month when she passed by Sarge's study he'd be arguing over the phone. She'd pause. After a while realized he wasn't arguing—it was simply that he spoke in a harsher tone than usual. Once she stopped long enough to listen. That current, he was saying, got to hit it right the first time, understand? That's crucial, got to hit it right that bastard. Fuck the distance. Hit that bastard right and to hell with the distance.

This sent her to the black looseleaf binder for another stare at the chart she'd already memorized. Her eyes followed the current's uneven curls and sidewindings. There it was, ice-cold rattlesnake streaming every way but the one you wanted to head for. On charts it was clearly marked. In water what marked it was its insistent, contradictory tug. No matter what, you had to fight that pull. Fight it in the opposite direction, sometimes putting in double effort just to keep from losing ground, or from being swept too far south.

Dorey lay on the sofa and shut her eyes. She could feel the swell and whirling undertow tug at her arms, could taste the salt. That clean cold throat-coating, tongue-swelling ocean salt. Then she'd left all that behind and what she felt now was different. She was beginning the last mile—measure it as straight distance and it was mile number thirty-two, consider miles added by necessary deviations from a straight-line course and it was mile number forty, forty-five, maybe even fifty. Well that didn't matter. Like Sarge said, to hell with the distance. What mattered was that this was the last one. This was the final stretch and nothing could or would stop her now because she could feel how close she was getting. She'd done it and was just about reaching the mainland and she was going to touch that mainland with her own hands.

Sometimes what woke her these nights was this feeling of sand in her clenched fingers. She'd swear it was the salt, salt

145

and the sun that had made her so thirsty and nearly crying for water. Then open her fists to see the sand had sifted clean away, only her palm's flesh glowed back in the dark. She hadn't reached there yet. Not yet.

That winter Ilana put some energy into decorating. It began with the cacti. Light for them was better in the easternmost dorm room where Dorey now slept. She couldn't put them on the window ledge without beginning to consider what the window itself ought to be framed with so soon there were long sashlike curtains there that pleased her a great deal. A rug seemed the next most obvious thing. Then there was the matter of getting cots out of the way, establishing one dominant corner for the bed and another for a dresser, another for a tall-backed leather reclining chair brightened by plush cushions. Dorey asked could she exchange those cushions for the ones out near the sofa, the ones from northern Greece. Of course, Ilana agreed, pleased to finally hear some input. For the most part Dorey watched her plannings and touchings-up with a pleasant smile, a ready hand when physical help was required and a carefully controlled kind of impartiality. If it were a cave, Ilana teased her, would you still care so little? Dorey thought seriously about that. In reply she shrugged and smiled. Her one demand was that there be nothing on the walls. She herself tacked a single white sheet of paper near her bed. It was on the wall at waist-height, you had to bend down to see it. WORK HARDER, it said.

"How?" Ilana asked when she saw it.

Dorey just shrugged. Somehow, she said, and Ilana laughed but not mockingly.

"My son Matt used to tack phrases up on his walls." Always when referring to him out loud, she had this habit of prefacing his name with "my son," as if Dorey needed reminding that that's what he'd been to her, or as if confirming the fact to herself. "He hardly ever removed anything, either, once it was up. His walls! They were a clutter. Something would catch his eye and he'd want it filed away or hanging somewhere close to him—he was like that, a collector."

"Like Sarge." Sitting on the floor, Dorey got restless and hooked her feet under the chair base for a few sit-ups.

"Like Sarge," she agreed, "like me." She smiled to stop the tears. "Unlike you, I see."

Ten, eleven. "Uh-huh." Twelve, thirteen, fourteen.

The bastards! Sarge was howling. You could hear him from down the hall. You could almost have heard him from the ice-smoothed edge of the lake.

"Bastards! Let them freeze their own balls off. Drown them in beer suds, those bastards."

He was holding the notice up to light as if that would change the words printed there. He'd thrown the rest of the mail unopened on his desk, thrown his coat across the room so it dripped melting snow in splotches. Sarge yelled another curse, then stalked down the hall saying to hell with them, to hell with them and their lousy race and their lousy beer.

When he stormed in on Ilana she had to pause. His rages were rarely loud ones and, when they were, they forced you not only to notice but to cease activity, as if the world and all its objects had been sucked temporarily into a vacuum created by his gestures. What? she mouthed silently. What?

"The sponsors! Goddamned sponsors!" He crumpled the paper, shook it towards her. "Late May instead of June. Let them get in that water in May, let them try. Bastards."

"They've changed the date?"

The letter was a neck he squeezed to death in his fist. "Know how cold that water is in May? Know what the temperature's like?"

She shook her head.

"Maybe low fifties. Maybe! With luck! Know what that means?"

Ilana had an idea of what it could mean. Gave her pause for thought too. Why? she was asking him, why the change, and he was rattling off bitter reasons. Always the athlete who suffered, he said. Sponsors dictated circumstance by financial whim. Seemed the brewery sponsoring this event had set up an international ad campaign to begin in May. Well they

147

wanted this race to coincide with their campaign's kickoff. Made plenty of sense if you were thinking advertising, but think of the water and then of the swimmers who'd be in it and you came up with a different story. He balled the sheet in his hand and tossed it ceiling-ward.

"What will you do?"

"Tough decision. Either way the risk's increased."

"Well why not let her decide. She knows her capabilities."

Right, he said after a pause. Right. That was what he'd planned on doing. Before leaving the room he crossed over to kiss her, and when he'd gone the door swinging shut carried a draft of cold in after him. Ilana bent to pick the crumpled paper from her rug. She smoothed it flat on the bedside table, read the words neatly typed and someone's official signature stamp underneath.

It was late January and snow had crusted several layers thick. His boots crunched doubly with every step. Sarge remembered winters when there'd been more snow but few colder—each successive snowfall had frozen almost immediately this season, laying down a hard-topped white sheen in preparation for the next. Strong wind blew off the lake. Icicles dropped from the pines with a sound like glass thrown on glass. He bent forward into breeze, his face frozen cold in the pale yellow sunlight.

Thickly wrapped in cap, scarves, gloves, coat, boots, Dorey appeared nearly formless walking along the lake's edge. Once in a while she'd pause, search the snow crust for small rocks and skim them across the white scrim of ice that thickened at shoreline. When he'd left the trees behind, Sarge stopped to watch. For a second she was motionless, eyes following a stone in flight. The only indication of life her breath clouding out consistently, dissipating in air. Breasts and hips hidden, she looked to be of indeterminate sex. Looked small to him, like a preformed adolescent, or a child. He coughed away the block that was suddenly in his throat. When she turned at the sound, he was more composed than he'd been all morning, knew exactly what the right approach would be. He was her trainer, after all, and she'd take her cue from him on a lot of things. If the news they'd received today made him want to burn down breweries, she would never know that.

"Powwow time!" he waved her towards him. "Looks like we're in luck."

They walked back through the pines together, both silent. She looked up at him expectantly. Into his study now for a little talk, he told her. He smiled assurance and his voice was affectionate. Occasionally he let his arm rest, very lightly, across her shoulders.

Settling comfortably into his chair Sarge watched while she eased out of her cap, gloves, coat. She was suddenly female. She'd gained weight in muscle since first arriving but looked slimmer. When she pulled a sweater off over her head her shirt tugged up to reveal the belly and he flashed on how she looked suited up and how she looked naked, all stretched and corded and branched out, like some amphibious tree still growing. Her hair fell thick and loose around her face, down the neck. She turned to sit across the desk from him, grinning.

"Big Mouth Bay," he grinned wryly, "is what you call cold and refreshing around about May."

"June, Sarge. June fourth. Six a.m."

"That's what I thought too. How does May sound to you? That's one, two weeks colder. Cold, damned cold. I'm talking Ontario cold. Lake Superior. Get the picture? Overexposure cold. But it is swimmable."

He told her the news from start to finish, the change, the why of it, the facts. Her face paled momentarily but then regained color, and her eyes focused on his were impassive, simply listening. When he'd finished she leaned back staring at the desk and he felt her struggle, quietly, in evaluation.

"What does that do to the field, Sarge?"

"Hell. I'm saying a lot of damned good swimmers won't be in that field anymore and that leaves just the toughest ones there are. You can bet on Beaujais entering no matter what. Tom MacIntyre. That Australian woman who popped up a few years ago, her name slips my mind. Right? I'd say it leaves maybe forty to enter, maybe thirty. All depends—"

"On the water."

149

"Right," he said. "Right."

He watched as her gaze shifted to the window, the icicle-tipped pines out there and that off-and-on wind sound. Somehow he knew what she was thinking, and with the certain instinctual knowledge came a kind of pride, he gave himself at least partial credit for her train of thought. "Yes," he said softly, "lake's cold in April. With a warm enough spring we can train in it. It's cold. Good practice."

"We'd move up the schedule, Sarge?" She massaged her left shoulder. Sometimes it stayed sore. "I could do it. I feel I could handle it."

"You can," he nodded. "We'd move up the schedule."

She flipped through the unopened mail on the desk, seemed to have forgotten what they were talking about. She plucked out a couple of envelopes addressed to her. It made him wonder all over again at what Tycho termed her isolation. Well it couldn't be denied. She received a fair amount of mail. From friends, she'd say, and shrug. But once in a while he'd catch her grinning over something. Once in a while even a laugh would escape, ring for seconds like a brightly colored cloud over the flapping page of letter she held. Then he'd shoot her a teasing, questioning glance. She'd look up and seem embarrassed. A friend, she'd say, no, uh-uh, an acquaintance really. All of them, they're good acquaintances I guess. Some from back in college. Ones I swam with. This one here—she'd wave the page a little stridently, face incredulous and, Sarge guessed, enjoying that touch of the dramatic—this one here is having a kid. A kid. I don't believe it. Hell, he'd say, still teasing, what don't you believe about it? And she'd smile with a touch of perplexity. Shrug. Oh, came the inevitable response, I don't know.

Most of the time, though, she did not share her reactions with him, and he figured that was because some essential part of her remained untouched by all these letters, these reports from what she'd begun to perceive as foreign territory. Because it was foreign to her now, in fact. They were swimming for time these days. They were surrounded by snow. He guessed nothing else really touched her much just now. And if it had that capacity, she'd removed herself from it

both physically and emotionally. There was a carefully con-
structed, well-designed barrier around her—she would not let
anything in. Once he'd seen her re-reading a long, densely
scripted letter, her face pale and intentionally blank. Bad
news? he'd asked, and she looked up startled saying no, uh-
uh, no, this one's from Carol. My mother. She's fine. Once
in a while she'd send letters in return. Not often. And once in
a while she'd get phone calls, long distance. He'd hear her
laugh sometimes, words muffled by the receiver at her lips,
and the sound always surprised him. Connected briefly with
some other voice from the world out there, other beckonings
from some other life, she seemed to him to be—for those few
moments—out of context. A friend, she'd say later, and shrug
again. It appeared not to touch or concern her. Merely a
pleasant interruption in the straightforward course of things
which, well-handled, was now over so that all might proceed
at the proper pace. Then he'd recognize her again. The chro-
nology of events, anecdotes she'd dropped here and there, the
history she'd given him: northeastern, suburban childhood.
Mother married a couple of times. And there'd been money
from somewhere, too—although she stressed, proudly, how
she'd worked all along, high school, college, off and on again
at shit jobs afterward—there'd been some money from some
relative or maybe from one of the divorces. Had to have been
because the better coaches could be expensive. So she was
trained carefully. Mediocre student, hard worker. Protestant
ethic and all that stuff—she'd really believed it all, though,
taken it quite seriously and with a near-innocent, near-gullible
belief in doing what the coaches said no matter what. He
could see her now: a quiet, ordinary sort of kid who no one
much noticed except when she smiled—then she qualified for
pretty. Or when she swam and the features were blanked away
anyway—then it was the physical strength that might draw
notice. Great form and just plenty of brute goddamned
strength, enough for a surprisingly good 800 freestyle at an
early age. Surprised everyone. She was supposed to be their
100 and 200 whiz kid. Surprised them all! she'd exclaim
proudly, the closest to boasting he would ever see her. Aside
from that just a disciplined adolescence. Talent for the shorter

151

distances that never seemed to go anywhere past a certain point. He guessed some of those coaches had been a little disappointed. Good college. She did decently, nothing spectacular. And then ran into Burns. That bastard. Sarge chuckled. Still—for all the facts he knew of her life—his knowledge of her lacked real depth, some missing pieces barricaded behind that blank expression or that made-to-please smile as effectively as if behind barbed wire. So that her life had reality for him only insofar as he was involved in molding it, training it. Here she was, Dorey Thomas, the swimmer. His swimmer. It was the way they felt each other, the only way. Beyond that he couldn't break through. Once in a while —like watching her now—he'd be hit full-force with the oddness of it, this impossibility of knowing her. It left him feeling unfinished.

She dropped her letters back on the desk unopened. There was a strange look on her face now, the bare beginnings of a smile bordering on triumphant. "Laughing River. I like that, it's a nice name."

Sarge watched intently. Leave it completely up to her— that's what he'd decided—and she sensed that. "It is," he said. "Has a ring to it."

"Nicer than Lac St. Jean. Or Lac Louie." On her face the smile settled firmly. He saw it wasn't triumph but defiance. "Or Michigan or Ontario."

"Right," he grinned, "that's true."

"Or the English Channel or the Bosphorus."

"Or Capri to Naples. North Channel of the Irish Sea. Or the Río goddamned Paraná. Or—"

"Anything," she said quietly, and her cheeks flushed now but not with chill. "Nicer than anything else in May."

Much nicer, he told her.

They were silent for quite a while. As he examined her face gone far away in thought, what passed over it was anger and then a kind of glow. She shrugged, smiled.

"Well. Well it's true then Sarge, we are in luck."

Inside him something crowed.

"Still want to go for it?"

"Uh-huh."

Good, he told her, let's get cracking. Some food then suit up and we'll get a little work done, huh? He was waving her out the door. He was drafting a formal reply to Canada reconfirming her entry, her status. He was marking up the training schedule, dialing the phone and leaving messages for Tycho.

"Think heat. The sun. It's right here beside you."

Facing each other, they were cross-legged on cushions while Sarge's hand spanned the air over her solar plexus.

"Relax. Center it, center it and just feel that heat. Relax. Relax those shoulders."

When she tried her hand went instinctively to the left shoulder. He didn't have to see her shudder to know she was in pain—the face was as blandly inexpressive as ever but looked slightly drawn, eyes a little clouded.

"Easy, easy," he said. "We'll rub it down later. Just relax, think heat. Heat, heat, the sun. That sun right here inside you." Lack of sleep. That was it, he knew. Problem was after the first week or so of a step-up in intensity the damned insomnia came back. Everything else was right as rain. Insufficient rest. If there was a substitute for sleep Sarge was hell-bent on finding it.

Sun, the sun. He repeated it, and then again. Sun. Heat. Heat. Think heat. Ovens. Ovens. The sun inside you. He made a half-whispered kind of chant out of it. After a while she shut her eyes and, watching her face relax, he realized he'd been rocking back and forth in rhythm to his words.

Minutes went by before she opened her eyes. Giving him a pale smile saying she liked that, yes, she liked that. It was almost an afternoon nap. But if that's where the sun was, then where was the moon? Sarge had to think a minute. Waiting, he tossed back at her finally, waiting for a good spring tide.

"No Sarge, uh-uh. You've got it wrong."

"Do I."

"Well sure. It's the other way around. With the tides I mean. The water waits for the moon."

"Right," he smiled. "And the swimmer waits for the water."

•

The phone was for her and it was Anne Norton. Surprised, Dorey answered almost hesitantly. Coming through clearly, Anne's voice was smooth.

"They're saying it's shaping up to be the toughest race of the season. As far as cold water goes, anyway. I thought I'd throw in my two cents' worth—you don't mind, do you?"

"No."

"Good. Ginny Adams—the Australian—they'll create a lot of hoopla around her but don't listen. She does well in rough water, nearly as well as I do. But my last season on the circuit I swam against her *a lot* up in Canada and she always goes out too fast, especially when she's cold." Anne chuckled. "In other words, don't worry—she's not a threat."

Thank you, Dorey said, I won't worry.

Now Santosuelos, Anne told her, he was another story. A good strong steady swimmer, always there at the last mile or so and in Mexico he was legendary for never giving up while conscious—he'd swim until he went under rather than not finish. Ditto Beaujais, a local gent with cold water his particular speciality and Quebec his native province—a tough nut to crack, very, very tough indeed. You had to think about Tom MacIntyre too, strong as a bear and they said he trained in-season in Ontario even when the temperature dipped to the forties. Yes, yes, it was a much smaller field than it would have been in June, only the best and the craziest were in, she'd heard less than thirty starting. Oh, and better not forget Parisi. That bastard. The biggest most muscle-bound lunatic alive and he had a habit of treating the women he swam against like dirt. "If you want to strike a blow in the right place, he's a good man to beat."

"All right," Dorey insisted, "but the water. That's the real factor."

"Of course. But someone has to size up the field while you're busy being a purist."

154   They laughed, talked swimming and ointments and diet, not much. Ear against the receiver, Dorey fixed her gaze on a small clear speck chinking the window's cover of frost. It

made her think ice and then glaciers, brought back the picture of those stalactites and stalagmites, some of them crystal-pure at the tip. Then Anne said good luck, remember strike the right blows in the right places and it won't take them long to wake up, they'll figure out pretty quickly who's back in the water. Thank you, Dorey said, thank you for calling.

"Well. Well look, I'll see you in June."

"Yes!"

Dorey turned and Sarge was there. When she left the room, he and Anne were talking.

"Thank you, Anne. Thanks for this."

"It's not the first time you've ever thanked me, Sarge, and let me tell you it won't be the last."

"I figured that," he said wryly. "How's your life?"

"My aim's disintegrated. And they'll run the Marathon without me this fall."

"Putting in some pool time?"

"Enough. *Bastante*. My shooting tabs claim I don't love them anymore."

Well swimming was one sport, he had to admit, that just didn't mix with others. He told her in the long run she wouldn't regret it, and she retorted she'd never done anything she'd regretted. Hear, hear, he said. He told her he'd given in to daydreams of the hotel in Quebec, night before. Sometimes at night he could feel himself floating through the corridors of the hotel, pounding on her door saying time now, time. Three a.m. champ. Time for breakfast, come on, let's get going. He could see the hotel dining room and kitchen, hastily opened at this off hour while swimmers and their trainers swarmed around burners, around tables, with various quantities of various foods. They'd talked it over and she preferred to sit apart from everyone else insofar as was possible, preferred to arrive as late as possible the day before—just prior to the pre-race meeting where they read the same old rules in several different languages. He thought it was a good idea. If she had status to regain let her gather strength for that task in solitude. Sure, he admitted to Anne, he was excited.

"Breakfast!" she made a disgusted sound. "I always ate

enough to feed a horse and without fail threw it all up an hour later. Never learned. Never!"

Sarge laughed. "How's the rest of your life?"

"Oh that." She paused. "All right." In the background he could hear a dog bark.

"Feel okay?"

There was no more running. There were weight circuits only twice a week now.

"Good. I feel good."

Everything was swimming. The substance of each day dissolved in water. Once in a while she hauled herself from the water to eat. She'd developed this habit of crawling out hands and chest first, legs flapping after. Reminded Sarge of a lizard, or a tadpole with only the front limbs grown in.

"Eat well now. Don't want you to wither away on us."

She did. Chewed everything thoroughly and inside her it became liquid, came out of her body water, out of her skin water. Time to get going now, he was saying, get back there, back in the water. Dorey closed her eyes during a couple of those tapering laps at the workout's end and it was no different than when the eyes were open. Same motion without sight, same stroke. She knew how many strokes to the end flip, knew her time to the second, to the particle of the second. Opened both eyes and just fog and water. No different. It was always there, only thing to be done about that was to swim in it. Closed her eyes for another sporadic night's sleep and what glowed back blindly was shimmering water. Closed her eyes sitting cross-legged on cushions and focused on that area where he kept claiming the sun was. She found a lake there instead. It gleamed dark greenish-gray in the fresh breeze of early spring, surface chilled and rippling. For warmth she made it a hot spring welling from the earth, boiling upward to ease both shoulders to rest. The steam shot up through the atmosphere. It congealed with dust, became clouds. It dribbled back down to earth as water, settled over the sunlight glowing from her solar plexus.

The first week of March it rained harder than Ilana remembered it ever doing. The lake flooded over, spilled up towards the pines. It rained straight down and without wind, made slush of the top layer of snow, then attacked the next layer and ate away so it diminished gradually like ice cubes left in a water-splashed sink.

Boring, that's what it is! Matt had always hated this part of training and let everyone know it. Swimming back and forth, back and forth, he'd complained, hour after hour and day after day, it makes a goddamned idiot out of you. There's nothing, nothing more boring in the world I'll bet.

"Do you get tired of it?"

"Swimming?" Dorey handed her the water jug.

"The monotony of it, I mean. I've always wondered."

"Well it is monotonous. No distractions."

"What do you think about?" Ilana could sense her struggle to reply, wondered why her replies were so often the result of some struggle she couldn't begin to understand.

"I don't know. A lot of things."

"For instance?"

Ilana wanted to turn around but didn't. She watered the cactus instead.

"I don't know, things, just things. I imagine things."

"What," she prodded gently, "what do you imagine."

"Ah. It's hard to explain. It's funny sometimes. I just go different places."

"You're not being very helpful," Ilana teased.

Standing next to her at the window, Ilana thought here they were, just about the same height. If she were by accident to brush against Dorey's shoulder, or leg, the feeling would be that of touching something very hard. This strength was not obvious. Clothes on, it was hidden. Clothes on, she was another woman and that was all. Ilana tried not to think about it, made her uneasy.

She traced delicate circles on the window. Saying look at that, look at that rain.

"The same sound." Dorey looked at her. "It's sort of dull. Isn't it. Same thing over and over. Like me."

157

"My dear—"

"No, Ilana, don't. Please." Her eyes weren't angry at all. There was something else in them that was foreign, Ilana couldn't read it. "Please don't call me dear. Don't call me that anymore."

There was the day nothing could wear her out. Not hours, not sprints, not miles. Chlorinated water spuming from nose and mouth she bobbed savagely out of the pool and, arms raised, shook fists in the air for victory. Right! he yelled, face flushed proudly. Yes!

There was the day she knew spring was about to happen. Warm traces in the air, no more snow. Soon the earth would be softening. That was the first day back in the lake. Dismally, shuddering at first contact, she forced herself deeper and deeper until cold lapped around her neck and she gasped to breathe. Sarge watched from the motorized rubber-sided skiff grinning. So cold it hurt. Couldn't move. Her fingers ached until they were senseless. He heard her moan. Then she lifted her right arm. Stroked. Stroked. Again. That's it lady, he whispered, watching, way to go, that's the kid, that's my baby.

There was the day she took out her old racing suits, realized they wouldn't do. No more. The Dorey Thomas before and the woman now, they were different. Same substance maybe, different texture. No more lightning streaks on suit or cap. Plain solid blue. Solid. Plain. Let the rest speak for itself. Papers in order, tickets purchased, reservations made, Tycho on his way to meet them with his rower's arms hanging large and firmly pumped by his sides. She'd put in ten hours in that lake one day last week, depleted glycogen and then spent the next few days replacing it with a vengeance. She was restless. Energetic. Nothing could tire her now. Nothing would, she told herself. One last bath. One last bath with bubbles, for relaxation. She poured it in. The water invited, cloud-topped, steaming. She stripped and examined her body in the mirror. This was good shape, everything angling up and out and everything necessary, smoothly stored, firmly placed. The pounds she'd spent days gaining she'd lose in hours. That was the point. It was all so systematic. Made sense. Gave her assurance. Yes, sure, this was good shape. Looking, you could tell. Inside herself, she felt it. Flesh and the water.

She opened the cabinet above the sink. Spotted scissors and held them in her right hand carefully. She turned full-face again to the mirror, grabbed a thick lock of hair laid across the back of her neck and firmly, expertly, she cut it off. Then another. Another. She did it evenly, calmly trimmed around the forehead, over the ears. Hair drastically shortened and of a length now to slip easily under tight caps, she smiled at herself, pleased. The face smiling back was the same but framed differently—or rather, less framed altogether, features unbordered and therefore more at liberty. Hi there, she said quietly. Hi there. Well what do you think.

"There you go, kid. Made of snow."
Sarge stepped back to look at her. Grease molded his hands into enormous white mittens and he shook some off, raised a shiny white index finger. Through her goggles she followed the deliberate line it drew in air until it pointed at the center of his belly. He circled it, delineating that core area while he kept his eyes on her face—it was the only part of her left unoiled, so she appeared to be wearing mime makeup in reverse—and he could see by the blank look that she was concentrating. He raised his voice so she'd hear through the caps.
"Here's where it comes from, right? The oven here."
She nodded carefully.
"Think solar plexus! Means sun network. Sun braids, twining out from the center here, this little oven of yours, right?"
She nodded.
"I'm talking heat. *Heat*. Just zoom in on the sun right here and you're fine." He could feel his heart pick up pace a little. 159
"You've got it right here. All yours, understand, no one else's. Keep you good and warm in that water."

Her mouth shut. He saw the oozy white line of her throat move as she swallowed. He hoped to hell she didn't throw up again, there wasn't a whole lot more of her breakfast left.

"Hey!" He jammed his finger straight up towards the sky and she snapped to attention. "Get right into your pace. Stay there and keep it up no matter what and don't change a thing for anybody else, understand. Hit that pace and stay there." He raised both fists over his shoulders. Grease spattered. "Remember. Anyone tries to dunk you, kick their balls off. Knock their tits off. Whatever." She grinned. So did he. "Right!"

"Okay, Sarge," she said. "I'm okay."

Bodies specked the beach getting greased gold or white or black. Some of them just used Vaseline. Whatever gave you the mental boost—realistically speaking, it eventually washed off whatever it was, just a little sooner than the rest of you. Sarge watched her. Feet slightly apart, dripping into the ground. She swung her arms gently and lowered her head. Shut them out effectively, he knew.

Down towards the shoreline's center Parisi gestured at his trainer. Above the tension, the bending and glinting grease of twenty-nine bodies shimmering against the backdrop of bay that morning, his voice rose.

"About ready?" Tycho grabbed his shoulder.

He caught one last full look at her, head lowered, concentrating. "What do her stars say today Johnny?"

"It's a good time for short journeys."

"You're kidding."

"Nope. No such thing as kidding where the heavens are concerned, you know that, maestro. She's fine." He caught Sarge's expression for a disappearing second and saw the flash of vulnerability there, pressed his fingers deeper into Sarge's shoulder. "She's been training with the best I hear."

"Right," Sarge whispered.

Dorey looked slowly up at them. When she smiled it was slight, but calm. She raised a hand, fluttered it, then brought it to her forehead for a gentle salute.

160 Tycho gave her the thumbs-up sign. He winked, and again she smiled. She turned towards Sarge.

What filtered through the grease, caps, goggles, suits to her was that she'd become, for these minutes before starting, the core of his universe. He'd seen her go blank without knowing that what she was really doing was the thing she called house-cleaning. She'd taken a minute or so, swept the insides smooth as fresh-cut plywood. Now he was the one concentrating. He was concentrating on her. Dorey felt herself radiate. For Sarge, she gained stature, and while he watched felt the substance of her own power without having to dig deep for it. This quietly surging sense of strength gave two words to her: of course. *Of course* passed across the blank board in her head. She stood as tall as she was, and relaxed.

Both men pushed off in the escort boat. Its prow tilted farther up while Tycho spun the motor to a low hum and took it out a fair distance, edged her slowly around in a half-circle so they had a full view. All twenty-nine were lining up on the embankment wall.

He removed his glasses, wrapped them carefully in two handkerchiefs and then snapped them into the leather case that swung from his belt. Everything blurred. Water to air. Figures on shore blurred to a long continuous stream of wavering color. In front of him Sarge's features spread to an indeterminate map, badly focused, lines hazy. Enough of that. He enjoyed the way the world appeared without his second pair of eyes, but he considered going too long that way to be an indulgence. Tycho reached into his tote bag for the goggles. Prescription goggles. He wore them when hiking. He'd worn them running alongside Sarge when they'd done that marathon in Iowa for the hell of it. The strap and rims were a moss-green rubber. He strapped them on securely. Now, thick-lensed goggles in place, hand on the motor gear, he looked like an old-time bomber pilot, or an overgrown grasshopper.

Sarge crouched in the dully rocking stern. He was all attention, gazing at the bodies lined there. They were still milling around a little, the count hadn't yet started. Towering above most of them was Parisi. His height and bulk made him swagger—Sarge had always figured, though, that on a smaller man his movements would have been tense, sudden. If he went out too fast today he could be worn down around midway. If he kept pace and used his brain then he'd pose a threat later on. Sarge ticked them off one by one, went down the line. Dorey was twelfth from the left. In the boat Sarge half-stood and then he saluted, held the gesture extravagantly in the air. If she couldn't see, no matter. He'd done it mostly for himself anyway.

"She looks good!" He slapped knuckles against Tycho's back, kept his eyes on shore. "Looks good, huh?"

Tycho watched his friend and then, slowly grinning, he nodded.

He nodded because it was Sarge who looked good. His face was sunburnt, eyes glittering with a vigor that had, for so long before, been missing. Tycho noted the slick, firm motion of his gesturing arm. Everything rippled the word health. Realized how glad he was to be in the man's presence again—it had that old edge of excitement to it, that feel of anticipation. For a second he forgot all the years that had gone. Sure, that was it. The glory of their long, long friendship for him had been that Sarge, at his best, made you forget history. Made you forget everything but the moment at hand, thus rendered it breathless.

"Hah!" It snapped out of Sarge a whisper. Tycho followed his gaze to shore. They were poised, ready to go. Any second now the count would start. Tycho held his breath.

Twelfth from the left, Dorey lowered her head again, swung her arms back a little. Ready to fly. She tensed, relaxed, then did something completely different. She became a still, concentrated beam, a ray of something, waiting to leap towards something else. Air was the bridge spanning the distance between what she'd become and what she'd leap into. Ten. Instantly free of clutter, she was slate-blank, slippery snowlike white on the outside, inside buzzing a consistent high-pitched static. Nine. The body next to her crouched low. She sensed rather than saw it, snapped invisible blinders in place to either side. Seven. Six. Someone at the line's other end had already jumped. Her guts lurched and she froze into place, wait, wait, must wait, be fair now, be fair. Four. Had she missed five. Three, two.

She blasted with the gun, exploded into air and arched

swiftly down, smashed cleanly through water surface with another explosion. This one she didn't hear. She was inside of it. She broke through, went down, curved upward spewing wild bubbles and that first stroke wound up around and down into the water, propelled her ahead and then another and another. The water was clear, too cold to feel at first. You could only gasp. She did. She yanked herself ahead furiously, kept her arms on line with invisible pulleys that each hand caressed in alternate rhythm. Dorey gasped to the side. Stroked stroked stroked stroked stroked gasped to the other side. Feet, arms, churned around her. She sprinted for clear space.

"Right!" Sarge flung arms up, rocked the stern. He choked with everything that swelled his insides out. They were off, and with it he felt a gush of relief before the immediate sharpening of tension.

Watching him, Tycho breathed again. "Right," he said.

Dorey sprinted for open space because then she'd be able to really swim. Needed room for that, lots of it. A body edged up on her right and she pulled away, imagined her arms like windmills alternately propelling. She liked to imagine them making complete circles. The water was cold and still and she was beginning to feel it on her face, against her arms, so cold it seemed to burn and the illusory tingling heat was invigorating. Wake flutter-kicked ahead of her, to the side. Someone rode her heels. She felt a stiff-fingered hand brush the ankles, looking for a hold. Fingers tried to grip. Trying to pull her under and bounce on ahead over her body. She put her feet together. They blended in a tail so they weren't feet anymore but a melded lashing organism at that opposite tip of her. She bent her knees and the tail dipped, snapped up with her hips and smashed into a face. No more grasping fingers.

She passed the body to her side. A woman. Time, she told herself, time to settle down now. Forget the group ahead. Around her near the surface the water was clear. Look straight down and it was opaque, you couldn't see the bottom but along it were mossy strings of colorless plant reaching up, swaying with the dense current. Dorey slid through. Kept her arms like windmills spinning from the shoulder axis. She

163

breathed steadily now with the roll of her body. The windmills weren't windmills but water mills. They pulled her along.

A B C D E she said, A B C D E. Ahead by several yards now several pairs of feet beat quickly just below the surface, six-beat, four-beat, gaining more distance on the rest. She settled for her pace right now. Figured the time she was making and figured she could pick up later when it got necessary. She ran through the alphabet again, got into numbers.

From the waiting boats, they'd looked like a flock of enormous birds taking off with a rush and flurry of wings, grease spewing the water in their wake like feathers left behind. Steadily, swiftly, the flock spread to something like hourglass shape—top-heavy and bottom-heavy. Then the top thinned and it was simply bottom-heavy. The pyramid pointed and at its point was Dorey, ahead of her a cluster who together made a big cherry on top of the cone spreading through water.

Dotting the bay to either side of them, escort boats hovered. One by one they shifted position, headed farther out as the pack moved and spread. To Tycho they were mother birds clucking watchfully after their nestlings, each dip of an oar another chirp of anxiety. Each prow was a beak poking through glistening water, nosing among the passing capped heads to claim the one that belonged to it.

"Let's go." Sarge stepped to the bow, balanced standing there. "After her, that's my baby."

The sun blazed a little higher. Eight o'clock. Sarge glanced back, then ahead, measuring. He'd be surprised if this pattern held all the way through. The group ahead stuck like glue and pulled farther away. Parisi wasn't one of them but that Australian woman whose name he kept forgetting was. He gave them another half hour at that pace, wondered when the few would start their kick away from the pack behind. That would be the first reckoning. They'd see then how well it worked, because his strategy with her had been simple. Let the ones in front erode themselves. Let the ones in back hold out and then put on sudden agonizing sprints. He'd thrown most of his eggs this time around into one basket: her pace. Except for that necessary scrambling sprint at the beginning, she'd just keep the same pace throughout. And if only she'd maintain this pace of hers, he knew she'd have some speed left at the end when things got rough.

The cluster of front-liners—Connery, Vanderhoff, Adams, MacIntyre, Beaujais, and Santosuelos—stayed there, the kickers he knew were in that crowd back there still hung back. Dorey'd hit her pace and, obediently, stringently, she was maintaining it. Occupied a unique place in the field. Grease was gliding from her arms, streaking the water white now with each stroke. Sarge counted. His pulse sped in sympathy. Sure looked good.

At eight thirty Connery and the Australian woman were battling it out with the others far ahead. Vanderhoff had fallen back and Dorey was gaining steadily on him. Another fifteen minutes and Sarge checked behind. Parisi'd started his break-away. The format was changing, shifting back there. A thick-clustered wide sweep of bodies constituting the rear. A group of several pulled away now, Parisi among them. Very slowly, they were gaining.

By nine she'd passed Vanderhoff. Sarge would have liked to stop her for a feeding but waited for a signal from her and there was none. He figured he'd have to trust her judgment this early on—she knew by how she felt now approximately what time it was. Lifting high, arching in that flamboyant, pointed spearing motion that pierced the water cleanly, her arms were bare of grease now and shimmered flesh-tone in the increasing expanse of sunlight. She kept it steady. Steady pace.

Quarter to ten and the water temperature dipped. At five to ten she stopped and tread. Tycho rowed them closer.

"Chocolate?" Sarge shouted.

"Uh-huh!" she was shouting too, louder than him. "Hot!"

Her hands shivered around the cup. She spilled it and the

dark spread momentarily through that clear surface before vanishing. Her head was pounding in rhythm with the stroke she'd just halted, and she heard Sarge yell not to worry, more coming up.

Fog spread on the insides of her goggles. She dimly saw the stick coming towards her, an arrow blunted by the steaming cup which she grabbed with one hand while the other arm kept treading. Must modulate her grip now, tight enough to keep hold but loose enough so she didn't crush it. Mustn't drop it again, she told herself, this heat was important.

"Keep it up!" he leaned over port. "You're damned good, lady."

"What place?" she yelled.

Sarge lifted six fingers. He shouted out the number. Shouted not to worry, shouted keep it up, shouted listen for the whistle. Lips nipped the cup's rim and fluid curled into her mouth, sweet dark heat. She got it all down in two long gulps. Signaled towards the boat with a wave how good she felt, and Sarge gestured back, shouted something she couldn't quite make out except to know that it was encouragement. She continued. The water slapped cold around her and met with the fluid streaking an internal stream of warmth from her mouth to her stomach. With each stroke she got a little more lukewarm, then cooled with rapid certainty until everything was numb.

By ten thirty Parisi'd moved up to within a few hundred yards and was closing the gap slowly, slowly. At eleven Sarge saw him stop for a feeding and whistled her in, too. Bay's temperature had dropped again. The sun was riding high burning his shoulders and he shouted to her how did she feel.

"Huh?" she yelled back.

Just after eleven Connery was pulled from the water.

166   "How are we doing?" Tycho sounded cheerful. Sarge could almost hear him whistle as he rowed steadily, easily, working up a cool film of sweat in the afternoon heat. "Captain?"

"Good. Watch for that Parisi though, I don't like it."

Tycho leaned into it, leaned back with it. "Mars is doing her a lot of favors right now, you know. And there's Venus sitting smack on top of her Moon. Everything's in working order."

Someone else was being lifted from the water ahead. Sarge caught sight of a towel being wrapped, flashing white in the sun like a truce flag. Another sorry flag was unfolded, the body lifted again from the bottom of the boat and cloaked. That Australian.

Sarge rummaged in the tarp for his slate. Checked his pocket for chalk. 2 MILES, he scrawled. Whistled. Whistled twice. Three four five times. Got to fifteen before she stopped, shoulders and head bobbing out uncertainly. Leaning over port so his entire naked torso swung out, he held up the slate. Behind them Parisi'd begun his sprint and was gaining rapidly.

"Now," Sarge muttered, and Tycho held oars steady in the water. "Now the fun starts, right?"

How do you feel? he was yelling to her. She was shaking her head, deaf. How do you feel? he shouted until his voice went hoarse. Finally she pointed to her head.

"Hurts," she blurted.

On the stick he passed her some sustagen mixed with aspirin. She got half of it down and Parisi swam by them. "Hold it," Sarge hissed. Tycho listened. "Hold it, I know that swimmer, he won't keep it up." Again he held the board high. He shook another fist in the air, and what spattered from his hands this time wasn't grease but the bay's dampness and the dampness of his own flesh.

"Go!" he howled. "Go! Right!"

Dorey's head dipped, arms curved into action. The oars did too.

A buoy marked the beginning of the last miles. She'd picked up pace. So had the current. It warned of a river mouth two miles away, riled the surface to small waves, darkened the surface clarity to a texture that was no longer crystalline. They'd been going for good time all morning, gloriously undisturbed by the slightest ruffle or rift. Except for the temperature, it might as well be a pool. Now the water made them pay for that pleasure. As always. The group ahead had held a pace of two miles plus per hour. Currents built slowly against them from here on in. Towards the end they'd be slowed, and that water would be going against them at a rate equal to their best time. Pretty soon. Pretty soon now, Tycho would haul in the oars and cross them on the boat's floor like weary bedmates. He'd hit the motor.

"Now," Sarge counted her strokes. His own arms ached.

"Now baby, now. For the good part."

Eyes shooting from him to her to him again, Tycho grinned. He grinned at the unmistakable glee in the man's voice.

There was the voice that said if she did not get out now she would die. There was the voice that said if she gave up now she would die. Her strokes walked the tightrope between voices and, for lack of any other option, Dorey kept going.

Below the waist she was numb. Above the waist torn to shreds. Saw an illustration in *Gray's Anatomy* of the pectoralis and latisimus. Her mind wrenched each muscle group from the page, dipped the throbbing membranes in buckets of ice and watched blood drip slowly, each pulse beat a sort of sob.

Sun blasted the bay with the fresh light of Canadian spring. Later she'd see how it had burned her shoulders and back. Waves popped against her stomach, slapped back at her reaching hands.

There were two voices, two sections of her body. And she had two pairs of eyes. One was the set of goggles strapped securely around her head, the fogged pair that could no longer see much and no longer cared. The other was the set of eyes that left goggles behind, left the discomfort, this unfortunate circumstance in which her body found itself. These eyes focused in on the sun, gazed on flashing yellow light, blinked in the heat. Reaching. Saw silver twinkle from her fingertips in the darkening rough pull of the water. Reaching. Closed and opened again and saw things ahead in the water that no goggles could have seen. Saw twirling blue and green and golden kaleidoscope segments glitter before them, went deeper into the puzzle of colors towards its center, the core which at first was orange and then pink and then a blushing, shimmering scarlet before it became a black hole of nothing from which yellow burst like sunlight. Reaching. Again she blinked in the heat. Breathed and water came in. Breathed and this time air. P Q R S T. Nine thousand nine thousand one nine thousand two nine thousand three nine thousand four breath. Saw fish the color of rainbows and thought that was pretty strange. Fish the color of rainbows didn't breed in Quebec, did they? Uh-uh. She blinked and the heat gave shape to a human figure. It was Ilana. Ilana called her and she reached for the image. Then it changed to Sarge. I'm trying, she told him, I'm going as fast as I can.

"Hah!" Sarge howled glee. The water roughened. It slapped back at them and she kept going, groaned to the side with her body's roll and picked up pace even more. She was gaining on Parisi with the water swirling and breaking roughly now, smashing against them, and they were both gaining on the diminishing cluster of swimmers ahead. Second to last mile. The current made miniature foam-tipped pockets of whirlpool action all around. Tycho revved up the motor.

Long before the trappers arrived, tribes in the area had called it Laughing River. The joke was squarely on the head of any swimmer who became enmeshed in its currents. Translated from Quebecois, its name was the Big Mouth. This made even more sense when you saw the banks containing it as it flooded into the bay. They were lined jaggedly with rocks, so the big mouth was blessed with two fine rows of teeth, sharp fangs that meant business.

Caught in the first suck and swell of the river mouth were MacIntyre, Beaujais, Santosuelos, Parisi, and Thomas. One would make headway only to be slammed back doubly for every forward stroke, sucked under momentarily, come up gagging and strike out again. It was the beginning of the last mile, which was a mile upriver, against the currents. It was a twisting spider's web of water that tumbled rather than flowed.

Beaujais, local boy and the favorite, lunged. That was the

169

only way to describe it—he lunged over some vortex and broke ahead. MacIntyre went under, came up yards behind where he'd been.

Santosuelos' crew went in after him. Sarge watched towels wrapped again, swirling bright red and green in the afternoon sun, wrapped around and around, the boat's motor coughing with greater force as it headed for waiting ambulances on shore.

Ambulances waited among the crowd lining both banks. This last mile upriver was a real gut-buster. It made Sarge perspire and he felt himself swell near explosion with a massive diversity of prideful sensations and undefined desires. Made him want to try it again himself. His throat choked watching her take a swing at the current, boxing waves, slugging back at the battering ram of tide.

Beaujais had it. Just as he'd expected. Only for all his talk and all his image-boosting, Sarge had to admit that on a gut-level he'd never expected her to do so well. Looked like she'd place third now. He'd thought maybe sixth, seventh, eleventh, maybe first among the women if she were lucky, maybe second. He'd expected her to place and grab some of the money but not so near top prize. She'd surprised him too. And now that she'd surprised him the way she had, done so well up to this point, he wanted her to sprout water wings and soar past Parisi, show herself off to everyone there and teach them all a lesson in case they'd never learned it before. His breath flew away for a second. Like most new believers, he wanted the world to join him in this newfound revelatory ecstasy.

"Go!" he shouted at the top of both lungs. "That's my baby! Now! Watch now, go for it, go for it, all right Johnny. All right Johnny, now for the real stuff, watch her now, watch and let's go for it. Hah! Go for it lady!"

She made her plunge during a relative lull in the flow. So did Parisi. Now he was putting on another sprint and, leaning over the prow so spray soaked his face, Sarge knew it was the last he'd be able to manage. Thing was to match him now if she could. Match him and keep him from struggling too far to a lead, that way wear him down first.

It pounded against her. Crushing in, slamming angrily, op-
posed to the rhythm of her heart. A long, thick body sprinted
now beside her. Dorey felt herself flood with one final burst
of hatred. Last sensation she was capable of. Why, she
sobbed, why. You bastard. Some voice laid a bet that she'd
never do it. The hell I won't, she said. Because she had to,
there wasn't any choice, if there'd been one she'd have taken
it. So she threw in the extra that wasn't really there, poured
herself ahead by reaching. Nine thousand nine hundred and
ninety seven. X Y Z A B. Breath. She spit out water and
wanted to puke. She sobbed to the left. Five strokes and again
to the right. Kept it up, went numb except for the infinite, increasingly loud boom-thump-thump that began in her chest,
rang in both ears, pulsed along her neck and the feelingless
subskin of each wrist. Reaching. Ten thousand twenty-one.
Threw in the extra and felt herself go dry but held on to that
final deadly pace anyway, felt it dragging her forward against
the river's bloodstream, and in this way she passed him.

Silver-gray sprayed in zigzag lines from her fingertips, each
hand a drill blasting through the barrier of gray. Muted sparks
flew back towards her face. It was a tunnel now and she had
no light or warmth. Hard to move. Your arteries froze if it got
cold enough. Each hand a pointing, spearing icicle tip poking
with impossible slowness through the oncoming walls of
water. The tunnel filled in behind so there was no going back.
It closed in on each side, from the top, from the even darker
bottom. Sparks snapped at her lips with each stroke. Ten
thousand one hundred and ninety-nine. B C D. Or was it R S
T. Was it eleven thousand now. Felt like night. It occurred to
her then that there was one way out of this mess and only one
way, and that was just to keep going. This barrier was also a
bridge. It was the only way. She took it. Set her arms and
hands to walking its planks.

The nasal, guttural murmurings and shouts of the crowd
lining both banks rose in volume. At the dock's roped-in area
Ilana waited, felt caught in a continually shifting tornado of
sound.

Here, this was an event of prime interest, one that gave annual birth to heroes. It was preferable that the hero speak a native tongue.

Beaujais fit the bill and had already been swathed like a mummy, eased with great ceremony to a stretcher and then was gone in a crescendo of swirling ambulance lights. Ilana pretended herself in the center of this noisy, liquor-spilling, sun-damp day. Like the core of a hurricane, she herself maintained silent calm.

She'd caught sight of Beaujais' face before the ambulance doors swung shut. He was a fairly young man, she knew, mid-thirties. What impressed her most was the aging effect of the swim—lines crawled across his forehead, spread from eye corners across his cheeks to connect with his mouth's shivering edges. The effect was a graying one. She recognized it immediately, telltale tint and markings of someone who had lasted through something. She sat on the stack of blankets, the stack of towels, crossed her legs, tapped her fingers to some nebulous tune she was remembering. Ilana wondered how long it would be now. She waited for Tom MacIntyre, waited for Parisi.

She almost daydreamed. When she heard the guttural humming roar pitch higher than before, bodies twist and spring with tension around her, she caught their rhythm in spite of herself and stood too, began to move forward along the dock as if sleepwalking and her cool fluidity increased in speed as she understood what was happening. It was like that still, unbreathing timeless space before springing from a cliff, that moment when she began to see.

Thick-fingered, burly hands latched firmly around her upper arms. Dorey couldn't feel them but knew she was being lifted. Up. Out. Hands slid struggling for a grip. Careful to swing her clear of the dock's edge. She'd thought of something just then, something important and she wanted to tell Ilana. Quick or she'd forget it. When her goggles came off the sun made her wince. Felt like she was lying there flat on her back on the light-sprayed, heat-soaked wood of the dock, but she

knew she was still standing. How could that be. Where was
Ilana. Hurry or she'd forget. The thing she'd thought of just
now with the last fly of sparks from that drill her left hand
made. Cap came off. One cap two cap three cap four. Inside
a laugh started. What was her time? Where was Ilana, now,
now, quick where was she. No good. Now she'd forgotten.
Dorey was on her back and she wanted to cry.

Did it, she said. Then she felt that glow.

The stretcher's sides curved around her. Fog over both
eyes. Looking down, Ilana noticed that beneath each eye was
a pale half-circle of swelling and beneath each swollen mound
a deep red indented curve, like a gash. The sun blinded.
Dorey shut her eyes, opened her mouth making sounds Ilana
couldn't understand. On the street of some city, Chicago
maybe, Ilana'd seen a mother shopping with her deaf son one
afternoon. They'd been speaking in signs. She'd picked up on
the sign for home. Home, she found herself saying now, don't
worry, we're going home soon. Found her hands making the
sign for home, fingers meeting to form a steeple.

Tycho swung over the starboard side and sloshed to shore,
didn't mind that water poured into his boots soaking socks and
chilling toes. He made it up the rocks and slipped onto the
dock sideways. Pulled off his goggles and replaced them with
the glasses he unsnapped from his belt. Grinning. Winking.
Draped an arm around Ilana and bent over the stretcher too.
"You'll be fine gorgeous, off we go. Touch of exposure." On
the way to the ambulance he was chuckling, saying thanks to
Venus, thanks to Mars, *merci* to the sun, *muchas gracias a la
luna*.

Sarge was a top-heavy rooster. Spray streaming down his
face, his chest, he balanced on both feet in the boat and
crowed.

"Well," said Dorey, "they pay money too."

Sarge laughed. He dropped the check on a fold of sheet
covering her lap. "You've got it. Beer money and a good time 173
thrown in, what more do you want?" All that fun for the prize
offered by this brewery. Sponsor spilling some bucks into a

few laps like malt beer dribbling from a keg tap, advertising a product none of the competitors used.

She didn't bother to look. Leaning her head back on the white-cased pillows, she shuddered a little. Painkillers couldn't kill all the spasms, they'd have to wear themselves out overnight. Her eyes stayed open, though, weary, a little dazed, glowing tip of pride edging through the artificial tranquility. "What time is it?"

"Nine at night."

"Can I leave tomorrow?"

"Morning."

"Good," she said. "Sarge, do I sound doped?"

"Punchy," he grinned. "You sound like you feel."

"Guess how I feel."

"I know how you feel."

"Like the best."

"Hell," he said, "maybe you are."

"Maybe."

Her eyes closed. He relaxed, thought maybe she'd sleep now but even with muscle relaxants he wasn't sure, her resistance to sleep was amazing. Tycho'd wrapped him in the old bear hug before leaving. Saying she'll be fine, come down for a checkup next week sometime. Saying I love you you old bastard and I think you're out of your goddamned mind, you and her both, couldn't pay me enough to do what she just did, and Sarge told him Johnny you're a fine one to talk. They'd both laughed. Then Tycho was off to grab dinner and a plane. Had to be in O.R. by the week's end. Coronary by-pass, he'd mentioned cheerily, an interesting case for sure. Sarge watched him whistle down the hospital corridor, stallion legs loping, boots still slightly damp.

She'd passed out in the ambulance and woken and passed out again in the hospital, come to, slept the rest of the day away and when they'd taken those warm wraps off her and given her some liquid she'd puked, then slept again, then woken and this time she'd been able to keep some baby food down. Her hands spread motionless on the sheet. He reached for the nearest one and covered it, flat of his own palm barely touching. After a while she wrapped all her fingers around his

thumb, like a baby experimenting with the sensation of gripping.

"Sleepy?"

She shook her head, opened her eyes.

"Want to see Ilana?"

"Ah. Yes, sure."

Her fingers eased from his. He stood and in the stark bedside light making shadows on white curtains she looked pale,
exhausted, funny glow battling through the haze covering her
face. "Hey Sarge. Thanks a lot. Thank you."

He leaned over. Like his palm, his lips on her forehead
barely brushed the skin. "Sleep champ, get some rest." He
was pretty worn himself. "I'll find Ilana. Tell her you need a
good bedtime story." She smiled.

She kept passing through a syrupy-textured cloud. Close
the eyes and she floated, opened them and felt her sunburnt
back. She turned her head slightly and it hurt. There was
Ilana, right at the side of the bed.

"Hi there."

"Rumor has it you want a bedtime story."

"Uh-huh." She chuckled and then something tightened
around her right shoulder. She twisted with the spasm. Before
it happened again she heard Ilana say she didn't have to do
anything but sleep now, just rest.

Dorey held her breath. When it stopped she broke the
freeze with a thin smile. "Let me tell you one. Want to know
what put Humpty Dumpty together again?" They laughed a
little.

"Why not? If you'd like."

"Well. Well sure. It's funny, you know. Back there today I
thought of something I had to tell you. It was like I remembered something I'd really known all along but thought I'd
forgotten, it was just suddenly so clear to me."

"And?"

"I forgot it."

She'd always figured forgetting was intentional. Why not
remember. Well she knew why not, it was because some

things were sort of a secret. You kept them even from yourself. Once you let a secret out it wasn't yours anymore, you'd
given up its power. Safer to forget. She tried to place where
she'd hidden it and pinpointed smack in the middle of her
chest under the glacier, embedded in sheets of ice. No wonder
it hurt to breathe just now. Maybe it would stay inside, now
as before. Try to find it, root it out. Talking seemed the ticket,
she didn't know why.

"I went back to live with Carol for a while."

Ilana leaned over to hear, responded by instinct. "After Seal
Beach?"

"Uh-huh. I didn't do much. Not for months! I'd take these
long, long walks. It was the first time in a long while I'd been
there. I mean, I stopped living with her pretty much when I
went away to school. Then Burns had me spend the summer
training so I didn't see her much, just once in a while to visit.
But I always thought about her a lot. I don't know. Worried I
guess. See. She was beautiful, really, she is—sort of fragile—
I think I always wanted to protect her. By then she was all
alone. And when I went back I guess she was glad in a way,
but Carol worried a lot, I know, she—well, I don't want to talk
about her and I won't." She stopped. She'd been going too
fast. Too fast and it made things spin. When she spoke again
it was slowly, her voice a careful monotone. "Anyway one day,
I remember, it was middle or late afternoon and I just felt like
going down to this gym in town and working out a little. I got
there and the place was pretty deserted, in the entire weight
room there was only me and this man. Well I watched him
doing leg presses for a while. His legs—they were beautiful.
They were long, very muscular and well-shaped and really
strong. I asked what was his sport and he said he used to be a
dancer, a ballet dancer. I could see when he got up and
walked around how well he moved and how graceful he was.
You know the way dancers move. Also he tossed his head
back as if his hair were long, like this"—she tilted her chin,
closed her eyes and gave a slight, pained backward flip, lips
shaping momentarily to kiss the air—"and his hands were
delicate. He used them like a girl. He was, well, I knew, I
could tell he was homosexual." She blushed. Her eyes rolled

shut and when she opened them Ilana was still there, listening. "Anyway he said, and what do you do, somehow you seem out of your element. I asked what he meant. He told me he wasn't quite sure and I said well I used to be a swimmer but I'm not anymore and he smiled then—he had a good smile, one of those ah-hah! kinds of smiles—and said so I was right, you aren't in your element after all, spending so much time on land now must seem abnormal to you. I told him that if I'd trained all those years for ballet instead the land would be my element, wouldn't it, and I'd be walking on land as well and as naturally as he did. He laughed then and asked how did I know he felt natural? After a while I decided to start working, so I did a few sets of lats." She moved her hands trying to reach above her head to grab the invisible bar, bring it down behind her neck, but they flopped back to the sheet. "When I got into the heavier weights he held me down by my shoulders. 'Your arms,' he said, 'are extraordinarily strong, like my legs. For what you do, your arms *are* your legs.' I asked him how did he know it wasn't the other way around? How did he know that his legs weren't just taking the place of arms. Well it was about the first good laugh I'd had in I don't know how long. Maybe ever." She wanted to fold her arms, tuck her hands away. They wouldn't move just now. "The two of us sat around there on the benches. 'No one should be out of their element for long,' he said, 'it warps the soul, don't you think?' I told him I guessed so. The way he saw it everyone moves with grace if they're in their proper element, and it doesn't matter so much what parts of the body you use as long as it suits the element you're in because it's all movement, just moving the most beautiful and efficient way possible to achieve a goal. So that he did his dancing on land, and I was a water dancer, and all the differences between us would naturally derive from the variance of the elements we moved in. But that the basic skills—I mean like endurance, and flexibility, and strength and style—would always be the same." Dorey's hands tightened, spasmed. She could feel the fingers lose sense of touch for one imagined moment, and panic growled just below the glacier but she stepped on it, drowned it out with plenty of ice.

Ilana reached tentatively to touch the rigid upper arm. There was no loosening, no response, and she placed her hand in neutral space between them on the bed. Watching Dorey's immobile profile, she saw that even dazed the clear-cut features—usually so quick to assume pleasingly attentive, bland expressions—were carved tonight from a very hard substance. The bedside light's intensity blanched her skin to a shade more pale than white. Ilana was reminded of a town in northern Japan where the winter festival was celebrated by an outdoor display of larger-than-life ice carvings. She'd seen photographs of the sculptures, one a dragon at whose base stood a young boy. In the photo his tiny breath seemed crystallized, and when she'd put the picture down Ilana imagined actually touching the dragon with bare hands, so for a second her fingertips felt burned by ice.

"I went swimming that evening." Dorey breathed, broke the stillness. "I was pretty out of shape. It was just me, too, no more giant."

"What?"

Dorey's eyes closed again. When they opened Ilana caught a glimpse of something approaching slyness in them, but then it was gone. "Uh-uh. I did all right. Swimming. It felt—I don't know. I don't know." She tried to shrug, winced. "Well that's that. Fair warning."

Ilana stayed quiet a moment. Then smiled and the smile was a question. She met Dorey's eyes firmly, held the gaze before they shut for good. She lowered the bed, made sure her head rested straight and flat on the pillows. Reached for a hand and held it gently in both of hers, pressing each finger in turn before laying it on the sheet again. She stood and smoothed her forehead. She shut the light and went to join Sarge.

By morning Dorey was sore but walking. They got an early plane out. Home by late afternoon.

III

THE CELEBRATION

T HEY CELEBRATED that night. Sarge dug out a bottle
of good Margeaux he'd stashed years ago. Spartan though
most of his life had been, when he opened the doors to luxury
he wanted it bathing his tongue with a taste worth remembering. The three of them grinned quietly at each other, all weary
and rolling in a cool haze of victory. He opened the windows
and made Dorey put on a sweatshirt. "Stay warm for a while,"
he ordered, emphatic and pleased as hell, "I want you warm
and dry, understand?" He uncorked the wine to let it breathe.
He fixed her some mineral water, squeezed in fresh lemon,
fresh orange slices. Booze was off limits for her and she was
obedient to a tee. Ilana poured the wine.

Sarge kept toasting. First his wife, then Dorey, then Ilana
again. Then himself, saying the hell with it, they hadn't expected that he'd leave himself out for long, had they? Both
women laughed with him, their voices echoing into the
chorus of crickets. Dorey heard breeze rippling over the lake
surface, through pines, tapping in rhythm like dancers' feet.
Sarge kept drinking. It got on to evening. It got on to night
and past her bedtime.

"To your health." He tipped the glass to Ilana. It was a
brandy snifter, real hand-blown glass tinged crimson, and the
wine reflecting even darker off its sides outlined his fingers
with red. They twined hands across the table. Dorey was on
her second goblet of mineral water. She saw that Ilana hadn't
touched her glass yet, but the bottle was nearly empty between a crumbling wedge of cheddar and bowl of black grapes.
"To your *pleasure*," he grinned at Ilana. She blushed quickly,
and through the pleasant cloudiness of everything Sarge noticed her eyes shoot towards Dorey as if in apology. Maybe
she thought they'd left her out. Maybe they had.

Dorey padded barefoot across the floor, switched off the
overhead so only the lamp stayed on. The light was dim, made
the wine in Sarge's snifter appear black, made one half of each

face shadow. Dorey saw Ilana's look change slowly from that worried apology to a smooth, half-glowing close-lipped smile. She got nervous and glanced at Sarge, then back to Ilana. She couldn't quite place what the smile was meant for. It was so slight. Like the silent sharing of an intimate secret, or some sort of invitation. She stood near the wall switch facing them, felt the fan of muscles along both sides of her spine twitch and flutter with discomfort. As they stared Ilana's smile diminished bit by bit, and unexpectedly Dorey felt in her chest a soft, insistent ringing like the vibrations of miniature tolling bells. Then something passed between them, a dull thud of recognition.

Sarge shifted in his chair, following Ilana's gaze as if it were a pointing finger. He chugged the rest of his glass like a beer-guzzling lumberjack, lifted it to Dorey. "You've got the guts for it, lady." When he set it down the snifter wobbled, tipped over without breaking and rolled to a stop against the cheese plate. He reached over to turn Ilana's face back towards him. They kissed. A long one. Dorey could hear their tongues. When they stopped Ilana ran a finger down his nose to settle on his lips, gently, and turned away from him to Dorey again. Her eyes were large, no whites to them at all, and the lines of her face totally smoothed by the half-light. Her lips opened about to say something but then stayed that way. Dorey felt her own lips open too and her head nod a couple of times, just barely.

Sarge was standing now. His bare soles slapped the floor. A gush of spring air blew in through the window screen, humming with crickets, hinting a hot summer. He rocked forward on his feet, and if it wasn't a straight line it got him to her steadily, inevitably, until he was rocking from foot to foot in front of her. Her shoulders quivered. Looking down his eyes were dark, softly lit. She tried to see past him to Ilana. With a thumb he tilted her chin up.

Sarge pressed forward so she was wedged between him and the wall. She twisted left, then right, repeatedly, without a sound. Watching, Ilana remembered a prize terrier her family'd kept when she was a child, barred from the house's upper level by a folding wooden partition they locked across the stair base every night. She'd woken up early one morning to find the first floor flooded and the dog shivering halfway up the stairs, tongue dripping blood. He'd gnawed through the wood. He'd never even whimpered.

Dorey tried to slip down but Sarge had her pinned. She could smell sweat beading on his chest. When he half-fell, half-slid to his knees, arms around her waist, he still had her against the wall but she stopped twisting then and her breathing began to calm. She touched his forehead lightly. She hesitated, then ran a hand across and it came away wet. She combed fingers through his hair. His shoulders were like two ledges angling out below her, and from the ledges' meeting point his head moved forward, palms slid to rest on either hip and he pressed his face against her, she could feel his lips through the worn denim.

"No," she whispered, "no. Uh-uh."

The ledges caved in and he crumbled sideways against the floor. Dorey crouched just in time to catch the back of his neck and ease his head down slowly. Then she rocked against the wall herself, wrapped arms around her knees and tilted her head back too, tired, more tired than she'd thought, shut both eyes.

"Dorey." Ilana's palm rested a second on her cheek.

She moved her face sideways against the damp softness. When her eyes opened, Ilana was crouching on the other side of Sarge, half smiling again.

They hauled him to the sofa. No easy trick. Sarge was a bundle you wouldn't want to bench press. Dorey gave the final heave, her elbows hooked under his armpits. She made sure he had a head cushion and balanced on the sofa's arm to watch Ilana ease his legs out straight, smooth a hand along the wrinkled shirt, fingers circling over his belly which rose and sank with each long breath.

"Thank you. Are you all right?"

Dorey nodded and something shivered up her spine. She watched Ilana watching her. Ilana sat on the sofa's edge while Sarge slept in steady enormous breaths that were like rhythmic winds sounding, unwakable.

"You don't really like him touching you?"

Her face was dull gold, ageless, framed with dark. Dorey shook her head. The shivering wanted to shoot out in words, wanted to shoot out somehow. She said nothing.

"Do you like being touched by anyone? Anyone at all?"

Dorey closed her eyes to see a wave. It was about to break over her, and her eyes would detach to hover in air just above the critical point and watch the rest of her shatter to foam. She opened them but Ilana hadn't gone away. She heard herself whisper that she didn't know. That she'd never tried it enough to find out. Then she thought she heard Ilana asking did she want to find out.

The wave splintered, bubbles spun across her eyes and bounced from her lips, seaweed gagged her throat. When she came up for air she breathed it from the center of the palm Ilana offered, her mouth opening against it. Ilana traced knuckles across her lips.

"Do you want to find out?"

On the sofa Sarge muttered in his sleep.

Ilana crossed over to shut the window and, from the hallway, looked back. She whispered to stay warm, it would get colder before morning.

When she'd gone Dorey watched him sleep. His shoulders and chest seemed to weigh him down, so his head propped on pillows looked out of place, at odds with the bulk of his body. His breaths were nearly perfect rhythm. She realized she was keeping time. One and two and three and four. Five and six. She rocked back and forth on the couch's arm. Nine and ten. Then she froze. She touched her eyelids and they were wet, touched her cheeks and then her tongue and it was saltwater. Seventeen eighteen nineteen twenty. She left the lamp on.

Twenty-six twenty-seven. Ilana'd kept her door open a crack, enough to see that a bedside light still shone in there. Thirty-three thirty-four thirty-five thirty-six. She felt her shoulders shove forward, reach for the right stroke, reach with the left stroke. Forty-one forty-two. The wave had started small, built size and momentum so she felt the vast suck of its undertow lashing around both wrists like lassos. Now it was back, foaming with that blue-white light seeping under the door. Fifty-nine sixty sixty-one sixty-two. Sounds came from somewhere below her throat, tiny gasps, gurgles fighting to breathe. Sixty-seven sixty-eight. Dorey felt her eyes fog. The door opened silently when she pushed it.

"Hi there." It sounded ridiculous as a whisper so she laughed, and the laugh got her across the floor to sit on the bedside. Ilana wore an old stretched shirt of Sarge's that came halfway down her thighs. She sat there, too, crossed her legs, and Dorey glanced away.

"You looked wonderful yesterday." Ilana's hand touched her shoulder lightly, tentatively, then jumped off. "You should be proud."

There was something Dorey'd wanted to tell her. Or maybe shout sounds that would be meaningless, but since Seal Beach she hadn't talked much to anyone and even now she didn't really know how to begin. So she stayed still, bent over elbows on knees. Looked at her feet, toes more pigeon than duck, curving in slightly. Her temples pounded.

"You must be tired, Dorey. If you want to sleep now that's fine, please tell me."

"I've got a headache."

Ilana laughed softly. For a second Dorey thought of girls in the locker room drawing hearts on steamed mirrors. When she laughed again there was a crack in the weightless trilling of the sound and Dorey looked at her then, saw the lips not quite in control and eyes too bright to be dry. "Dorey, I'm sorry. What's happening here?"

Pain nagged. "I think," she said, "that you know."

Ilana considered it a moment so the gentle laugh stopped, and in a blind way she didn't understand Dorey felt sure of something and wouldn't break the gaze between them. It was Ilana who moved first, though, reaching to rest both hands along her cheeks. When the sheets ruffled with a crisp white sound Dorey thought of rain. "Fair enough," Ilana whispered. "I've always wanted to ask. What happened? At Seal Beach?"

"Well I cracked up."

"Was that it?"

Dorey shrugged. "Sure. Sure it was." She took each of Ilana's hands in hers. Their hands were well-matched, practically equal in size. She held them away from her face, down against her outer thigh. They were warm and moist in the cold dryness of her own. Maybe if Ilana's fingers melted into hers their warmth would seep through, travel slowly to the center of her chest where the glacier sat. It was frosty and stiff there, jagged-top see-through blades of ice. "Look, it's difficult to explain. It was this feeling I used to have of being a giant. I'd worked up an image of myself, big bad giant, taller than the men and taller than the waves. It sounds crazy, well maybe it was. But I really did believe this. For however long the swim was, I mean. I was gigantic, many many feet tall, enormous muscles." She chuckled, then stopped. For a second she'd lost the words. "Well. When I trained for the Catalina Channel it was a double crossing, you know that, I trained for months. I trained so hard I couldn't eat enough to maintain weight unless I ate almost all the time, just swam and swam and ate and ate and ate and then I'd sleep. I trained so hard my periods stopped. There wasn't anything extra to bleed. This slow practice swim one day, it wasn't colder than usual, maybe a little rougher but nothing to stop me. I was doing well, I felt fine. Then there was one wave and I caught it right at the critical point and I just stopped. Everything seemed to stop. All I felt was my body, all of the sudden it wasn't much of a giant's body for sure, I saw that clearly, my body frozen in the middle of this wave. I thought I could see bubbles and each separate particle of whitecap. It was like the wave had split apart in front of me, like I was seeing it in a series of stills, you know, some science course lesson on the composition of a wave. And I felt—" Dorey stopped. She started and knew it didn't matter, there was no way to describe it, but for Ilana she'd try. "I got very small. Very human. And I felt that if, if I kept moving, you know, I'd disintegrate and crack apart into the wave, and all these millions of pieces of me would go swirling around and disappear. So I stopped moving." She saw Ilana's face listening, still except for the eyes. They noticed her own eyes and noticed her mouth. "I just stopped moving for a while."

Ilana's fingers closed slightly around hers. The touch was a questioning one and Dorey stared between her feet again. Words froze partway up her throat. Her hands wanted to return the pressure but were frozen still.

Maybe she'd better keep quiet for a while and calm down. Stand and detach both hands. Say look I'm tired and what's going on here makes me nervous Ilana, let's stop. Maybe she'd better. What if she were to do it now, stand and leave? The weight shifted coldly between her breasts. It hurt. It hurt too much.

Their eyes met and stayed there. Dorey set herself to breathing regularly. Mustn't panic now. Still, she had the feeling she was in a dream that she wasn't really orchestrating. Ilana was in command somehow, and now Dorey just kept still and waited for whatever was supposed to come next. She didn't think of it. It hovered deep somewhere, an unspoken want towards which she was moving as a matter of course. Formless, bright, nameless, it simply waited for her arrival as she was waiting now, and suddenly she had the sense that she'd been moving towards this place, this moment, very naturally, moving towards it a long time. Her shoulders went up, then down.

"When you lift your shoulders that way it looks painful."

Dorey grinned, saw Ilana grin back and heard herself saying well Ilana, no one's ever loved my shoulders enough you see so they hurt sometimes for lack of love, and that's why they're so broad, it's like they're swollen or ready to explode, because they do such a good job of plowing through the water and I guess don't feel really appreciated. Then she was shivering. Ilana was offering her a head massage, cure for headaches. Dorey asked was it a cure for chlorine on the brain too.

Ilana moved behind her on the bed. She spread both sets of fingers across her forehead, drew them to the sides and began gently rubbing her temples.

"How does this feel?"

Dorey didn't answer because her mouth was twisting soundlessly, and she felt her face twitch out of control, chin try hard to stay firm.

"Relax. You're very stiff, you know, lean back."

Dorey did and her head rested. Maybe it would break open and let all that hovering light in. She felt it start to split from the center down, told herself she had to stay in one piece and then told herself that was a lie. The head massage swept farther down to a neck massage and then a shoulder massage, Ilana was saying something into her ear, and Dorey covered her face with both hands to hold it together. Ilana's hands were unsteady too, long fingers questioning, across her shoulders.

"What happens next?"

"When I imagined it," Dorey whispered, "next it was easy, just moving, just easy moving like floating or like falling." She turned to look at her. "Is it all right?"

Easy moving. Ilana took the cue. Keep things moving or maybe she herself would quit now, back away from the door she'd opened to a room full of possibilities. Her hands were shaking but she guessed that was all right. Keep it moving. For this one time—if never before and never again—she accepted full responsibility.

She'd been trained so that particular movements would become part of her reflexive repertoire. One might have been the motion she used to pull Sarge's old shirt over her head, cleanly, gracefully. She took Dorey's cue and kept things at a good pace. Maybe her voice shook and she guessed that was all right too. "Why don't you take off your clothes?"

Dorey stood very slowly but without hesitation. Ilana watched her undress. It was done the way she did everything else, clearly and with little flourish. Still there was a certain elegance about each motion, a simple directness and self-assured efficiency that had a grace all its own. Her fingers shook visibly but never fumbled. Ilana found herself admiring. With each article that was taken off she realized how much clothing diminished her. Naked, she was at first sight sufficient and firm, on second sight much more. The lamp reflected an inverted triangle of light that broadened over her

188

breasts, angling at the shoulders, and from the hips' slight curve her body followed that upside-down triangle shape. Muscles that on a man's physique would bulge and ripple were on hers apparent in a different way, rounding unobtrusively with smooth hardness beneath the skin, so the overall impression was one of mass with no unnecessary part to it, of strength that was far from brittle, a well-coordinated power. It was the kind of body that—though perhaps ideal only according to the standards of her profession—made others seem impoverished by comparison. Watching, Ilana's throat caught with surprise. She hadn't expected to be moved by the physical. She'd forgotten how much Dorey herself was invested in the purely physical. Now, naked, she stood with an unselfconscious dignity Ilana hadn't foreseen. Without clothes she seemed taller. Almost in her element.

Then she smiled. There was the Cheshire cat look Ilana'd seen once before. It reformed the dimensions of her face, for that instant, into a new exotic whole from which all banality was banished. At her sides her hands turned, palms up. Well, they said, well here, what do you think. When the smile faded she was pale again and she was moving very slowly towards the bed, leaning over so Ilana's face rested on her shoulders. When she reached around to press both hands against Ilana's back the sensation was at first a shock that tingled through each fingertip. She didn't think, only sensed semiconsciously that she'd stepped into a new world. Instinctively she eased in by reaching, top first. That wave. You opened your mouth and swallowed so it dug a pit inside you, bubbles splintered to white air inside you and hollowed you out so you were nothing but the water flooding into the pit that had once been you, water inside, water outside, no one and nothing to drink it in much less dance. Uh-uh, no. She wasn't going to think. She eased to the bed top first and they floated in a heated, pleasing light. Maybe she was saying something or maybe it was Ilana, someone whispering into another ear in another language, she wasn't sure. What she felt surely was Ilana's body shivering uncontrollably along the length of hers. Ilana holding her, or rather holding on to her, as if afraid she'd vanish, and

189

opening her eyes Dorey saw her fear and then understood, so for a second they were still.

"Don't cry Ilana, I won't die out there. I'm not a boy."

In the dark Ilana watched her. Bodies in darkness have a light all their own. If she made her eyes slits she could break this glow down to whirring specks of light, an aura humming along every curve in the dark. Hardly a giant. Ilana could have curled herself around protectively but didn't, better not to disturb her. Dorey didn't sleep enough. Hadn't for a while, she'd told her, not since Seal Beach. Ilana tacitly volunteered herself for the night watch. She'd done a lot of volunteering tonight. A lot of volunteering in the belief that she was doing it for Dorey, a half-truth at best. It was all right for now. For later she didn't think. If she closed her eyes all the way she'd hear the halo of their pale bodies hum an almost silent chorus. It was a good idea, this one of being a giant. All mothers should be giants. There were four months to go before she'd jump into that water, and Ilana knew nothing she could do would be giant enough to save her from the cold that would strip that glow, strip all those manners, strip the beautifully conditioned covering down to bone. Watching Dorey, she was afraid for a minute and cold welled up inside, bringing with it her brain's snapshots of frozen water, all the old bitterness. No, she hissed, no, go away. I won't let you hurt her. Dorey's eyes opened, glistening a little in the dark.

"Your shoulders must hurt." Ilana brushed them with her fingertips. "Shhh. Relax."

"Sometimes I feel so tired, Ilana."

"Then come to sleep."

Dorey shook her head. Ilana leaned on an elbow and looked down at her, wanted to tell about the nights she'd heard her pacing, heard her walking a straight line from bed to door and back and forward, on and on. "I hear you sometimes, when you can't sleep. Walking."

"Well you're awake too then."

Something like a sound tightened Ilana's throat. It hurt and never came out. To put Dorey to sleep for an entire night, that was her goal. Real rest could be valuable, more so than raw meat or time trials. Let Sarge take care of the day while she took care of the insomnia—it was only fair. So she seized control again, this time without shaking, slid her hands down along the open body, and her lips, slid her own hips forward.

It was sleep. Dorey felt her eyelids easing to close, arms tremble to rest, shoulders sink and she was counting. One stroke two stroke three stroke four. It was easy and she remembered things: Carol in the backyard. She was sixteen. Carol patting her head with a hand that looked fragile but was the strongest gripping hand Dorey'd ever known. You're crazy darling, she'd said, crazy, but go on ahead and do what you need to do anyway, there are worse ways to live. Her smile had been tender and desolate, her face pale, turned up to catch moon glow in the night.

"Shhh." Ilana held her head against both breasts. She hid it there. "Relax."

Nine ten eleven twelve. Warmth spread in tiny embers to toetips and fingertips. No more cold for tonight. It was gone, she couldn't recall the last time it had gone so completely. No more cold. This sleep was going to be good.

"Rest," said Ilana. "You can sleep if you want."

She mumbled that she was sleeping already. Then she let go and floated.

Ilana held her. She watched. This was the dead time of night, that limbo between moondown and dawn when everything hid and nothing promised relief. It was during these hours that long swims failed. Spirits cracked in the hopeless pitch-black fatigue of it all. Between waves, blanketed by cold, the only light false rays from boatside that couldn't be perceived anyway except as parts of shadows, the only consolation your thoughts fragmented by the weight of an absolute solitude. Ilana held her and watched. She watched the rest of the night and was still holding her when the door pushed open for morning and behind it stood Sarge. Dorey slept and Ilana remained motionless, awake, eyes wide. Looking straight at him, she touched a finger to her lips in warning. Dorey's sleep was precious. For a moment she thought maybe they'd both stopped breathing. In all the world that morning only the body she held was breathing. And it must not, it would not, be woken. Sarge looked gray. She saw the tinge of her own skin mirrored in his. He'd squinted at first. Now just stared. Then he backed out into the hallway, closed the door again, and she heard his feet go away.

"Good morning."

It was full sunlight. Dorey blinked. What, she whispered, eyes shut again, what time is it? Where her hands closed the sheet was damp.

"Almost eleven. I thought you'd sleep around the clock."

She jumped then and Ilana was sitting fully clothed on the side of the bed. Pressing into the texture of her clothes, Dorey's flesh tingled rawly. Ilana wrapped arms around her. Exposed, she felt cheated then and hid her face against Ilana's neck, gave in for a moment to confusion and the panicked thump of her heart.

"Eleven? No."

"It's all right!" Ilana spread both hands against her back, fingers pressuring reassurance. The skin was smooth, cheek against her neck soft and cool from sleep. What these sensations aroused was not erotic—the feeling was for her a vast and pleasing tenderness. It poured out through her encircling arms, fresh supply waiting inside. So for a second, meeting this other body on the full crest of the tenderness it brought about in her, Ilana was the more vulnerable. Just for a second. "It's all right."

"Is it? It's all right for you?"

"Shhh. I watched you sleeping a long time, you know. That was lovely."

192   "Eleven." She dropped back on pillows, breathed deep and the air was fresh, cool with that touch of increasing warmth to it. She brought Ilana's hand to her cheek, spread it palm-

down over her face. She inhaled softly against it. "I never slept this late."

"Never?"

"Uh-uh." She caressed each finger in turn, folded each carefully towards the palm and placed the loose fist she'd made against her neck artery so Ilana'd feel the pulse. Around Ilana's wrist her own hands trembled slightly. "Well. I don't know. I don't know how to do this Ilana, or what to say."

They looked at each other silently, unnerved and a little shy. Watching, Ilana felt instant tears and blinked them away with surprise. Then she leaned over and very lightly kissed her forehead. "Are you okay, dear? How do you feel?" Where her lips had been was moist, tiny imprint centered over the highest form of spirit.

"I want you to be happy. If you told me how. That's all Ilana. Could I make you happy—" She paled. Hands shook more now and she twined them around one another, forced them to be quiet on the sheet. "If you told me. I want that. I could."

"Don't you know? You did."

"Ah." Dorey blushed. "That. Sure. Well that too. Listen, it's more though. I'd like to touch you perfectly. Just touch you every way, then I'd see you—I don't know! I can't explain exactly." She closed her eyes a second, saying she wished she knew how to be right now. How to explain what she meant. It's all right, Ilana said gently, everything's fine.

"So we could see each other. You'd know me then."

Ilana thought she understood. For an instant she had the sense that whatever tables there'd been had turned—she was no longer completely in charge. Asked herself was this more than she'd bargained for, and the answer came back simply, immediately, no, no, there'd been no bargains made. She felt relieved by her own answer. Still, she'd become overnight an active participant in some new scheme of things, a scheme partly of her own making. This active role was strange to her. Examining Dorey's face, Ilana realized it was the first time she'd appeared rested. Without that familiar sleepless strain her features seemed subtly transformed, the face itself slightly different overall. So along with the fear Ilana allowed herself a full moment of pride, pressed both hands against the smooth cheeks, not just to reassure Dorey but also herself. "People really knowing each other, that's a tall order. That takes time."

"Distance." Dorey looked up at her, eyes asking. "If I want it this much it can happen. It's possible."

Possible if. Gazing up, the eyes still asked, and Ilana knew they were searching out her reply. Then she felt lightweight, lithe, momentarily released from the pull of gravity and incredibly strong. Anything could happen now. Anything. No more rules. She was walking a thin wire between cliffs and didn't dare look down now to see if there was water below or not. It was the knowledge of this new responsibility she'd assumed that balanced her—she felt almost giddy with a sense of her own power.

"What do you think Ilana. Will this work for you?"

The tenderness came and Ilana wanted to hold her again, watch her sleep. "Somehow," she said. "Somehow. Let's try."

Late now. The day impended. Ilana wondered where he'd gone and wondered should she go find him. Then she felt stubborn and dug in her heels—no, knowing that it was for Dorey different than for her—she wouldn't rob the morning of its completeness. She thought of telling her that he'd seen but didn't.

It was Dorey who pulled back first, gently detached her hands. "I think you ought to go, Ilana. I'll wake up now."

"You've already woken up," she teased. "Are you shy?"

"Well yes. Yes, a little."

The real shaking didn't start until she was in the bathroom, turned on water for a shower and waited for it to warm. The swim. Whatever soreness she felt now around shoulders, arms, thighs, gave her Laughing River back in bits and pieces, the ice-battering tunnel it had been and pictures she'd had in her head, what she'd been reaching for towards the end. Then she remembered exactly what she'd wanted to tell Ilana before the sunlit spin of the dock beneath her back, the finish and glow obscured it. She'd already said it though. Last night.

It ripped through her like the jagged edge of something—the night, how it had felt—so standing there in steam fogging from the shower she began to shake and couldn't stop. Easy. Like she'd imagined it had been so easy, and her imagination had gone through the ease of it so thoroughly and with such attention to detail that she'd neglected to imagine the aftermath. But she was sure that—had she done so—the imagined vision would be nothing like this. Not this lacerated burning making her shake out of all control. Ilana. It was Ilana and remembering how she'd touched and been touched, that spun through her insides now. No she hadn't imagined this, she could not have. It was unique, bitter release, like the first time you cry or the first time you win. Or like nothing else. Just nothing.

Ilana! it hissed out loud with the steam. Dorey rubbed both palms on the mirror's clouded surface and cleared a dribbling circle. Said her name softly then the way she'd said it last night. *Ilana.* Different. Different for Ilana than for her, she knew. What that might mean she wouldn't think of. Still it hovered just above the bright fountain of her confusions now, a cold dry edge of despair. To swim. She had to swim and that meant Sarge. Sarge whom Ilana had caressed last night too while he slept there on the couch in a way that said she adored him. That she wanted him Dorey didn't doubt. Well he touched too but differently, that was where the disparity appeared between Ilana and herself, and how could she be with them both together anymore? Or lie to him. She'd chosen, until now, not to reveal much of her life so far as emotions went—the basic facts he knew. But swimming meant Sarge and to actively lie while she swam wasn't a possibility.

Dorey stepped into the tub. She closed eyes and turned her face up for the full force of the water. Somehow, Ilana'd said, somehow, let's try. Sure. Well there was no way to tell now what that might entail. Dorey let the water fill her mouth, blurted it out as if her lips were a water pistol's barrel. Another shot and she'd exiled all threat from inside, remembered only that slippery, burning, shattering sensation and the long easy uphill, downhill sliding that had been last night, words mostly forgotten and that sense of breathing stopped along with the floating loss of time. No matter what its aftermath did to her now she would ask for it again and no one would stop her. Sometimes you had to be offered it. Once you knew, though, you would seek it. Like the first swim in open water ever, someone had to invite you along. Then you'd look for the lakes yourself. Or the saltwater shorelines.

Sarge sat at the table over a cooled mug of tea. He'd opened all the windows as far as they'd go. When Ilana came quietly into the kitchen, he didn't look up.

She was offering him more tea. He waited for a note of something in her voice—what, he didn't quite know. But whatever it was he didn't hear it. Tea? he asked calmly. Tea. Yes, thanks, he'd have more tea. She steeped it in a fresh mug and placed it in front of him. He saw her hand stop briefly on the table, letting go of the handle. It was a lovely, long-fingered hand. She put a basket of something else there. He didn't look up to notice what. Then the smell came to him. Wheat toast. That smell was fresh, sighing off the hot dark bread. Sarge sniffed at the tea. He let it get cold again.

Ilana was putting other things out, more utensils, other foods. He heard footsteps and counted them coming closer. Then the sounds stopped but he still counted. When he did look up there was Dorey.

She paused, paled slightly as she looked to him and then Ilana. Back to him. But her eyes settled finally on Ilana. Hell. Whatever she might have tried to pull off he could see now she wasn't capable, there'd be no convincing lies from her in appearance or action. He sat back and just watched the two of them. For a second neither moved. He noticed how good Dorey looked. That healthy high-colored shine on her face beneath the momentary pale wasn't sunburn but rest and plenty of other things he hadn't seen there before.

"Hello," said Ilana.

Sarge cupped the table edge in one palm. He lifted up and over and everything capsized. Mugs slid with a ceramic scrape, broke on the floor, hot tea soaked bread in puddles. The crash hadn't finished sounding when Dorey stepped instinctively in front of Ilana. Arms thrown back shielding her she faced him, thrusting slightly forward as if to dive, or butterfly. Her eyes were a dark mixture, some desperation, some defiance. Many things, most of which he didn't read, he couldn't. He was so outside of it all. He just stepped over broken plates on the floor, then was out the door.

Leaning against the counter, Ilana felt tired. Well of course, she told herself, she'd been awake the entire night. Turning, Dorey was careful not to touch her. But on Ilana's face no warning appeared, just open exhaustion. So after a while Dorey brushed her cheek softly with fingertips, saying well, well, this isn't working for you right now is it. What happened?

"I wasn't going to tell you, but he saw. Early this morning he walked right in." Ilana watched her panic, then freeze, all in seconds with no more indication of turmoil than the jaw tightening shut. "I apologize. I should have given you some warning but then I didn't know what to do either. You see this is all new to me, too. And I didn't want, oh, to *spoil* things— isn't that ridiculous."

No, Dorey told her, no, not really.

"I'd better clean up."

"I'll help."

"Don't bother." Ilana laughed, sad little sound. "It's my mess, after all."

Dorey crouched, started mopping up with paper towels. "Well, Ilana. Mine too then. Here, here's a towel."

She found him at the dock's edge, bare feet dangling numbly into water. She knew he heard her approach and knew he wouldn't turn to look. The air was warm, dark green shadow of pines mellowed to a more sun-bleached tone. She walked slowly because she was afraid, kept walking anyway because one thing she knew was that fear, like pain, was simply another factor to be accounted for.

The water shimmered placidly today, once in a while rippled by faint wind. Mostly clear, though, and mirror smooth. She'd have liked to swim but no. Let the muscles rest. He didn't move and she sat beside him.

They said nothing. She felt minutes pass, took off her shoes, rolled up the jean cuffs and let her toes dangle. She wished she could speak like Anne Norton. Speak well and a lot, have that familiarity with words, phrases pouring out like whip cracks, bubbling over one another so that everyone felt at ease and everyone listened.

It blurted out finally, a harsh-sounding plea.

"Don't hurt her. It's got nothing to do with you."

Without looking he half-smiled. "Great biography you've got there. You just left out a few things."

"No Sarge. Look. I didn't really know. Maybe if I was sure before I would have said something. Maybe. Said something like look Sarge, look"—she laughed and her voice shook audibly—"this is the way it is and she's a beautiful woman, what can you expect?"

"Sick."

He looked then and when he saw the tears—not quite spilling but there for the first time he could recall—he grinned, chilled with satisfaction.

"No, Sarge, no. Don't say that to me—you don't know." She swallowed the tremors away. Sunlight curled across his hair, down the slope of his shoulders, and she thought he looked nice that way, wondered how he could look so good and hurt so much at the same time. Hurt inside himself, hurt her. Well okay. But not Ilana, that's where it had to stop. Facing him, she spoke firmly now. "It's not that. She's beautiful. It's a pretty thing." She smiled gently—he'd never seen her look better. "It's so pretty."

He was of two minds. One was to tell her to beat it, push her away with disgust. The other was to grab hold of her shirt near the neck and rip to expose her entire upper body. He wondered what she'd do. If there were marks on her abdomen, around her breasts, remnants of kisses. He wondered how they did it, could imagine some things but not with Ilana as participant. That's where the images got hazy and that's when he wanted to rip. Just rip. He rubbed knuckles against his temples. Dully, his head pounded.

"Don't hurt her. Please."

He barely heard it. Ilana. How could he hurt Ilana. She was secure somehow, floating far from his reach now, and his adoration was an additional barrier between her and any harm he might do. If he raised a fist he'd have to drop it just as quickly. He'd have liked to tell Dorey that he'd rather put the fist on an oven burner or smash it through plate glass. But she was almost pleading, saying please don't hurt her. He had to promise. Sarge shook his head.

"You're crazy. I won't hurt her."

"I'll go away. Do you want that?"

"I don't care," he said, "I don't care what you do."

"Ah." She wriggled toes up and out of the water. "Right." Bare feet numb, she stood. He heard her soles slap sharply along the dock until the sound vanished. When he looked around she'd gone.

Sarge rubbed a hand through his hair, over his forehead. Goddamned hangover. It had been years. He let himself stretch backward and out on sunburnt wood, heat searing. Wet soaked against the back of his head. He sat and turned to examine that spot. It was her first footprint, heading away from the water.

"Where?"

Ilana'd removed her gloves. Wet clumps of dirt still clung. Dorey sat too so her toes played with the earth. Away, she was saying, just away.

"He won't hurt you, I don't think. I'm sure."

"Sarge! No, of course he won't." Ilana stopped, understood what Dorey's concern had been, then she wanted to cry. "What do you want to do now? You can tell me, you know."

"I should leave, Ilana. Do you want me to stay? If you want that I'll stay, I will. I promise. Are you afraid?"

The garden smelled alive. Ilana breathed in with relief. Almost the tropics. "Afraid? I don't really know." Some parts had begun to bud. There were tiny green nubs poking through the near-black earth.

They talked a little longer. Ilana sat with a natural kind of ease, looked to Dorey like some Hindi rahnah in prayer you'd imagine finding small statues of in an open-air market in, say, Calcutta. After a while she noticed a sad look shadow the face, Ilana reach towards her and she curled around on the ground then, rested her head against Ilana's stomach.

"Am I your baby now?" It was said lightly but seriously. She was no good at saying things without meaning them. Understanding that about her, Ilana had to reply in kind.

"Sometimes," she said, "sometimes."

"Like now?"

"Yes. Along with other things that you are. One of which is not a boy."

"Good. I'm glad about that. I'm glad. Are you sure?"

"Sometimes."

Well she was honest.

"Uh-huh." Kneeling, Dorey pressed a cheek softly against the upturned forehead and pulled back to look carefully. She took note of lines all rendering the face more exotic somehow, as if they were a celebration—rather than a scarring—of age. "I'd better go now, Ilana."

She started for the house at a quick walk that turned to a run. Watching, Ilana stood suddenly. Something she ought to be saying now that hadn't been said. She wasn't doing a great job anymore—no, wasn't handling things so well right now. She wanted to make this right, make it better, didn't know how. Worry hung there darkly until she realized she was somehow reveling in it, escaping into motherliness again, wanting to make everything fine for everyone—that was all. Another tall order. The night's weight settled on her along with exhaustion. Ilana didn't know if she was up to it, this task of knowing her. Only she'd taken the jump and there was no way to recall that and she didn't want to. So she went towards the house.

"What I want." She stopped at the entrance to Dorey's room. Dorey was throwing things into her bag. There was money on the bed, car keys that jangled when she picked them up because her hands shook. Ilana saw them clench. "What I want is for you to come back."

"September," Dorey said blindly. The bag trembled against her knees. "That's four months. Well I wish I could swim today."

To concentrate on one thing, and one thing alone. It had to be a simple thing, Dorey knew—a movement, repeated rhythmically. Or a note, also repeated until you lost count. There was staring at one bland object long enough so it became everything in your field of vision. Either that or you stopped seeing it completely. And both offered the same result: you could then cease thought.

That's what the road was, and driving. Because it was smooth, clear of distraction, the route familiar. Dark gray split down the middle by that white line. Concentrating, she was aware enough to drive but her insides were freshly erased. On the open hilly land were pines, through the small towns were maples and crudely pruned hedges. She noticed but remained fixed on that line. After a while she was humming. Song to the moon.

The day got darker, chillier, into evening and night. The land became flatter, trees sparse and finally nonexistent, towns larger, then they were suburbs. Ahead huge shadows of buildings, tiny window lights twinkling like multiple blinking eyes on monsters' faces. The air was no longer fresh. She rolled a window higher. First toll booth yanked her away from the blankness. Then the blackboard inside her was suddenly vulnerable, unprotected from the crazy proliferation of messages that chalked across it in many colors.

Entering from the north, she wasn't sure of these routes and so drove more slowly, nervously aware of traffic and of car lights, bridge lights rainbow arcs under the countless building lights. She stayed in the right lane. After a while there was a smell of water, along with increased breeze and chill. She drove parallel to the Hudson, ignored possible turnoffs into the network of city streets. She decided to follow it all the way. Worst that could happen if you just followed was drive in circles but you'd still be on the island. Go down to where the Hudson curled around and lost itself and then you went across to the East River, followed that up. The Harlem. Back around. There was some comfort in that. She relaxed a little. You wouldn't want to be caught in some of those nastier currents there, waiting for the tide to turn in your favor.

At the docks she slowed, jumped at horns blaring behind her and pulled over to the right-hand side, signals blinking. Along the waterfront people walked. They stopped sometimes, some of them held hands, threw lit cigarettes into the water, gestured towards waiting dark cruisers anchored off the wharf. Cars flashed by. An undercurrent of noise rumbled up against the dull lapping of water, the low indistinct murmurings of people moving past and a barrage of odor. She couldn't shut it out anymore—not the smells, the lights or the people. Sitting there she watched couples, decided to evaluate them from the back—when one was taller, broader-shouldered, or had a protective-looking arm around a partner it was very often a man and the slighter one a woman but you couldn't be sure. Two men leaned against the railing up ahead. One lowered his face, rubbed it gently across the other's sweater-covered chest and for an instant they clasped hands.

She pulled carefully into traffic again, inched the car to the left-hand lane and looked for a turn. She'd steered away from the waterfront and now crawled through narrow curving streets that were more like village lanes. Eyes roamed side to side in search. Not swimming, not driving, here the best way was to walk. Get rid of the car. Beyond that she didn't know, or think.

A dark, well-polished BMW pulled out of its space ahead. She parked and for the first time in hours that motor was off, lights shut, wheel warm but still in her hands. She rolled down the window again so noise flooded in. Dorey leaned back and just listened—feet scraping cement, taxi horns, the mumble, that indecipherable collage of voices. No more river sounds. No water here. She locked the doors. Took her bag, her money, got out. Then something froze inside and she felt that sore weight around the shoulders. She sat on the car's warm hood, dully, watched people go by on the sidewalk.

Night air cooled against her. Dorey realized she'd been sweating. Two women went past, one wearing nylon shorts that had a soft sheen in the light from street and restaurant windows. Her legs sprouting out of the shorts were long, leanly defined, and each step had a lengthy spring to it. Her shirt was sleeveless, arms very thin, shoulders fragile. A runner. Distance. The two of them grinned at Dorey as they went past and, faintly, she nodded, looked elsewhere.

"What?"

She barely recognized herself speaking.

They'd turned around and were asking directions. She shook her head, had to ask what another time. What were they looking for? The runner said it again. It was the name of a restaurant, maybe, maybe that was it. They were visiting, the other explained, from out of town. She had an open, pretty face. Dorey shook her head again. No, she was saying, uh-uh, not me. No I don't know, sorry.

"Are you all right?"

The couples walking past were moving formations of light. Their faces lamps, and each pair of hands held formed a light bulb swinging between them.

"Are you all right?"

"What?" Dorey opened her eyes. "Yes. Yes thanks. I'm okay."

"You sure?"

"Uh-huh. Yes. Thank you. Thanks. I'm all right."

They were gone and she slid to the sidewalk. She swung the bag over one shoulder, started walking, turned a corner, then another. Seemed to her she was going in an opposite direction from all the people out tonight but surely that couldn't be true. Calm down, she told herself. Breathe. She wound around some more corners, stopped at two phone booths and the second one had a phone intact. She fished change from her pocket. When the dime slipped in there was that buzz. Straddling her bag, she opened it a little and pulled out some note paper, ran through numbers scribbled randomly across it and tossed it back in. She took out a small address book. Breathe. Thumbed through to the N's, repeated the number to herself. Breathe. Replaced the book and dialed Anne Norton's number, cupped a hand over the uncovered ear, and waited out several dial tones.

"Hello?"

It was a man's voice. She paused a second. Then hung up, panicked. She leaned back against the phone's glass shelter, felt herself shivering even though the air wasn't that chilly. Breathe. No she couldn't. Uh-uh. Breathe. Her memory for numbers was good. A few times exposed to one and she'd have it. She slid another dime in and dialed, steeled herself for the answering machine but none clicked on and she felt panic start again. When the voice spoke, she forgot to inhale. Then it spilled out abruptly.

"Listen, it's me. It's Dorey, Dorey Thomas. I did—I can't explain. Look. Something happened."

"What?" said Tycho. "Where are you?"

"I'm here. I don't know. I left the car somewhere."

"Okay, okay. Mercury's a little haywire tonight, you know, just relax. Can you see a cross street? Something specific—"

She glanced around, found a signpost and told him the streets. Just stay there, he said, just stay right there, I'll come down now and meet you. Don't move.

"Help." That wasn't her, she told herself, wasn't her at all.

"I'm leaving now."

"Tycho. Help me."

Three steps led down from the front door. Three led up towards the other rooms. One wall was completely blanketed by books, many of the titles in foreign languages. In this way alone the room was reminiscent of Sarge. Dorey avoided glancing at those bookshelves, ignored the furniture altogether and sat on the floor. After a while, Tycho did too. They talked a long time. Or rather, he listened to her when she spoke and also to the long silences in between. Once in a while her hands rose, and the fingers would flutter an almost wing-like motion, delicately. At those times his eyes were drawn to her hands.

"There's an ancient theory, I think it belongs to the Greeks." Tycho thumbed circles in the rug. "Which states that in the beginning were spherically shaped entities, each one blissfully complete in and of itself. Due to some great environmental trauma—ordained by the gods but, you'll have to excuse me, I forget exactly why—each sphere was split into two equal parts and each part that had once belonged to a whole went spinning randomly through the world, totally lost. Well, the story goes—of all these spheres, some split into a male part and a female part. Some two male parts. Some two female parts." He looked at her intently, concentrating. Through the sunburn pale strain was beginning to show. Well it was late. "So from that time on, each separated part was obliged to search everywhere for the other part of the sphere. And when two parts of the same original sphere met, suppos-edly they'd recognize one another immediately—as if each were looking in a mirror. Then they'd unite. That was the only way they could fulfill their destiny."

Her smile was tired, only half there. "I like it. It's fair." Where, she wanted to know, where had he heard of this the-ory. He paused then.

"A friend told it to me," he said finally. "A friend who be-lieved in it. At the time I treated it as sort of a joke—no, with plain contempt. I guess underneath contempt there's always a kind of terror. Anyway, my attitude was pretty painful, I think, to us both, and it wound up hurting. It hurt very badly." He cleared his throat. "Do you understand that?"

She stared fully at his face. After a while she nodded.

"Your friend Bob? The one who was your partner. Double sculls?"

He smiled quietly, asked how did she know.

"Well I asked Sarge once. About your face, I mean, how it happened. He told me who did it. When you said this just now"—her eyes stayed with his—"I guess I knew."

When he listened closely he could hear her nearly struggle

to breathe, as if something heavy were throttling her. Carefully, he inched towards her until they sat cross-legged, side by side, arms nearly brushing. He reached to lay tentative fingers on her shoulders.

"If this bothers you, tell me."

But she didn't say anything or open her eyes, and then his long arms went around her and, gently, he guided her head to rest against his chest.

"I think if you'd cry," he said, "you'd breathe easier."

He wished she'd cry. Wished so much that for a moment he wondered whether he had a vicarious stake in the matter, this business of her crying. He felt his own throat go desert-dry and wondered did he want her to cry for herself or was there more to it than that. Him looking to take a free ride on those tears she still hadn't spilled, save himself the effort, after all these years.

Mr. Gallagher, they'd asked, why the shift in interest? Astronomy to medicine. It seemed to require some sort of explanation. So he'd sat there dressed in what his father would have called his Sunday suit. And he had tried to come up with a respectable reason and tried to avoid letting the real reason spill out.

I am precision-oriented, he wrote, being an astronomer. As my record indicates. I find the application of precision in, for instance, a process such as surgery to be infinitely more socially contributive than the application of mathematical precision to the measurement of changes in inorganic matter.

This was acceptable.

What he wanted to say was something like: Because it's the logical extension of astronomy. The human body is a map of uncounted galaxies in microcosmic form, and all those stars out there are an enormous representation of the human body. In the biological entity of the body there's death happening all over. And out there energy. Light. Life's essence contained in what we call dead matter. Because before going outside I want intimate knowledge of the inside that's taking me there.

That is why. No shift in interest. Merely a deepening. We compartmentalize all experience into illusory divisions with neat labels, anyway, the divisions are random and the compartmentalization a grave psychic error.

He kept that to himself.

Tycho wandered until past two. Relaxing with rhythmic breathing exercises he'd follow the trail of his thoughts until they blocked him, then uneasily stand, stretch with care and walk. He moved like a prowler in his own apartment, socks sliding a hushed friction over the carpet. When he came for the dozenth time to the closed door he paused. Then eased it open so a dim strand of light sprayed into the room, illuminated her sleeping profile and the blankets bunched along her body. Watching, he felt like a thief. No problem sleeping tonight. She looked anything but restless, utterly sunk in sleep, nearly motionless.

In sleep there was no male or female way to be. This androgynous quality Dorey shared with children. In the dull light she changed back and forth from woman to adolescent boy. He changed her. Each blink of his a wand, each swing of the wand a transformation. Tycho closed the door gently.

He wandered to the bookshelves and pulled out a few Deutsches Ephemerides along with other material. At the small desk in his bedroom he measured a circle on large sketch-pad paper, did some quick calculations and sliced the pie twelve ways, each angle notated by degrees. At the center of the circle was another. This one was blank.

DOREY THOMAS, he wrote in the smaller contained circle. Beneath it her date of birth and the exact time, the geographical longitude and latitude.

Always, he was surprised by the amount of fire element there. So much opposition, she was all fire and water, fire drastically muted by that T-square friction but Saturn slowly, slowly easing off by painful degrees. Tug of war between Uranus and the Moon. Venus circling inexorably around, staying overnight with the Moon, going on ahead towards some rough flirtation with the Sun and Mars. He examined it, everything made sense. Then he drew another circle around the larger one and spent a long time calculating.

Looking at his calculations, Tycho frowned. He went over them again and they were correct. He adjusted his glasses, blinked fuzzily at the figures, then plugged each calculation into its rightful place on the new rim of the twelve-pieced pie.

When it was done he stared, took in the entire map. Nervously his fingers tapped the oddly symboled sheet, caught a rhythm, and he'd have sworn that through soundproofed walls and windows he'd heard the beginning rush of predawn traffic from the streets.

Tycho pulled out a large sheet of tracing paper. Setting it over the chart, he roughly sketched a hexagon. On various points of the hexagon he drew twelve circles, and in each circle a symbol from the underlying chart, along with a corresponding Hebrew word.

He placed a fresh sheet of tracing paper over both. On this he drew a human body.

At first the figure looked sexless. After a while, though, it was clearly female. At various parts of the body—the feet, knees, genitals, the abdomen and heart, palms, fingers, shoulders, throat, eyes, ears, and forehead—he transposed symbols contained in the underlying hexagon's circles. To each symbol he added another word, also in Hebrew. These words were names of tribes. There were twelve of them.

Above the figure's head Tycho inked in a name, this one in English. DOREY THOMAS, he wrote.

He removed his glasses and for the first time in hours felt tired. He glanced half-blindly at the figure sketched in front of him. A couple of rooms away she slept.

Tycho opened a drawer, pulled out a map and laid it over everything else. Then he drew a red line from Punta Provechosa to the middle of the San Antonio Strait. Already-scribbled markings indicated the current there, and the new red line he drew followed these markings along in a northern direction for some distance before pausing, stabbing across the current and lunging in arrowlike segments for the mainland shore.

•

"Hell Sarge." Matt flexed his fingers, or tried anyway. They were frozen. He soaked into the towel. "That new girl out there today, what's her name?"

"Dorey Thomas."

"Yeah! Well she can *swim*, Sarge. I mean, she can flat-out *swim*."

"Right." Sarge rubbed his back, his arms, through the layers. "She's good and you're better. Here. Drink some of this. Good swim Matt. You did well today."

He crouched over the softened heap of blankets they'd laid on the ground, over Matt wrapped in towels shivering on the blankets. July sun burned his back browner. He knew the kid didn't feel a bit of that sun, he was too chilled. Sarge lifted Matt's head up to the Styrofoam cup—hot chocolate with a healthy dose of glucose—saying easy now, easy, get it down slow. He slapped him gently on the shoulders, rubbed them again well, made his usual fuss. Good swim. Third place. Well the kid was young, it was a damned good showing. Around them the crowd was chaotic. First four in the field had finished and the next few were far behind, but this mob was going on Labatt's and high-pitched summer fever and he bet most of them would stay for the last finisher, many hours away.

"She spooked me Sarge. I kept turning and there was that red streak! How'd she get it on her cap? She kept just riding up on my left the whole goddamned way—"

"Old trick! Just relax."

"What was my time?"

Sarge stroked his hair. He forced some more fluid down, tossed the cup away. "Ten hours forty-one minutes."

"Not bad." Matt smiled faintly. The words came out with loud distortion, so this close he was almost shouting. "Catching up to the old man."

"I'll say."

"There!"

The kid grinned in that crazy, semidelirium he'd fall into towards the end of a swim. Sarge turned to see if he was staring at anything solid and when he turned the sun slashed across his eyes, momentarily blinding. Around were shouts, babies crying, men swearing and pervasive beer odor mixed in with the cold new smell of wind-driven lake. She was on her feet and trailing by, a few yards away. Limping, legs shaky, but walking. They'd draped her with towels. She hadn't yet taken off her cap, just pulled goggles up to rest against the forehead. Her trainer and a couple of others hovered around, big hulks all of them. Made it difficult to see her.

"Lightning." Matt laughed.

Sarge saw that custom-designed red bolt jetting down the cap's side.

"Hell Sarge that's funny. Look how small she is."

It was true. Not that in and of herself or, say, among women she would have been considered small—although even there she would not have been considered large either—but here were mostly men, and big men at that. The contrast was striking. In comparison she was little. On land, small, and absurdly female.

She noticed them looking and stopped, nodded slightly. Her face was dazed. It was sunburnt and dripping. It looked scarred. Standing there, she smiled.

"Any more towels Sarge?"

"Cold?" There weren't any more. He stretched out on the blankets himself, pressed against his son's shivering body. Best source of heat there was, actually, another living body. It seemed to help. He felt the kid relax some, spasms diminish. The body was almost as long as his but imperceptibly slighter. All in all, it gave the impression of being fragile underneath. No heat retention. Sarge pressed forward more. He wrapped him in his arms.

If you could see through dusty shutters, if you'd stood outside the window to Matt Olssen's room, you'd have seen Sarge alone. He was lying on the bed there, arms crossed over his chest embracing someone invisible.

The walls were a mess, haphazard collage of posters, newspaper clippings, ribbons and letters and photographs. A lot of the photos were of young women. All were pretty or in some way appealing, all had wide-mouthed smiles and large eyes. Matt's type.

The desk was meticulous, odd contrast to the walls, its blotter barely stained. A few books stood at one corner. A dictionary, some poetry paperbacks—Keats, Milton—his taste had been distinctly classical. Two other texts lay flat across the blotter, side by side. Standing, Sarge read their titles for the thousandth time. One was a treatise on the supposed lost continent represented by architectural remnants discovered on the ocean shelf off Bimini, smack in the Bermuda Triangle. The other was an oversized hardback illustrating the works of Hieronymus Bosch. Its cover was a section taken from the *Garden of Earthly Delights*. Sarge hesitated before reaching to open it. The title page was inked at one corner in a rapidly scrawled, light-handed script. *Cute guy*, it read. *Race you to the garden no dunking allowed. Anne.* Sarge shot a glance at the black-and-white photo of Anne Norton that stood framed on the desk. She was giving one of those smiles that split everything wide open. Matt's unrequited love. Or maybe sometimes requited. Sometimes requited could mean unrequited, though, Sarge reminded himself, especially when you were young and wanted everything. Hell, he wasn't young anymore and he still wanted everything. Only this one thing he could not have, his son alive again. He could not have that ever and the impossibility of it dazed him. He closed the book, smoothed dust from the *Garden of Earthly Delights*.

"That was his favorite creature, the one right here." Ilana pointed. He examined the tiny demon she'd singled out before turning to meet her eyes. They were large and somewhat Oriental, sadness bright inside. It occurred to him this was the first time they'd been in Matt's room together since his death. For a moment Sarge felt oddly violated.

"I wish you'd go away," he said.

"I want us to talk."

All right, he told her numbly. All right, in a little while. She nodded and lightly touched his arm, which didn't yield. Before turning to go she gripped it more firmly, pressed her cheek against the sleeve. She was gone as silently as she'd entered.

Alone, Sarge stepped softly to the bed again and looked down at the impression his body'd made. Standing there he

211

was suddenly aware of his own weight. Little fat to his bulk, age or no age most of it muscle and brutally conditioned muscle at that. But heavy it was. In that second his own mass overwhelmed him. He sat on the bed. Shoulders and broad chest sagged forward, head drooped into the large hands.

Stars! The stars! Over and over in water he rolled. Something filled his mouth, something soft but substantial. Swollen to mouth-size. It was his tongue. Stars! What's that champ? The fish? Yeah sure there's fish Sarge, this is the tropics.

Stars flitted. Teasingly they sparkled then danced away. Hill and valley of each wave's swell soared from a bottomless source, rolled over him as he rolled over in it, spun him up then down at the tail end of a crazy waltz. With each swell stars flickered in scattering groups of light. What filled his mouth was his own salt-caked tongue. Stars dancing. Feverish now, he reached for a few and they twinkled just beyond his grasp so his arm fell back down futilely, then up and around to reach again, turned into a stroke. Another. Stars. Dancing. He reached. Then he was swimming.

On the table a few black grapes had dried. The empty green-tinted bottle was still on its side against a plate of stale cheese. Sprawled on the sofa, Sarge ignored that. He measured, instead, the number of steps it might have taken from here to the door. Because now he was remembering things hazily, and his last memory was walking towards Dorey as she leaned against that wall. He'd wanted to do something. Run a hand down her. In those clothes she'd looked more vulnerable than she ever did naked.

Ilana started to speak but he interrupted without really intending to.

"Tell me Ilana, did you like it? With her I mean." He gazed tiredly, eyes frankly questioning. "I'm curious."

Sitting at the sofa's opposite end she was silent, touched her forehead to soothe the ache there. After a while she sighed.

"It was lovely. Different."

"Better?" He couldn't stop his lips from curving into a slight hard sneer. She seemed to ignore that, looked instead to his eyes.

"Don't," she said gently, "don't. Not when you know what the answer is."

He relaxed some then, even though he guessed he'd known all along. "I'm still curious Ilana. Just wondering why—was all this in your head for long?"

Not really, she told him tiredly, not consciously. And the whys of it, well, they had nothing to do with him. He laughed then. Saying sure, sure, that's what Dorey'd told him too. Nothing to do with him at all.

"Then tell me. Where do I fit in here?"

She hesitated before shaking her head. "I don't know Sarge. I barely know where I fit in right now—that's the truth."

He believed her. Asked what were her plans exactly? I'll wait, she told him, just wait. Her voice shook. And him?

"Let me tell you something, Ilana." He leaned farther away from her. "About me. I committed myself to this project, right? This swim. I want it. Understand? I want it. And her, she's a swimmer, one of the best of the best—know what that means? Not all this muscle, not so much this shit"—his arms outstretched, hands flagged and flexed so the thick bulk rippled all over—"as a good heart. Strong heart for the pain. So when it starts she keeps going and when it gets worse she still keeps going. That's all! The heart here! Just heart, this heart—" The words strangled. He'd been tapping the left side of his chest. His eyes were wet. "So you do what you want," he whispered. "I want this swim. More than anything else right now. More than you. See, she wants it too. Needs it. Maybe almost as much as I do." Sarge stood. Head drained and pounding, he paced. He turned to Ilana. "Where did she go?"

"She wouldn't tell me. But she'll be back."

"How do you know?"

"Because," she said softly, "I said I wanted her to come back."

"You're pretty sure of yourself there, aren't you?"

Bugs whirred high-pitched metallic sounds. Outside they bumped faintly against the screens. She remembered one dive from seventy feet. It had been perfect. Perfect because she recalled no pause between the sequential movements, it was all a long fast graceful flash of motion through air. Bad dives were the ones where something stood out in your memory afterward—a slight spread of the legs, perhaps, on entry, that tiny imbalanced twist here or there. But this one had been perfect. Later she hadn't remembered even breathing. Back-flip. Jackknife.

"Now let me tell you something, Sarge." Her voice was calm, almost effortless. Sure of herself—well she was. He'd been sure of himself always, and so instinctively, and now he spotted it immediately in her. This was what it was then, this kind of certainty that happened once you claimed something as yours by right. "She needs to sleep at night. I think you'll agree. I can take care of that, you know. I can because I want to." Empty, her fingers strayed. They tapped like moth wings on her knees. "You know, since Matt I've thought a great deal about this, caring for someone and what that means. I think I don't stretch my limits enough sometimes. Not since he died. Or maybe even before that I didn't—I cared only on my own terms and never really tried testing the boundary lines or car-ing for someone on their terms instead, or maybe some com-bination of the two—oh, I don't know, it's difficult to explain and maybe I'm too tired. But I do know this. I've given myself permission to try. I'm going to love her and I'm going to do a good job of it. That's all. That's all." Her arms sagged towards her knees then, voice softened. "It's not too much, Sarge, not really. It's not much time at all."

For a while they said nothing.

When he sat his look was questioning mingled with a weary kind of regret. Reading his expression, Ilana was surprised.

"I'm not sure," he said quietly. "I don't think I can be with you while you're doing this. Whatever you're doing. I don't know if I can."

She nodded, reached for him. She held one of his hands in both of hers, and as she caressed it he returned the pressure only slightly. She spread his hand against the upholstery and stroked each long finger. It was like the rest of him—enormously strong, large but with good shape, a kind of refinement that overcame most suggestion of brutishness. Her arms trembled dully and wanted to rest.

Sometimes she'd look back and see things—her life—spread clearly before her like a map, or some multipaneled painting. A pond, a cliff. The tropics. Dark-haired boy. Family. A picnic. Umbrellas. Mountain range or two for background. All impressions, dashes of watercolor, no room for pointillism in this picture of her life. Then across the sky shot a projectile of some indeterminate form, a comet of many bright colors. This was her husband, and his path obscured everything beneath, above, around, so her life was a background for the flaming missile that was him. She'd chosen him, accepted that willingly. Now she'd stepped back just a little and could see, if she peered carefully enough, some of the details his journey had camouflaged. She didn't cling to them. Simply noticed them, for the first time, and could see clearly that she would not have chosen otherwise—what he'd contributed in terms of light and warmth and texture was irreplaceable and utterly singular, overwhelming. It was just that, without him there for the briefest moment, other, smaller, darker images became apparent. A young woman. Sand. Some waves. Herself, moving among them. She wondered whether it was for some intrinsic value, in these other things she now saw, that she was willing to risk losing him—or was she willing to risk that simply for the odd clarity of vision itself. She didn't know. He could change her with a small motion sometimes. Gravely, she leaned down to kiss his hand. She curled there on the sofa, let a cheek rest against the back of his hand. Then neither of them moved, or spoke. They were silent and still like that for a long time.

It had been a sleepless night for Anne—they'd had another fight. There was something a little different about this one, though, more extreme maybe. On her way to the pool she tried to make some sense out of it. His sudden flashes of desperation that led to his own brand of violence. Came from fear, she knew—it always did. Still she felt tired, insides scraped raw. When Dorey called it was a welcome diversion. And she'd been planning on a good swim anyway. Great, she said, sure, what brings you here? And by the way congratulations. I heard. Everyone's heard. You did it, you know, you really went out there and blew it all apart. Congratulations, Dorey. The reply came back well thanks, thanks a lot. She was in town for a medical, she said, just checking up. No, Sarge wasn't with her.

Meeting at a specified corner, Anne was glad to see her. She felt her own exhaustion a little more but refused to let on, talked rapidly as they made their way to the right building, wove down a couple halls to the locker room. Once there she kept on talking. Hyperactive, someone had called her once. She'd scoffed. Hyper? Wrong, she corrected them, the proper term is *manic*. There was more grandeur in mania.

In the locker room they undressed. And Anne talked.

"Anyway, I said to him, 'Don't knock the breaststroke Coach, my father says it's the oldest stroke there is.' Imagine a nine-year-old brat mouthing off to *him* that way." Anne stripped, laid each piece of clothing separately on the bench while she talked. First the shoes, the socks. Jeans. "He took it in his stride though, give the man credit. He invited me to sit and have a serious talk with him about this *entire proposition*, which appealed to me of course, and there we were sitting at the side of the pool when everyone had left, and here was the best coach in the state trying to convince this brat that I was —still am? right!—to try the backstroke instead. Just try it. Hah! He was a gentleman."

"Did you?" Dorey straddled the bench. She twirled the lock combination and her hands shook again, slightly. Well talking took all of Anne's energy, she wouldn't notice.

"Did I what?"

"The backstroke. Did you try."

"No! 'No way,' I told him, 'I want to swim breaststroke. I want to swim breaststroke at the Olympics, I told my father and he says it's a good idea.' " She fiddled with the top blouse button, pulled a locker open.

Dorey slipped her own lock into the handle. She hauled her shirt up over and off, hid fists inside the crumpled material, pressed down on the bench. They still trembled. Anne winked carelessly.

"I think he must have been tickled by it all, here was a brat telling him what she had in mind, sometimes I remember and I can't believe it. But he had *craft*. That's the making of a good coach I guess. He spent quite some time considering. At least he made it look that way to me. Then he asked—very gently, mind you—what exactly I had against the backstroke. And *I*" —she patted her left breast gleefully—"said the first thing that popped into my head, which was a phrase I'd heard my oldest brother Bill use once and I'd always wanted to say it myself. 'Because I won't take anything lying down,' I told him. That was the clincher. All right, he laughed, fair enough, we'll see, he'd like to speak with my father and if everyone seemed agreed then he'd also like to coach me. And I'd have to get up early every morning to be there on time with the other girls. 'I'm never late,' I told him. 'Never.' At which point he became immediately stern, all business. You know the type. 'You'd better not be,' he said, 'that's the first rule.' " Anne grinned triumphantly. "I never was."

"Me neither."

"Yes! I could see that in you. So *serious*."

Dorey blushed. "I was. I was that. Well, I am."

"No kidding. Hey, want some?" She squeezed Vaseline onto her hands and offered the tube to Dorey.

"Thanks."

"When I die they'll cremate me. That's what I want, no two ways about it. Just up in smoke, and when they peek into the jug I'll bet they find chlorine powder instead of ashes. It's bad for the skin, so bad. Almost worse for the hair, though. Have you slept, by the way?"

What? Dorey asked, suddenly upset. Anne focused on her for the first time that morning.

"Have you slept? Not that it's any of my business but I

thought your hands were shaking for a while there and then I thought, ah-hah, maybe you didn't sleep last night. Exhaustion. On top of the race, you know, sometimes it takes a while. Oh what am I talking about. You know all that."

Standing, Dorey pulled everything else off. Clock on the wall said seven twenty-five. She grabbed at the locker door to hold those telltale hands steady. You could smell chlorine but nothing else.

"I slept. I slept well."

"Good." Anne's eyes darted elsewhere. All her buttons were undone now and she parted the blouse delicately before letting it slip off, folding it to the bench. Above her right nipple was a mark, blue-tinged at its center and reddening around the edges. Nothing playful.

"Did you?" Dorey asked.

"Did I what?"

"Sleep well."

Anne caught the direction of her glance and moved almost involuntarily to cover that bruise, then dropped her hand and just nodded. "No," she said quietly, "no I didn't."

The lockers were that dull metallic color like orange peels. This early they were alone. Before seven forty-five it was mostly just the pros and the fanatics and everyone had a lane reserved. Out at the pool all you'd hear would be an occasional splash. In here their voices echoed and, when there was silence between them, you could hear showerheads drip on the adjacent area's tile.

"I'm sorry," said Dorey. "You must be tired. When I called—"

"You didn't wake me."

Dorey hung things in the locker. Everything just so, she'd done it this way forever, socks folded next to shoes on the top piece of shelving, pants on the right, shirt the left, bag at bottom and lotions waiting in the bag's side pocket. She got out a couple of suits, pulled on one and then the other. While she did Anne observed her the way she always observed—took in everything without appearing to at all. She shook her own hair back and it got damp and heavy on her neck. Most bodies looked clumsy in these places, caught between unrelenting lines and bleached to putty texture by the damp fluorescence. Dorey looked good though, her touch of awkwardness having nothing to do with physical motion. That's what it was, some kind of discomfort Anne couldn't place. Hard one to figure out. She shrugged. Dorey'd suited up and was sitting again, waiting. Her hands were steady now, Anne noticed.

"I'm holding up the show."

"That's okay," said Dorey. "It's all right."

Anne stood and removed all the rest. She looked tiredly at Dorey's double-suited body that followed her own curves so similarly. Compare torsos and they were sisters. She stepped into the first suit and eased it carefully over that breast. When she did so Dorey looked intentionally away. Then Anne had something figured out, she just didn't know quite what yet. Time, she told herself, give it time. Her brain would click in on target. She had faith in that. That dead-on faith you had for a bull's-eye. String, nock, aim and hold, release, follow through. She missed target practice.

She got into another suit, this one blood-red.

"Do you want to do distance? Or quarters?"

"What about just a few miles."

"You're on. What time do you want to make?" She grinned. "Better than Parisi? You did it, you know, you really went out there and did it. How was it?"

"Ah. Interesting."

"Do I get to hear a blow by blow?"

Well okay, Dorey told her, sure. But later.

She was getting anxious, wanted to be out at the pool. Just be there and then somehow things would seem okay for a while, she knew. When Anne leaned over the bench to retrieve a shoe her back made a perfect arc, bridgelike.

They both locked up.

Along empty rows of benches their bare feet stepped silently. They passed the mirror and Anne caught a side glance, saw Dorey looking too and she laughed then.

"Ah-hah. Is it vanity or curiosity?"

They passed into the shower stall area.

"What?" Dorey turned it to warm. These questions stinging out all of the sudden made her uncomfortable.

"Your fascination with mirrors."

"Fascination?"

Water spurted. From the next stall Anne's voice echoed. It was blurred by the shower's force, amplified by tiles.

"Fascination. For lack of a better word. I caught you looking."

There was that frozen feeling again. Dorey turned the knob to hot. "Looking," she said weakly. "No, really. Really. Not at you."

"*What?* I meant at *yourself.*"

Her sunburn, she'd forgotten. Quickly rolled the knob back to warm and breathed relief. She shut it off and stepped out, plucked towel, caps and goggles from the wall hook and watched curtains parted in front of the next stall. Anne emerged as if stepping out on stage to take the spot, suits and skin drenched and hair dripping.

"Okay." Dorey faced her. "I was looking."

"There!" Anne gave her the A-okay sign. "A little narcissism never hurt anyone. In my case a lot, that's just the way it is. But I always thought there was a touch of it in you somewhere —there had to be." She grabbed her own towel and tossed it over a shoulder as if it were a cape, or long sash. "For all that world-class time in that bitch of a bay—you *ought* to be a little narcissistic, don't you think?"

"I don't know."

"Don't you?" Her voice softened. "You know, I'm just trying to figure you out, that's all. If it bothers you tell me to go to hell and I probably won't listen anyway, but I guess I'm looking for your ego. It's there, isn't it." She swung her goggles around, shook out her caps to keep them from clinging. "I'll tell you what, forget about this, all right? I feel lousy this morning."

"Are you okay?"

Behind them drips sounded. The locker room door swung on its hinges and there were rustlings from in there. Seven forty now, things would start to get populated.

"I want to swim." For a second Anne's voice was a little unsteady. "It's good you called. To tell you the truth, there's nothing else I'd rather do this morning. And anyway"—her tone brightened—"I'm waiting for that blow-by-blow. I know that water, it's the kind of swim you write home to your husband about, right? Or your boyfriend." She met Dorey's gaze and smiled casually. "Or whatever."

"Where is she?"
Tycho held the door open and stepped aside.
"Come on in. You look tired."
Stalking through every room, Sarge looked like maybe he'd glance under the beds, or in closets, to find her. In Tycho's bedroom he turned wearily to catch Tycho standing out in the hall, watching.
"She went swimming," Tycho said softly. "Just this morning."
"In a way you didn't have to call. I could have guessed she'd come here. Don't ask how, just intuition." He tossed his stuff down and sat on the low-framed bed. "Know what I used to wish, Johnny? That I'd just go crazy. After Matt died, I mean, I used to wish for total insanity. Seemed like a blessing."
Tycho sat too. "You want to talk about it?"
"No. If she got here last night I'll bet you've had an earful."
"I mean Matt. Maybe we can talk about Matt now."
"Go to hell."
"No thanks." Turning, he jammed both hands under Sarge's knees and lifted so the legs swung, off-guard, onto the bed. Tycho slapped a calming hand against his shoulder. "You know I like the cold. Get some sleep captain, huh? Get some sleep."

"You on permanent vacation these days?"
Tycho's long legs spread like prongs out of the armchair. "I've scaled down the practice pretty drastically. And no more surgery. Not for a while."

"No kidding. The stars warn against it?"

"Not exactly. They just told me it was time for something different."

"Different."

Sarge sprawled on the carpet, using the sofa as a backrest. He'd done that since Tycho first knew him—it made Tycho wonder whether Dorey'd picked up this habit of avoiding furniture from him.

"Different. The next reasonable step, I guess you'd call it."

That and the bare feet. Sarge, he wanted to say, my friend, look at how you're emulated. Sarge you've been unofficially adopted, be proud.

"Well, what the hell is it?"

"I'm not quite sure. They didn't specify." Tycho grinned. "So I'm just rowing these days. Just rowing."

"Is that it?"

"Maybe."

It was midmorning and no buildings were buried yet in shadow out there, sunlight heightened everything and a fresh kind of warmth poured into the open living room windows which even city air couldn't quite putrefy. Filled Tycho with a kind of nameless longing—nostalgia maybe, a sort of pain that felt alive but dimly recognized, like an old memory or long-suppressed desire. He told Sarge some of it. The rowing, how it seemed the key to things for him now, why, he couldn't say. Just his intuition saying to row, pursue that motion relentlessly enough and suddenly things might become clear. Or perhaps the clarity wouldn't be perceived suddenly but would seep through to him inch by slow inch. Either way clarity was what he sought now. The next step. Because he'd spent so much of his life concentrating on the heart of the matter, and now maybe what was left was to use his own matter to arrive at another heart. "It's strange, Sarge. This realization came to me one morning that of everything I've experienced in my life, the accident"—he motioned towards his nose—"psychologically obscures everything else sometimes. It's affected me more, inside here, than a lot of other major experiences. I remember it more clearly, you know, than the first time I made love! How do you like that? Not that it's for anyone to like or dislike, maestro, I know. But that says something, doesn't it."

Sarge nodded. Saying hell Johnny, poor bastard. Then he laughed dully. "Look who's doling out sympathy."

"Empathy. Why not, if you've got it to give."

Sarge was on his bare feet now, stalking again hands in pockets, back tight beneath his clothes. Tension, all that tension. Sometimes Tycho wanted to cry for him, but crying was something neither of them was too good at. So he simply concentrated on remaining open, heard his friend's occasional statement. Sarge answered a lot of his own questions— it was his way. Tycho listened, guessed he might not be any good at crying but at listening, well, that was something he could do.

"Ilana." Sarge's fist tapped the wall.

"What is it, Sarge? Apart from all the standard guidelines of behavior, I mean. What exactly bothers you about it?"

"What do you think?"

"I don't know! I can imagine for myself, or try anyway, but I can't say for you."

"The hell with you," said Sarge. "Jealousy, goddamn it."

"Jealous of her? Or of Ilana?"

"The hell with you Johnny." He turned and sat suddenly like a big statue crumbling at the knees. "Both of them. I'm jealous of both of them."

"There," said Tycho.

Sarge closed his eyes and sunlight paled his face's bronze. He still looked fatigued.

"Do you really think it's sick?"

"Hell no. I just said that to hurt her."

"It worked. She's afraid of you losing respect for her. No. Of rejecting her."

"What the hell am I supposed to do? Celebrate?"

"Oh," Tycho breathed, "I don't know, captain. It's complex. It's difficult."

The sun burned a hole right through the back of Sarge's head. He could feel it, feel his hair turning whiter, losing color by the second. "Christ Johnny, I'm tired."

"Sometimes love comes to you. To anyone. Sometimes. All

a matter of timing, Sarge, when your time comes nothing stops you from opening up to it. Does that make sense? Sometimes it comes disguised as a woman. Sometimes a man."

Sarge gave a questioning glance. "You believe that? For yourself?"

"I'm not sure. I don't think so. But maybe that's due to conditioning. Or maybe I'm not evolved enough yet—I don't know."

Sarge shrugged. What he wanted to do was sleep. "Hot day, huh?"

"Go stretch out for a while," Tycho said gently, "get some rest."

The floor of the room was sand and the bed a kind of flotation device, in the corner was a small insect and the insect watched him. While it watched it grew.

Matt's bones jangled over him. Some green flesh hung sadly to a few joints. Daddy, said the insect. Daddy.

He woke up sweating through his T-shirt and hearing Dorey's voice. She was there in the front room talking with Tycho. He felt washed clean by the familiar sound of her voice and then the pain slammed him full force again, along with that sense of betrayal.

What had he half-imagined all those hours watching her go endlessly back and forth in water. The countless sets, reps, the different schedules and intervals, all those baths ago, those massages ago, the muscles taped, skin greased. Swinging her in his arms. Sure he'd imagined things lifting her into a bath, from tap water to pool water to lake water and the next step was to give her to saltwater. Swinging her in his arms both of them dripping water. Maybe he'd wanted to climb in too, strip completely, step off the edge just once. Easy. It would have been so easy, way back when he and Ilana'd done it a lot that way, in a bath or a secluded spot of water somewhere, warm water it had to be, slow water, he'd just reach for her with both hands and slide her on top of him.

Sarge stood and opened a window, took off his shirt and let

himself cool. He showered, borrowed Tycho's razor and shaved, drew some aimless designs on the mirror. He changed and felt healthier. Voices murmured through the walls. Sarge opened the door. There they both were, Tycho in the armchair as if he'd never left, and there she was too on the floor gazing immediately up at him. She was all his pain, all his betrayal, and sitting there she looked good despite everything. Damned good, there was just something beautiful there to him. He couldn't have made her better out of clay.

"Want to come home?" he said quietly.

She nodded.

Did you ever love a man?

You mean this way. Maybe. No. No, I don't know.

I find you very virginal sometimes. No, that's not the right word. Idealistic. You see, I used to think it was a kind of naiveté on your part but now I think I was mistaken, there's a certain brand of emotional idealism that masquerades as naiveté. My dear, if you expect too much you'll always be betrayed, betrayed badly.

Ah. No Ilana. You're wrong. You're wrong about that.

Am I?

Uh-huh. Sure. Why do you believe things like that. Are you going to hurt me?

Shhh.

It's all right if you do. Betraying's different. That means lies.

"Idealistic." Ilana smiled. "Very."

Sarge hadn't stayed long once they got back. He just dropped her off, then was on the phone and away to Washington. See about some things, he said. Put in some distance while I'm gone, a few days' worth, huh? He asked her how much money she had up front now, was it what she'd calculated originally? She told him a little more, showed her own calculations and then threw a checkbook, savings book, green bills and change out on the table. Well he could have it all, all of it she said, plus the prize money. He looked through some. She'd saved a surprising amount over the years, couldn't have been from the swims. I worked, she told him almost apologetically. After Seal Beach, I worked. Anywhere. I just saved everything. He didn't press her on it, there wasn't time. Told her good, maybe they'd need it. Do it right, no fooling around.

Somewhere in the house was Ilana, she could feel her, and he seemed oblivious to that fact. Dorey put invisible nails through her limbs so she'd stay motionless in the chair. Be back in a few days, he told her. Work.

"Uh-huh I will Sarge, you know I will."

He was out the door without stopping to shave. He had a small carrying bag and briefcase, had thrown a jacket on, and the sunlight gleaming off his hair when he was halfway out the door made him look good again so she followed him up to the road. They had to wait for a cab from the nearest town. It took a while.

"Are you tired Sarge?"

He shrugged. He waved a little when the cab pulled away and Dorey watched until it was into the trees. She rooted up yellow-flowered weeds on her way back. Their stems were milky and warm in the warming afternoon, had a thick bitter taste when she crushed them against her tongue.

After Matt died he stopped sleeping with me for a long time. I'd get up in the middle of the night and wonder where he'd gone and then be afraid to look because what if I couldn't find him. One night I decided to look and I found him outside lying on an open sleeping bag. He was in deep sleep, utterly still except for his breathing. The smell of pines was very strong.

You were lonely.

Oh it was more than that—despair and this sense of futility, I wanted so much to be dead but didn't have the courage or whatever it takes to kill myself. He looked beautiful that night. So still. Like a big strong dark statue. Then later I realized he'd looked nearly lifeless, and I thought perhaps that's why I found him so beautiful, I'd fallen out of love with Sarge and in love with this idea of death and of being dead because somehow maybe that would get me to Matt.

"Ilana." Dorey curled Ilana's hair around both her fists in white-swirled balls like yarn. "I think you're beautiful alive."

Look. It's getting dark out. I ought to tell you now because I'm feeling very honest and maybe won't feel this honest again soon. I don't want this swim to happen. I'm afraid.

Ilana come here.

When it starts to get dark I feel it most, I feel my own age crawling up on me and there it is, nothing to be done about that. Fear's strange, so strange, it's tangible sometimes like a taste or a color. Sometimes I feel it less for myself than for someone else. You. I'd rather dive through a loop from sixty feet up—ah, you're laughing, but it's true, it comes from being a mother. I don't want you to step into that water and I know you will. It's all right Dorey. It is all right anyway, everything.

They were on the carpet. Dorey pulled a blanket up around them both. There was that slight chill of evening. "Well. Maybe you keep mixing me up with Matt somewhere inside. But listen, women are better at swims like this. Our bodies. More endurance, I mean. Women are superior."

"Superior? Do you really believe that?"

Dorey nodded seriously. Saying gently don't be so surprised Ilana, you said yourself I'm idealistic, maybe that's part of it. Women. They're made more for the water. We just fit it somehow, I don't know. But it's true. Look at the records. The distance. Well never mind. Do you miss him now? Do you miss Sarge. I don't know what to do, Ilana. When he comes back.

"Do you miss him?"

"Dorey." She heard birds nesting from the trees. They'd fan wings to shelter their babies, cluck and puff to twice normal size. I'm afraid to lose him, you know. And I might, but it would be for this kind of pain that has nothing to do with you right now, it's something in me and it's something in Sarge. I don't know if both pains are the same. I think they're not. He doesn't want to be with me now.

Because of me.

Because of *me*. And him.

Ah. That's just part true. The rest is me.

My dear, you shoulder too much responsibility. I know you're strong, so strong, it's not noticeable until you're close up and then it seems striking. To me. But if you'd permit it again I could take care of you sometimes, you know, you might be able to feel some of my strength too and relax. Don't you feel it. There. There. Do you. My shoulders aren't as broad as yours but they're not frail by any means. While you were away I think I decided something. I think I decided it's all right if you're my child sometimes, that's just part of the way I feel although not all of it or even most of it. But a significant part, yes. Is that all right? Is that all right with you? And I'd like to, now, to give you something perfect. Something *superior*. There. Ah. All those muscles and you're still very soft, that's remarkable. I understand myself a little now, do you feel that. Shhh. Shhh. Lie still.

Outside the last bird wings beat. For a while there wasn't any wind and everything hung suspended, damp and quiet. Felt like it could rain.

Before Seal Beach she'd talked a lot. Never fluidly, never brilliantly, but enthusiastically and a lot. Since then rarely. With Ilana it was different. She forgot to censor. Well, most of the time. They'd turned out lights. Night breathed in and she was thinking of Sarge in a way that ached. Flashes of Sarge once in a while knifed her thoughts so the spoken words would stop, painfully, and patiently Ilana would wait. She felt her waiting. That presence was calming. One night, Dorey told her, it was right after Seal Beach, I did something before I went to bed that night.

"I did it, it was a little strange." She gave a small sudden laugh and glanced at Ilana, then looked away uncomfortably. "You're going to think I'm crazy, you know."

"Maybe, maybe not. It's okay."

"Well I went into the hallway closet where Carol kept her sewing supplies and I found her pin cushion and got a needle. Then I went into the bathroom. You know how in biology class in high school sooner or later you have to prick your finger for a blood slide. I was always good at doing that, I hardly ever even flinched. Anyway what I did over the sink was I pricked my finger with the needle"—in the dark she stretched out an index finger, jabbed towards it with the other —"and squeezed. To make the blood come out faster. See. What I thought was how it's mostly water anyway, right? All that bodily substance and most of it's water and a lot of it's red. Well I kept squeezing so the blood kept kind of popping out on my fingertip and then I wrote 'water' across the mirror with it in these enormous, drippy letters. Looked like the title of a horror film." She laughed. "Then I washed it off and I rinsed my hands in the sink, and I splashed some cold water on my face and then I just kept splashing it and splashing, I couldn't stop. After a while I felt better though. Then I went to sleep."

There was breeze across the lake now. It hadn't rained after all.

"No," said Ilana softly. "No, I don't think you're crazy. Here. Like so. Can you sleep now?"

She could.

"Cut it off. Just *everything*—I expect to be shorn. But it's got to look appealing, too, leave a little here." Anne tugged at the hair flowing thickly against her neck. She smiled for the brilliantly lit mirror. "And here."

Joe took that threatening stud pose that said he disapproved. He pouted.

"What's wrong?" she asked impatiently.

"We've spent months growing it out."

"I changed my mind."

"That's not like you, Anne."

"Oh come on! What do you mean?"

"You're not capricious. Once you decide to do a thing you do it. No. I don't want to. You're not going to walk out of here"—he twirled the scissors deftly, tapped the handle against his chest—"walk out of here and tell the world Joe did that to you."

The hair-drying lamps around them fired occasional mirrors

with hot circles of reflected orange glow. Anne caught a whiff of conditioning lotion and her nose wrinkled. She explained to him that she was on a tight schedule, time was of the essence and she had none of it for explanation or apology. Still his face was sullen.

"Joe. It's important."

"*Beauty* is important, Anne. There's something lovely about you now, really, you have this way of sitting that turns ordinary chairs into thrones—"

"Flattery gets you zero, pal."

"It's the truth!" he snapped bitterly. "Take it off and you're another dumb jock."

Anne sighed. "So be it."

Grimly he went to work. Her hair was thick, wet, dampness making it darker against her forehead, obscuring its fair highlights. After a minute he paused, shears and comb poised delicately above her as if about to perform neural surgery.

"Do you think I'm too feminine?" His voice was shaky.

A thick damp lock stretched out with the comb. Clip, went shears.

"I think you're feminine. But what do you mean by *too* feminine? Too feminine for what?"

"For the planet earth."

Anne laughed. Told him the planet earth probably didn't care who was feminine and who masculine, it was too busy with volcanoes and tidal waves and anyway, the earth had no right to judge since earth itself was female but who would call it feminine. He clipped methodically, gave her a narrow-eyed look.

"Please explain."

"The earth is the womb. The sky's the *fertilizer*. It's standard symbolism. From the ancient mystics on up through the alchemists I guess, et cetera, father sky, mother earth. In Spanish the heavens are masculine and the word for earth feminine—"

230   "Well, do you think I'm too feminine?"

"Joe. Can you blow that smoke away from me? Whew. Thanks. No, this is the way I see it, I think anyone can be feminine and anyone can be masculine and those qualities shouldn't be defined by sex. There."

He sighed. "You're so squeaky-clean liberal, Anne."

"What do you expect?" she grinned. "My oldest brother is William Randall Norton the *Fifth*."

"Money," he coughed, "money. At least you're not a fascist."

"Just a dumb jock."

Another lock pulled flat out, another subtle click, click. He was tapping away gently, reluctant to see the inches go. He shook his head but continued.

"Let's save it, Joe."

"What?"

"I'd like to save the hair. Why don't you just cut it into a bag or something?"

"Oh," he said, "I'll tie a blue ribbon around it too."

"A good dumb jock color. As long as it's blue."

In the end he couldn't find any that were blue but did come up with a dark violet one. Ah-hah, she told him, if it was not first-prize color at least it was the color of royalty, didn't he think. Joe agreed. He tied it carefully around the neck of the bag.

Scissors snapped with a fresh calming sound from every direction. While her hair dried beneath lamps—what was left of it, anyway—Anne realized that to Joe she was in large part a head. To shear that head of its hard-won glorious mane— and her hair was thick and richly colored, she admitted its beauty proudly—was to him a kind of crime. That the beauty of the head region might be forced to take back seat to the functioning of the rest of her body was not natural to his way of thinking. He wasn't thinking rough water or bathing caps and he wasn't thinking triceps. She grinned and the Anne Norton grinning back was Anne Norton the swimmer, pure and clear and nothing else.

She tossed her head. Felt different. Nothing brushed silkenly on her neck or cheeks. It felt a lot lighter. Her face changed now, more revealed. She noticed where she'd gotten older. It was all suddenly obvious, and while in one sense she guessed she'd have been considered prettier before, she felt very apart from the weight of all the hair that had been so pretty, felt—in a way—free.

Joe adjusted the heating lamps again. He lit another St. Moritz and with the first puff winked apologetically. "What will you do with it all? Store it in a cremation vase and mourn?"

"I'm giving it away as a gift."

"How kind. Well." Standing behind her chair, he examined her reflected image. "I did my best. What do you think?"

Anne was silent.

"That's beautiful," she said finally, firmly. She nodded towards the mirror, then twisted around in the chair to look up at him. "Don't you think. It's all functional, Joe, just functional and that's what counts." She gazed back at the mirror and blew a kiss to herself.

Joe held a hand mirror up behind her so she'd see the back of her head doubly reflected. "Are you swimming across Lake Michigan again?"

"What? *Michigan?* No, no way."

"Why not? You look ready for some sort of action."

"I am. But Michigan's in the past."

"What's in the future?"

Anne shrugged. Her eyes did their swift dance away. Cups of coffee steamed on tables, there was a low hum of hair dryers. She smiled. "I don't know, Joe. I forgot to rub my lamp this morning."

"Too bad for your genie."

On the street she turned once to see him watching from the window. It was a storefront window, the interior mostly obscured by huge potted tropical plants. Among the waxen green leaves he stood. He waved once, sadly.

Anne kept walking. Sometimes when she shut her eyes the city was there before her. Uptown. Midtown. East Side. She'd spread herself all over it. West Side. Downtown. She could smell hot dogs and mustard and hear the slap of racing flats on reservoir earth in the summer. Or feel that sweat from inside saunas, see boats chug slowly up the East River. She remembered the time and moved crosstown more quickly, finally hailed a cab. The bank was air-conditioned, made her feel a little lightheaded. At the teller window she reached to caress a leaf from the potted plant near the counter and found it was plastic. She jerked her hand away.

"Norton," she repeated flatly. "N-O-R, yes, that's right."

She played around a little with the trust fund and got things rearranged to her satisfaction but it took a while. Then she tucked money away and on the sidewalk hailed another cab.

Anne had read once, long ago, about some tribal custom of the Navajos. Or maybe the Hopis. Maybe neither and she guessed it didn't matter to whom this custom belonged so long as it existed. When a member of the tribal community committed an antisocial act, the custom was to surround the offender and shower him with gifts. The more heinous and violent the crime, the greater the gifts. In this manner the perpetrator was once more urged to become a member of the community. He was absorbed back through this elaborate process of begifting.

At the right places she did some shopping. She knew what she wanted and it was merely a matter of evaluating, comparing qualities. Gold was waterproof, and one of the things she purchased was a waterproof wristwatch that also functioned as a stopwatch. There was a silk-rimmed hat too, she'd written down the correct measurements. Some other things. She charged it all. Anne didn't bother with prices, never had. The one thing she bothered with was overseeing gift-wrapping. Everything had to match what she'd had in mind. About that she was quite demanding.

It was hotter than usual for this time of year and on the streets bodies stifled. Traffic spumed clouds over fenders and hoods, stopped bumper to bumper along the avenues at red lights. It took quite a while for another cab. Anne persisted. She was good at that, endurance. Finally one swung over to her side and she was heading downtown.

On corners you could smell flowers. That reminded her. She had the cab stop and bought roses, the deepest scarlet she could find. The layered wax paper slowly became damp around the stems. Getting out of the taxi finally she had to maneuver for money, hitched things under one arm with difficulty, entered the building and on the second floor landing had to stop and refocus. For a minute she didn't feel able to continue. Then she picked everything up again and went one more flight.

"Hey pal, calm down. What's up?" The mutt made a fuss and she set things on the rug for a little roughhouse, pulled his ears, pounded his chest, shook paws and slapped his rump playfully. He nibbled her hand without biting hard.

Anne found his rubber bone and tossed it gently so he'd gnaw for a while and leave her alone. She went through all those wrapped gifts in insulated bags and dug out a square hat box. Why they stuck round things in square containers she didn't want to know. She listened for sounds but there was only the squeaking of teeth on rubber. Crouching on the rug, she pulled the lid off and removed the hat carefully by its rim. Just as carefully she set it on her own head. It was oversized but she liked the feeling. She'd have to check it out in the bedroom mirror. Quietly Anne picked everything up again and, hat loosely shadowing her face, she headed for the bedroom.

At first she didn't notice him, he was so still at the drafting table. On his stool, deep in concentration, his back was turned, and when she stopped in the doorway she saw he had on those khaki trousers that were too big. They hung around his waist, flapped on his thighs and calves so his legs dangling off the stool looked for a second like a little boy's.

"Hey! What happened to your meeting?"

"I sent my rep instead." He didn't turn around.

She crossed silently to the bed and dumped everything. Then to the mirror, tried to arrange the hat in some semblance of style and gave up, lousy fit. A fop. She smiled.

"I got you a few things."

"Huh."

"You're not curious."

He turned then and when he saw her set the razor-point pen down.

"The hat's for you." She kicked off her shoes, sat on the bed with wrapped boxes, and did her best to tip the brim politely. "But you can't have it until later. You have to open the rest of this stuff first."

"Is that an order?"

"Yes."

Quietly he slid from the stool, approached the bed with care. She saw that he'd lost a little weight during these past few weeks and so seemed slighter, but it was more than that. He appeared younger somehow, too, almost diminished. Rick perched tentatively on the edge of the bed. He held his hands up to her, palms out.

"Ink," he said. "Is that all right?"

"I like ink."

"But will it stain?"

"Just the wrapping paper."

She watched intently as item by item he unwrapped everything. He did it meticulously, laying paper with its loose strands of tape on the quilt. Once in a while he glanced up to see her watching, face shadowed beneath the too-broad brim, her expression unreadable. After a while it was all there on the bed between them among semi-crumpled wrappings bearing expensive trademarks. There was the waterproof wristwatch with an inset that blinked seconds and tenths of seconds. A set of oils, red tones, rust colors and crimsons, several brushes of varying numbers. There were other things, all silks and gold and Shetland wool. There was a waterproof windbreaker, designer cut, navy blue. In her lap she held a brown paper bag tied with purple ribbon.

"Put on your wristwatch."

He did and time clicked silently against his wrist, gold dully glowed.

"Here."

Rick took the bag from her hesitantly, making sure there was no accidental brushing of fingers. He held it in his own lap, unopened.

"You know," said Anne, "an expert told me once that there are these vast ruins under water just off the coast of Bimini. In the Bermuda Triangle by the way. They think it's what's left of Atlantis but of course no one knows for sure because of

235

course the more conservative elements of the modern scientific community tend to disregard phenomena with a mythological basis, one of the self-imposed limitations of our age if you ask me. As a result these ruins just stay there unexplored. No one can get funding to explore them, not officially anyway. Rick. You don't even have to dive for this one. Why don't you open it?"

Untying the ribbon, his fingers were clumsy. He wondered why they'd gone numb and wished he could touch her instead. He stuck a hand in, pulled out a couple of locks, looked from the thick shining strands in his palm to her shadow-brimmed face and back again, his own forehead puckered with questions. Calmly, she lifted the hat off and set it just so on his head. It was a perfect fit.

"Benton Harbor," he said, "it was that short then." He held the strands out towards her bunched in his fist. Like his face, his voice had in it a childlike desperation. "Once it's not attached to you—hair—does that mean it's dead?"

"Yes, I guess so. Of course it grows back though, *fast*, let me tell you. Like amoebas." She grinned. "Or starfish arms."

She reached for him and he made the plunge across wrapping paper, scattered long-stemmed roses, and crushed boxes. The hat shadowed both their faces. It brushed her neck, tilted darkly over her breasts when he kissed them. He smoothed lips on that spot where the bruise had been, now faded, and what came out of him was a half-sob.

"Killed."

"Sweet man," she held his head gently against her, caressed his neck under the dark silk brim, "don't you know. Things die all the time."

"What's she like?" Rick wore the wristwatch and hat and nothing else. He rubbed thick lines of charcoal on the sketch pad with his fingertips, once in a while glanced at Anne to get his bearings.

"Who?"

"Dorey Thomas. Look, try to hold a little more still, Anne.

Just stay—well, you can breathe, you know. I didn't say not to breathe."

"Thank you. Thanks a lot. It comes as a relief."

When he wasn't looking her hand crept across the sheets, patted the dog's head and got drooled on. He growled contentedly.

"Well?"

"Well what, Rick?"

"What's she like?"

"Dorey Thomas? She's strange."

The quilt was a mess of paper, roses, and charcoal smudges. Stub of charcoal poised, Rick stuck his tongue at her and wiggled it. The phone rang.

"Shit."

"Don't answer it," she said.

They let it ring a long time. Then it gave one short half-whistle and stopped. He grinned.

"Hold it, Anne. There. Great. What do you mean by strange?"

Anne thought. For that moment she was still, naked, cross-legged and regal against a background of pillows. The light thick capping of hair gave her a starker appearance, drew more attention to the face's individual features, the full lips, fine line of the nose, the broad forehead—sign of good blood and intelligence she'd always said, tapping that forehead, a sure sign of royal lineage, let me tell you—and it highlighted her eyes.

"For instance. Sometimes when she talks—and she doesn't do much of that, take it from an expert—she sounds sort of stupid. No, that's not the right word. Bland. Monotonous. And yet I just get this very strong sense that she's really intelligent, somewhere underneath, she seems to understand a great deal and have interesting thoughts on everything, she just doesn't tell you what they are."

"Can you give him his bone or something? Please. If you don't sit still—"

"All right. All right. Come on pal, get your bone. Find your bone, where is it? Find your bone."

"Thank you." Charcoal dusted his ankles and the sheet. "What does she look like?"

"Ah-hah. Maybe that's partly where the strangeness comes in, I'm not sure. You'd probably think she was pretty. Dark hair, pale skin, nice eyes and nose and mouth and she can walk and talk too, just think—"

"You don't like her."

"No! No, that's not true—I think I really *do* like her. Honestly. You know what it is about her, though, she's kind of flat. That's it, yes. Her presence, it's very flat, I think maybe she's just asexual."

"Asexual?"

In the midst of the black-shaded figure, his fingers paused.

"Yes. She's really not very feminine, not at all. But on the other hand she's not masculine either. She's just—"

He waited, and after a while looked up to mark that for the first time in his memory Anne seemed at a loss for words. He watched her eyes dart uneasily, and while the rest of her was immobile stole the opportunity to sketch in a little more. The hat bobbed snugly with his head.

"Just what?" he said gently.

"Just a *swimmer*. It's as if she's"—Anne giggled and her eyes brightened—"as if she's underwater all the time. Everything, all her movements, are at this very *measured* sort of pace and so are her reactions. Do you know what I mean? So whatever there is, really is, inside there, you just don't catch even a glimpse of it when you're with her. Hardly ever, that is."

"She doesn't sound anything like I expected."

"What did you expect?"

"That she'd be a little like you somehow."

"We're *built* a lot alike, actually, you'll be surprised." Anne grinned with satisfaction. "Although I'm taller. But up here" —she tapped the royal forehead—"there's no one on earth who even resembles me."

238 He had to agree.

"In the water, though," her voice softened, "she's incredible. It has to be seen, has to be. I kept thinking when we worked out together that *this*, this was what Greta Andersen must have looked like or maybe Florence Chadwick—I'm just talking about stroke now and how high she rides with her kick, it's terrific, it's absolutely beautiful and she's pretty fast when she gets down to business and you know Rick, you know, there's hardly a ripple left behind. It's *pure*. You know the old formula of form follows function. Well that's her. Yes! Yes, form follows function, that is Dorey Thomas." Leaning forward, she glanced at his half-completed sketch upside down and then resumed her position. When she spoke again her tone was wistful, made him look up suddenly and examine her eyes. "Do you know who I think she reminds me of most in the water?"

He shook his head.

"Me."

"Oh," he said cautiously, after a pause, "does that upset you?"

No, she was saying, no, not particularly, it was not that which upset her but rather the idea behind it. "Seeing her swim alongside, I realized something all of the sudden. Do you know, I've never seen myself swim, I've been inside of it all the time. Of course. But I realized there was nothing left —of me, of my style—nothing captured or recorded from what I've done. Oh there are newspaper articles, sure, and some photographs in archives somewhere and a few records, et cetera, but once you do something like a swim that's it and you've done it and then it's over. It can't be filmed like a road race, no film or video could ever really, I think, catch a swim the way they do track and field, because the element's so foreign. The water. So swimming with her I had a chance to watch her go from a very close approximation of her perspective, because there I was keeping pace, and what I realized was that watching her swim was, in some way, the closest I'll ever come to seeing myself."

Rick rubbed the paper gently. He examined it before holding it up for her inspection. He'd given her a Robin Hood hat with quill feather. Anne Norton in charcoal gazed back at the Anne Norton sitting there naked on the bed in living color.

After a while, she moved the sketch pad calmly aside and leaned forward to kiss him.

The lake rippled. Across the water Dorey could see more pines at stiff guard, tops pointing darkly into the sky like pyramids. It was that time when stars went out. Somewhere something splashed. Lake creatures were dark like lake bottoms and lots of them nocturnal. Such splashes were telltale, therefore rare. Once she'd gone up to that lake with Burns, third or fourth time he'd taken her for an open-water outing, and she remembered floating placidly on her back one Sunday afternoon after a swim and taper-down, and emerging on shore some kid playing by the water's edge pointed to her back screaming. So she'd glanced around at both shoulders to see them speckled thickly with leeches, and both arms, both legs, her neck. Burns was there with his powders and oils and lit matches, saying think this is bad, other places they're four times as big, once I had to bite a few off. That's right. Yeah, bite. With my teeth. Like a dog.

Dorey picked up a few damp stones and threw one. She couldn't see its dive but heard. If you think women are superior then you must see yourself as such, Ilana'd said. Especially since at what you do you're one of the best among women, doesn't that make you superior to most women as well? Dorey'd mumbled something about how she didn't know, it wasn't as simple as that. She tossed the next stone. Burns always told her when you were good you could afford to be humble but don't get carried away with humility. Still, look at Anne Norton. Anne was better than good and she wasn't humble, at least didn't appear to be. Well maybe she was humble somewhere, in some important way, and maybe while she'd been looking for Dorey's ego it was under her nose all the time, waiting minute by minute and year after year right there in the water. Dorey rubbed her shoulders. Keep the circulation going. She threw the last stone hard and far. This time there was a longer wait for the sound of entry.

In the dark she knew. It was not a question, really, of superiority when there was just you and the water. You couldn't prove anything against that and the most you could do was last in it for a few days maybe, a pretty pathetic period of time when you thought about all of time. It had just reached out and smacked her one day. Think you've been great all along but it's all a joke really, you're fragile, what holds you together isn't much, just this skin and bone stuff and this muscle, these nerves here. Think you're a giant. Huh. Think so. You can be undone just like that kid, like that. Easy. Here. Here is some humility. Not anything you have to strive for, understand. It's just what you are, humble in comparison, nothing else you can be. Pretty small. Would you like to dance. Went crazy, they'd said. Everything was fine and then whammo, went nuts, just like that. And the reports she'd sneak glances at. Psychotic episode, depressive personality, borderline, schizoid. Schizoid with repressed homosexual tendencies. No, she wanted to tell them, no, uh-uh, don't you know none of that matters. Crazy, they said. Well maybe. Maybe. Still they said that on land. Had they ever been inside a wave.

Dorey pulled off her shirt. Knees soaked through by the wet earth, she searched by touch for another stone. Finding one she stood. She tied it securely in the shirt's sleeve and then, beginning slowly, she swung the weighted shirt around her head. Swung faster and faster, it made whip sounds in the dark, then when she'd stopped feeling her arm at all released. Hearing the faraway splash she applauded.

She headed back towards the house. It was just about summer, dew drenched everything. The sudden enclosed stillness of indoors seemed hot after the cooling damp. Sarge was away again, this time for four days. Washington. There was a boat now, had to check it out and then of course arrangements. When she went down the hall she found herself pausing at his door out of habit, trying to sense if he was awake or not. He'd come back from the first trip still tired. Stayed just a week and put her through the wringer with sprints, sprints, sprints, and a couple of long lake swims, then there was another phone conversation one night and he was away. Do some intervals on alternate days, he'd said, you know the schedule. While he

241

was home she swam like a maniac. Avoided looking at Ilana whenever possible, but some nights she'd be in the hall and stop there in front of the door to his room and she'd glance from his door to Ilana's and back again before pacing restlessly into her own room, open the window and breathe deeply waiting for sleep.

Tonight Ilana's door was wide open. Ilana half-slept, folded in the sheet like a wing-wrapped moth. This sleep for her was a limbo because she felt herself dreaming but was also conscious of the room, the air, funny how you could hear air at this time of night, it was as if all the starlight that had faded left invisible remnants behind buzzing not quite inaudibly. The past couple of weeks she'd found herself suddenly attuned to these insignificant physical sensations even in sleep, and because of that she'd felt a change take place in her. Her sensitivity to the physical heightened, some part of her intellect deadened. She'd begun to move moment by moment these days, without much thought. Instinctively. She hadn't lived primarily by instinct since before becoming a mother. When she stopped to take note of that it felt like backsliding, more than just a little terrifying and also, somehow, exciting. What is it, she whispered to Dorey, half asleep. What is it dear.

Ilana felt herself drifting away, then back again. A woman sat on the edge of her bed. Maybe she'd dreamed her up, too, along with the sound of air, but she didn't think so because she could reach out and touch skin there, a naked female torso and hands that matched her own. Maybe they were her own body and hands she touched. She drifted.

Once upon a time.

"I'm listening," said Ilana.

"This is a story."

Someone rocked back and forth on the bed's edge to a steady, monotonous rhythm. Then the lulling motion stopped, the voice speaking was sad. Asking, do you think I'm crazy too? No, Ilana smiled, no I think I went crazy myself a long time ago, I think I'm a bad judge of sanity.

"Ah. Well do you want to hear a crazy story? We can both pretend we're sane—"

"Bravo."

Once upon a time. Except this was in the future, it *is*, I mean. Or maybe it just happened so long ago it doesn't matter when. It was a war. It was the worst. Everyone had to hide if they could. Anyway, there was a woman—she was pretty strong, she was in good shape!—a swimmer.

The face that glowed above Ilana in the dark changed expression suddenly, shifted back again, then transformed to still something else as if the features were melting, or as if all the hard-sculpted stability of the mask had become liquid. Ilana tried to wake up. Felt for a moment she didn't know that face anymore, it was an embodiment of someone or something else, and then along with that half-dreamed prickling of unease came an undeniable sort of fascination. A *swimmer*, said the person sitting at her side, a good swimmer. She had a baby.

"A baby?"

"A girl. She had a daughter. So she knew they had to hide, Ilana. Where do you think they went? Where would you go?"

Ilana shook her head. Saying she didn't know, it depended on the circumstance.

"Uh-huh, that's right. That's good!" she gestured with excitement, gave a smile of approval. She was Dorey again. Ilana woke up another hazy inch, relaxed a little.

Well I'll tell you. There was this sewer system that went under the whole city. The water was pretty deep down there, you couldn't stand up in it but you could swim. She made this basket for the baby with straps and everything. It went across the back of her shoulders. That way she bet she could swim and still carry her daughter mostly out of water. Because she knew she had a good strong kick so her upper body rode high. That was important. This woman put on all her suits and all the caps she had too, she knew it was going to be cold down there, and a pair of goggles. She just wrapped her daughter in blankets and strapped her into the basket. Then she strapped the basket like this, straight across her shoulders. She went in at night. That's when the water was at its lowest. She spent a long time calculating that so she'd start out right. She knew, she knew all about water. She followed the water. It was cold,

243

it was so cold and dirty. This was a night swim. Remember in a sewer there's never light anyway. Just the dirt underground and water. She was afraid but she knew there wasn't any choice, not really, it was follow the water down here or else die up there on the ground and then her daughter would die too, so this was the only thing she could do. That's when you do what you couldn't normally do, when you just have to. Sometimes things touched against her in the dark. Slime. She wanted to scream every time. Only she didn't. The baby slept. That was good. If she'd been crying maybe they would hear from outside. She kept stroking the way the water flowed. Once in a while she reached out to make sure they weren't headed into a wall. She tried to keep count of the strokes. That way you can tell what time it is. But she got tired and lost count, she couldn't help it, she'd been up for so long. It went on forever. That's what she thought anyway, and the basket started to hurt really badly. On her shoulders, I mean. It got hard to lift her arms.

"Dorey."

"I'm right here, right here."

Don't worry. It's okay if you sleep Ilana, I'll just stay right here, I won't leave. Sometimes now she thought she heard sounds from aboveground. I don't know, like people screaming or things falling maybe. But maybe she imagined that, she was delirious. She kept wanting to drink the water but knew it might kill her. She kept swimming. Then she thought there was some light ahead there, she didn't know for sure anymore, see it was at that point where you don't know if it's hallucination. Well it took another few hours maybe, maybe more. Her teeth were chattering, they bit into her tongue and she kept swallowing blood. But she swam to where the light got stronger. It was real. Then all of a sudden, just like that, there they were in a river in the daylight where this part of the sewer system flowed into. She was lucky her goggles were so fogged. She couldn't see the banks of the river, they were stacked high with bodies, and she thought they kept bumping into floating logs or garbage. But they really were hitting floating corpses. Well. She wanted to crawl out on land then, she wanted to so badly, all she thought about was touching the ground and then she would stop being thirsty and so hungry. Only she knew she couldn't. She just knew to keep going, that was all. The baby woke up and started to cry. They had to go into the water after her. When they found her. But that was later.

"Who?"

"The ones who were after her."

The men who were killing everybody, them. See, Ilana, she made a mistake towards the end there. Well I don't know. It was a mistake for her but she did it for her daughter. The river forked off at one point. One fork went on ahead through some woods. The other went on to the ocean. She felt that she was going to die soon, she couldn't last much longer. So she stopped at the fork. There was shallow water there. She hit the bottom with her knees and undid the basket straps, then she sent the basket with her baby in it down the fork going for the ocean. When she stopped like that, they saw her. They were watching from land to see if any of the bodies floating there were alive. Anyway they pulled her out with grappling hooks. They couldn't catch the basket though. That's a true story I think. Do you think it's a happy ending? Ilana, I know you won't go on a boat again. You won't be there. Well that's all right I guess, that's what you have to do and it's okay, don't worry about me. It's just a day. That's all. One day and then it's over. If the current's bad and we don't hit it right maybe a little more, thirty hours at most. Like a trip where you wave and say I'll see you tomorrow. Look there, the sun. Just about. Last night you kept staring at me so strangely, as if you didn't know who I was.

The sun streaked her face and breasts. Ilana opened her eyes, saw her sitting there and reached to hug her.

"Dorey."

"Hi there." She stroked Ilana's hair. The way Dorey held her was encompassing, protective.

"Did you have trouble sleeping?"

"Uh-huh."

"You're a little muddy here."

"I took a walk this morning."

Ilana was crying.

"Ilana," she said quietly, "all this, does it hurt too much?"

"The truth of the matter is," said Ilana, "in some way, I need you now. And want you."

Inside Dorey sunlight burst.

Do you know who I am? You do, you dreamed me last night and before. That first morning in October you woke up I was just outside there at the doorway, standing against the screen like a shadow. Remember, Ilana. I waited there like I waited before and all those years wanting, waiting, just the swimming and working and waiting. Didn't talk much, just to myself in the water. Maybe you dreamed the rest of me. The Dorey out of water, on land, she barely existed before. See what you've done. I was waiting so long, Ilana, and wanting. I worked so hard. Do you know. This is part of what I waited for.

It was June sixth.

Anne leaned out the car window, waving.

"I dare you, Sarge. I dare you. Get me into better shape than I'm in, just try."

Bending to kiss her through the open window, he squeezed her upper arm playfully. There was no give.

She grinned. "Nautilus."

Driving in from the road, she'd caught a view of the whole set-up, house that expanded to hold more than a dozen extra bodies, long corridor attaching to the poolhouse. The grounds leading everywhere to pines, lake breeze blowing across grass, and that spectacular garden, a track just up the road. Perfect, she'd thought. She'd have chosen to train here, sure. No fighting crowds to reserve lane time, or skimming magazines that told you the only swimming records worth reporting were set in pools by Olympic wunderkinder. Hauling some of her stuff from the car, Anne had to smile. She'd been one of those herself. "It's good to see you, Anne."

He lifted a couple of suitcases out, and when he straightened sunlight showered him, emphasized the black thick hair 246 and his dark-toned face and arms. He seemed a little tired, or uneasy somehow. It didn't matter though, the old guy looked terrific.

"You"—she linked arms with him—"are pretty incredible looking, you know." He blushed, smiled with pleasure. Funny about men, she thought, except for the most vain—and who wanted to bother with them—they weren't trained to accept any estimation of their physical beauty. Call them pretty and they fell apart. Too bad. She'd always guessed that if times were different and roles more easily reversed in public, she'd gladly stand on street corners with a bunch of women to whistle at the men walking by.

Anne's smile teased. "Ilana's got good taste."

Uneasiness flooded around them. Anne tried to shrug it off.

"Speaking of which," she said innocently, "how is Ilana?"

Okay, he said. Then he was silent, walking with her towards the house. She didn't pursue it.

Sarge stalked at the pool's edge. He glared down towards Anne, and if she couldn't see him clearly she could hear and feel it.

"Put some *guts* into it, damn it. What the hell are you up here for anyway?"

She pouted.

"You don't have the raw talent to go out there and wing it."

"Sarge." She gestured nastily. "Don't you have any new words of wisdom?"

"If you'd make some decent time you wouldn't have to listen. Or talk. On your mark."

The whistle screamed. She bolted right in, a good set this time, he could tell. He grinned. Coaching, training. How to get the best out of a swimmer. She responded well to that high-demand pressure. Pepper it with plenty of tension and a lot of noise, continually setting specific standards of performance, and you'd gotten to the place where her motivation lived. Everyone different. You had to be sensitive, to know that. He'd never have raised his voice with Dorey, for instance, except to let her know he was pleased—with her it was there on the surface, the willingness to just go all out and really hurt, as if she were anxious to hit that sky-high point of pain and the sooner the better. Thing with her was knowing how and when to hold her back. But Anne you had to dig out flamboyantly. Sarge figured he'd just be Jekyll and Hyde for a while. Strange, though, looking at them out of water you'd have thought maybe it would be the other way around. He guessed water had that effect—made some extroverts while they were in it, others introverts who withheld their best effort —and the type you were in water sometimes couldn't be predicted from the type you seemed to be on land.

Anne busted through to the set's end and hung on to a gutter ledge. Water spilled from her nose. She hated it. She'd forgotten how much she hated it.

"Quit fooling around!" he goaded.

"Go to hell, Sarge."

The whistle blasted again and she shot cleanly through that water like a shark near blood. Sarge beamed satisfaction, clicked the stopwatch almost as an afterthought to confirm what he already knew, it was her best effort today.

"Getting there!"

The whistle shrilled. She couldn't feel a thing except rage. Good thing about sprints, that flat-out rage, turned the water to red right in front of her eyes. Hated it. She'd forgotten how much.

Some time later she was crawling in slow motion from the water, moving across the floor in a dripping, reeling cloud.

Good, he was beaming, nice work.

"Out of my way, Sarge. I've got to throw up."

"It's warm today."

Hand on the anchored rowboat's gunwales, Dorey grinned and even through goggles Anne could make out the mischief in her expression. It caught her off guard. She didn't see Dorey's other hand sculling swiftly to splash water.

"Hey!"

"It's warm. Aren't you coming in?"

From the stern Anne dove. Where she disappeared the surface foamed in circles, swells glittering silver with sun, black in the shade. She bobbed up gasping a few feet away.

"Damn it!"

Dorey laughed.

"Damn it!" Anne moaned. "You trained here in *April?*"

"Uh-huh."

"Whew!" Her arms were treading swiftly to stir up a little heat, legs half-circling an egg-beater kick. One thing about cold water, you had to be there.

Dorey hung calmly from the boat. She seemed composed to Anne and not at all suffering. The goggles protruded from both eyes like a bizarre mask, and despite the cold Anne giggled a little to think that she herself looked that way too. Behind goggles you were interchangeable with anyone else.

Breathing got easier. Anne began to feel her limbs again. Still, it was cold. Now she understood the Laughing River victory better and, despite herself, was filling up with respect. Not that it was anything she couldn't have done. Rather, it was because she knew what went into the training that she had to be respectful.

"April." Anne splashed back and smiled.

"Well," said Dorey, "you were looking for my ego."

"Ah-*hah*."

"See the buoy out there. We can loop around and back—"

"Like Lac Louie?"

"Well sort of. But together." Dipping her face in, she filled her mouth and spouted. She was smiling. Anne couldn't remember seeing her so relaxed, not even in a semideserted city pool. In open water what billowed from her like an unseen halo was formidable self-assurance. Loop around and back, she was telling Anne, go fairly easy, two complete loops to the mile, okay?

"You're on."

"I'm breathing to my right. Every two strokes."

"Let's go," said Anne, "face to face."

The water was dark near the shore and dock, clearer once you got out towards midlake. Lake water. Anne spit some out. It was her least favorite to swim in. The bitter cold, the darkness of these surfaces, both qualities she detested. Still she'd done well on the circuit in summer's full stride, competing up in Quebec where they had the last word on cold water. Good training ground because it was so tough and dense and gave

249

you so little. Ahead, her hands sliced water as if detached from her. She kicked gently and breathed to the left. Dorey's face breathed back at her. She'd set an easy pace and, already numb, Anne felt a hint of gratefulness seeping through to her insides—courteous in the water, yes, she guessed you could say that about Dorey. There was no competitive edge here, tension had sloughed from her.

Mozart. The viola quintets. C minor. Anne hung on to that initial chord, it was sad, so sad, and vibrated. No instrument like it, no. She'd chosen viola at a late age because it seemed to her to be what she called a well-rounded instrument, and by that she meant it reverberated with rich, broad tonalities. And she wanted to play. Instead stroked monotonously. Metronome. She was freezing to death, this stuff was pretty ridiculous. An identical face breathed back at her. Freezing. The water clung dark and icy, made her fingers clumsy blocks. No hands like these could finger delicate notes now. Steadily she stroked, breathed to the water and the air and that other face moving effortlessly alongside her own. A part of her hung above it all and ran her bow across a small open tin of resin with a silky clean squeak, looked down at the two bodies moving rhythmically through dark freezing lake and giggled. Ah Norton. You're probably nuts. Maybe back home the doctoral committee was disintegrating again. Maybe those arrows at the indoor range were rotting in her locker, no tournaments this year, her hands were clumsy these days. No marathon for sure. Not even glory this time around. Norton, she said, Norton, you really are nuts sweetheart. Just for the pleasure of the saltwater to come and all that nausea stretched out over the course of a day. Lovely. She breathed, thought she saw Dorey grin but it couldn't possibly be. Sure here you are Norton swimming in this lake with this woman whom you don't really know. And for what. She breathed. At the buoy they changed sides.

Only Anne stayed there, circled it, reached out an almost reluctant hand and then just hung on. She pulled goggles up onto her forehead. The buoy swayed.

Dorey paused, then did a quick reverse. Anne smiled. Lifeguard training. Well she'd done that summer-at-the-beach number too and still remembered the guys' cars flashing like their teeth, like their tans, and the smell of vinyl oiled with Coppertone or vaseline when she leaned back against it. Dorey approached the buoy, finally rested an elbow on its rim. She cocked her head.

"It just occurred to me."

"What?" Dorey said.

"I've got no idea"—Anne struggled, decided the hell with it, full speed ahead—"no idea who in the world you are."

Dorey was silent, expressionless.

"All right," said Anne, "what's the story?"

Against the buoy, water lapped. They weren't moving much now so cold crept up on them and, at just about the same time, both stirred up a little heat kicking casually underwater. Their palms rested on the buoy, slapped the water's chilled opaque surface. Sunlight reddened their shoulders.

"The story?"

"Yes. What's your story, *muchacha?* Because I'm going to be looking at you I don't know how many times off and on for a pretty long stretch in some pretty nasty water, and I guess I just want to know who it is I'm looking at."

Dorey gave a funny smile. "At nobody," she said finally, "okay?" She surface-dove and came up yards away, headed swiftly back for the dock by herself. Anne watched water rise in domelike bubbles around that simple, strong kick of hers. Then she got angry and slid goggles back in place, set out after her. The water was cold as ever but this time Anne didn't feel it, she was too busy sprinting to catch Dorey Thomas the way she'd done so often before she'd forgotten how often, busting gut just to catch up to that woman ahead who kept that maddeningly unchanging pace. Anne put on some Olympic Trials speed. Norton, placed first in the 200 breaststroke to qualify. Right. She translated that into freestyle and, a few feet from the dock, caught up.

Clinging to wood, Dorey turned.

"Cut it out," said Anne. "You owe me."

"What?"

"A good story." Anne smiled angrily. She was surprised at how angry she sounded.

"Well I don't tell stories."

"You owe me, lady. I'm not getting in that water with a lunatic you know. Are you? Crazy, I mean. Well are you? Rumor has it, maybe you've heard. Why don't you set my mind at ease."

"All right," said Dorey, "that's all true."

"*Bull*shit!"

It rang on the water.

Anne's feet were numb now and, clinging to the dock post, she laughed, yanked off goggles, tossed and heard them plunk on the dock. Then she hauled herself up, sat there at the edge dripping. She pulled a couple of caps off and threw them over her shoulder. The sun felt good. This was her element, heat and sunlight. She gazed down at Dorey. After a while reached to offer a hand.

"Come on. Let's be friends, I dare you." Her palm hung, open and empty. "Want to arm wrestle?"

Dorey paused, treading. Then she grabbed hold of Anne's wrist and let herself get pulled partway up. She threw off her own goggles and caps and they sat there silently for a few minutes, soaking up heat.

"You've got fingerprints, don't you?" Anne teased. "And once you had an umbilical cord, right?"

Dorey grinned a broad, long-lasting grin. "Uh-huh. Once."

"And a birthday—"

"Yes."

"And a mother?"

"Ah." Dorey's voice got softer. "Everybody does."

"I guess that's *true*." Anne stripped a twig. She sharpened it against the dock, swiveled it in air like a broadsword and then it was a spear that she aimed carefully, tossed up towards the sun, watched angle down to vanish with a tiny splash. "But you could have fooled me. My mother barely existed in our family, you know, all I remember is my father, he was so dominant. She just took a back seat, sort of followed when she could and went to the right parties with him I guess. She played some golf—"

"Babe Zaharias?"

"Not quite. But she was pretty. *Was?* She's still alive, what am I talking about? Well! I guess *that* says something, doesn't it?"

They were walking up among the pines. Dorey kicked through needles, silky sharp against her feet, for some reason the texture just now reminded her of sand.

"With me," she said, "it was the other way around. Carol, my mother. She was always there. She encouraged me." It was more than that, she knew. More than just that but how to really explain what it was like to be so close, so close to that private pain of a mother when in fact you were only a daughter. "When she—when she was in labor with me. I found this out much, much later. She was in labor for nineteen hours—"

"Nine*teen?*"

"Uh-huh. Nineteen hours, three minutes and twenty-one seconds." The statistic sounded proudly in the woods' hush.

Anne laughed. "You sure had some good training to start with."

"Me?" Dorey frowned. "I meant Carol. I was talking about my mother's—"

"Ah-hah! But don't forget yourself—all she had to do was push and not pass out, right?"

"Wrong."

"Oh, okay. I'm simplifying, of course, I've never had children and don't intend to and so much for that. But listen, even if what she went through was worse than a hundred miles' cross-country skiing on lousy surface, say—stop laughing! I'm serious!—aside from what she went through, don't you think it was a lot rougher on you? You being the one who had to get *out* of that mess in the first place?"

Dorey considered it. After a while told her maybe, she didn't know.

"No," Anne demanded quietly, "that's not good enough. What do you *know?*"

"Well. That you can't say I went through anything aside from what she went through. We were tied together. You too." They looked at each other openly and a little uneasily. "You were tied to your mother for a while."

"A shorter while, I'm relieved to say. Nineteen hours?"

"Uh-huh."

"No wonder," Anne chuckled. "No wonder the 1500 bored you."

Dorey laughed. Saying lucky thing it did, too, she hadn't been much good at it anyway. Not for indoor competition. Just an edge too slow, that's what Burns said, and now, chucking pine cones and breathing in the summer afternoon, she guessed it was just as well after all. Except it was funny, wasn't it, the way different people came to the same thing in different ways—here she was and she'd never have ranked too well even nationally in her best indoor event during her best season. And here was Anne with an Olympic medal. Dorey stopped, blushed. She'd been talking a lot. She couldn't remember the last time she'd talked this much to anyone but Ilana. Then she grinned. An Olympic medal, she repeated, and a rich daddy.

"Ah-hah! You've got it!" Anne beamed. "A very rich daddy. What about yours? You've got one of those too, don't you?"

"Uh-huh. A few."

"Sounds interesting."

"I guess."

"No way!" Anne's eyes sparked back. "I'm not letting you get away with that one, either. Tell me."

"What?"

"About the *daddies*. A few of them, right? Now that sounds like a good story."

"Well," Dorey smiled reluctantly, "not really. I could tell you their names I guess. Look. That doesn't matter. What matters is my mother, why she bothered with them in the first place. I don't know, I think she couldn't be alone. Maybe she felt she would die without one."

"One what?"

"A daddy. No. I mean a husband. A lover. Well they were all decent guys really. It's just that—I don't know—"

"You do too!"

"Okay! Okay!" Her voice lifted with annoyance, face darkened. For a second Anne thought maybe she'd gone too far but then saw Dorey considering, struggling without malice. "Whatever she was looking for," Dorey said quietly, "she didn't find in any of them. But she kept trying. I think maybe she wanted someone to take complete care of her. Well no one ever could." Her face paled slightly. She met Anne's eyes. "No one was big enough for that. I mean, strong enough."

They sat damply on grass, talking. Leaning out the full-opened window of his study, Sarge caught a glimpse of them there and watched a moment. Dorey looked excited about something, she was gesturing with her hands the way he'd seen her do maybe once before, and the sight of it caught him off guard. Shoulders arched, arms outspread like wings, and those fingers fluttering while she said words he didn't hear. It was a little like seeing a strange bird about to take off in flight. Sarge pulled back inside. Into a well-polished tortoiseshell. The map was spread on his desk and weighted at all four corners. When he felt that familiar raw ache in his chest, he sent it away. Still, it came back. He'd brought it back by clicking an internal camera shutter to seal this picture of her inside along with the others. Something about that broad-fanning arch of the back, hands caressing air delicately at the ends of those long, strong arms. It was the striking swift grace of that movement, along with the blankness of her back, that made him conjure up the rest of her. All the rest of her he didn't know. Whatever thoughts dug in stubbornly, unexpressed, behind the face. Or the way her breasts looked dripping water.

Between her teeth Anne twirled a coarse strand of grass. The sun felt great. Stretching out, she luxuriated. For all her expensive taste, she didn't require much for that feeling of luxury, just a few simple elements. It was what lots of people liked about her. It was what made her look at Dorey sometimes with a far-off glimmering of recognition. Form follows function. Inside herself, Anne figured she believed that.

"You don't have to answer, you know."

Dorey told her maybe she wouldn't. But first she had to know what the question was.

"Right. Oh well, why not. Damn the torpedoes."

This was the part Dorey'd been hating all along even before

it happened. She froze a little, got that intentional slate-clean expression going that gave nothing away, and looked at Anne, waiting.

"All those times you beat me—were you ever afraid you'd lose?"

She relaxed. Not what she'd anticipated at all. She leaned back on the grass herself, enjoyed the full heat of sun on her thighs and shoulders. "Uh-uh. I didn't think much about it."

"What *did* you think about?"

"I don't know. The alphabet."

"I'm serious."

"Me too! Really. Really, lots of times I started just sort of going through the alphabet. See." She held up fingers, counted them off with her eyes closed, twenty-six times. "Then I'd get tired of letters and I'd start numbers."

"You mean," Anne scratched her head in perplexity, "one two three et cetera?"

"Yes. Guess how high I got to once." She blushed. Anne waited, mouth open with surprise. "Seventy-eight thousand twenty-six. That's three thousand and one alphabets."

For a while they were silent. Anne listened to birds chatter. "What happened after that?" she asked.

"Ah," said Dorey, "I finished. Second. That was Australia."

"Personally," Anne laughed, "I'd hum to myself."

"Music?"

"You bet. Mostly Haydn. But towards the end there—my last season on the circuit, I got onto this Mozart kick. And when I started doing 'Aase's Death' from that Grieg piece, you know, *Peer Gynt*, I knew! I knew it was time to pack it in."

They both laughed. Well lots of times, Dorey told her, I just lost count. Most of the time. Then I'd think about other things.

"Like what?"

"I don't know. My life. Just remember things."

Anne shredded a dandelion. She blew tiny yellow particles off her palm and they melted against the sunlit air. Ever think about sex? she asked. The question hung like dead weight, an unanswered challenge. If she'd thrown some gauntlet, Dorey was steadfastly refusing to pick it up.

"Ever think about sex?" Anne repeated. "I know I do. I just get *fixed* on it for a while, that's how I tell the time, when I start fantasizing I know I've been in at least seven hours and the wilder my imagination gets the longer I know I've been in." She gazed at Dorey, scrutinizing. "What about you? Ever think about men?"

"Not much." Grass prickled against her back. Dorey blinked up at the sun, eyes defenseless.

"You like women?"

"I'm in love with somebody."

"Oh," Anne said gently, "congratulations." Stretched full on the grass, she shut her eyes. Her hook had come up with the fish it wanted and now, dangling that line into water, she felt it go taut and for a moment didn't know what to do.

Dorey breathed in with relief. Well there. There it was. She was glad it was over and felt clean and loose inside despite the shakiness. Each breath could be honest.

Anne had bounced back quickly, though, and was sitting up, motioning to her. After a while Dorey sat too. "Hey," Anne smiled, "this is the way I feel about it—I know nobody asked me but I'm going to say this anyway—and it's true, really true, I honestly do believe this. If you've got what it takes"—she winked—"to give Beaujais and Parisi a run for the money in that kind of water"—she gave a victory thumbs-up signal—"I don't care if you do it with a baboon."

The face staring back at her stayed blank.

"Is that what it's like for you?" Dorey said.

"What?"

"Is that how you think about doing it. With baboons?"

Anne stopped.

Whew, she said quietly, did Dorey want to take a swing at her or should she go ahead and do it herself?

"No," said Dorey, "uh-uh, I don't hit women."

Anne reddened visibly. Then they looked at each other and laughed, both nodded in some sort of appreciation neither understood.

"Bull's-eye," Anne grinned. "Should we swim?"

"Just to feel out the water. Not for time. A couple of hours maybe."

She stood, offered a hand but Anne pushed off the ground on her own. She turned to Dorey and nodded slowly, saying humility, Norton, humility. She reached a little clumsily and then they shook hands.

In the evening Anne wandered. Things were pretty strange around the place. Sarge and Ilana barely acknowledged each other's presence, she'd see them pass in the hall on occasion without a glance. See Dorey and Ilana at opposite ends of a room, eyes studying the floor, the wall. Or Sarge speaking with Dorey once in a while, giving some pointers, encouragement, stressing a few facts about the swim, and Dorey'd look up at him and reply in that same tone of voice. She was no good at hiding feelings, Anne figured, despite that blank face she'd put on in the water. Stripping off her own goggles once at poolside, Anne caught a clear glimpse of Dorey's face looking up to Sarge while he spoke. The face was remarkably soft for an instant, and vulnerable, and what spread across it unmistakably was a sort of misery for which Anne could think of no cause.

Restless, she tucked her worn copy of *La Celestina* under one arm and turned the corner. She was thinking about Rick. She didn't like it, the way she thought about him all the time, that prickling, tingling sensation along her arms and thighs and belly. It was supposed to be off the record, this one. She'd always been able to see the end of things before, how long something would intrigue her. A few months here, a year or so there. Sometimes an off-and-on intimacy born of friendship, mutual appreciation, even that sibling feeling—like with Matt. At least it had been that way for her, for him she hadn't known, and something always kept her from asking. When you didn't want to know the truth it was simplest to not ask. That was about the only form of running away she permitted herself. With Rick she'd thought plenty of times that the end was imminent or that it could at least be identified as centering around one or two major variances in need. But now she'd thrown something extra into things with him—what, she didn't quite know herself—and the end was no longer clearly defined. Nor was it clear that he was her match, or that between them existed the kind of parity she'd always idealized. He was whatever he was, equal, inferior, or superior, in various respects. So when she thought of him now, it was without comparison or contrast. It was wanting his presence—not a desperate need, but a confirmed want. For Anne, the consistency of this feeling was new.

Lights had been turned off or dimmed in each passing room. It was a silence that made her think about Matt for the first time in a long while. She reached to brush hair off her neck but there wasn't any. Purely classical. Blinking away the sadness, Anne grinned. She turned another corner, passed by the kitchen and glanced in. Nobody there, but through the room's open window she could hear voices. The words came through indistinguishably at first. Then she stopped to listen and with difficulty could make them out. It was Dorey's voice, she guessed it was coming from the garden out there.

"I know I said that. Well I was wrong. It's not all right."

Anne leaned against the wall. She could hear Ilana's voice replying but couldn't understand what she'd said.

"Why won't you?" Dorey pleaded. "It's just a boat. It's just one day, that's all."

"I told you—"

"You don't even have to watch."

The wall prickled along Anne's back. She waited. Crickets were buzzing out there, filling up the silence.

"I can't, dear. I'm sorry. Forgive me but I can't do that for you. I am sorry. I would. I would if I really knew how."

What filled up the silence now were whispers Anne couldn't make out, hidden sounds, maybe somebody crying. Who, she couldn't tell. It was the faraway sound of a faint sob muffled against someone else's shoulder.

Careful not to let footsteps be heard, Anne moved away down the hall, into the dark. There was the part of her that withdrew from it all, acknowledged with grace and dignity what was none of her business and wanted to know nothing more. Live and let live. Then there was the part that spun around inside with a speculative kind of astonishment. She wouldn't have guessed this one. Not in a million.

Sarge rested both feet on the desk. The guitar fell easily across his lap, right hand hooked over to strum, left sliding along the ivory-fretted neck fingering chords. By the time he noticed Anne out in the hallway waiting permission to enter, a mild grin had spread across his lips and he paused just briefly to nod her in, continued while she took a seat. What he'd begun in E minor changed key. After repeating the passage there was a major resolution.

"Not bad." Her sunburnt face grinned gently. "You ought to change that B string, though."

"Been meaning to."

"Do you mind if I try?"

Sarge passed the guitar to her across the desktop. Its polished dark surface caught light, shone.

"You know, Beethoven said"—Anne settled back with the instrument tilted carefully over her thigh—"that the guitar is a miniature orchestra unto itself."

"Right. He was right about that."

"I agree." She strummed an open chord. It's amazing when you think about it, she was saying, the tonal richness along with real elegance. Which in another way was to be expected, didn't he think, considering that the instrument itself was an outstanding example of male and female principles being successfully united.

"What?" Sarge frowned. "You mean the shape?"

"Only in part. What I think matters more"—she picked out a triad, plucked each member of the chord separately before strumming—"is the unique musical character. Look at it this way, Sarge, it's so *complete*. It doesn't need a woodwind section. Or cellos. Or anything else to sound magnificent, not anything."

"Hell," Sarge chuckled, "you make it sound like a god."

"A *demi*god. An androgynous one. Like Bacchus." She laughed. "Or Hermaphrodite."

He gave her a look of mock confusion. "When did you say you were going to be a doctor?"

"At this rate, never. But that's beside the point. Maybe that's not so important after all, you know, maybe things change at different times and life just comes running by and you let it take you along to wherever it's going. Right? New *experience*, Mr. Olssen—"

"Hell. That's not your philosophy, Anne, all this flow-along-with-fate crap."

"Quite right." She stared at him fully. "It was Matt's philosophy though. We used to debate it a lot." She watched his shoulders tense, his entire face set in the act of pained listening. "He told me once that he thought setting goals was fine up to a point, a good way to achieve things for sure. And he —what was it he said? I want to get it right—he said that sometimes all of this racing at world-class time for all of these goals tended to obscure the present. So that we hotshots jump right from the past, or the latest accomplishment, straight into the future. I used to fight him on that." Her fingers beat the guitar surface with tiny hollow thumps. "I used to tell him that swimming was different. Because when you're doing it— you *are* living life while it's happening, there's absolutely nowhere else to go and there's absolutely no one else you can be. And I used to tell him"—her fingers plucked—"that in order to live, really *live*, what you need is concentration. Just to keep on doing something well, and concentrating the entire time, because when you let yourself get distracted that's when you start swimming in circles and that's when they pull you back on board and *that*, that is like dying. So being alive in the real sense—and that means the extreme sense, feeling yourself and what you're doing fully—is a very serious proposition. Death happens when you're distracted."

Sarge shut his eyes. Yes, he said after a pause, I see.

"Now *I*"—she embraced the guitar, tapped a fond hand to her chest—"am very serious somewhere inside here, let me tell you, all joking aside. Like you, Mr. Olssen. Like Dorey Thomas." Her eyes had firmly focused. They never left his face. "Somewhere inside, Matt wasn't. Somewhere inside he didn't much care for all that extremity, you know, and all that concentrated seriousness. He was kind of a prankster and I guess he was really pretty young for his age, after all, very youthful. Sweet guy. He was adorable, Sarge, and beautiful. He didn't have what I'm talking about, that seriousness, not really, not at all, and didn't even know that he didn't. And I thought he was fine anyway. He was my friend."

Inside Sarge something lunged and he reached forward, until she'd extended a hand over the guitar and they pressed each other's hands on the table.

"Mine too," said Sarge. "Christ, Anne, I miss him."

They took a walk late. Sarge knew every inch of ground by heart, led them the shortest path towards the lake. Once in a while they linked arms affectionately.

"This man of yours."

"Rick."

"Right. You love him?"

"Afraid so."

Sarge crushed pine stems. The perfume spilled out sticky on his palm, he opened it to the night. "What," he said gently, "are you afraid of."

"I'm not sure." Anne sighed. "When I was on the circuit everything was generally pretty clear to me. There'd be a swim coming up, I'd train for it, in season I'd be flying here and there for this race or that—everything else and I guess every-one else took a lousy second or third place to the swims. Now things are different. Maybe I'm still adjusting." Her laugh whipped through the heavy warm air. "Norton adjusts again. Listen, Sarge, it's complex. Love makes things messy."

I know, he said.

She shrugged. "Ah-hah. Play on land and you get dirty, Sarge. You get sweaty all over."

He gently pressed her elbow in his, nodded silently. The lake glimmered moonlight back to them. Sarge let it cool his toes.

IV

ICE ANGELS

TAKE IT EASY,'' Sarge urged quietly. He shifted gears and eased the car to a stop. "Take it easy."

But she was out the door before he'd turned off the ignition, and her track shoes blurred speedy markings on sand. It was the southern part of the state of Washington, hilly, hot, August hot. The hills were ocean-carved rock, rising barely enough to hide the flat crescent of boulder-scattered beach beyond, the shoreline and waves. They couldn't obscure sounds though. Watching her sprint up a sandy mound to disappear from sight, he sensed it had been the sound of those waves that gave her extra speed.

"How splendid," Anne said, "are the accommodations?"

"You'll feel pretty royal, Anne. We've got almost the entire ground floor."

The sun melted the chrome-lined hubcaps to a silver shimmer. Sarge hauled stuff out of the car and she gave him a hand.

"Who's on the other floors?"

He shrugged. People, he told her, just people. Anyway, it wasn't of concern, nobody'd be swimming in that water except them.

Anne frowned. "I want to stay incognito."

"Go ahead."

She leaned over a couple of boxes, examining the labels. Then she grinned up at him affectionately. Chocolate bars.

Anne slid onto the car's hood, winced at metallic heat burning her thighs. He stood close and she touched his shoulders gently. "What are you going to do about all this?"

This? he asked cautiously, motioning at boxes, suitcases, knowing it wasn't what she had in mind. He wondered how much she'd been told or guessed. But something inside him didn't care any longer, there was only one thing to care about right now.

"I'm thinking about September. This swim. Beyond that I don't think."

"At all?"

"Not at all," he said firmly.

Her arms went around him, and he rested an unshaven cheek against hers. He rustled a hand through her short thick hair, pulled back and gazed with appreciation.

"I'm glad you're here, Anne."

"Funny. My father told me that once. It was an important moment in his life."

Sarge picked up a couple of cases of glycogen. "What was he up to?"

"Dying," she said, "He was dying."

The hotel sat on a low rock cliff above the sea, wooden balconies and stairways framing its walls on the interior courtyard where there was a rock garden. Windows here and there had been opened, and despite the signs of occupancy—everything kept neat, wood and shutters well-stained, towels draped casually over lounge chairs near the garden—the sound of breeze ringing through wide open windows gave you an empty feeling.

"Captain."

Tycho leaned over a balcony rail grinning. He came casually down the steps.

"Not bad for a retreat. I want you to know I could be in Los Angeles now, there's a convention. I was supposed to present a paper."

"I thought you liked the cold." Sarge opened his arms. "When you said retreat I thought Wisconsin, Johnny. I thought Minnesota. Johnny, meet Anne Norton. Anne, Dr. John Gallagher. You've both heard of each other."

Tycho's arms were large, hard, tanned a dark red-brown that nearly matched the color of his face. Looking, Anne figured there was a good story here.

"I like your boat with wings."

"You've seen it."

"I've seen it."

Tycho laughed. It was the strangest boat he'd ever seen, he told Sarge, asked where had he managed to dig it up. Sarge winked, said he had good friends in strange places. An ordinary, good-sized private craft with double cabin, the boat had been through some custom-designed revisions once upon a time and had been fitted with aluminum arms of sorts, two per side. Each arm was flat-surfaced, exterior edges rubberized, wide enough to step out onto comfortably. These arms lowered, by lever, flat-out into the water from the ship's sides like wings. At the tip of each wing were pontoons rolled of aluminum. So that someone from the boat could hop onto one of these lowered wings off the port or starboard ladder, walk out to an aluminum-drummed tip, and sit. Reach out maybe, with a feeding stick, or talk face to face with a swimmer there in the water.

"What do you think?"

Sitting on boxes, Anne ignored them and tossed back her head, let the heat soak in. Saltwater. Rough-water swimming. It was her favorite. She could taste it.

"Oh," said Tycho, "it's a beauty. Ilana called just before."

Sarge didn't respond.

"For you."

"Hell," said Sarge, "where'd my swimmer go? I'd better find her."

Dorey sat and closed her eyes. You could keep time by it, that pound of waves. Around her everything stretched a bleached gray-brown, coarse sand and, near the breakers, deposits of smoothed rocks glistening in their perpetual bath of foaming water. Seventy miles up the coast was the mainland shore of the San Antonio Strait. The water was the same.

She opened her eyes to the sun's glare. Having arrived at this water, she felt calmer now than she had in weeks. In some way, years—no matter what else had happened. To think of Ilana, or of her absence, wasn't really bearable so she simply didn't think. There was too much at stake. She'd worked too hard to let that interrupt her concentration now, here, where it mattered most. The swim. Somewhere a gull honked bleakly. She didn't even hear Sarge's footsteps in sand.

He sat.

"My mother used to tell me stories. She'd dangle me into the water, wait for a wave and let it wash over me. Then she'd lift me up for air."

Dorey dug her hands into sand. "Were you scared?"

"I don't remember. I guess I was too young to remember. Hell, if I was it didn't stop me later." He squinted at her sitting there, eyes half closed like some kind of Buddha. "Interesting person, my mother. Her people were from Turkey, some of them, some of them from Rumania. She was born in Palestine. That's what they called it then. After the Second World War she called herself Israeli."

"Was she the one who taught you? To swim, I mean."

"No, that was mostly my father and a couple of good coaches. Anything you want to do badly enough you'll teach yourself anyway. Right? But I guess you could say she was the one who introduced me to water."

Seaweed dried darkly along the sand's damp part. Gulls picked through it for bugs and dead fish.

Dorey laughed suddenly. He started at the sound.

"What's up?"

"I don't know Sarge, I was just thinking. It's funny hearing you talk about your mother. I never thought about you having a mother."

Hell, he told her, everybody's got one.

"My mother," she stretched arms up to the sun, "was a good mother. Only she kept marrying men. About three of them. I think she was afraid of being alone."

"She alone now?"

"Uh-huh." Heat brought moisture out on her forehead. She could smell him now next to her, a distinct male smell mingled with salt and dry seaweed. "I used to always want to take care of her. I mean, somebody had to. Well that's what I thought." Again she laughed. Umbilical cords, she whispered to herself, umbilical cords. She grinned at Sarge. Her hands formed a scissors.

268   "Come on," he said quietly, "let's do some work." When they stood, sand showered silently from their clothes to the ground. She linked an arm through his and he was surprised

but then patted her hand very gently. The water sprayed. Waves curled like giant tongues, licked out at them.

They'd all begun to look different, skin toasting by daily degrees to a ruby-tinged light brown. Waking before the five o'clock alarm one morning Anne noticed her own thigh, dark against the stark white bedsheet, and for a second it appeared separate from her, unrecognizable. This is it, she told Dorey later, we're changing. We belong to some other race now, don't you think. Cautiously, Anne hugged her.

Gulls shrieked. Sarge leaned over the rubberized edge of the inflatable to grab both her wrists. One, two, and with the third dunk he pulled her easily on board.

"Good work." He layered her with towels.

Rick swung them around, headed for home. He'd arrived that morning with a receipt from the kennel and visions of a forlorn Boston Bull howling through him. Sarge shook hands while his eyes measured, put him to work immediately. Now Rick had loosened up, felt good handling the vessel, exhilarated by sun and spraying salty wet.

Towel-clad, Dorey stayed at the inflatable's opposite side. She set her goggles down and examined him a little shyly, wanted to like him. If you feel uncomfortable with the man, Sarge had told her, he won't step on that ship I promise. Sure. But Anne wanted him there. Dorey blushed when he caught her looking.

"How you doing?" Rick said clumsily.

"All right."

"You look terrific in there."

The inflatable rocked with swells, breeze sounding along its gunwales like spray from water pistols hitting a balloon. She shivered underneath towels and pulled them closer around her.

"Uh-huh," she said. "Well thank you."

She felt Sarge's hand through the towels rubbing upward

along her spine, all five fingers spanning the area between shoulder blades. Good work, he told her, good work. She grinned for him. Then blushed, meeting his eyes, and when he felt her pull back just barely his fingers stiffened. He didn't know what to say. His throat groped. The words came out softly, he was surprised it was his own voice saying them.

"Mind if I touch you?"

Beneath terror, water rhythmically swelled. She invited the terror to play. "No." She shivered. "Sure Sarge, go ahead."

"Crazy kid." His hands reached under towels and bumped into hers so they laced fingers.

"He needs a towel." The words chattered out. She nodded towards Rick, saying tell him Sarge, tell him. The sun. He doesn't know.

"Hey." Sarge got his attention. "Know the myth about the kid with waxed wings?"

"What?" Rick squinted at him. The harbor was close and they slowed.

"Icarus! Flew too close to Apollo and got a hell of a sunburn!"

Dorey laughed.

"Yeah?" said Rick.

"Well, your wings are fried. Better get that shirt back on."

"Oh," Rick muttered, "shit." He glanced at a shoulder and saw scarlet.

Sarge grinned. "Cold, wet sheets if it blisters. Anne'll love it."

Steering them between anchored yachts, Rick glanced occasionally at Dorey Thomas. She seemed remarkably silent, he couldn't get a reading on her. There was nothing striking about her face. He had to remind himself hers was the same body he'd watched cut through that water for the past four hours like an expertly wielded X-acto blade. Out of water, he couldn't quite see her in 3-D—not yet, anyway. His lips were dry and about to split. For the first time that day his head pounded with sunburn and heat.

Dorey didn't think much about it but suddenly she'd made a C shape under all the towels, leaned forward against Sarge's chest and pressed. Look Sarge, she was saying, is it okay now? She asked in a whisper the wind could have taken away. "Sarge, I don't lie. Not to you." She felt his hands close around hers to show that he knew. He was proud, he whispered, damned proud of her, hell did she look good out there.

"How do you feel?"

Cold, she told him and he held her.

Curtains puffed inward with the night. Sarge smelled damp salt. He dreamed.

When he heard knocks he left bed and slipped on trousers, saying just a minute. Though he went around half-naked like this every day, now it was feeling like an intimate way to look and his chest, all of him, very revealed. Still he appeared casual, looming in the doorway.

"What's up?"

"Were you sleeping."

"So what."

"I've got something to show you. Can I come in?"

Sarge stepped aside. He was careful to leave the door open but when he turned she'd shut it. He flicked on a light. Salt air billowed in again. It brushed sun-tinted strands of hair over her ears, so for a second it looked as if she were wearing a helmet and the helmet had begun to sprout small wings. Dorey winced in the light. What's up? he asked again, sat back on the bed's edge and couldn't stop a yawn.

"Can I turn this off?"

"What's the matter?" he teased. "Seen too much of me?"

"Uh-uh. Sarge."

"Yes?"

"Do you want to sleep with me?" He blinked in the light. Her face was nervous and patient, waiting.

It was a windy late August night. Sarge was dreaming, he figured. He smiled.

"The thought," he said softly, "has crossed my mind."

"Well will you?"

"Is that what you want?"

"Well I want to be close to you if I can. I don't know if I can, that way. I want to try though."

She looked dusky and glowing. Looked terrific, he'd have liked to tell her that. Hot wind blew across his face and he wasn't dreaming and still she stood there, hand readied at the wall switch. He thought a minute.

"You're the coach."

It blurted from her. "What do I do?"

"You're the coach," he insisted softly. Then smiled, his voice gentle. "Use your imagination."

Under the tan she paled. Well turn around then, she told him.

Sarge stretched out facing the wall, and when he opened his eyes again she'd shut off the light. Mattress was lousy, always made you feel you were perched on the edge of something. He tried to relax.

"Are you turned all the way?"

"Yes," he said.

"Don't look."

He looked at the wall.

It was difficult, not turning. He wanted to turn in the dark to see. Wanted to stare hard to make out what her expression would be, tiny hint of a grin or maybe that blank mask she wore when concentrating, that almost vacant thumb-sucking look. In two and a half weeks she'd be swimming across the San Antonio Strait because he'd created her for that express purpose, and he wanted to see her now. Clutching the sheets his arms ached. Delirious, he told himself, too much sun. He wanted to turn around.

"You're not looking, are you?"

No, he said, no, he wasn't looking.

He heard a belt buckle clink, then more quiet. Somewhere a stray gull screeched, sound blending into the slamming of waves on sand. The mattress bounced with another body's weight. Was it as simple as that then.

"Well how do I look?"

"Hell. I can't see you."

"Don't turn around!"

He didn't.

"Use your imagination," she whispered. He obeyed and she waited.

The wall spread dark across his field of vision. In seconds he'd adorned it with images of her. Slack-jawed face running in water, breath clouding out rhythmically. Faceless, hairless, smoothed away beneath suits and rubber and that flamboyant arch of hers into a dive like coiled spring stretched out suddenly, slicing water surface with a high-pitched splash. Bundled up formlessly along the lake in winter. Funny how defenseless she looked in regular clothes, somehow diminished. Or the invulnerability of her smooth back, gaping sightlessly at him when he'd opened the door to Ilana's room that morning. Christ. All these images he had of her, he hadn't known there would be so many.

"How do I look Sarge."

"Good," he whispered, "to me."

Okay, she told him, you can turn around now. Sarge hesitated. Then slowly he turned. She'd taken off her shirt, that was all, and lay there facing him with arms crossed firmly over her breasts. They were so nicely formed, her breasts, ample but in proportion. He allowed himself the luxury of imagining her arms flung back and breasts uncovered for him to see. They were also tanned like the rest of her, and he wondered when she'd gone out there naked in the sun to get evenly browned like that. Maybe those unaccompanied early-morning swims he'd expressly forbidden. Sure. Now he was wondering where that quivering in his own chest came from. Because he was her trainer, hell, he'd seen her more naked than this before. Those post-workout baths, muscles taped, bare skin greased, the massages. Sarge wanted the light back. With light he knew how he'd see her, eyes shining large in that sun-darkened face and her hair would have a reddish glow.

"What do I do now, Sarge?"

He could feel her tension like some stiff halo around her entire body, thought to reach and touch but on second thought stayed still. What he wanted he didn't permit himself to imagine. Any minute she might turn away in some kind of fear, he didn't know. "I'm just here," he offered, "I'm not going anywhere." He closed his eyes and there was that deliciously soft moment like electricity when he felt her breasts crush gently on his chest. Then he permitted himself to imagine a few things.

He thought of Ilana and his imaginings stopped. What jumbled up inside now was the vision of Ilana meeting his eyes that morning when he'd pushed the door open expecting to see her. Ilana asleep. Ilana alone. Ilana for him alone. That's where his sense of betrayal had sprung from, then, she'd shared herself without his consent. He wondered had it always been like that, had he isolated her in some subtle way, straitjacketed her with his own pain. Since Matt died. Maybe before. He'd held her, somehow, apart from Matt and Matt from her, kept them separate, each, for him alone. Caring on someone else's terms, Ilana'd said. He moved fingers gently through Dorey's hair. It was suddenly clear to him what she'd meant. Well it had taken long enough, he told himself, long enough to see. Not that the pain was gone or ever would leave, but now he understood something and so the sense of betrayal slid from him like an unwanted outer skin. His heart went pumping a little faster. A swimmer was here, she was no dream, and this lump of sudden realization blocked his throat with a dull ache that turned to longing.

"Sarge. This doesn't feel right."

"That's because the top of you's doing one thing and the bottom another."

"Uh-huh. Mermaid."

He laughed. "Not exactly. Want to move the rest of you in a little?"

"I'm afraid."

"Want to?"

"Yes." She hesitated. "How come it's not easy?" Her voice was a little plaintive. She moved fully against him, he could feel her bare feet brush towards his.

He stroked her back. "Tired, champ?"

"I'm so strong, Sarge. Nothing makes me tired." She could feel him breathing. It was all right. It was nice sometimes, kind of nice. "Are you?"

"Once in a while."

"Now?"

He held her tighter. She didn't protest.

Then he felt his age. Everything sagged. He moved a cheek across her hair, wanting to sink into the softness there, moved his forehead tiredly against hers.

"You go to sleep, Sarge," she said gently. "You go to sleep now. I'll stay here."

He woke off and on to find himself in varying stages of arousal. She seemed to sleep too and in the dark her face was shameless, childlike. He could feel the slow heartbeats that moved her left breast against him in rhythm. He woke once in a sweat, breathing hard because she was touching him. Her touch was light. Almost too gentle, didn't match his urgency. He kept himself still.

"Sometimes," she whispered, "it's so small."

"Getting bigger."

"Ah. I know."

He was stripped, pants folded neatly at his feet. She'd done that and remained only half-naked herself. He wanted to ask why but didn't, let her hands alone in that rippling motion they had all over him.

"Is this okay? Is this good for you?"

"Know what," he said, "I think you're goddamned beautiful."

"You were swimming all winter. I watched sometimes when you didn't know."

She rummaged along his chest for a nipple. Bending over, she kissed it, moved lips across to the other. He touched her arms and the hardness of them was a shock. He wanted to move towards her himself and on top or maybe just allow his own hands and mouth to caress too, but something told him no so he stayed still while she crouched above him, fingers

275

fluttered over his thighs, found his cock, hands alternately slid and gripped firmly. It took a long time.

What he wanted was to be inside her. He'd push deep in and then deeper then maybe keep going because there, there was somewhere to go to, inside her was a place he'd find and leave himself there. He closed his eyes to imagine himself inside of her. Then he was hovering, waiting, staying still while she made things happen. Against every instinct that said move forward he kept still, and what moved towards him now just beyond the hovering point was a bright blasting wave that would carry him along. All he had to do was wait.

He opened his eyes to see her examining his face with an expression on her own that was solemn, openly curious, and something else altogether. Whatever it was he couldn't read. Things were spinning too quickly. Eyes open, he was separate and no longer inside. He was going to spill out nowhere. He was going to spill out into nothing and dry and die. He reached for her face to touch. He sighed. Gave her absolute control.

"I love you Sarge. I just love you."

Here, he said, here.

He came into the nothing her cupped hands formed. Her hands curled around to catch sperm, trap it in both palms and keep catching until it ran down her wrists and there was no more coming.

Too much sun, Sarge told himself, must be the sun that made him dizzy this way and covering the sheets with sweat, muscles quivering reluctantly like he'd just woken from a dream or broken out of fever. Some memory tapped his shoulder. He'd seen her once before like this, long ago at night hands turned to catch the wet and it formed pools between her fingers which she inspected, licked a curious tongue at and pulled back with surprise, making a face. He'd seen her like this long ago, hadn't he. Rubbing it over her torso slowly, carefully, rubbing it under her breasts only what she'd been massaging into her skin back then had been rainwater. She passed both hands over herself again. She rubbed them across her mouth, down her neck.

"Come here." He opened his arms.

The eyes lowering towards his were tender and triumphant. Beyond that they were dark, thoughts unexpressed and lost forever to him and forever separate. He wanted to tell her he loved her but that wouldn't have been true—rather, it would have been something less than the truth, and he lacked words to describe the rest of whatever truth there was here. When his hands felt between her thighs she trapped them gently, firmly moved them away. He guessed those were her terms and accepted reluctantly. Her arms relaxed along his. Silently they both drifted towards sleeping.

It was late when the sky cleared. What showed full-face was a full moon. It was icy white and large in the sky, calling in a spring tide. On sand, water swelled. It foamed along the beach leaving smooth-worn quartz and seaweed behind. Out past the breakers moonlight shone calmly on a rippled surface. It washed everything mirror-silver, cold white, without transparency so the water seemed solidified that night, and pure, like an unbroken expanse of snow.

"There's a letter." Sarge waved it. Already nine thirty a.m. and the fog was wet along his shoulders. In T-shirt and shorts she sprawled on sand, hair blew in the slight breeze and she looked at him calmly. He was confused. He'd woken up alone that morning, and only stiffened sheets and the cool light-headed sensation inside him hinted proof.

"Hi there." She patted the sand next to her, offering a seat. It's calm, she told him, pointing towards the water, there's hardly any wind. Look at the breakers.

"Feel okay?" he asked cautiously.

"Uh-huh."

"Good. Here's your mail."

"What about you?"

"What?"

"Do you feel all right?" She took the letter without looking at it.

"I feel pretty strange. Not bad, understand. Just strange." 277

"Ah," she smiled shyly, "me too." She reached for his hand, pressed it against her belly and shielded it there with both of hers. The letter lay dusted in sand.

Later she'd tear open the envelope to slowly scan several ink-scrawled pages. She'd rest her head in the backboard his arm made. Sarge watched the shoreline change. Sometimes wind stirred up some pretty spectacular medium-sized waves, nearly decent enough for surfers, but for the most part things were calm and shrouded, and out beyond the breakers water glistened a deceptively warm-seeming, gray-tinged green. When he pulled back from visions of water what he felt was the line of her body resting gently against his arm, and his heart picked up pace. How many beats per minute. For the hell of it, he placed fingertips at her neck artery.

Later she'd stand slowly and set the letter carefully under a rock for safekeeping before heading to the waves. He watched her go. No swimming for the next two weeks and more. She'd begun her regiment of eating, plenty of carbohydrates, hoping to load on an ideal twenty pounds for good measure. He'd settle though, he told her, for fifteen—minimum. Now, watching her face the water and kick feet through it, bend to dip hands into it, he could feel tantalization crawl through her, streak up the beach, and grope its way inside him. He'd have liked to swim today himself.

Sarge glanced at sand and some flapping pages caught his eye.

—*your gift*, the segment of page read, *for productive solitude, which is remarkable*—

He looked away. Then couldn't help another glance.

—*be there to watch you. I'm alone now and learning to*—

He didn't look down again. Whatever it was Carol Thomas had learned was none of his business and he guessed he'd never know. Then Sarge was wondering again who Dorey looked like—was it that first father or did she have the face of her mother Carol, or was it a mix of both. Like him. Father's build, bones, facial structure. Mother's coloring, mother's eyes. He had a crazy urge to tear up the letter, obliterate all traces of this parent because for just a moment he wanted her all to himself. Then he chuckled. Hell, she'd never have passed for his daughter. Too smooth-featured. Too distinctly American.

Later he'd follow her down to the waves, letter in hand. He'd place a careful hand on her shoulder and she wouldn't freeze or move away.

"Miss her?"

Dorey looked at him painfully.

"Miss Ilana?" he asked.

She nodded. She shut her eyes. He could smell nothing but salt, filtered through with damp morning fog. She caressed his arm. "It's got nothing to do with you. Not with any-thing."

"Hell," he nodded. "I know that by now."

He kissed her forehead, then her cheek. They were light kisses, and chaste, like innocent butterfly wings brushing against something. She was smiling although still painfully. This swim Sarge, she was saying, this swim, it's going to be the best. Ever. It will, it's got to be.

"The best," he said. He ran down a few facts for her. September fifth, it looked like, the fifth. He'd been checking twice daily with the coast guard and they had Tycho consulting the stars—he grinned—and calculating, calculating away. If all predictions held steady they'd head out for San Antonio Island September fourth, and they could use the coast guard facili-ties, dining mess and rec room and bunk rooms too. They'd send Tycho a day in advance to position the boat offshore. He'd run through things down to the last detail, he told her, with the coast guard. Fellow named McNeil stayed there on the island throughout the summer, monitored weather, kept an eye on things, radioed daily reports to passing coast guard vessels. He'd be expecting them. She nodded patiently. Sure Sarge, she said, I know. That's great.

"In the meantime, better eat plenty."

"I will."

"Fifteen pounds, understand? Minimum."

She lifted his fingers to her cheek and cradled them, then released and his hand got lost, just for a minute, in breeze.

When he'd gotten it back he handed her the letter. She stuck it in the waistband of her shorts.

Sarge slept by himself that night. He figured she wouldn't appear again and wasn't expecting her to. She didn't.

"Better eat." Sarge grinned. He spilled some more onto her plate. "Get nice and fat."

It was six o'clock.

Anne shoved a small wrapped packet across the table. A blue ribbon curled around it. Dorey looked up, fork in mid-air. She glanced at her watch and then back to the plate, to the gift, to Anne and Sarge and the other faces there. This eating had become a chore. She regulated it by schedule. There were another five minutes allotted for the completion of corn and whole wheat bread, and potatoes came after that.

"Come on." Anne's fingers tapped the table impatiently. "Open it."

Dorey did. The ribbon fell away and she tucked it under the edge of her plate. Then the wrapping paper. It was an enormous Swiss chocolate bar.

Anne beamed. "Dessert."

"One of many." Sarge was threatening her with more corn. She had to hurry. Then she'd dropped the fork with a clink and was laughing.

"Thank you! Thanks a lot." She squeezed her abdomen. "I'm so fat."

Rick tickled Anne's side and winked across the table. "You're not the only one."

"Hey. Hey cut it out, Barton."

Eat, Sarge crooned. Eat. She'd weighed in this morning at one forty-three, a fifteen-pound gain. He had to trust it would be enough but he'd have liked to see a few extra pounds in addition to all that, you couldn't be too sure and fat was the best insulation.

"Tomorrow." Dorey's fork poised again. She gave him a funny smile. "It's all coming off tomorrow."

"Right."

"Just like that." She snapped her fingers.

"It's a hell of a way to lose weight," Anne cracked. She and Dorey looked at each other and laughed. "Years of conditioning just for a crash diet. If *you're* not going to eat that chocolate bar, give it back Dorey. That's great chocolate."

Dorey shoved the corn and potatoes aside, the salad, bread, bananas and cereal grain and glass of water. She unwrapped the candy bar and, laying it on the table, took a clean knife. She divided it into equal sections, one for everyone at the table.

She was suddenly the center of a quiet attention. She stood handing out identical pieces and took the remaining one herself. It oozed slightly between her fingers. They looked at her and Dorey blushed.

"Thanks." She nodded towards Anne. Thanks. To Rick. Thank you Tycho. She blew him a kiss off of one chocolate-smeared fingertip.

"Sarge."

Across the potatoes steamed on food-crusted plates, mineral water, carbohydrate-ridden milkshakes, she leaned forward and this time it was with grace. One set of fingers stroked his cheek leaving faint lines of chocolate. The ceiling lights were harsh but for a second when her lips pressed his forehead he felt enveloped in some dim-lit mellow glow. Watching, Tycho nodded. He was agreeing with the stars. Sarge stood too, reached for her, and then they'd both shoved chairs aside to embrace. It wasn't a bear-hug of friendship and it wasn't an embrace of lovers either, but Anne liked the way it looked and she applauded.

"All right," said Rick, "that's the first illustration."

Dorey pressed back with as much force as she could. His arms might have crushed her but didn't, and there was an exhilaration in that, how strong she was and how much it was proven by how strong he felt too. They could touch each other and it was all right. It felt good to Sarge, more natural than a lot of things he'd done in his life.

281

•

A window stayed open. September night chilled and the breeze brought salt, damp odors of sand. Dorey fell asleep immediately. Her thoughts had pinpointed to one bright blur. In the morning she would not remember a single dream. She'd wake up in the same position she'd fallen asleep: on her back, pillowless by choice, arms outstretched and everything relaxed, eyes motionless beneath lids and breathing slow, regular, the only sign of life in an otherwise remarkable calm that held her body for the night like a drug. Remembering the air's possible chill, she'd pulled a sheet and thin blanket over at first but then threw both off and slept naked. With the extra weight, she was particularly sensitive to heat.

Anne slept on her left side, legs frozen silently on the mattress in running stride. Rick threw a leg over hers. His hands cradled her breasts. After this, she'd told him, no more major projects except the Ph.D. and of course the Marathon next fall, viola, and she'd work back up to tournament level with the longbow indoors over a period of months. Aside from that she guessed she'd take it easy for a while, a good idea, didn't he agree. He ran a hand down her and said of course. When she'd been asleep for a while he whispered to her that these illustrations would be the best, he promised. She would be proud, proud of him. Promised.

Sarge didn't bother trying to sleep. He sat in the dusty rec room with all lights off but one. Hell of a place for a tour of duty. Still, maybe the coast guard were used to these kinds of places, dismal islands otherwise unused and unwanted. There was a TV that didn't work, a radio that did but he left it off. The furniture upholstery was cracking.

He'd spread some charts on the table but didn't glance at them. Sarge just sat massaging both temples. He hadn't yet looked at the water, not really. Coming over in the boat, he'd felt some part of him freeze shut. This was the San Antonio Strait. Sure, he told himself, sure. Only it still didn't make sense to him. He still could not permit himself to feel it in his gut. The San Antonio.

That water was gray. It reached up at you. Now, sitting on cracked upholstery, he found himself listening, straining for the sound of waves. As if they'd come crawling up past the shoreline this time. As if they'd stand there at the window, waiting for him to open it. Stand there at the door. Each one poised, cold and gray, ready to envelop and carry him off, pulsating with the beat of his son's heart and of his own. For a second Sarge thought he'd heard it—crash of the waves, a long, far-off gull screaming itself to sleep. Maybe the drift of wind on sand. He'd forgotten what it was like to be here. And while he sat he felt himself opening a little to the long-remembered horror of it—this loneliness here, on an island, with thirty-two miles of heart-freezing gray waves between himself and the mainland sand. Sarge cupped hands over his ears to make the sound you'd hear in the opening of a conch shell—rushing water, swirl of the waves. And he knew what he was listening to, allowed himself to feel it finally. It was the San Antonio Strait he heard now above and beyond all the other water clamoring in his ear. The San Antonio Strait licking gray tongues up at him. And here he was, waiting. The water struck up, poured past his waiting ear, filled his head. The San Antonio. It danced out and up, invitation to dissolution, beat at him like the sounds of his own death. Sarge was waiting, and afraid.

"How do you feel?" Tycho sat across the table.

Sarge opened his eyes. "Meditative."

"Good." Tycho curled the edges of the chart between his fingers. He seemed to want to say more but remained silent for quite a while. When he did speak it was softly, asking, well captain, what's your alternate plan in case of bad weather?

Sarge gave him a tired look. "That won't happen. We've got the latest reports, no chance of anything major. Not even light rain."

"Do you have an alternate date?" Tycho pressed.

"Hell no." Sarge frowned. "You don't go into this kind of a thing planning for anything but success, Johnny." His eyes narrowed. He asked Tycho why, did the stars know something he didn't?

Tycho hesitated, then shook his head. "No Sarge. They don't know anything. Just call it my propensity to worry."

Sarge laughed. "It's strange, Johnny, how the rest of you shuts down for a swim like this. I feel"—he tensed, leaning forward—"I feel like I've just tossed Ilana into the background somewhere. It's like she doesn't matter now. I think of her and can't feel much."

"Numb?"

"Sure," said Sarge, "maybe that's it." He spoke carefully. "She called this morning."

"Is she all right?"

"She sounded all right. Wanted to speak with Dorey." He glanced at Tycho, features strained beneath their bronze coating and eyes hurt. "I wouldn't let her. I said it would be hard on her emotions just before the swim, better save it."

"Did you mean it?"

Sarge shrugged. "Part of me did. The other part wanted to do it for some crazy kind of revenge, though. Or maybe I was angry at her myself, Johnny. For not being here."

Tycho's eyebrows arched in surprise. Oh, he said, so you'd rather she be here. Sarge nodded. Sure. Despite himself. Or because of himself. Or her, Dorey. Hell, he didn't know. He just didn't know anymore.

Wind whipped along the beach out there. It raised sand and some splatted against half-open windows, sifted through to the floor. You could hear the waves. Sarge listened, eyes closed.

"Let's get some sleep," Tycho suggested. He folded the chart himself, slid it across the table to Sarge. "Tomorrow's the Dorey Thomas crossing of the San Antonio Strait. That's a big event, maestro. That's a major symphony to conduct. You get some rest."

284

By ten fifteen a.m. McNeil gave them an all-clear for the weather. Nothing nasty coming up, he smiled. August was too rough this year, everything's played out. He lit a Marlboro with glee as if to reward himself for the good news, took that first exquisite puff and leaned way back in his swivel chair. He sipped stale coffee, tousled his son's hair. Al glared at the floor. He didn't like the old guy tousling his hair like that as if he were still a kid. It was the freckles, he sighed to himself, the freckles that did it. Once you had them you were labeled cute for life. He wiped his nose on a shirt-sleeve. This burden of cuteness was no fun.

"You know the signals by heart, so keep an ear open."

Al nodded angrily. "Sure."

"That coast guard ship. It ought to be in sight at all times. Listen for Thompson. Listen for Shaler."

Al could have said it in his sleep. Again he nodded. Sure, sure, I know.

"Everything goes the way it looks, you won't hear a word from them." McNeil grinned happily. "You'll do fine, Al."

Al knew he would. He'd been around boats all his life.

At eleven that morning Al hauled his small canvas backpack down to the jeep, checked the contents before tossing it in the front seat. Swiss army knife, some extra rope, his net, suntan lotion. Maybe this year the freckles would die. A change of shirt, canned soda and plenty of sandwiches. They said they'd feed him but he'd seen the stuff they ate and would stick to tunafish on a roll. A sweater, a slicker. He sat in the driver's seat, gripped the wheel, admired his own grip. He admired hair speckling the backs of his hands, how it grew thicker and darker along his arms.

McNeil finished some paperwork early and was out at the jeep by eleven thirty. He whistled when he jammed a key in the ignition, pleased as hell. Al, he whistled, I'm proud of you my boy. Al blushed. He wanted to die for a second with that intolerable mixture of pleasure and embarrassment. A slight wind had started up, almost unnoticeable departure from the morning's complete calm. By the time Al's blush faded the engine was hot and they were heading quickly for Punta Provechosa, ripping up dust along the way.

·

Dorey smeared Vaseline on her lips and handed the tube back to Sarge. Hot sun today.

She pulled a sweatshirt over the suit, settled sunglasses on her nose. Her bare legs glowed a dark tan.

The jeep spun up to them. McNeil waved. "Hop in. My boy's there with the rest of them, he'll get everyone out." Sweat darkened his shirt down his chest, around the neck. Plenty of dampness in the air and it wasn't just from saltwater. Sarge looked around but there were still plenty of gulls circling, everything smelled like comparative tranquility. He trusted his instinct about these things. Felt a little uneasy now, but that was due to the expected tension, he knew. They had a beauty of a day and night cut out for them.

Sarge opened the door for her. Before sliding in himself, he bent down for a kiss. It was light, lips barely brushing her cheek, and when he sat she squeezed his hand in both of hers. McNeil talked a lot. Babbled about the coast guard ship, about his son making cross-country at junior high school, second year straight, and wouldn't you know it the kid dropped off the team when his fluff of a girlfriend broke up with him. Mourning, he called it. Well he didn't want to butt in with his son's affairs, hadn't so far and swore he wouldn't, but he'd lay ten to one that a year from now the kid would regret it in a big way. McNeil lit himself another Marlboro. He'd figured a long summer out roughing it with the old man would do him good. Good for a young guy to be around boats and the sea, roughing it. What did Sarge think. Maybe, said Sarge. Maybe but you couldn't tell with kids, they lived in their own world of pain and triumph, that's the way he saw it. Hard to touch them when they were growing. Hard to see them the way they really were, after all.

"You're right," McNeil puffed, cruised around a clump of thorny weeds that had grown into the road, and spumed up more dust. "You've got something there. It's the damnedest thing, I can never figure what's going through his head, that boy."

286

"Getting born," Sarge muttered. "Over and over."

"What?"

Nothing, Sarge told him.

Dorey let breeze cool through the sweatshirt. Underneath she felt naked. Slipping into the extra suit would be almost a relief, she was used to it now. She concentrated on the suit, its color and texture and all the added warmth. The suit would give her pleasure. Eyes half shut, she smiled.

"So you're a cross-country man." Anne spread her towel and settled down while he revved up the motor. "And good at it too, right? Do a lot of track work?"

"Some," he mumbled.

They sliced through a wave, got drenched with spray. Both gasped. It was cold. Cold.

"Whew!" She shivered, remembered to breathe fully and it calmed her. "I've got it. The ten thousand, right?"

He blushed with pleasure. "Some."

"Good man!" she applauded. "What's your time?"

He told her and spray chilled them both, dampened their hair darker. She told him her P.B. for the marathon. That's not that good, he said apologetically. For a runner no, she defended herself, for a swimmer it's not bad. Al guessed she was right.

"I hate swimming."

Anne laughed. "Why?"

"It's boring. You get cold. Who needs it?"

"Oh I don't know, there are some good things about it—"

"Like what?" he said bitterly.

"Like if you're cold enough and bored enough long enough, you start seeing other things. It's like watching a movie going on in your head, and you can be the director—"

"Yeah?"

"—and the camera, and the *star*. It's not like the rest of your life because there's only you"—she giggled—"and you are whoever and whatever you can be, right there in the water."

Al considered it. "That's dumb."

"You're right," she replied calmly. She licked salt from her

287

lips. The boat was in sight now, anchored beyond the shore-line's waves. "It *is* dumb. Dumb means unable to speak or make sounds. You can't talk when you swim. No one else hears your heart beat, you know, there's only you in the water. It's got nothing to do with running, it's a very isolated thing. Like falling in love."

"*What?*"

The look he gave her over his shoulder was the kind that said you were totally out of context, out of time, and worthless.

Anne smiled gently. She was glorying in this, she'd always wanted a younger brother. All those older ones had been no fun after a while. They were too big and too many.

"Like falling in love. Because both are isolated experiences when you do them. Nobody else in the whole world under-stands what exactly you're going through, and let me tell you there's no way anybody else can go through the same thing and feel it the same way, right? So when you do a swim"—her hand caught spray, arm flung gracefully wide over the water beneath them—"a swim like this one that's about to happen, if you're the swimmer you're really alone. Everything you feel whether it's wonderful or horrible or whether you want it to go on forever or just want to roll over and die, it all belongs to you and there's no one else to share it with. Like when you love somebody, I mean when you're *in* love with them, there's no way to communicate everything you really know inside."

Al slowed. Almost there. Gulls circled overhead, made a perfect O, and one dove swiftly to come up with a wriggling fish. "Yeah, well I don't know," he growled. The hazy-glowing sunlight caught her hair and it glittered different shades of brown, red-tinged, blonde-tinged, perfectly offsetting the open-faced cheerleader features. Al glanced over his shoulder with admiration.

"Hey!" she was waving to someone on board. He gazed towards the boat and saw that guy. What was his name. Rick. Some asshole name. Probably got to fuck the daylights out of her every night. Twice a night. Al sidled the skiff up closer so she'd get an easy foothold on the three-rung rope ladder hanging between those weird pontoon riggings. He watched her thighs pump up the rope, swing over on deck, and Rick caressing her shoulders. She turned to smile and wave. Al ignored her. He revved the motor again, headed back for Punta Provechosa. Engine gas sputtered hotly and faint fumes mingled with the omnipresent scent of salt. A five-footer slapped his face, spilled over the gunwales as he neared shore. Felt right. It was despair.

"You missed a spot." Dorey motioned with her chin. Sarge rubbed Iodex gently around her left nipple. After a while it became erect, pointing towards him. She was all black, glistening, looked tar-coated. He wiped hands on a grease-laden towel and pulled the first suit up over her coated torso. Sarge went through signals with her. So many whistles per direction. So many whistles meant feeding time. Stop and he'd make sure she would clear the pontoons. There was nothing to worry about.

"Ah. Well. I'm not worried."

She smiled faintly. He greased over the first suit thoroughly, then pulled up her second. He cleaned his hands well before fitting her with a fourth cap. Her head looked white and enormous, fetal. Her hands were grease-free and held the goggles delicately. She spit into them, then slipped them on and got a good fit.

"Let's go."

The ground was granite-strewn sand. Against the granite crust of shoreline, waves busted open. A little bigger than they'd been this morning but still all right, she'd clear the rocks fine, swing out and around and swim past those breakers for the boat with wings.

McNeil leaned against the jeep's door, waiting for the show to take off. Knee-deep, Al had roped in the boat and also waited. His face was red with sun and the tint of his hair, flushed by freckles.

"Good luck there!" McNeil gave Dorey an upraised fist of victory. She nodded vacantly, turned to Sarge.

"If I throw up a lot, just the vanilla cookies."

"Right. No chocolate." They'd been over it countless times.

"Or the broth."

"Broth," he echoed, "I know."

It was twelve fifty-six by his watch.

"See you later." She stepped towards the water, entered it, waded past Al and leaned forward into a few breakers. They were milder than on the rocky side of the point, three-footers, no more. The whitecaps washed her thighs. Swirled a little black grease away in ivory foam. Dorey waded out until the water level crept against her ribs. Farther out. Numb and it chilled her breasts. The nipples would sink away now, try to hide, she knew. She dove into the next wave head first, and salt shot up her nose with that frozen clean taste. She swam easily, clawed herself out past the breakers, caught a big swell and rode it and then she wanted to laugh with the bitter cold tingling deep-rooted rise and fall that carried her. She let it dwindle and stroked out farther. This was it. The water. Just like that she'd begun, it seemed easy. Uh-huh, she thought, here goes. Just like that.

Sarge shook hands briskly with McNeil and muttered some thanks while he kept an eye on her. He tossed the sack of supplementary supplies into the motorboat, told Al to get on in, and gave the boat one strong shove out through the waves before he swung in himself, drenched and nearly capsizing them. "All right. Let's get going. Want you to stay to her right now, understand. Six feet to her right." It was a good few minutes before he felt his toes again. Above spray and freezing green-hued water, the air had thickened to bear down on his shoulders with humid weight. Through it all, sun burned hazily.

This was it, Sarge told himself. Almost had to remind himself. This was the swim. She'd just stepped into water at the point they'd agreed upon. It was as simple as that.

She made good time out. He watched her carefully. When the boat was in sight, wood, aluminum, and fiberglass gleaming, he whistled and she stopped obediently. Boarding now, he shouted. He shooed Al up the ropes and took the skiff around himself. They detached its motor, then hoisted it to the stern and lashed it. Sarge was on deck. He whistled three times. Looked down at her and waved. She waved back, turned due east and started to swim.

From the anchored spot off Costa de Piedra they headed due east. Before the first feeding the coast guard clipper *Lazarilla* appeared off the starboard prow, maintained its distance and cruised parallel to them. A male figure showed occasionally on deck, waved. After the second feeding they headed northeast, a subtle shift in course. On deck the wet heat burned. It bounced off wood and waxed rope. Shimmering light blanched the water surface and the water rippled calmly. Sarge chuckled happily at it—there were scarcely any waves to speak of, once they'd cleared the coast it was smooth sailing through that near-smooth bitter cold gray. He monitored the centigrade reading, translated it to Fahrenheit: 54.7 degrees and steady. Chops maybe one, maybe one and a half feet average. No sweat.

"Great!" Rick leaned over for a look, wiped forehead on a sleeve and whistled. He turned to Al. "Ever seen it this calm?"

"No." Al took a walk. No one had said he had to be polite in the bargain.

He dug through his pockets and found a couple of pennies. Deliberately threw them, one, two, as far as he could overboard without a wish.

Sarge blasted the whistle. Then he took off his shirt. It was hot for September, on the whistle cord his hands slid. He bunched up the shirt and ran it across his face and chest.

She'd stopped and he gave the five long, slow whistles agreed upon. Five strokes reverse, they said. She backstroked easily. Her arms were grease-free, sun-red against the icy glitter. Let's go, Sarge nodded to Rick. The lever got pulled slowly, carefully, and Tycho eased to a complete stop as the wings spread, one on each side of the boat. They were metal arms twelve feet in length, the width of an old-fashioned gang-plank, two arms per side about six feet apart. At the edge of each arm, a sizable rolled drum you could brace yourself against. The wings lowered until they'd settled gently in water. Rick released the lever.

Sarge swung over onto the aluminum walkway.

"Here, captain." Tycho poured out preheated liquid. Thousands of calories, thick chocolate taste. He handed it to Sarge, passed the feeding stick overboard. "Say hello for us."

Balanced easily, Sarge stepped out on the first pontoon. He set the cup of hot fluid in the stick's steel-looped end and braced himself firmly before holding it out to her. His legs dangled. Waves lapped mildly up around them.

Her teeth were chattering. He could hear.

Going great! he yelled a couple of times.

"I feel good," she said.

Below her was nothing. Dorey squeezed the cup against her lips, held it there for a second without drinking. She could smell steam. Then one sip, two sip three, and she'd started to feel below again. Her feet, ankles, even the toes. Five sip six and seven eight. She jammed the cup back in its loop. Didn't want to let it sail off all alone on that vast icy expanse of green-gray saltwater.

Her teeth stopped chattering. "I feel good Sarge!"

Below was nothing. Just cold and gray. It was this deep, unsupported nothing and swelled in small chops around her shoulders, she the only thing in it.

"This calm keeps up," he leaned farther towards her, "you're going to make some beautiful time."

"Uh-huh. I know."

She waved and took off. Sarge signaled to Tycho. He walked steadily back, handed the stick up over the side and, on rope rungs, stepped up. The boat started moving again with a purring, easy glide. Rick worked the lever. Wings lifted by careful degrees. In the stern Al stole a glance at Anne while she stretched on deck, sunbathing, reading some book in Spanish. He dug in his pocket again and this time threw a dime. It spun through the air, spattered twinkling silver against the surface before vanishing.

"Make that fifty-four point five degrees," crackled the radio, "and steady. How are you doing? Over."

The hotel room was small and air-conditioned, and it was across the street from the hospital. Once in a rare while an ambulance crawled silently uphill to the emergency entrance, flashing lights turned off. Port Johnson was a small, quiet city. Business was local, the tourist trade nonexistent. To the north and south, to the east, pine-studded, shrub-studded hills shimmered in bleaching September heat. To the west was the Pacific, squeezed between mainland and an offshore island thirty-two miles away into a stretch of water called the San Antonio Strait.

The room had a too-soft bed. A clean, bare night table stood by the bed. There was a bathroom, a desk to write at. The television carried local stations but remained off. You could see the hospital through the window just by pushing aside heavy drapes. They were dark green, matching the bedspread. By the window was a green-upholstered armchair.

Sitting there, Ilana shut her eyes. She was tired and leaned against the headrest. Sometimes she'd jump a little as if waking, open her eyes to blink at the glaring white building across the street. Her eyes would close again, then she'd force them open. Must not sleep, she told herself, no. It was only a matter of hours, at most until tomorrow afternoon. She could stay awake those mere hours longer.

On chair arms, Ilana's hands relaxed. She pulled herself from a cloud again, focused on the bedside clock. She ticked off seconds until in her head a whistle blasted. Chocolate sustagen. It would be heated and poured out by exact measurement into a Styrofoam container.

How do you feel? Ilana asked. How do you feel? You're doing well. Here. Here. Drink it all.

Cold.

Here, I'll hold you then. Hold you and I promise you won't be cold anymore.

She finally stood and opened the window. Sea breeze blasted in with a heavy wet thickness.

Better.

Better now? Of course. See how easy—

—Uh-huh—

—Like floating or like falling.

Anne let the book rest spread open across her face. She'd stared at the title page for about ten minutes before realizing her concentration was shot, finally just used the book as a sun shield, thick hazy air like this you could fool yourself into thinking the rays wouldn't affect you much, and even with a great tan like the one she'd worked up you could come away with a second-degree singe. Protect the face. Always. Like a pretty boxer.

"What's that?"

She lifted the text and squinted. Al nodded towards the cover.

"It's Spanish, huh?"

"Right, it's a collection of stories."

"Like what?" He stood glaring down, lounged back against the gunwales and coiled clamped rope.

"Like *San Manuel Bueno, Martir.*"

"What's that?"

"It's the title of a story. It means Saint Manuel the Good, Martyr."

He tssked scornfully. He'd gotten more color on his face and it made him a near-violent red. "Sounds too complicated."

"Too complicated for what?" she challenged.

Then she'd started to be aware of an old familiar feeling in the pit of her stomach. It made her uneasy.

He looped a hand through some rope, clenched fingers around it and with each motion he felt his biceps flex a little, wondered if she could see too.

"Aren't you going to watch?"

Anne sat, shrugged. "I'll see soon enough. I know what it looks like, you know, I've been there before."

"Are you going to swim?"

"Probably." She recognized the sensation fully. The boat rocked noticeably now, and her forehead was damp. Anne placed the book with care on the towel she'd spread. "It depends on how she does later, especially after dark, that's usually the most difficult part."

She stood unsteadily.

Norton, she shook her head at herself. Norton, you sure don't have much of a stomach. And she'd been careful at breakfast, too, careful to take just dry toast and tea. Well if she'd known it would attack anyway she'd have had a decent meal. Eggs, oatmeal, a shake, the works. She felt worse and took a slow walk towards the prow.

Rick wondered what had changed at first and then realized it was color. The water wasn't green-tinged anymore. He glanced up to where sun ought to be, now obscured behind a haze of gray. The water was gray too.

At ten to six Sarge licked a thumb and held it out for an informal measurement. He judged the wind, said something to himself that no one else heard.

"Shaler here," said the radio.

"Hello," Tycho replied.

"Temperature's holding. Fifty-four degrees Fahrenheit."

The boat rocked.

Sarge leaned into the radio. "What have you got on that wind?"

"Up to sixteen knots, blowing you southwest, mister."

"Right in the face," Sarge muttered.

Tycho did some quick figuring and they shifted course slightly. He didn't like it, they were being pushed too far south as it was but—he shrugged—perfection was unattainable any-
way. There were too many factors involved, too much water, too much weather, too many faces.

295

Sarge sat on a pontoon and offered the stick out to her. Waves smacked his knees.

"Water temperature's up," he shouted.

She lost the cup in waves.

"Ah!"

"Stay there! More soon!"

Water slammed over the aluminum walkway. He had to straddle it and slide, hang on to rope at the boat's side to steady himself.

"How's she doing?" Tycho asked.

Sarge's shirt was drenched. All right, he nodded. Some of the plain stuff now I think, it's rough out there Johnny. Sealed container in hand he slid out again, jammed it into the stick's loop-end, sent it probing over the chops towards her. She was six feet away. If he'd stretched out in water he'd have been able to touch her.

"Sarge. I'm sick."

A wave broke over her.

"Drink it," he ordered.

"Is it hot?" She spat saltwater.

"It's hot."

The wind was pretty substantial. It had already begun to dry the ends of his hair.

She was reaching. "My stomach."

"Drink this," he coaxed. "Drink it, that's right, right, that's my baby."

"It's hot."

"It's damned hot."

She let the cup drop, mostly empty, foam away with the white-flecked gray chopping up against her.

She waved to him.

"You look good!" he shouted. "You look good to me!"

296   "If you're going to rain, then rain." Anne was discussing things with the weather. Listening, Rick recognized that she'd come around to the bargaining stage. If you rain don't do it

too hard. And if you've got to do it hard then at least don't last too long, okay. Give her a break. What am I talking about. Give *me* a break. This stinks.

"Maybe it's working," he said, "the water temperature's up to fifty-five."

"An all-time high," she groaned.

"Feel better?"

"Feel disgusting."

"It's sundown," he said. "You know you always feel better during the day."

Whatever twilight there was had been shut off by the sky's haze of gray, so no blood-red streaks of light bounced off water, there was no subtle pastiche of color on the western horizon. Everything just got darker. It happened by rapid but barely discernible degrees. Soon everything was dark. Just like that.

Tycho flipped levers until the boat was girdled with light. Parallel to them, the *Lazarilla* appeared darker. Once in a while the cabin radio crackled with Shaler's voice, or Thompson's. Wind kept steady. They'd thought maybe by seven it would diminish. Tycho readjusted his course again, just slightly. It was dark now and he had to think of the swimmer first, and of the cold. It would be better to let the wind have its way for a while, not fight it quite so much. They'd head east of course, but tilt a little more to the south. It would just take longer. More distance, that was all.

"Is it chilly," Anne said, "or am I imagining things."

"Come here. It's a little cold."

"Think it's going to rain?"

The boat lurched and she rolled her head miserably against his chest.

"Feel better?"

"Uh-*huh*," she lied.

Something cracked at the base. Something splintered from above and all around. It was ice. Picture this Carol, she said, there's this ice, a big block of it. It's black. Like a monolith.

Inside there's a body. Suspended animation, that's what they call it, they freeze you. See. Well when you wake up and start to move that cracks the ice. Ice gets white when it cracks, those icicles that drop from the roof in winter, you know how they shatter and suddenly they're not see-through anymore. Anyway the ice cracks. Well that's what you do to cold water. When you swim in it, I mean.

"Come on now," Sarge coaxed. "Drink. Drink some."

She went under to avoid the next wave's force. His mouth was moving, somewhere out there in the dark. She fumbled with caps. Tried to roll them up over one ear.

"Drink. Understand? Drink."

"You go to hell. I'm busy."

"So I see," he said gently. "Why not stop for a drink."

"No, uh-uh. I'm talking with Carol."

Sarge looked up at the pitch-dark sky, felt a wave slap over his lap before he felt what was coming from above in soft insistent drippings.

Hell, he said softly. Rains in hell too sometimes. Straddling the pontoon, his legs were numb. It was as if all the nerve endings had been removed and he could see them floating, suspended, in vials of saltwater.

"You're getting some rough stuff now," Thompson radioed in. "What have you got, six-footers going there?"

"About," Tycho replied.

"This'll blow. This'll blow over, you wait."

"Any time frame on that?"

"What's that?" The voice disappeared in static. At the controls Tycho kept his stare straight ahead, ran through some more statistics, and decided he would not further alter their course. Rain spewed over portholes, thumped measured hollow sounds on the fiberglass, rapped like rifle shots against the pontoons.

"When?" Tycho said after a pause. "When does this rain stop—any estimation?"

"It'll blow, guaranteed. Gale season's over."

"Oh," Tycho nodded. "If you say so."

•

Al spread a tarp at the stern. He wrapped the tentlike flaps of his slicker around and pulled another section of tarp completely over himself so he looked like a roadside beggar, or supplicant monk. He'd thrown on the sweater and was warm underneath, dry and protected. He chose the stern because that's where they'd lashed the skiff and he figured it was his job to keep an eye on it. Sure they said gale season over and he'd never known it to storm seriously in September, but this was the San Antonio and you were never sure. He could have told them all that.

He huddled there comfortably, blending into the dark without a sound. After a while he searched through the small canvas backpack next to him and found a tunafish sandwich, wrapped in aluminum foil. Al ate with good appetite, then went for another. He thought about watching that woman swim but then shrugged. Swimming was boring, he didn't care how long it took or how far it went. Nothing like the 10 K. He wondered where Anne had disappeared to and felt that ache he'd spent the summer getting rid of.

Al finished the second sandwich. It had begun to rain harder, didn't look like the wind was diminishing any. Now the air had chilled, rain cutting through its hot heavy weight.

Huddled there, Al watched things go on. Nobody noticed him.

"Soup. Here." He was shouting so maybe she'd catch a little of it. He'd left the feeding stick behind and just leaned full out over the water to hand it to her. She wasn't biting.

"Come on now kid. Come on champ. Get it down. Here. Take it." He swallowed saltwater, gagged. "Take it. Take it and drink. You're looking good. It's night and you've been making damned good time."

That was a lie. They'd slowed. The wind, the turbulence.

She bobbed up. Shouted. He had to cup a hand behind one ear, funnel it towards her to make out the distorted words. She was saying the same thing over and over. Finally he got it.

"I'm sick."

"You're nice and strong there."

"I'm sick Sarge."

"This is medicine."

Dorey backed away. Then she'd lifted the right arm, Y Z A B breath. Her hand had fallen off but she didn't want him to know. It happened sometimes near the north pole. Capillaries froze, blood stagnated and turned to ice. Entire limbs fell off. Her feet had dropped hours ago. Didn't want to let him know, he would dive for them then. Her feet. She stopped. She was crying for her feet.

Drink this, someone said.

Icicles shattered, splintered like musical notes played through the air at random.

Drink this, it's good stuff.

She stopped. The voice had a nice sound, like chanting.

Who? she said. Who's there?

A friend. Drink up kid.

She did. It burned her fingers. Then she was throwing it all up with the next series of waves.

"What time is it?"

"Nine-o-five at night. Don't worry. Don't you worry about the time."

At the cold's core was shivering nausea. She ducked under to watch her other hand detach and sink. Poor hand. There was no helping it. It sank out of sight. Footless, without hands, she was treading in the direction of the voice.

"My stomach." She started to cry. "We're going the wrong way Sarge."

"We'll get you there, lady."

"Wrong way. Not even halfway yet."

C D. E F.

Leaning over to see, Anne felt lousy but kept her eyes open. Time to watch. Time to take a look and face up to what is happening here. She'd never watched before.

Light-flooded, the waves licked up, spun a silver shadow

across the entire lit area and you could hear erratic pounding against the boat's sides. In floodlights rain flashed like clouds of grain falling from a silo. Anne's insides lurched again. She could see her now—the white rubber-sheathed head that turned predictably for air, and the arms. Problem was she wasn't making much progress. The stroke looked strong all right, still strong after so many hours. It was the turbulence holding her back, waves and those winds. Waves. Some of them were at least seven-footers, she was sure of it. She felt sicker.

"Hey!"

Sarge leaned over the gunwales. His face was set, unreadable. He turned to Anne, T-shirt nearly dissolved against his chest, trouser legs wet and caked with salt.

"Hey. When does this let up?"

"It doesn't," he said wearily. "It doesn't."

Anne glanced at her watch. It was eight minutes past ten. So late. She hadn't thought it was so late. Her own hair was drenched. Clothes clung underneath the slicker. How many times could you play the streichquartette in D minor in your head and how many times could you think of chocolate bars?

"What about a pacer, Sarge?"

"Go inside," he shouted back, "get some rest."

"What *about* it?"

He turned palms up. "This swim's off."

"Based on what?"

"The weather."

He had a hard time believing it himself. Just as he'd had difficulty that morning—was it as short a time ago as morning —believing it had actually begun. It seemed so simple, such lack of real ceremony, she had just stepped right in and then for those first hours it seemed easy, too easy, like dreaming. Sarge laughed with a salt taste in his mouth.

"You're kidding, Mr. Olssen!"

"I'm not kidding."

Some part of him still believed he was jumping the gun. He went through everything again in his head. They couldn't shift course anymore, they'd already made too many adjustments to the wind as it was. They were smack in the middle of a gale they'd waited through August trying to avoid, and the improbability of it happening now, in September, on his own carefully plotted, intimately planned D-Day, made him want to laugh, or sob. He had a choice. He could keep her in and let her go an additional unspecified number of rounds with the waves, in which case she'd wear herself out before they hit that current mid-channel, still a good three hours away at least—and there was no guarantee that even by then the rain or winds would let up. In and of itself, that current was tough enough. It was a killer. The past eleven months he'd spent training her to last through the cold until she hit that current and then fought it out—that was all. He assessed her. Stroke still strong. So she was a little crazed out there, a little delirious, she was still eating and throwing up only about every other feeding and he figured she was strong enough right now so if he kept her in she'd stay strong a few hours more. Sure he could keep her in. He could. Sarge shook his head. There wasn't really that choice, was there.

"Go inside, Anne. Go get some rest."

She looked at the water, waves and rain and Dorey swimming in it, and Sarge saw tears in her eyes. She was understanding the situation and understanding he was right. It wasn't fair. Not at all.

"Oh Sarge. What a shame." She stepped closer to huddle against him.

He stroked her hair. "Beat it," he said gently. "Tell Tycho to get on out here."

The wind flapped her slicker around like a whip. Watching from the stern, Al thought it looked like an exotic cape. If he shut his eyes almost all the way, he'd transform it into shimmering red velvet.

"She'll hurt," said Anne. "She'll be so hurt."

"Right," Sarge hugged her, "I know."

302   "No chance?"

He shook his head.

•

The wings lowered. Dimly hearing a whistle shriek, she hesitated before stroking backwards out of the way, then hesitated because this wasn't feeding time yet. She was only on the twenty-seventh alphabet for this hour. Blind, she rolled the caps up over her right ear. She rode the intermittent swells by instinct, after a while you caught the ocean's rhythm and could predict these waves. Something tapped insistently on her head. She faced up. Rain. Her teeth chattered uncontrollably.

You've gone eleven miles, the voice told her.

She cried.

I'm calling this swim off.

"No," she yelled.

You won't make it, he coaxed. It's not you it's the goddamned weather. It's the goddamned weather and no one was predicting this, nothing's your fault.

"No," she told him, "uh-uh."

She backstroked. Four five six and then was treading again. Now the voice was farther away, indistinct. Like in those crystal caverns she'd read once you spoke and your words echoed around wildly, bounced from wall to ceiling and broke apart on the ice formations so you couldn't understand a thing.

"No," she said. She'd made up her mind. When you started something you were meant to finish it.

We'll try again. Another day. Come in now.

"You go to hell," she yelled. "Tell her I'm all right out here."

Who? Sarge leaned over, hands wave-battered and devoid of sensation. You know who, she was crying, you know, you go to hell. It occurred to him then that he did know who, and he wanted to laugh for one bitter moment. Ilana was a couple thousand miles away.

She stayed just beyond his reach and he guessed that was intentional. She ducked waves, bobbing up again and turning with blind instinct to face him. And for a moment he was uncertain. He'd never really allowed himself that luxury of indecision in crisis before but he did now and it immobilized him. He was thinking of Matt. Remembering the kid's face.

303

He was thinking about Ilana and cursing himself now. Where the hell was Ilana. However anyone might choose to be along on this ship, because of their fear or despite it or for any other slew of grand or petty motivations, she had the best goddamned one he could think of and for just a second Sarge blamed the weather on Ilana, too. He shouted out over water. Coaxed. He talked sense and he told a few lies. Uh-uh, she said, no, she wasn't coming out.

"Come on up, captain. What's the story?"
Sarge hauled the ladder in after him.
"She won't come out, Johnny." He grinned regretfully but the look was touched with pride. "She's feeling too strong."
"Well," Tycho tossed a couple of towels around Sarge's shoulder, "the coast guard's saying this won't let up, you were right. It looks like September's not immune to gales."
"I'll get her out."
Grab hold of her, touch her once like that, and she was officially disqualified. He knew she knew. He pulled off his shirt, dropped it on deck with the towels.
"Need a hand?" asked Tycho.
"Could be. Stand by."
Sarge kept an eye on her. Damn but she sure could swim. That stroke wasn't getting her much of anywhere right now but it was strong. He glanced at his watch. Ten hours of this stuff and she looked good. He wanted to kick the boat apart. She'd started to swim again and now, slowly, the pontoon arms were being raised, he imagined them groaning, wearily. Cautiously the boat moved ahead on course, parallel to her.
"Give her time," Sarge muttered.
He was coiling rope attached to the end of an inflatable flotation device, the bright-colored tube kind that could wrap around a body and snap shut.
"Give her time."
He waited. She'd slowed a little more now. Chops slammed against the boat's sides and rocked them. The rain made background static. Sarge hesitated before blowing the whistle.

When he did it eased the boat to a stop, brought her to a slow cautious tread again, brought everyone out on deck. The rain slapped nastily against each slicker. He didn't have much to say, didn't want to stare too long at the faces, or imagine what his own might look like. But Tycho's hand was on his shoulder, and he shrugged.

"Everything went fine. Everybody did a perfect job, right?"

"*Right*," Anne nodded emphatically. Her face was pale.

"This weather wasn't supposed to happen." He spread his hands and rain washed them. "So much for supposed to."

The wings were lowered while he kept his eye on her, knew that even though she couldn't see or hear anything clearly she'd sense something was up, and she was strong enough and still sharp enough to stay out of reach if she had to, make things difficult. He told Tycho to keep an eye on her. He headed for the cabin and his goggles, a couple of caps.

"Hey mister. Here."

Standing between him and the cabin, Al held out a neatly rolled bulk of mesh. It was a fishing net.

"This way's easy," Al blushed. He looked even skinnier, wrapped away inside the flapping rubberized folds of his slicker. He offered the net up to Sarge. Sunburned, freckled, his face stuck from the slicker's hood with a quality about it of perpetual, surly apology. "I use it for big fish all the time."

Later, crawling out along a pontoon with one corner of the net clenched in his teeth, Sarge understood something. Perfectly parallel to him on the other metal walkway Tycho slid along, prescription goggles strapped firmly over his eyes and the net's other corner in his own mouth. He understood something and wanted to tell Tycho. So when they'd both settled firmly in position and held their respective ends in hands instead of mouths, Sarge shouted to him and it came out a strangled sound.

"Johnny! Know what?"

What? asked Tycho.

What I hate most? I hate my own guts, Johnny.

He turned to Dorey, whistle shrieked about twenty times into rain-spattered waves and the wind. You're looking strong!

he told her. Had to repeat himself a few times, very loudly, slowly. His throat went raw. You're looking good, wind's supposed to blow over in less than an hour, can you stick it out?

She came in a little closer, nodded.

We'll get you there, he coaxed, get you there, don't worry kid now don't worry baby. Time for a feeding I think. Some broth? Want some broth. You look terrific. Here. Right. Make you nice and warm again, champ. Cold?

"Now, Johnny."

The net swung up, swung over. Lashing through the floodlit night it seemed for a moment to glitter. Then it bit through water, dragged under the swell of waves, went taut. When they hauled it closer they paused, both men weaving back and forth on their pontoons from the waist up, legs clamped so firmly around the aluminum they might as well have been plastered there. Below the surface, the net thrashed furiously.

"Count of three, Johnny." Sarge took in slack. "One. Two."

Three and the filled net rose. It twisted up above waves. Floodlights bleached struggling contours of the dark-suited body inside it.

Later, sliding inch by slow inch back along the aluminum walkway, net corner wrapped around his arm and clamped in a fist, Sarge felt coils crawling up from inside like razor-sharp claws. Hated them. His own guts. Felt how unrefined they were, how deep they'd grown and how unredeemed, how low. He and Tycho attached the net ends to waiting hooks that held it more firmly against the starboard side.

"Get a move on!" Sarge yelled to Rick. "Get her on deck and some towels, will you. Hot towels."

The body wrapped in the net had gone limp. Still he could have sworn that, had he leaned over a foot or so to his right he'd find her conscious and the goggle-blinded face, battered and swollen past familiarity, hissing poison at him.

"Okay, Sarge," Tycho cupped his hands for a funnel so he'd be heard. "It's okay now."

306   On hooks, the net rose. Tails flapping helplessly, dozens of tiny night fish fell free of its mesh, dropped back to the water in exhaustion.

"Arctic Ocean."

Anne had to lean closer.

"They breed there. In ice."

"I know what you mean," Anne said generously. "Listen, don't feel too badly about this, don't, it's got nothing to do with you."

They wrapped her in more towels. Out on deck the rain kept up. Now they were cutting a straight path across at top speed. Soon they'd hit Port Johnson.

"Ah," Tycho murmured, "that's it. Nice pulse there. Very nice."

Swollen, her eyelids closed the small remaining gap. She went through a hole. It was cut in ice with buzz saws, the kind they used to saw through the Arctic Ocean's frozen-thick layer so divers could slip in. Those divers were strong, chests puffed with muscle beneath their skin-fitting black insulation. They went into the water backward. One puncture in the insulation and they'd burn to death within seconds. Because cold, when extreme enough, had the same effect as extreme heat.

"Tycho."

"What is it?" He bent down to hear.

It was slow breathing there under ice in the cold. How cold. Maybe thirty-three degrees. At first you just stayed still, suspended by a rope attaching to the hidden surface world, then slowly righted yourself from that upside-down position. Flippers moving tentatively at first, tenderly, you'd start to see. The only sky was ice. Through it, bitter snowy sunlight filtered from above in patches. In intermittent light, delicate-tailed, tiny-finned fish flitted like flying fragments of stars. Icicles hung from the sky. Pointed spears and large hanging sheaths of ice. Stars reflected in the ice like multiplying mirror images. You'd move carefully. Here in the coldest water on earth that protected a universe apart, universe of crystal caverns where ice shot down from the tangible sky like flame tips. Then you'd hear it: the slow, measured boom-thump-thump of your heart, the rasp of each breath's suck and release. You alone with the sounds of your existence. You attached to some other place by that cord hitched around the waist. Move carefully now. Don't break a mirror-plate of ice.

"Tycho."

"I'm listening."

Face-mask pressed against a block of ice, looking in, you'd just concentrate on the sound of breath and the methodically slowing rhythm of your heartbeats until they came less and less frequently, then almost never, but louder and stronger each time. Your legs curled up towards your belly. Thumb curled up trying to find the mouth. Shuttered gaze pressed against the ice to see microscopic creatures. They had the delicate ice-etched contours of miniature snakes and centipedes, and, embedded in ice in the Arctic Ocean, they were living and breeding. Had done so without changing form for thousands of centuries. Lovely, delicate, prehistoric and varied in form. Some appeared to have wings.

"Angels," she said.

Sarge lay next to her towel-wrapped body, arms around her for heat.

"Almost there," Tycho promised.

She reached suddenly for Anne.

"Shhh," said Anne.

"I wanted it," she cried. "So much."

"I *know*."

They docked.

She'd lost ten pounds and was now sleeping endlessly. Tycho stayed awake at the bed, once in a while reached over the rails to turn her from side to side. He kept changing compresses. Already the swelling was receding.

"Tell me one thing." From across the bed Sarge held his gaze. "Did you know?"

"Know what?"

"The weather. Did you know before?"

Tycho sighed. "There were indications." He checked her pulse again, watched liquid potassium drip through the I.V. He removed each compress. She looked like the fighter who'd lost by decision. Twelfth round. Fifteenth. At any rate, quite a few.

"I don't understand."

"Would you have listened?" Tycho settled back in his chair, and the half-light made his face crazy battered stripes of red and pale. "Or stopped everything dead on the basis of some intangible indication? Look Sarge, it was a disaster out there and it wasn't your fault either, it just happened. Accept that, why don't you?"

"Damn it!"

"She's strong," Tycho smiled. "She's a beauty."

"Damn it," he whispered, "damn it."

"Next week, captain."

Sarge shook his head.

"Listen to me."

He snapped to attention. He felt how bloodshot his eyes must be, lips cracked from coatings of salt.

"Next week," Tycho said firmly.

They were silent, reading each other's eyes. Then Sarge nodded slowly, an odd cautious look crossing his face. "What's the date?"

"The fourteenth."

"Too late," Sarge frowned. "Too late and too soon all at the same time. Know how cold that water's going to be? It's dropping each day, Johnny. She won't be up to it by then either, too soon."

"No," it came out sharply. "Listen to me. The fourteenth."

Sarge was quiet for a good long time. Then, "No kidding," he muttered.

No kidding, said Tycho. He grinned. Nodded towards the blank white ceiling.

Restless, Sarge walked. He paced the room, stepped stiffly down the hall with each chilled thigh aching protest. He passed empty metal carts, movable polelike trolleys with empty I.V. bottles attached, nodded at an aide lounged against the wall reading some magazine, an on-duty nurse walking by. Sarge was tired and feeling his age. Sore muscles. In the vacant waiting room he paused, contemplated sitting on the couch and realized his body was not responding on target because it was shaking all over. Particularly the hands, arms, the knees. He perspired, itchy with salt crawling like ants into his pores. It was the thought of sitting that made him shake that way, he knew, because he had a vision in his mind of lowering into a chair and the physical act of lowering reminded him of swinging off gunwales. In his heart it was always water you sank into when you sank. Always water and always cold, and the anticipation made him shiver. Then he was sitting suddenly, eyes blurred against both fists.

"Was it very bad?"

He blinked. Against the light her features were indistinct so she was nothing but a female figure, slender and tired and gazing down at him.

"Pretty bad." His voice came out cracked. "It just crept up on us, Ilana, there wasn't much warning. It was pretty bad."

She crouched, her hands resting gently on his knees. His vision fogged and he could have sworn her face was free of age. Maybe he'd been hallucinating after all. She was a couple thousand miles away so far as he knew.

"There's a hotel." She nodded beyond the wall. "I've been waiting."

Sarge wanted to tell her. That water had taken something from him long ago. You had to keep a sharp eye on it, had to, otherwise it would steal from you every time. He'd thrown Matt in full of life, then maybe relaxed his guard for a moment. He hadn't known the kid well enough, hadn't understood his limits. That life was dwindled, then suddenly gone completely. His son had been kidnapped while his back was turned, and gazing at the mirage in front of him Sarge felt his eyes full of water and reached to touch her face, expecting his fingertips to caress only air. When they touched flesh instead she was no longer ageless. Through water he saw her clearly for the first time: his wife, mother of his child, a woman also separate from him—so if there was no way to see a child just as he was, there was no way to see a lover just as she was—except in moments like this, when every illusion had been deadened and all expectations failed. He wanted to tell her he'd kept an eye on things this time, hadn't relaxed his guard once. Because of his vigilance they'd survived and he wanted to tell her how glad he was, so glad, that they were all three of them together again, and alive.

"She'll be okay," he said.

Her cheek smoothed against his before pulling back. "I was afraid for so long."

"Still?"

"Oh." She smiled. "I'm still afraid but maybe I've grown used to the feeling. At any rate, it doesn't matter anymore."

He spread her palm against his. Looked down to see their fingers form the contours of a many-armed starfish. There was no living proof remaining of what they'd created, it was all dissolved in saltwater, and when their palms touched the sensation was for both a shock—like a body strolling easily through night air crashing, unexpectedly, into an unseen pile of leaves. Both guilty. They were co-authors of death.

"September fourteenth," he spoke quietly, "is nine days away. If she wants we'll go for it again."

"You ought to get some sleep."

"I'm glad you're here, Ilana. That water." He lost the words, swallowed everything that bubbled up from inside. "Hell. I hate that water. You should see her face. I feel it in here, right here." He tapped his chest, he was crying. "Here's where I feel it."

She pulled his head down onto her shoulder. "Don't, dear. Don't hate it too much. You can't control things all the time." She told him the room number and gave him keys, said to get some rest. And to take her umbrella, it was still raining outside.

Some time just before dawn, Anne woke in tears. She listened to the continual splash of rain on panes and roof gutters

and, beyond the rain, dull sounds of surf pulsing along
beaches a few streets away.

In the marina boats would be anchored close, tarpaulin-
covered. They'd look like shrouded pieces of furniture in some
hurriedly deserted mansion.

"What is it," Rick whispered after a while.

The mattress sagged at its middle. He rolled closer to her.

"Michigan." She shivered. "It was cold."

Rick kicked off the sheet. Listening, he waited.

"You always think you'll make it," she said, "until you
don't."

"Was there a moment when you knew you wouldn't?"

Her head shook emphatically in the dark. "No! No way. I
kept believing I would, really, really, I just needed to get there,
Rick. It was a profound need of mine. Then I opened my eyes
in a hospital and realized I hadn't made it. I felt robbed. It
was like being gutted." She wiped her cheeks on a pillow. "Let
me tell you, it's a good thing I came to when there wasn't
anyone around. I wanted to die. That's what I wanted. It
seemed like the only alternative because when I planned on
Michigan, and when I trained for it, I told myself I needed
this swim in order to live. I needed to complete the crossing
and that was that, nothing else would be acceptable. So I
came to alone, I was hurting pretty badly at that point, and
here I was in a situation I hadn't counted on at all. You never
plan for failure. Succeeding meant I could live. I guess for a
while there when I knew I hadn't made it I preferred to die,
honestly, there was so much emptiness, Rick. So much."

Lying very close, he wanted to touch her and was careful
not to.

"I couldn't move, either. Everything just hurt. Then I heard
footsteps, and I thought someone was coming to check up on
me and inside"—her hand covered a breast—"I more or less
snapped to and I said to myself, Norton, you had better listen,
you needed to do this more than anything else in the world
and you didn't get to succeed at doing it and this need of yours
is unfulfilled and maybe, maybe it will never be fulfilled, understand? And if you want to live, lady, then you will have to

live with *that*." She laughed a little. "The footsteps went right on by my room. Another raw deal. I just made up my mind then. I decided I could and would live with it. Anyway. I had a dream about Michigan, so I was crying."

After a while she got out of bed and went to the window, opened it a little so the sound of rain burst through forcefully. She pressed her face against curtains.

"I'm glad," he said.

"Glad?"

"That you made up your mind."

"I am too!" her voice was clear now. "Otherwise just think, no Dr. Norton. No Big Rick Barton." Listening, he cheered. He smiled inside in a way that hurt. No longbow, she was saying, no Boston Bull. No streichquartette. It was nice now, didn't he think, nice anyway, even without those things, just being around before morning.

Yes, he told her.

A little light came through soon, gray, rainy, and he watched it outline her dimly against the curtains. Standing there, she seemed temporarily motionless. Seemed smaller to him than before but somehow more regal, gone far away in thought and quite, quite solitary.

Ilana leaned over. The beaten face swelled back at her. She looked up sharply at Tycho, but when she spoke it was gentle.

"Go away, Doctor."

He nodded wordlessly, brushed her shoulder in passing. Then he was gone down the hall.

She changed the compresses often. Reduce as much swelling as possible before morning and pain would be reduced too. Ilana made that her task. She dabbed the lips with salve. They were puffed and broken, it would hurt to talk. Ilana didn't let herself think about that. This face belonged to someone she didn't know—that's what she told herself—and her near-complete removal from intimacy with it allowed her hands to remain steady and to function.

The body moved. Puffed eyelids quivered, dreaming.

313

It was 4:30 a.m.

The body shuddered, in sleep repeated an incoherent name. Ilana pushed down the bed's side rails, sat in Tycho's chair. She couldn't make out the sounds and told herself she must listen better. She bent closer. For a second she thought she had it but the sounds stopped. For a second she thought it was her own name being repeated. Then she felt herself shake slightly all over with fatigue, no longer removed and so no longer safe.

At a little past five the body lunged weakly to one side. Ilana helped it turn to the left, away from her. Keep turning, she remembered that. Stop water from collecting in the lungs. You could drown in bed, too.

Ilana watched the back facing her. The hospital gown split open along the spine. The skin peeking through white curtains was dusky red-brown, followed the backbone up to disappear beneath dark hair curled on the neck. Ribs rose and fell with slow breaths. Ilana stood, reached over to remove compresses. The face appeared not so distorted as before, and recognizing Dorey in those sleeping features Ilana looked away quickly, sat again and told the panic to leave.

Please be all right, she asked the silent body.

Wake up, said Ilana. Give me another chance.

She closed her own eyes, felt her head nod forward easily. Easy. It would be so easy just to give in now and sleep. Like those Klondikers who'd never made it back to their trading posts in northern winters, discovered days later frozen solid and curled into the snow, asleep and dead, tranquil smiles on their faces. After a while the cold and need for sleep became a sort of stupor, like opium, the snow an inviting and delightfully clean white sheet. To be enveloped, give up the burden of maintaining an existence separate from it—that's what beckoned from the vast white. Knees caved in towards the sinking chest without sensation. Let me in, you'd say to the snow. Ah. So warm. Lover. This is what I've wanted. Then you just went to sleep.

314   Ilana snapped to attention. Somewhere were sounds.

"Ilana."

By itself the body had turned towards her. The face still swollen, cracked and battered. Ilana reached to brush the forehead lightly with fingertips.

"Ilana. You're here."

She nodded.

"What time?"

Ilana told her. Dorey tried to lift an arm, motioned vaguely in the direction of her mouth. Ilana wet a tissue. She squeezed water onto the lips.

Outside shoes squeaked along the corridor. Everything was light gray now, and through sealed windows came the steady sound of rain. Ilana heard metal wheels click, supply carts being rolled.

"Ilana."

"What, dear."

Dorey looked at her fully, eyes dark and unreadable. Pain, Ilana thought for a moment, then wasn't at all sure. The words were surprisingly clear.

"Poor Ilana. Your hair."

"What?"

"Your hair's all gray."

Ilana glanced at the bedside mirror. It was true.

"Great!" The shutter clicked. Rick advanced film.

Dorey pulled her bare feet up onto the armchair, knees to chest. She glared at the camera.

"That's *enough*." Anne stared dismally out at the incessant drizzle. Fifth day of high winds. Fifth day of what they'd been calling unseasonable rains. Scratch the predictions, she'd scowled at Sarge, just scratch them for this year, right? She turned to Rick and her tone softened, teasing. "You know, I was never a fan of photography."

"Me neither, *señorita*. Just think how oils will brighten up a canvas based on this stuff, though."

"What'll you call it?"

"*Waiting.*"

Dorey grabbed a chair cushion. She threw it vehemently at the ceiling and it thudded there, flopped down. After a pause Anne applauded. They laughed.

Rick turned to Al, who also sat on the rug, back propped against the wall. When Rick spoke his tone was conspiratorial. "Natives are restless."

Al snickered. "Tell them to calm down," he suggested, "calm down or next time I'll haul them both out in the net."

Dorey looked at him.

"If you do that again," she said calmly, "I'll kill you."

Al's smile went away by swift degrees until his face was pale beneath the tanned freckles, thin, and very young.

"Hey! Hey, relax." Anne turned suddenly to Dorey and then scowled at the two male figures lounging against the wall. "*I'll* kill you first, hotshot. Both of you." Her arm swept the room's dead air, wrath spun out and encircled Rick also, as the camera shutter clicked to store her in mid-motion. "Do you hear?" She'd raised her voice. "Do you? All of you *witnesses*. With your thousand-dollar cameras."

Sarge held out a hand. Perfectly balanced, Ilana touched it lightly and stepped on deck. Behind her, the dock stood solidly, attaching to land she'd left behind. For a moment she felt dizzy with release.

"See these?" Over the gunwales he slapped raised pontoon riggings proudly. "They lower into the water. There's a lever. You can even walk out when it's calm."

"And talk to her?"

"Right. You can talk to her."

Slowly, she walked from stern to prow, under riggings, around the cabin. Water slapped gently against the boat's sides. A small yacht, sails furled, motored past them at turtle pace and the young man on board waved casually.

"Going to try for it again?" he yelled to Sarge.

"Hey?"

"The San Antonio!"

"The fourteenth!" Sarge called back, then stopped, surprised. Funny how word got around. Like telepathy, invisible wires buzzing unusual news to everyone in the area. They'd made no attempt at publicity and he hoped there'd be none, she was too shy of that stuff as it was. Even Barton's photography had gotten on her nerves these past couple of days. Still he couldn't stop himself from replying. Three days away. He walked along deck, following the yacht's slow progress and looking down to the eager, dark-haired face turned up towards him.

"Are you the coach or something?"

"Right."

"You too?"

"Oh," said Ilana, "I'm the coach's wife." Then she paused, leaned over gunwales. "And a close friend."

"Well good luck, huh. It takes balls." He blushed. "Excuse me, lady."

Ilana laughed.

He waved as the yacht drifted out of the harbor for free space, then put a couple of fingers to his mouth, whistled shrilly and raised a fist, saluting.

Ilana's hair was a thick gray shining mass that tumbled onto her neck. Dark strands ran through it. Sarge watched its curls shiver in pleasant breeze until it looked electric silver. He realized with a shock that she was beautiful in a way he'd never noticed, standing there on deck apart from him, her hair suddenly all gray.

"Coming along?" he asked. "What about it?"

"What do you feel?"

"Difficult. Everything hurts." He shrugged. "Hell, I just love you. You do what you have to, Ilana. I hope it's yes."

"There's something, I want you to do it for me."

"All right." Ilana touched her hand briefly and they kept walking. Sunset was just over, sky out on the horizon bordering San Antonio Island vaguely pink at its edge.

"Well. I don't know."

"Tell me," Ilana coaxed. "What is it?"

Tide lapped at them a few yards away. Dorey could hear breakers thud on rocks at the beach's southern tip.

"Lie to me."

"What?" Ilana said softly. "I don't understand."

She took both of Ilana's hands in hers. They were so warm. "When it gets bad, during the swim I mean. If you talk to me. Tell me—I don't know. Tell me I'm almost there. Almost. Don't tell me how far it is, Ilana. Just say I'm almost there." She sighed, relieved. "Just keep telling me that no matter what."

Ilana peered to see her face. The features were obscured so for an instant she had the feeling it could have been anyone here in front of this water with her, any swimmer. Softly, she shook her head.

"Why?"

The face smiled. "I'll believe you. Then I'll keep going."

"If you know I'm lying?"

"Ah. I won't know by then. I'll just believe it's true." Some last flickerings of twilight gave the lips a death-mask's grin. "See. You never lied to me."

They went down to the water. Ilana removed her shoes and let both feet freeze in the wet. "Here, Dorey. It's a perfect egg shape." She handed over the smoothed stone her toes found. "You haven't gained back all of that weight, have you."

"Uh-uh."

"How do you feel?"

"Good. I feel good, Ilana."

Dorey waded out almost to knee level. Each step was high so the foot raised above water, and watching the sure, fluid toe-first point of each foot back below the surface, Ilana was surprised all over again by the sudden delicacy of motion. She didn't know her really. Not yet. A wave rose, drenched her to the waist. Dorey laughed. She turned to Ilana, back carelessly facing the expanse of water, and stretched both arms skyward. Ilana thought for a minute she'd grow wings. Then she'd take off, leave her stranded here on the sand to get older, wingless and childless.

318

"Ilana!"

"What dear?"

"That feeling! When you climb out of the water. You know you did it. It's better than anything."

Yes, Ilana told her, yes it must be.

"Well will you?"

"What?"

"Lie to me."

"I'll try."

Dorey waded back to shore. When she was close Ilana noticed the smooth egg-shaped quartz still in her fist, and reaching out lowered her face to one of those broad shoulders. The neck her cheek pressed against was strong, smooth. It was young.

"The last time," Dorey whispered, "it was bad, Ilana. I got hurt."

"I know."

"No more giant. Look. I have to get across this time."

Ilana pulled back a little to look at her. When she spoke her voice had a reassurance she didn't feel. Well, she told herself, let this be the first lie then. "I know you have to. So you will."

"Uh-huh."

"You know," she said carefully, "you're the one to do it."

"I am."

"Yes. Of course."

"I'm going to this time. I will."

"I know you will."

They walked some more. After a while stars speckled the sky. The air was touched with cold.

"Guess what, my periods stopped. Before Laughing River. April."

"It's okay, you know."

Dorey nodded. She jiggled the rock in her fist.

"Tired?"

No, Dorey told her, not really. She guessed she'd eat some more though and then go to bed. "Will you stay with me tonight?"

"I hoped you would ask."

"I'm glad, Ilana. Look. I'll be there." She reached and her fingertips fluttered against Ilana's cheek. Feel that, she said, it's nice. It's soft. See. You gave something back to me.

"I did?"

"Uh-huh. My sense of touch. This last time in the water, I missed it. You. Well," she smiled tiredly, "come by when you want. I'll leave the door open so remember to lock it."

"Of course."

"Remember. I'll show you what I missed, Ilana. I will."

V

TOUCH

At 6:05 a.m. the sun had risen. Air temperature was seventy degrees and rising. Water temperature was fifty-three degrees Fahrenheit.

Dorey was greased and suited. She set her goggles for a good fit. Turning to Sarge, she suddenly pointed an accusing finger that, when she grinned, turned into a gun and her thumb the trigger. Bam, it went silently. Then she kissed its invisibly smoking barrel, aimed it again. Sarge dropped the plastic ointment container, hands up.

"Got me."

"Do I?"

"You've got me."

"The second time," she smiled calmly, "the second time things work."

Along the milder shore of Punta Provechosa, Al waited patiently with his outboard. McNeil stayed in the jeep. You don't have to go along again, you know, he'd told Al, we can get them out there and motor back in together. No, Al said, he wanted to go. So McNeil kept to himself in the driver's seat and looked a little gloomy, seemed almost to have shrunk, or aged.

Walking out, Sarge was careful not to touch her. "Breakfast feeling all right?"

Beneath the grease and goggles he could make out an apologetic expression. "I threw up."

He gave her a grin to stop any anxiety from showing. "Thought you liked raw eggs." He checked his watch. Glancing up he noticed Ilana seated on the hood of the jeep, hair catching sunlight to sparkle silver. She'd strapped a bag of supplies over one shoulder and, when she saw them, smiled and waved.

He watched Dorey head towards the jeep. Her gray-greased back glistened. He couldn't hear what she said.

"It's all okay, Ilana. Everything."

Ilana just nodded.

Dorey's fingers fluttered. "I'll see you tomorrow."

Water sucked at land, at the rocks along it. It churned everything up and laid down a new surface, then crept back before the next surge. It made rocks smaller and smoother by microscopic measurements every minute of every day. It swept firm earth into soaked chaos. This was cold water that made you numb. This was water in which average human beings did not live for very long. It was rough water. Saltwater.

Dorey stepped into the water.

She took another step, slowly. Began to feel her toes again. Then she stopped just to look. It was that beautiful clear green-gray tint that made you remember warm things. Dorey stepped deeper, up to the knees. Shallow now, and receding. The tide would take her out past the breakers. This water made you think of coral reefs and sun and still it was so cold you almost couldn't believe it existed in the same world as the sun, on the same day, under the same sky. She stepped again. Ilana, she said. Then she wanted to jump out backward to warmth, seventy degrees and rising, and the land where Ilana was. The place she was going Ilana couldn't be in so with each step she lost her more and more.

Then something inside her clicked, the door to all that shut and was securely latched. Dorey breathed. Felt good. A little underweight, she'd have preferred to weigh another ten pounds and it was true she'd peaked for the fifth, not fourteenth, but this was a peak they'd worked on a year and she guessed she could ask it to stay through another day. She breathed deeply, went forward until water crept up her thighs. It was calm here near shore. The alphabet. She'd start out with the alphabet this time and run through that for the first two hours just to establish pace. She'd planned it all carefully. Alphabets for the first one hundred and twenty minutes and then she would do numbers up to three thousand. Then there was the tape Tycho'd sent up. She'd memorized it through those earphones. The tape was forty-seven minutes long. If she went through it song by song once, filled in the remaining thirteen minutes by calculating flip turns to every tenth stroke, that took her another hour and by then it was time for feeding. Then alphabets again. And later she'd be dreaming somewhere else anyway, no need for alphabets. Cold. She stepped waist-deep. She was ready. She had to walk out a way, feel it get shallower, then the suck of breakers on sandbars, then the pull tugging her towards them and she went along for the ride, sidestepped whitecaps, caught a swell and was no longer on her feet but kicking, lifting the right arm high, all of her in water.

The sun becoming higher and brighter drove Tycho into the cabin. He'd step out once in a while with a baseball cap's brim shielding his face, leave Barton—who knew a little about boats and could be relied on to follow instructions—at the controls. He was generally careful not to expose his face to too much sunlight, even rowing he wore some hat or other. Come night and he'd be back out there full-time, though. He'd never heard of moonlight harming scar tissue.

At the controls Rick chuckled. The sound made Tycho look up suddenly. It's a good day, Rick said without turning around. A good day. Yes, Tycho told him, it is.

"You're a doctor. Will you tell me something?"

Yes? Tycho waited.

"These swims. How much do you depend on the body? And how much the mind?"

"What do you mean?"

"For success. How much of it's just a strong body?"

Tycho understood. He sat back, manuscript slipping shut on the table in front of him. "Oh, you're speaking percentage? What part of it's physical and what part the psyche?"

From behind, he saw Rick nod slightly.

Tycho had to think. It was a difficult question: Given several people of, say, equivalent physical condition, throw them all simultaneously into a situation of extreme demands and some of them might make it while others failed. So how could you tell why life stopped functioning for some? And was it at the point when effective physical functioning ceased that it was also determined who would survive and who would not? Who had whatever the extra was that sustained when physical capacity had long since been depleted?

"I don't know," he said quietly. "I really don't know."

After a while Rick shrugged. "Me neither."

It was just after seven a.m. She'd stopped for her first feeding.

"Don't."

Defiantly, Rick clicked the shutter. He advanced film and smiled. "Thank you."

A golden brown back was turned to him. He admired the body's slinking, sulking motion along deck. At one of the life preservers hanging amidst rope coils she wheeled around.

He took the picture.

"Tell me, Anne. What do you have against photography all of the sudden?"

"It's not all of the sudden."

"You're always talking about video tapes and film—"

"That's not the same."

"What do you mean?"

"If you don't know, I can't help you."

Anne took refuge in the stern where Al sat on towels, tanning lotion smeared liberally across his face. He was carving some figure out of wood with a Swiss army knife. "You shouldn't play with knives," she snapped. He looked up immediately, wounded. Then put the knife away. Anne paused. "Hey. I'm sorry."

"No sweat." Sadly, Al examined the half-carved figure before tucking it under a backpack flap. It was a crude, angular attempt at a full-breasted, long-torsoed woman's body. "It's no good anyway."

Anne slid a little to one side with the ship's sway and righted herself. She told him she was sorry, really sorry, she had no right to say things like that. She had this habit of getting angry and of treating everyone around as if they were her loyal subjects and it was no good, it was a lousy way to be, she knew.

"Oh, you're not so bad." Al grinned. Then he remembered the globs of lotion on his face and grabbed for a towel, wiped it nervously. "You're okay."

"Thanks. That's the nicest thing anyone's said to me all day."

"It's only eight o'clock. Stick around." When he heard the words echo he blushed profoundly.

Anne laughed. "You're smooth, ace." She blew a kiss and then he laughed too, turned a deeper scarlet but somehow the fact that she'd gently defused him came as a relief.

The sun speckled his back with sweat. "I feel pretty bad about something," he confided.

"Shoot."

"When I made that crack about the net. I just feel lousy about it."

Anne waved that away. "Don't worry. I'll bet she's forgotten all about it, you know."

"No." He shook his head miserably. "No, she won't. I just know. And if she's out there—there, you know, and it's dark, what if she thinks I'm really going to use it?" His eyes searched Anne's. She was surprised at the desperation there.

"Listen," she said gently, "let me tell you—take it from an expert, okay?—tonight that's going to be one of the furthest things from her mind. Do you know what she'll be thinking about by tonight?"

He shook his head.

"Food." Anne patted her stomach, winked knowingly. "She'll be thinking about eating and how to stop feeling so cold. That's all. So don't you worry."

"You think?"

"I know."

"I feel so bad."

Anne examined the sunburnt, freckled face. She was surprised again to see tears waver in his eyes. They looked at her, asking something, before glancing self-consciously away. The tears never did spill. They just hung there unwanted, stuck around sullenly, boy's tears.

Whistles blew and the ship slowed to a stop. Just after eight. Anne stood to hang over the gunwales, searched out the

327

white-capped head pausing now among slick, rolling waves, aluminum wings lowering towards her.

When Sarge reached up it was Ilana's hand he gripped. "Cold?"

He was drenched. "I'm okay. Everything's all right."

She handed him a towel, took the feeding stick away, and looped it carefully through rope latches on the gunwales so it looked like a blunted harpoon waiting to be used. She told him the *Lazarilla* had radioed in to say that water temperature was holding steady and so was the humidity.

"Good. She looks good out there."

Ilana nodded.

"Swims like a dream."

"It's what she does best." Ilana leaned over to watch, the way she'd been doing for the past three hours almost without pause. Her eyes had already begun to ache. "It's where her pride comes from, Sarge."

"Right! She is that, she's proud."

Ilana eased the towel gently from his grip and offered it like a cape to a bull. Sarge lowered his head. She rubbed it dry.

With each roll of the boat she got a free-floating feel of being completely detached from earth. Each was like the initial jump from cliffside and, as she balanced easily, Ilana felt all that litheness she'd thought years had left behind returning. She wondered what had kept her earthbound so long, when her natural milieu was that airy limbo between land and water. The waves were four-footers. She watched, eyes shaded by dark glasses, skin sheltered under a hat's wide brim. Between swells the blank white head turned for air every two strokes now, arms arched up and spearing down in perfect timing, machinelike. That was Dorey Tomas out there, someone she'd grown to know and still didn't know well, not really, because to know her well would have taken more time. Was it always that way. These torrents of half-knowledge, as if behind the illusion of the body you pressed against lurked a multitude of shadows—and the very act of holding and of loving made the shadows impossible to reach—the body, the illusion of it anyway, always there in the way. Well she'd lost all the darkness of her hair for this. Ilana guessed there was no more reason to be afraid of whatever might happen, or of shadows. For a second she had the urge to leap into water.

From behind, Sarge's arms went around her. He was damp, big, securely rooted, and Ilana felt a rush of pleasure and relief that he'd touched her again. Then she knew what had held her earthbound for so long. When she reached behind to touch his cheek, her eyes were sad but dry.

It was time for the third feeding.

Of all the planets spinning that day through the planetary system, only one had on it the vast collections of liquid water called oceans. Descending to a certain depth, the human body would begin to compress. Eventually the external pressure of increasingly dense water would force the body to cave in. This was long, long before it hit bottom—the ocean floor —a longer distance than up Everest and longer than the 10 K. At bottom the floor was in a state of constant geological change. Shelves were crumbling, valleys deepening, plains and ridges shifting. The changes echoed up through pitch-dark cold, past levels where plants grew bleak white without sun, and sucking fish swallowed molecular configurations of plankton that glowed in perpetual night. The echoes bumped off ascending layers of shelf sloping into dry-topped continents. They spun up in zigzags, rumbled through decreasing blackness and density towards the first gray glimmerings of light. Bouncing, enmeshed in one another, the echoes of change sliced through to water surface. There they met air, sun, wind, and rain that fed water to the water. Meeting this, the echoes struggled along the surface as currents. Like the floor from which they'd ascended, they were in a state of constant change. So the current that ran parallel to the main-land shore of the San Antonio Strait could not be predicted long-range. It was subject to forces other than wind, or rain. All it did was writhe around itself, each of its multitudinous

329

echoes struggling, snaking brutally along the ocean surface in a long, south-flowing stream.

At four minutes past ten in the morning on September 14, Dorey Thomas was swimming along the ocean surface at a rate of about two miles an hour—which, considering surface temperature and relative turbulence, was damned good time to be making. So she had swum nearly eight miles into the strait of San Antonio, heading east from Punta Provechosa. Another eight miles away, just about mid-channel, the current waited. It meandered. It would take her longer than just another four hours to reach there because, although she did not know it, the water temperature would soon drop by one degree and that would slow her down. Her change in pace would at first be unnoticeable, but by infinitesimal increments she would continue to slow until, at nightfall, her pace would appear drastically altered.

At five minutes past ten she stopped, backstroked methodically and was treading in water. It was time for her fourth feeding.

"That's where you're wrong," Rick snapped. It was his turn to pace and he did it tentatively, sensitive to the deck's seesaw motion. The encased camera dangled around his neck. "It's not still-life."

"Then what is it?"

"*Light*, Anne. It's sunlight." He paused on his way to the cabin. "For your information." Then he'd gone inside.

Al finished the torso. He gave the belly button an extra whorl and carved down, started tenderly on the figure's genitals. Anne leaned over.

"Let's see."

"I'm not ready yet."

"Just a sneak preview."

Proudly, he held it out.

"Nice! Only"—she pointed between the figure's thighs—"that's a little inaccurate, just a little. The split doesn't go up quite so far and anyway it's not really *split*, is it, you want more of a fold effect there. Like lips."

"Lips."

"Yes! A mouth without teeth."

He grinned, then was immediately serious. "It's got to look soft."

"Yes it does."

"Really soft." He held the wood in front of him, squinting. If he shut his eyes nearly all the way it became flesh-colored and larger, thighs beginning to open in measured, skin-fluttering motion. He looked up in time to see her stand unsteadily, walk towards the cabin and disappear inside.

Al shrugged sullenly. He checked his watch. It was nearly eleven o'clock, the sun had begun to really blaze. He put on a white visor and tossed a T-shirt over his shoulders.

"Listen. It's like this: We're still seeing light from stars that blew out long ago. Thousands of years ago. And what we see is the image of the star that the light creates, not the star itself, follow me?"

"Yes of course."

"So maybe somebody out there with fabulously advanced equipment is gazing through it onto planet earth right now. Only what they're seeing is something you did years ago! Because images travel at the speed of light. They're out there millions of light years away maybe, and they're seeing"—he grinned mischievously—"little Anne Norton breaststroking away at the Olympic Trials—"

"Oh cut it out!" She smiled despite herself.

"They are! And they're taking that picture, maybe. Well," he patted the zoom lens gently, "that's what I'm doing too. Right now. In a manner of speaking."

She thought about it. Yes, she told him after a while, yes she could see his point. But this close to the actual event his presence with a camera altered things. The camera changed the event itself in some way, didn't he think.

"Sure," Rick said, "but so what?"

"I don't know."

"It's light, Anne. Just sunlight. It's taking the sun and seeing it write a history book."

331

After a while she smiled and kissed him. Okay she told him, sure, but was it really tangible evidence?

By noon Anne's stomach felt lousy. Dorey stopped for her sixth feeding. Anne had a glass of mineral water.

Well, Dorey told herself, see, you should have put on more weight. You're already cold.

She told herself she'd been colder before. Quebec. That year at Lac Louie. Or Ontario some days, sure. D breathe E F breathe G H breathe I J.

There was one sound in the world. It was flesh on water, each splash the same. It rang against the layers on her ears. S T breathe U V breathe. Each hand already numb. One of those hands would touch sand tomorrow and she wouldn't feel it at first it would be so numb but then a quick jolting sensation would quiver up the arm of the hand that was first to touch. K L breathe M N breathe O P.

Colder before and weighed less. How many fingers? Burns used to say as a joke. If you can count to ten you're okay in my book. Which direction you going? Know that and you're all right. Keep going that way that's all that counts, he said, I don't care if you freeze your butt off. Keep that pace and concentrate on where you're heading. Keep that pace and worry about yourself, forget the rest of those jokers in there. Let the water take care of them, you concentrate on where you're going and the water you're in.

U V breathe W X breathe Y Z breathe A B. That stroke of yours, Burns shook his head, distance stroke, distance, that's what you're doing there in this measly little pool. Maybe the 800 this year they'd said. Said that to Carol. The 800. Q R breathe S T breathe. No. She wouldn't slip back to then. Not to childhood or triumph. Not to despair either. This was it— now. Only now, the now was all that mattered. No backsliding. Not yet. Now was just the getting there, stroke, stroke, breath, numbers and the alphabets. No pools here no mothers here. No books here no lovers. Not now. Then was before. There was no past here, only water. Water always shifting, always in the present. Breathe. Don't slip back. Not now. Not yet. A B breathe C D. Burns. Remember. Old guy. Mean old guy. Said women were the tops at this stuff in his book, more endurance, less complaints.

Carol. It's cold.

No, she told herself, no you can't go back to then. Not now. Too early. Stay here. K L breathe M N breathe O P breathe Q R breathe and she caught herself, shivered smiles to herself, she could count to ten and go A to Z breathe A B breathe C D breathe and she knew, she was sure, of the direction. East. She was swimming the San Antonio Strait, she was going to cross it and touch land at the end. S T breathe U V. Pale lovely Pacific. It was frozen green-gray and not a fish in sight.

D breathe E F breathe G H breathe I J. Time for her feeding now. She stopped to tread and then the whistle shrilled once twice three times, up to five so she backstroked and was treading again. Cold but it was all right. You're okay, she said. You know where you're going, where you're crossing to.

It was five after one in the afternoon. She grabbed for the cup.

Tycho opened his eyes. The boat rocked in rhythm, he heard waves slap its sides and the whistle that cried like a gull through his afternoon meditation.

"Sarge?"

"Out there." Rick motioned with his chin.

Fitting into a baseball cap, Tycho stood and balanced on the seesawing deck, tilted up out of the cabin. Sunlight shot across his vision as a hot yellow streak. They'd stopped again and he checked his watch. Just after two o'clock. He leaned over to see.

Sarge crawled along the pontoon, washed by waves. He held the stick in his hand like a spear. Tycho watched the broad arch of his friend's back over the aluminum drum, saw him reach and extend towards the bobbing white-topped fig- 333 ure treading there in water. Grease had long since washed away, and the flesh of her shoulders, arms, and neck peeking through water occasionally was sun-brown tinged with red. She was reaching for the cup, hand missing it, reaching again. She was drinking and Sarge talked to her.

"How are you, dear?"

He touched Ilana's arm. "Okay. It's a hot sun. How long have you been here?"

"Forever."

"Get some rest."

"Doctor's orders?" She smiled tiredly. "I'm all right, Tycho. I'm all rested up and ready for this, don't you know? Look. Look at her swim."

You're hungry and you ought to eat, it said. Here, eat this. She did. Couldn't see her hand reach for the liquid but knew it was out there somewhere, heading in the right direction and shuddering uncontrollably like her teeth. What went down hurt her lips and tongue. They were puffy with salt and raw.

Remember where you're going, it said. East. Remember stay here for a while because you haven't hit that current yet. Important. Stay.

Carol.

Not yet.

It was cold.

When the moon goes high in the—

Stay.

She did. Lifted the right arm, stroked, stroked, breathed to her right. She swallowed saltwater. Then something forced its way up from her stomach, all the heat vomiting out of her. She had to stop. Rolled over on her back, shaking. Couldn't keep it down. I'm sick, she said. Sarge I'm sick. Oh come on, it said. It was a voice she'd heard before. Come on, don't be a cry baby. You're just fine. You know the story. You're strong so stop sniveling.

She rolled back over quickly, lifted the right arm, the left, breathed, again. Swimming. There now, see, that's better, that's the way it is meant to be. You're doing well, see how well.

Who are you? she asked.

Dorey Thomas.

Well it's good to meet you. Thank you. Thanks a lot. Dorey Thomas the swimmer?

The swimmer. Listen. Let me tell you a secret. All these terrible things, they aren't happening to you. The cold. The sick feeling. These things are not happening. Not to you. They are happening to me. So relax.

I'm sick.

Stop complaining. Come on. Faster. Don't you want to make good time? Well then. Let's get moving.

Here, all here. Hands arms neck head, bench press, lats.

What about your legs?

Leg press. Hamstrings quadriceps. Not much good at it.

That's okay. Keep kicking, you know you're strong.

Yes. Well I do. Thanks. When the moon goes high in the sky I also rise and my eyes are tired from so much looking at the sea. No. That's not the way it goes. Before dawn I also rise and my eyes. Breathe. Are tired. Breathe. Okay now. Sure I'm still crossing the San Antonio Strait, I am in water. They said try the 800, Carol, just try—

Not yet. Stay here. You have to.

—the 800, the Regionals. See how she does at—

Get back here.

—and they were surprised weren't they.

Dorey! Dorey Thomas! Stay a while.

She did. One two three four up to ten. Alphabet once more, one more time just to make sure. Hands arms shoulders neck all right. Breathe. Torso yes. Breathe. Thighs calves breathe. Toes count them. How many, Burns? Count to ten and where are you heading? East in the strait of San Antonio. To touch sand tomorrow. Uh-huh.

She was okay. She knew where she was and where she was going to and there was someone out in the fog now, telling her try this, this is broth. Broth and a vanilla cookie, try it champ. She did. It was three o'clock.

335

The *Lazarilla* radioed in that water temperature was down to fifty-two and might drop more before dark. Might but they doubted it. Then again, this was the San Antonio. You couldn't be sure.

"Cold." Anne shuddered. "I hate it."

Ilana watched the sun's progress. It was west in the sky now, worst afternoon heat over, and though she'd been drinking plenty of water she felt numbed by the sun, a little dazed. Maybe it was simply that she'd been focusing on that white dot swimming through water for so many hours. Focus on anything long enough and you went somewhere else.

"She looks good."

"Yes she does," said Ilana.

"She *is* good. She's just got a lot to her, don't you think."

Ilana turned to Anne. "Yes I do think so."

Him too, Anne was saying, lazy gesture washing towards Sarge as he huddled alone at the prow watching his swimmer. Him too. You know I always told Sarge you've got good taste.

Coolly, Ilana met her eyes and they examined each other boldly—neither flinched. Looking back, Anne had that open expression that was at times actually guileless. Ilana waited until she was sure. Then she'd accept whatever had been intended. After a while she decided it was a compliment and smiled. Thank you, she said, I suppose you're right about that. "And thank you for being a friend to Matt. I don't think I ever told you before but I'm glad you were his friend."

"I am too. Friendship. It's the best way to be, I think."

"Sometimes," Ilana told her. "Sometimes."

It was almost four. Ilana brushed softly past Anne and took a slow walk. She was feeling unsettled—not seasick, but a little fragmented and nowhere near hungry. Just after Matt's death she'd gone for days without experiencing hunger. Finally Tycho paid a visit, shoved a plate in front of her piled high with everything and said listen damn it, you'd better eat. So she had. It was as simple as that.

"Hello." When she touched Sarge's shoulder he turned. "Tired?"

He shook his head. "Thinking."

"It's almost four."

"Right."

336

"I can feed her this time, Sarge, if you're tired. I'd like to."

Minutes later, she'd changed clothes. Ilana imagined herself sliding along aluminum, feeling for a grip. Would it be like climbing cliffs. She'd balance the feeding stick and hot cup in one hand. If there were cookies or any other solid food it would be wrapped in plastic. She focused on the image of herself doing this. Once she had a clear picture of how she would appear, she knew she could do it easily. It was a matter of visual cognizance—for her, all movement was.

She stepped down rope rungs.

That's when she felt the cold. Spraying against the bared top of her chest it was salty and numbing. Gasping, she'd forgotten what it was like. She took her time before crouching to sit, slide along those few feet out to the pontoon's end with careful balance while her legs hung, feelingless, in water. The waves had diminished during the last hour. None washed over her. Still, it was cold.

It was a cold that gave her the feel of death. Loss of sensation from the toes up. She wondered had it been that way for Matt. Must have been. Always the extremities became numb first. So death crept in on you like some unseen marauder, or an uninvited guest. Turned young men's faces blue, made that long gashlike slit in the chest. His chest opened, blood frozen and the slashed tissue inside paling with exposure against jagged-cut edges of breathless, unmoving skin.

Braced against the drum, she looked up. The face staring blindly in her direction, bobbing between waves, could have been anyone's. Could have been but was not. Somewhere, in the blank line of the nose, the opened mouth, Ilana searched out a lover. Thought maybe she'd found her. Then she was leaning over to reach, extending the cup-tipped feeding stick across water. She spoke clearly. Had to repeat everything until the words stopped making sense, but finally she was heard.

"Ilana?"

She was relieved. Yes, she said, yes it's me. What Dorey said next was unrecognizable. The sound came out all swollen. I don't understand, Ilana said, again please, tell me again. Dorey did. Finally Ilana thought she understood.

"You're okay?"

"Okay."

"Drink this, Dorey. Here. To your right. Your right. To the right. Drink this. All of it. To the right."

"I'm a little crazy now Ilana."

What, Ilana said, tell me again, I'm listening. Listening. I am. Tell me. Again. I'm sorry, one more time. Once more. Crazy? You are? Crazy but okay?

"Uh-huh."

"Good. That's good. It's the best way to be."

Ilana I'm a little crazy now, it happens like this a lot but I'm okay. Still here. There was something I wanted to tell you. Can't talk. Feel sick. Well a little. Still here. Something I'd like to tell you now while I'm still here in the water.

"Later."

Ilana understood. She began the slow slide back to ship. Around the midriff of the feeding stick, her fingers shook with cold.

Tycho calculated carefully, then shifted course to the north. It was a subtle change at first, east to northeast, but by the time the eastern sky'd begun to darken they were heading nearly due north. In the west the sun was dark orange and just starting its fade. Air temperature was sixty-eight degrees and falling. Water temperature was fifty-two point three degrees Fahrenheit and winds were with them this time, blowing from the southwest. Waves were erratic. Some five-footers. Still they were, like the winds, slamming along in the right direction.

Just before twilight was the time when ghosts rode echoes right up to the surface of the San Antonio Strait. They were the strait's lost spirits, and most had left their bodies behind in its water over a century ago. Along the perimeters of the current they hovered silently, huddled close together without touching in the deepening gray.

There's another, one said in Spanish. Pointed soundlessly. Dorey looked up. They were conferring about something, it seemed. Her. She didn't understand the Spanish, it was being spoken too quickly. Still she caught a couple of words.

Another what?

Otro nadador. Another swimmer.

But this one's a woman.

Nadadora. Estará lo mismo.

No. Perhaps it won't be the same.

Perhaps.

They were silent again. Looking up, she thought she'd caught a hint of her name being spoken but no. Only gray tranquility that clamped over her now like a snow-cold glove. What was there in the world but the sound of water, those relentless splashes ringing against both her ears until she almost did not hear them because everything had become them. Her arms stroking water. Her arms causing splashes. Arms rendering her ears deaf. Watching, the spirits stepped from their perch atop waves. One sat on her shoulders.

Knock knock.

Go away.

Knock knock.

Who's there, she sobbed.

Guess.

Go away.

No I won't. Guess.

I don't know.

Do you want me to tell you? Do you?

Please, she said, you don't understand. I have to concentrate now.

Knock knock.

Who's there?

Matt.

Who?

You know. Matt Olssen, me. Remember me? I beat you in Quebec.

Not by much.

Hah. Want to shake hands?

The hand crawled over her shoulder. It caressed the raw line of her neck. Fingers found her lips and pried them apart to poke into her mouth. The fingers were salt-tasting. They were bone. She screamed and kept swimming. Then the weight on her shoulders lifted, mouth emptied, she'd thrown up again and was swimming north, chattering teeth biting once in a while into her tongue. Her toes were gone.

She concentrated.

Now came a noticeable tug from the east, water just slightly more turbulent and its direction confused. Closer. Getting closer. The skin along her spine burned. Its burning was a bright line of flame in ice, a tingle of expectation. That current. She swallowed more water, threw up the rest of last hour's feeding.

Fog on her goggles darkened with evening. North. She concentrated. Counted each splash up to ten and then started over. In front of her yawned an enormous mouth. Its lips were full, slime-smeared, its insides black and cavernous and it had no teeth. Whoosh, it went. Sucking. It sucked her to the east now, lips glistening. She fought to keep heading north and it laughed. So little, it mocked. You're so little.

Who are you?

Water.

Oh, she said. She was afraid.

Someone else was talking, that swimmer. Better concentrate. Just concentrate now, that's right. Keep the pace.

But the water.

Keep that pace. Cut out all this whining, huh? Remember this isn't happening to you, it is happening to me. Remember.

Dorey Thomas. She wanted to cry with relief.

Right. Let's get going. We can do it.

Too small.

No you're not.

She paused, confused. Small. But you're bigger than me, are you a giant.

No, said Dorey, I'm something better now, don't you remember?

I'm sorry, she cried, I forgot.

Think a minute. Let's swim now. Uh-huh. Just think.

Something better? No. Well I don't know. Tell me.

You haven't really forgotten. Do you want me to tell you anyway?

What? she stroked. Stroked. Breathed. What are you?

Dorey smiled. I—she glowed proudly—am a water dancer.

She breathed. Then wanted to throw open her arms with a burst of recognition. Ah, she said. A water dancer. Well so am I.

Well then *concentrate.*

She did.

It was five o'clock.

"Here we go," said Sarge.

Tycho gripped his arm briefly. Sarge shivered in dark, threw on his windbreaker. In the cabin voices crackled over the radio, coast guard clipper lights glowed on, and across the entire dark expanse of water what you'd have seen from bird's-eye view were two lit vessels, cutting through black thrashing water along with the whitecaps. If you soared down closer you'd see a swimmer, too, human body stroking alongside one of the ships, stopping every hour to be fed. The body had been heading north for more than two hours. Now it began a shift northeast, faithfully alongside the boat escorting it.

"Here we go."

"Right, captain."

"Well you bastard. Been watching the stars lately?"

"Up there." Tycho pointed. They both looked, the first couple of stars had glittered into view. Tycho slapped his back roughly, roughly rubbed it. "Just wait for the moon, she's the real beauty tonight."

"What do you mean?"

Tycho winked. Wait, he told him, wait and see. It's on her side tonight. "Get on a sweater or something, why don't you. No use getting sick before it's necessary."

Sarge wondered what he knew. Then Tycho said it for him. "Swimming later?"

Sarge nodded. "If I have to."

"I thought maybe there was a reason."

"Trained all winter."

"Oh," said Tycho, "I know."

"Do you." Sarge grinned back, odd light in his eyes. "The stars tell you that too?"

"No. Dorey Thomas told me that."

Sarge shrugged. Leave it to a woman. It was seven o'clock and he went to feed her.

The water was like giant hands slapping you around. Deeper they got into the current's flow, the more random those slaps became. Tycho guided them slowly in on a northeast angle so she wouldn't fight it head-on, and the loss of speed would therefore be less drastic.

Anne suited up.

She'd have liked to eat something but the idea made her sick right now. She decided to use lanolin and focused on its application. Rick snapped a few photos. He'd rolled in some high-speed Ektachrome. Finally she gave him a petulant look, saying if he had shot it all so to speak would he mind doing her back now, and grinning he replied he wouldn't mind doing any part of her at all. Very cute, she said. Then winked and they were friends again.

"Grease, your majesty." He kissed the back of her neck. He dipped into the jar and smeared heavy globs over her shoulders, back, the backs of her arms. He knelt to swab it thoroughly along her legs. In the half-light, her skin glistened gold.

It was eight o'clock and they stopped again. Anne pulled up a second suit. She put on a few caps and wiped her hands grease-free before delicately reaching for goggles. She turned a cheek to him and he kissed it. They walked out on deck together. The camera hung uncased around Rick's neck. Just off starboard, Sarge was feeding her. Occasionally a wave washed over him, wind rippled his hair into a damp dark nest. You couldn't hear what he was saying, but she'd rolled all the layers of cap up over one ear and was trying to listen.

"Good luck." Al had come up behind.

Anne swung around. I *am* luck, she wanted to say, don't

you know. Instead she grinned. "Thanks. Twenty minutes. I'll
see you in twenty."

Out there Sarge was balancing, turning. He signaled her on
in. Anne spit into the goggles. For her, there was always that
moment before hitting the water when she felt herself rotating
in air, around and around. Hands held her, anchored her to
some remnant of earth. They were the strongest, surest hands
she'd ever know, and the only absolute impossibility in the
world was that those hands would let her go. She stepped
quickly down the ladder. Gripped the top rung while one foot
rested on the bottom rung and the other foot dangled free-
floating, in dark night air. She released one hand and half of
her swung out free. Let go and you'd broken every rule, just
like that. Let go and you'd unleashed something foreign, elemental, utterly uncivilized and—for most who deemed themselves alive—long since buried. Let go and there was no
telling what in that instance you'd created, what kind of monster, or rage, or unquantifiable desire. Anne focused on an
imaginary pinpoint speck in the water below. Then she let go.

Numbed on impact, she backstroked frantically, turned
over, cut into the tumbling water with a few quick strokes and
stopped to tread, gasping for breath.

"Pick up pace a little, I think."

To her right was Sarge. In front of her, another swimmer
who tread obediently, waiting.

Anne breathed deeply until she could speak. "All right
Sarge. No problem." The boat lights blanched water surface.
Everything was that silver-white color, and the skin of the
swimmer before her looked bleached, shivering hands pad-
dling in water, shriveled and worn. "Hey!" said Anne. "Do
you want some company?"

Through fog came dim outlines. That swimmer. Dorey'd
seen her before. They'd talked once a long time ago. She
smiled. She smiled and waved.

"Let's go. Face to face."

"Anne," Dorey said, "hi there."

Anne didn't understand. Come on, she invited, want to
swim? They did and somewhere a whistle blew. Its sound was

343

long and nervous, shrieking across the dark troubled surface. Anne felt out the pace, achingly slow and she decided give it five minutes, then step things up. The current tugged them south, slammed against them with its heavy weight of cold. Come on, Anne willed silently, pick up that pace a little, just a little. A little. After a while they did, imperceptibly at first. She'd pulled them back up the speed hill slowly. At least over a mile an hour, she decided, had to be. Had to try. She breathed out cold. It twisted her feet and cramped them, wave motion made her sicker until she felt boxed in and the only out was that rhythmic, predictable turning of the head to see another face like hers gazing blindly back for a second in water. Anne bubbled out dark breath. She turned to air, turned back to water and the cold she hated.

The current pushed them south.

By nine o'clock Anne was towel-wrapped and still shivering on deck, and the *Lazarilla* radioed in confirming that, yes, water temperature had risen and was just about fifty-three. Fifty-two point eight to be exact but it was a marked rise, they ought to be happy about that one. Wearily, Sarge smiled. Ilana watched him consulting with Tycho and wondered why. Then they stopped for the fifteenth feeding and this time it was Rick at the controls again, Tycho lowering himself down the ladder, supplies in a waterproof sack slung around his neck. Above, stars were clear and there were plenty of them. Glancing up occasionally, he outlined constellations.

"I'm sick," she said, "it hurts." One salt-scarred hand pointed to her head. Tycho leaned over, found that if he listened carefully he could, in fact, understand her the first time around.

"You have a headache," he explained. "It's to be expected."

"Well I'm pretty sick."

"I know," he said carefully, "you feel that way. But you're still very cogent. Everything seems to be working—"

"—my stomach."

"Biologically, you're in great shape."

"Uh-huh." She pointed to her head.

"I've prescribed some medicine."

She started to cry.

"Some medicine," he insisted, "which is sure to work." He poked the stick out slowly, broth steaming in a cup at the end. "Drink it now."

"Hurts."

"You have to drink all of it, or the effect is diminished."

Hands shaking, she reached, couldn't grasp it, and he brought it directly to her mouth and tilted until he saw her swallow.

"You look very strong," he said. "You should feel this medicine shortly. It's time-released."

She cried a little more, then was swimming again.

Sometimes what she imagined was a beam of light attached to the topmost cap emanating from her forehead. It was similar to the kind worn by coal-miners, spotlighting the dismal route ahead.

Sometimes she worried about sharks, then remembered that none had ever been spotted here. This was the San Antonio Strait. She guessed they preferred less difficult water.

Sometimes what happened was the cold went completely through her, pierced her chest, and rode out somewhere in the vicinity of her spine. It came in waves like gusts of wind. Each wave of ice was electric shock.

She'd slowed again to less than a mile an hour. South-flowing, the current pushed them. Tycho tilted them slightly northeast again, readjusting until she'd snapped back on course. If it was going to take this long, he decided, they ought to be consistently on the right trail.

"Here, dear. Here's some food."

The voice's faint sound filled her with longing, and a sense of expectation for which she could not account.

"Who's there?"

"Ilana. This is Ilana."

She stopped. Tried to think. Then she had it and gave a

grin that split her lips but they were too numb to feel it. "Ah. Are you my lover?"

"Yes."

"Still?"

"Yes," Ilana lied.

Dorey swallowed some liquid and spat out the rest. Blindly, she backstroked a little. Water swirled into her mouth, she felt it creep down her throat and mix unsettled with what she'd just consumed. Most of it water anyway. *Lover.* Why not. Bugs had them. Sharks had them. Animals had them men had them and so would she. A lover. For a second she felt part of what she floated in, inside of it as it was inside her, integral aspect of the water-covered world. For a second, there was peace. She felt her eyelids sink down and she turned suddenly, listened carefully, heard the whistles signaling which direction. Bear left, the signals said. Arm raised, muscles felt torn. Arm raised. Breathe. She went on ahead.

"Get that stuff away from me." Freshly-suited, Anne waved the lanolin jar at Sarge in warning. But it was too late, the smell of food got to her and she was out the cabin, racing to the ship's port side and leaning over, miserably.

No tolerance for nausea. No tolerance for cold. And of all the professions on earth, she'd managed to choose the one that would subject her repeatedly to both. The nine-year-old brat racing at high speed for the locker room toilet after a workout and the woman standing here now, swaying with this boat, were in many respects still the same. Both boasting they could stand just about anything as long as the goal was clear, and big enough to hold her enthusiasm.

In the dark Anne straightened. She wiped her face on a towel. Wind cooled her down. Then she knelt for the jar of lanolin, recovered it, good thing it was plastic. What she'd have liked most to do just now was stretch out in the sun, let her carefully disciplined love of luxury take over. What she wanted least was to get in that water, and she knew she'd do it anyway and that after a while it would be all right. The nine-year-old brat might have said at times she was doing it for her father. The woman, twenty years later, that she was doing it for Sarge. Somewhere inside, both knew better. Anne Norton never swam for anyone but herself. She'd always figured it was the best reason there could be.

"You all right?"

She turned to Sarge.

"What time is it?"

"Eleven."

"I'm ready. Come on, Mr. Olssen, hell is freezing over."

Spirits watched. In the night, two bodies moved through water. The bodies were living and both female. They swam face to face, once in a while one would pick up speed and the other would naturally match the new pace.

Swimmers, said the ghosts. They're very small.

Stars watched. The moon rose. It was a delicate arching sliver of cold silver, dangling in the sky. Hid the rest of its face in shadow, lightless.

Once in a while boat sounds would ring across water. Mostly, though, were only the sounds of the water itself, water rushing on water, slapping wave on wave on water, current dissipating in small whirlpools of foam here, striking out at itself there. It pushed south, and the unnamed boat with wings and the coast guard clipper *Lazarilla* and the two swimmers pushed just slightly northeast, losing ground on the northern front but gaining it on the east.

At twenty minutes to twelve Anne Norton was pulled gently from the water and before she sat on deck leaned over to notice the remaining body still struggling, swimming slowly but somehow firmly, in the direction she'd pointed and at the pace she'd set. She grinned with satisfaction, wrapped herself in towels, stumbled to the stern just in time to throw up. She pinched her abdomen. She'd lost weight already. Anne thought longingly of chocolate bars and threw up again.

At midnight Sarge got the feeding stick ready. He'd put on a white T-shirt and in light-flooded night looked to be moving

347

in slow motion out there on the aluminum walkway, shirt flapping around the strong waist, ghostlike.

"Ilana!"

At one in the morning she was treading, trying bleakly to yell.

"Ilana!"

Ilana stepped down the rope. On metal she balanced. Something rang dully in her head and at first she thought it was the incessant rhythm of exhaustion but after a while she knew that, no, it was something else altogether, some realization she was wavering at the edge of. When water washed over her thighs she shuddered. Fifty-three degrees and steady was cold enough. Personally she liked it in the eighties.

Out along the pontoon she'd left a boat behind. Whatever she was heading for was different, she knew, than anything she had done in the past. And perhaps it was weariness that brought these tears to her eyes now, here, in the middle of an ocean at an hour past midnight but she didn't think so.

"I'm here."

"Ilana."

"Yes."

Features blanched, swollen, unfamiliar, the swimmer faced her by instinct and reached, hand dropped weakly, splashed the water.

"Ilana what time is it."

Ilana thought before answering. When she spoke it was with care. "Oh, don't worry about the time. You're doing fine."

"One o'clock? It's only one o'clock?"

"No. I don't know."

"Then," the voice slurred, "how do you know it's not."

Ilana took deep breaths. "Because," she said, "you are almost there."

"What?"

"You're almost there. Get going now, don't you feel good about that?"

"*Liar.*"

In the head-splitting light, Ilana rubbed her cheek with those long fingers of hers. The fingers came away wet, whether with sea or tears she didn't know and didn't care.

"Liar. You're lying to me."

"Dorey. I've never lied to you. Not ever, remember?"

Dorey paused silently, treading. Well it was true. Then it could not be one o'clock and still the middle of the strait if she were almost there, could it. Maybe the stars had already faded. And it was nearly dawn. Well maybe. Ilana was there. She reached. No, they hadn't lied to each other. She remembered. No betrayal.

Almost there, Ilana coaxed. Almost there so don't you worry about the time now, not now, you just concentrate on swimming. Just swim now, all right? You're fine, you're doing very well, believe me.

Dorey believed her. It was Ilana saying these things, after all, Ilana who didn't lie. She ate part of a cookie they'd crumbled in liquid but threw it up. She guessed if she were almost there she had just better swim. Ilana was right. Sure.

So somewhere after one o'clock in the morning Dorey Thomas, more than halfway across the strait of San Antonio, gave up on time. She let it leave her. Realized, once she felt it slough off, how much energy she'd been expending keeping track of alphabets and Spanish words of songs, keeping track of feedings and what they meant in relation to distance. Now that she was no longer spending precious calories on thoughts of time, she could concentrate on one thing alone: stroking through water, maintaining the specific rhythm of a pace she'd worked towards all her life. There was no further purpose in this—no goal of time towards which the strokes could be counted because she'd lost track of time and, losing time, lost sight of all specificity. The space between where she was each instant and the shoreline she struggled to approach was now immeasurable. The only goal left her—if it could indeed be called a goal—was the rhythmic continuation of strokes through water.

She concentrated.

Each stroke an end in itself. There was no other purpose in

the world than this, she knew, to stroke through water and that way keep going. Every stroke the same so every stroke was an infinity of strokes, in the dead of night each infinity measured by the sound of a splash.

The first thing it seemed to be was a scream. After a while, though, Ilana realized it was that white high-pitched static of exhaustion. She realized it was silent.

For Anne Norton, shivering down the ladder at two o'clock on the morning of September 15, it was also silent and came to her disguised as waves crashing on imaginary sand. She'd picture a beach, stretching long and blank towards the east. On it, foam sparkled. When she blinked behind goggles she was hanging from the rope ladder ready to drop into water that glistened, in boat lights, like a shimmering reflective mirror.

Anne dropped into the mirror, went through its other side. She surfaced and looked at a reflection of herself. Something had happened though, the glass warped. This face staring sightlessly back at hers was swollen and not quite her own. In all other respects they were the same, like two similarly colored stones smoothed to matching dimensions by water.

Ten minutes ago, Dorey Thomas had spilled out on the snaking eastern boundary of the current that ran through the San Antonio Strait. The farther east she swam the calmer water surface became but now, at two a.m., she'd stopped. What confused her was this lessening of motion around her, this diminishing of turbulence. Inside she heard no sound at all. Now she paused, treading in water she could no longer feel, and through blinding clouds made out the dim outlines of herself.

Anne raised her left arm, sliced it down into water. Watched bubbles sputter out white in that pitch-dark below the surface. She started slow. From another mouth, bubbles spilled back at her. Michigan. It had been this cold. No. This was colder. Pulling you out now, they'd said. Oh no you don't. No. Pull me out and I will kill you, bastard. Want this. Need it, you don't understand. Let me finish. Just finish. Yes, this was colder than Michigan. She breathed. She went by instinct and tried to measure, slowly began instilling rhythm into the mutual motion, rhythm bringing with it a slightly quicker pace. Colder. Left arm, right, and breath again. She hadn't finished but just about dropped dead instead, that dead-weight sinking sensation. Red eyes opening in a hospital she'd wished they had left her there to sink. But they left her injured and breathing, rolled on her side in a white bed somewhere in the Midwest to blink eyes open and contemplate the monumental failure of it all. Breathe. Stroke. Stroke. A swimmer breathed back at her. She'd said to herself in the midst of one muscle spasm or other okay, okay, learn to live with it. Live without having what you need, it is the hardest thing you will ever do. Michigan. But this was colder. And she knew, now, there wouldn't be any more Michigans and there wouldn't be any more of this stuff, no way. Those weeks afterward, Benton Harbor, back home, something inside her capsized. Then built itself back up and left her transformed beyond her need. None of it because of her—that was what always got you down, if it had been a failure on her part she'd at least have been able to crack up, but no, she wouldn't even be granted that small release. And by that time, all those spasms later and cracked skins later and hospitalized days later and hurting grins later and tears later, she'd just sat there back home and laughed. Thought of the water and how cold it had been, shivered, laughed, listened to traffic screaming by on streets below and refused to answer her phone until she couldn't stand not having a handle on things again, not shooting the breeze with whoever it was, and then it didn't matter who or how many called, the voices were all human and called her back to life on land. None of this late great Anne Norton stuff for her. She'd elected to live. Would realize later how conscious a choice it had been. Then he'd sent those illustrations.

Whistles blew. Anne slid away. Goodbye, she said to the image gliding alongside her. Bye.

Hauling herself up the ladder, she couldn't hear what they were saying at first. She ripped off her goggles and caps when she thought she knew, blinked at Sarge, stood there shuddering dripping ice-water on deck. Something about the temperature dropping. Looked bad out there. So slow. Too slow.

"She can't make it," he said.

She was slamming fists against his chest. Shocked, he tried to blockade her with those massive arms.

"Screw you, Sarge, screw you. You're the one who can't make it. Bastard. You lousy bastard."

She was crying but you couldn't tell. It mixed with all the rest of the saltwater beading her skin. Anne was strong. She'd always kept in great shape, one of her trademarks. For her, off-season never existed. If it wasn't pool workouts it was running. Nautilus. She was stronger than a lot of men and it took every ounce of Rick's strength to pull her off. Still she grabbed for Sarge. Eyes spat hatred.

"She's okay. You let her finish. You just let her finish."

He stared.

"Let her finish or I swear I'll kill you."

She meant it and Sarge took a walk. He kept his eyes on the swimmer in the water that had just dropped to fifty-one degrees but was calm now, night air windless, current behind them. She was going slowly—too slowly, it seemed, to ever make it now. The water's floodlit glare bounced back at him, bleached his unshaven face a phantom shade. Looking at the water, Sarge was afraid and started to cry.

Carol, remember that day. I was little. Walking into the kitchen. He put an arm around your neck and kissed. He winked at me. It was raining. I had a jelly sandwich.

Remember at the beach. I climbed on your shoulders. That way I was over the waves. You bounced. You played horse.

Dorey reached for sun. Just as it was about to envelop her it faded. Something sat on her shoulders. It seemed a weight from outside, like a leaden shoe. She wondered who was stepping against her back. Wasn't fair.

Carol?

Think we're there yet?

The weight got heavier. Much more of that and her shoulders would cave in, she knew. No more giant. Back when she was a giant maybe she could have carried it. Maybe. No. Because she'd been a giant, and even then all it took was one wave. One wave and poof. Giant broke in two. Humpty Dumpty.

Well I tried, Carol. For you. To be that strong. See. You needed it. But it wasn't possible. I was barely strong enough for one. See when you stop being a giant it's so lonely. Lonely. Still lonely. All right. But I can touch now. Getting there. Stronger now. I guess. I know. And no giant. No. Just going for it. Going for broke. Free, you said, it is possible to be free. That's the part I liked. Believed. Still do.

That frozen feeling in the center of her chest seemed to waver then, massive glacier teetering on the edge of some vast cavern before it tipped, crumbled, dissolved and she reached, reached, breathed easier now from the center of her chest where the sun glowed hot, bright, unsmothered by ice. Still the weight crouched, gripped with monkey hands on her shoulders. She breathed out sun and heard the hiss of melting ice down in the cavern there. It was a sound almost of lament, far-off wails heard in some jungle, a dark female cry. Dorey listened carefully. Her right, she knew, to stop for just this second and understand something. The glacier had been water after all. Frozen water. Not permanent. Not indestructible. At least she was less destructible than ice. Hot blood inside stronger than the cold. For now. Strong. She could breathe easier. And it was her right to listen, to hear the dark sounds of dying. Or, pounding against it, her own pulse-beat. Dancing. And know she was alive.

The lie. It was a lie Carol. That I was doing it for you. Sure. It was for that glow. What's left under everything. Get rid of everything else and you feel it. The glow. Not giving up. Making it through. That's all. Alive. Cold but feel that, that glow. Alive.

The weight pressed down. Everything hurt.   353

How much longer?

Remember? What you told me once. What I believed?

By the beach. I was twelve. You told me that day. You can be free darling, it is possible if only you're willing to pay the price and the price is very high. Simply a choice. You must need it more than anything. You must want it more than love.

It was too cold to feel anymore. She'd dropped down below the earth into water and was starving, filthy, no chance to clean right now and no strength left to stop. Just keep going. She'd dropped down below where people didn't go unless they had to, where nothing changed but the wind and time didn't exist. But something sat right there on her shoulders, crying, insistent. Sounded like an infant. Dorey pulled out the scissors. Sorry, she said, I am sorry. She'd have cried but nothing left. Sorry. I would carry you now Carol if I had the strength. Except I'm not a giant anymore. Just enough left for me. Forgive me. Forgive me. I have to make it. Carol it's what you wanted.

She cut.

The scissors dropped, sank out of sight. From below rose blade-shaped traces of blood, and between Dorey's shoulders the cord flapped, spliced, oozing, with nothing at its other end. She picked up the pace slightly. With each stroke the cord shriveled and dried until it was nothing but dessicated, unneeded skin, and the skin washed away from her by saltwater.

"How much longer?"

"Not much. You're almost there."

Perched on the pontoon, she said it mechanically. It was four o'clock and stars had died, moon vanished in an ash-colored sky.

"But how much? How long?"

"Keep going," she said, "you're almost there."

In clammy predawn, Ilana felt her shoulders droop. The lines on her face she could just about feel through her skin. How deeply they'd etched themselves. Winds had calmed to nothing so what shrouded the water now was a vast stillness. Even their voices seemed muted by it, echoes nonexistent. Parallel to them the *Lazarilla* had slowed. If you squinted from deck you could make out figures standing still, watching. They hung there over the rails. They froze like shadows in the dark.

"Almost," Ilana whispered. "Almost there."

It was true. When the sun rose they'd see the mainland shore and see it was close. Now, though, it was hard to believe things were on the verge of dawn. They seemed, instead, to be on the edge of some black well, a sewer of ink into which the world would slide.

"Go away," she sobbed. Her tongue filled her mouth. "I don't believe you anymore."

Ilana leaned far over. She shoved the half-finished cup back towards the face. "Please believe me. Keep going. You're almost there."

Dorey rolled over. Hands reached for goggles. Then she slid into a backstroke before rolling over again, faced the voice that hounded her right back into the cold, goggles intact, hands clenched below the surface.

"Ilana, what are you doing to me."

She started to swim again.

"Go to sleep." Bending, Sarge brushed Anne's hair from her face. "Good job tonight."

"So tired."

"You go to sleep."

"Three miles?" said Anne. "Wake me up. I want to see her finish."

Her eyes closed. She'd lost weight, Rick could feel it when he touched her ribs. Sitting on the edge of the bunk he turned to Sarge. "She'll hate me but I'm going to take her picture anyway." He nodded towards the sleeping body, swathed in blankets and still shivering in dreams even though the air temperature was warming rapidly. "I think she's the most god-damned amazing woman."

Sarge smiled. It cracked his face like the carved mouth on a pumpkin. "Go ahead. Let her hate you. That's about a hundred times better than having her bored with you."

"Don't you think I know that, Olssen?" Rick tapped the

camera lens. His voice was proud. "She's still with me, right? Sometimes I even feel like I understand her—do you know what that's like? She"—he caressed the space above her sleeping face—"is still with *me*. So I'm a goddamned record-breaker."

"Right," said Sarge, "top prize."

He pulled off his shirt and untied his shoes. That left only a suit. When he went to join Tycho, a camera clicked behind his back.

Tycho looked immobile, the tired eyes scanning, figuring. To the east where they were heading the sky'd begun to lighten. It was blue-touched gray. Tycho looked up briefly to notice that Sarge's eyes were red with exhaustion and the beginnings of tears. He turned back to the course.

"Why are you crying?"

Sarge shrugged.

"It's better," said Tycho, "not to waste energy. Here." He reached for a chocolate bar, cleanly tore the wrapper away and broke it in two, keeping half for himself. "Eat this." His expression was cool, matter-of-fact, and unsympathetic without being cruel. Sarge took the chocolate. He let it melt a little on his fingertips but sudden panic flooded him, he was wasting this food, and without thinking he popped the entire thing in his mouth, chewed just a little before swallowing. It tasted like some kind of heaven. Licking his fingers clean, he felt safer and he was ready to swim.

Barton took over and out on deck Tycho watched as Sarge emerged from the cabin. Except for the suit he was naked, the body glowed a dusky shade in deck lights, rippled with muscle developed over a lifetime and tuned up secretly during the past year. What Tycho noticed was that more than ever he appeared bull-like, some minotaur with fins. The vast triangular expanse of chest and arms looked unreal for a second, like an illustration of something—looked, somehow, impersonal. Sarge spotted Tycho, headed for him, face tired but recognizable. Tycho just opened his arms. An odd pain thumped alongside his own paradigmatic heart. He loved the man.

356

"Swimming?"

"Swimming."

Tycho helped him grease up. Soon the dark-toned skin was white. Tycho slapped his back with a few more globs.

"Auditioning for polar bear?"

"Polar bear of the year award, Johnny." He flexed his arms. "Time for a swimming lesson."

"I'll be watching."

Sarge was at the stern, talking with Ilana while Tycho kept an eye on the water and the swimmer. His own neck hurt from looking. Head turn, stroke, stroke, head turn, stroke, slow and painful, limbs numb, quivering in fifty-one-degree water. She was barely moving now. They were progressing at less than a mile an hour.

"Jesus," said Al. Leaning over the gunwales, he'd been watching a long time. The crudely carved female torso hung from his belt by a string attached around its wooden waist. It swung there with upturned belly, nipples perpetually erect and stiff thighs spread to reveal those folds of lips. "Hey."

Tycho kept eyes on the water. "Yes?"

"You do this kind of stuff too?"

"Oh, no," said Tycho. "I row."

"Yeah?"

"Single sculls."

"What's that like?" Al's eyes fixed on the water too. He breathed in rhythm now. His legs ached. That kid they'd brought up from L.A. to demonstrate, he said in the marathon you felt like your legs would fall off there towards the end and that was just on six-minute miles, none of the flashy times. Al wondered how her arms must feel. Maybe they felt nothing.

"Interesting," said Tycho. "It's solitary."

On the eastern horizon corpse-gray spread and spread further until the sky above grew perceptibly lighter. "You think," Al coughed tiredly, "you can get anywhere you want if you're strong enough?"

"I don't know. A part of me believes that, yes."

"You think you can get any*one* if you want them enough?"

Tycho smiled softly. He shook his head.

357

"Why can't you?" Al's voice had cracked and, glancing, Tycho noticed he needed a shave.

"I don't know."

"You don't, huh. I was afraid of that." He looked down. The small wooden torso teased against his thigh.

At three minutes past five it was Tycho who crawled out along the pontoon holding a Styrofoam container filled with lukewarm baby food. Here, he coaxed, here. Her teeth chattered. The sound clipped dully through still morning air. In the east the sky'd begun to glimmer yellow.

"Later," said Sarge. He reached up over the side. Ilana gripped his hand. He realized they were shaking hands firmly, solemnly, like friends sealing a contract. When her hand had left his, Sarge thought of other things. First he focused on water. He focused on the water and then on the oven inside him. It was less an oven than a volcano of sorts, hot incubating bed of lava which he'd feed himself at will. Gripping rope, his hands shook. He wondered why and then knew it was because he was afraid. He was afraid of water. He was afraid of jumping into it, remembered Bachmann. Was this water special water. Different from any other water. Was it separate from all other water on earth because it had his son's heart thumping faintly through it and a piece of him along with it.

Sarge focused on her. His son was dead and he'd never have him again. Dorey Thomas was alive and swimming across the San Antonio Strait and he was her trainer. She was three miles from touching the mainland sand. That was all. She was a swimmer swimming. Water changed with the rain. He couldn't know that this very same water had taken his son. That had been years ago. Maybe it was not the same water. Even though all water was the same still it was not the same, and so he could be afraid of water and realize he'd been all his life without knowing it, realize that the San Antonio Strait in his head would always be there, death-giving, terrifying, and forever apart from the reality of the water before him now. 358 There was no San Antonio Strait in the absolute. It changed by the day, by the hour. And the swimmer in there was not his son nor daughter and would never be his lover. Still she was a swimmer—and in that, the most essential sense of that, she was his. He'd nurtured the part of her that would survive.

Sarge let go. He dropped cleanly into water. Poured lava out of him, out and out, ice penetrated but not to the core. There was at his core something red, bubbling and alive, that the ice skirted around and couldn't cut through. Gasping, he waited. Then the boundaries were established. Cold crawled around but past a certain layer wouldn't enter. Through the density his arms cut slowly. He swam out to where she waited. He stopped to tread a few feet away.

"Hello."

The skin of her face was raw and swollen. She was blind, deaf too, effectively muted for all he could understand of what she said. Something inside him ached just to touch her. That was forbidden here. She was the swimmer and must cross unaided, touching was a violation. Sarge stayed where he was. Facing her, more than an arm's length away, this was the closest they would ever be. She was effectively isolated by cold and pain and her own desire, and the world she occupied now could not be touched, it was surrounded by water.

He saw her head wobble slightly, begin to fall forward. Sarge splashed at her. "Stay awake!"

She did. She started a listless breaststroke. He slid alongside between her and the pontoons, passed Tycho without looking his way. Sarge was all concentration now. He focused on her and willed her awake for the rest of this crossing however long it took.

Dorey stopped, legs began a leaden sink. He flailed arms again. He beat up quite a fuss.

"Stay awake!"

The swollen head shook stiffly. She rolled onto her back.

"Awake!" he ordered. "Let's go!" He splashed some more at her, caused her to swallow it and sputter and then he heard a sob. She'd turned face to the water and lifted the right arm, breath, stroke, and another. Slowly he moved alongside her. Ice crept against his bones, dulled sensation. Sarge stabbed it back with the life inside him. He jerked it out and poured it out on ice and the ice screamed while it melted and then some more ice formed, hovered at the oven gates, waiting. Stay awake! he told her. Around them was ice water, sleep-inducing, that would coat you like snow and deep-freeze the pump that was your heart. What they had against it was the liquid inside them, blood bouncing strongly back to help the heart generate heat, bouncing from all muscles and capillaries, running through veins keeping the engine alive. Outside was cold water, life inside them hot water, both bodies of water held apart by the thinnest partition of flesh and bone. Wear down the partition enough, Sarge knew, and the inside water dissolved into the outside surrounding it. He swam. Stay awake, he warned her. Stay awake lady, stay awake baby, stay awake now champ come on kid stay awake come on. It would be so easy sometimes to allow the dissolution of boundaries to take place. And he wasn't going to let that happen. Not now. Not to his swimmer.

After a while, if you stood on deck you'd see both bodies swimming at the same pace. Sometimes they'd stop, one yell and splash at the other and then they'd continue.

In the east, you could see the mainland shore. You could see hills rising black into sky. The sky was yellowing there, then light gray, then blue-gray as it crept west. Soon the first flame-orange mound of sun would appear between hills.

One by one, lights on both ships in the San Antonio Strait went off. On the *Lazarilla* shadow bodies belonging to voices heard by radio all night straightened, stood tall and male, and silently waved. Off the escort's starboard side the swimmers moved, capped heads turning gently towards one another in unison. Arms lifted, shoulders rolled. Once in a while red skin flashed against the dawn-lit water.

At six o'clock Ilana stepped along the pontoon. She balanced perfectly the entire way. She was feeling weightless this morning, insides clean, determined and vacant. She was all emptied out.

She could smell the air change texture and content. If she concentrated, she could pick out the first hint of land odors.

Ilana imagined tree green, and the wet of earth when you first dug in. Mid-spring. That's when you could do some real planting.

"Dorey."

She leaned over tiredly.

"Dorey."

She was looking for the Dorey Thomas she had tried to know these past months. There didn't seem to be a trace in the body bobbing weakly before her. Had you shown Ilana a photograph she wouldn't have been able to make a positive identification, and if you asked why she herself was there she might have laughed in perplexity. Because she'd done it all by instinct—opened a door last autumn asking who are you, opened arms, given a breast when instinct said it was needed. Now she balanced by instinct too. She couldn't have said why. Just that to do so, right now, answered some instinctual want inside herself, or a need to prove herself still capable of some kind of love—the definition didn't so much matter anymore. She could still nurture. And her songs, though no longer nursery rhymes, could still put a child to sleep.

"Dorey?"

No trace of a boy here, though. Not much trace, either, of anything female. There was just that beaten body treading water. Ilana looked. She took her time. She tried to find somebody familiar.

"Ah." The body was talking. Words unintelligible, even Tycho couldn't have deciphered them. Behind her, Sarge had stopped. He nodded to Ilana. Glycogen, he said, glycogen. Tell Tycho. Make it hot.

Ilana signaled to the ship. She began the careful walk back for liquid food. The body in water still faced where she'd been at the pontoon's end, still talked incomprehensibly, blurting thick sounds. Ilana, she was saying, that's you. You're going to leave aren't you. When this is over. Go away from me. Look. It's all right. It's all right anyway. Everything. See. Ilana. Am I almost there. Almost there and then I won't be able to touch you anymore.

"Tycho. He says glycogen." Looking up, she thought in the

361

dim morning light he'd changed. Thought for a split second that he'd donned a cape, sprouted large dark wings. One of the wings clutched a dark and gleaming wand of sorts that he tapped against gunwales, waved elegantly through air, said abracadabra and immediately transformed it into a steaming white cup of pure liquid glucose. Then he was smiling bleakly down at her, just Tycho again with the reddish scarred face, and she took the cup he offered.

"Not much longer," he said gently. "Remember."

"Thank you, Doctor."

"It's nothing."

She stepped back out.

Ilana. You won't be with me anymore.

"Here, dear," said Ilana. "Here."

"Ah."

"You're almost there."

She inched her head forward. The cup waited, she could smell it. Lips tried to find the rim and they swelled around it.

"Almost there," said Ilana.

Sweet liquid burned down her throat, hurt her tongue, and she tried to scream. Another sip. Another. Had to. Then it hurt too much and brought back the nausea. She shook her head. No. No more. Too sick. Almost there, that's what Ilana said and Ilana wouldn't have lied. Well she'd better not waste time then. Couldn't afford to throw up. Precious energy spent.

"Going," she said. Ilana understood. She looked to Sarge for reassurance and he nodded. Let her go. Believe it or not she's all right.

Dorey stroked sideways in the water, then she'd stopped and was treading again, facing the pontoon. Ilana leaned forward. The repetition was patient, methodical. Ilana listened harder. She could feel her ears straining as if both were hands reaching for something just beyond reasonable grasp. In the patience, the repetitious care with which the words were repeated for her, she got a glimpse of something familiar and of something enduring and realized that, apparent or not, this enduring center was alive in the body speaking before her. It was what had pushed so far, so hard, for more than a day now, had done so without sleep or the relief of being warmed by touch. Dorey, she said. Ilana smiled, relieved, finally recognizing her. She listened. Then she had it.

"Ilana. Do you know me now?"

"Yes," said Ilana, "I am proud."

"See you," Dorey blurted.

When she began to swim again, Ilana let her head sink tiredly to her hand. She was older physically and irrevocably. Hair all gray. Too old to bear children. Too much of that water inside had dried up by now. Still, what she'd recognized in Dorey—or what she'd finally recognized as Dorey—was there in her, too, she knew. What was it but a capacity for some incessant kind of behavior. An incessance that made you put one foot before the other when you no longer wanted to, or made you send one arm stroking when nothing was left to propel it. As if the instinct to survive lived deeper in them than desire itself, deeper than consciousness. That was what she'd recognized, this instinct as base as blood, and like blood it ran through both of them.

Sarge climbed out of the water. He hung for a minute on the ladder's bottom rung, pulled off goggles and blinked. Watched her swim. Unbelievably slow, each stroke still had to it a certain elegance. Or maybe it was simply that the strokes continued after so long which made him proud, and held for him a certain fascination. Sarge watched, then shut his eyes. Shivering fingers tightened on rope while he hung there in the morning. That was to him beauty, and strength in the ideal. He knew it. That reaching for something. It was his way of moving through the world. For an instant he experienced a strange, removed sense of peace.

Sarge pulled himself up and over, sat on deck in the first streaks of sunlight. No grease remained on his body and his skin shone raw, quivering with cold.

"It's all right, captain." Tycho bent over him. "You did what you had to. It's okay now. It's good."

Sarge made a fist. He rested it gently along Tycho's cheek. The busted old healed-over tissue pulsed against his clenched

363

fingers. It was warm. Sarge took his hand away. Saying right. Saying thanks, you bastard. Tycho tousled his hair fondly. Then he took a walk.

When Ilana knelt next to him on deck offering hot towels he seized the end of one to pull her towards him. "Getting there," he said. He told her when all this was over he'd like to be close to her again. However that was. Maybe they could try.

In the last mile, the water calmed to a lovely stillness. It reflected a cloudless sky, tinted the sky's reflected image slightly green. Flame-gold sun crawled above the horizon. It was a perfect day.

The closer they got to shore, the more the air changed. It was heavier, less pure. It was sweeter. Gulls swooped against the sky, struck water for fish. They'd rise, small catch flapping in beaks, their wings fluffed to shake off water. Sometimes they'd circle. One would break away, torpedo the water with a scream of triumph.

Dorey heard one thing now, one series of sounds. It was the breathe, stroke, stroke that coincided with the boom, thump, thump of her heart. That heart constituted a powerful sort of engine. Fifty beats, normally, was what it took to propel her through a minute. Sometimes less. And now it seemed to her to have slowed considerably, immeasurable time stretching between each pulsation, each pause delineated by the suck of a breath. There was nothing else in the world but this. Each stroke took her farther away from what she'd been before. One stroke a lover. One stroke a giant. The strokes disappeared with the water they propelled through. She left them all behind. So what she headed towards was unknown, the land she touched would be a strange one. She'd arrive bereft of all the elements by which she could quantify the shape of a day, or qualify her place within it. Arrive stripped, therefore different.

364

As they got closer there was some noise. Anne Norton came out on deck. This was the last mile and she wanted to watch.

She was the first one to hear it, too. Then she squinted eastward and made out boats. People on them. Some tiny figures
perched on bare lashed masts, watching. They were waiting.
Hey, she told Sarge, guess what. Cat's out of the bag, you
know. She pointed.

"Over," the radio crackled, "there's a guy here who wants
some pictures. Mind if he boards?"

Tycho shrugged. Standing there, his hands shook slightly.
They were tired. It was Rick Barton who bent towards the
controls, spoke back to the *Lazarilla*.

"Go to hell," he said cheerfully. "This stuff's copyrighted."

"*Huh?*"

Rick ignored that. Camera swinging around his neck, he
went out on deck. He stopped to make sure he'd put in a fresh
roll of film.

On deck, Tycho waved the wand in his head. One wave and
stars sparkled, then vanished. Another wave and the moon
rose in broad daylight, ran full-force into the sun until both
had melded to a pale hot light. Obscured by the light of day,
stars glittered above them and their contours mapped out a
body in the sky and the body they mapped out was reflected
by the body down here today swimming through the San Antonio Strait. On her tired sunburnt arms, stars winked disguised as drops of water. Stars shot from her elbows. Swollen,
filthy, beyond exhaustion, he saw her moving slowly through
the water and what he saw was light. It bounced back into his
eyes, rumbled in his chest and spilled down towards his groin.
Then it circled up and around with the flow of his blood. It
stopped at the neck momentarily. Then pushed higher. Tycho
had to concentrate to breathe. He did. He was all right. Just
tired, he told himself later, just the weariness and the waiting,
which had brought on that dizzy spell.

"Keep your distance. Please." Sarge had to use a bullhorn.
His voice was too raw. The closer they got the more boats
putted out to meet them. Not an overwhelming number of
vessels but enough, hell of a lot more than he'd ever have
thought of and they were all shapes and sizes. Made him
nervous. So he kept repeating that, keep your distance.

Please. Keep your distance and be careful, she's pretty tired right now. They hung back, obedient. The faces on them were curious. Plenty were young faces but looked slightly worn, strained with a looming anticipation.

At 7:38 a.m. Dorey picked up pace a little. Water on the outside of her goggles had gotten lighter. She guessed sand. Then something inside her cracked open, bled out. Silently, breath spilling back into saltwater, she felt sounds coming from her totally muted by water. She was crying. She didn't know why. Just for the pain, maybe, that had turned to ice long ago, or for all those things that were now lost. Every stroke stripping more and more of it away. She was changing. That meant leaving skin behind. Her head wanted to bust open. Well she'd sleep soon, once she got there, sleep and it would be okay then. Okay and maybe she'd never do this again, not ever, not unless she had to. Right. Only if she had to. She promised herself. Muffled, Dorey was sobbing. It hurt. She needed to drink water. To bathe. She was hungry.

The water grew even lighter, goggles clouds in front of her that brightened the closer they got to the sun. She wasn't hungry anymore. Not dirty. Just trembling, she was just trembling all over with a happiness that seemed absolute, it was hot like fever, kept her moving in the foreign light of a strange kind of ecstasy. The 800, something whispered. Come on. You can do an 800.

She started to.

Come on. You are almost there, you know. Dorey. Keep going. Come on lady. Come on baby come on kid come on champ keep that pace come on. Too much for you? No. No, well, I'm glad to hear that. Glad, understand. Come on. You can do an 800.

She did.

What flew by her now were visions of sand. Her fingers clutched at sand and each time it was a mirage. She cried and kept going. Then her left hand hit a mirage and stuck. Fingers moved against the mirage. They burrowed in deep. Her fingers clawed at the grainy texture and squirmed with the unfamiliarity of it, this sense of touch. Other hand groped

366

sightlessly forward. She reached and the right set of fingers touched too. She was on hands and knees in sand, head above water, and what washed over her back was sunlight.

"Did it," she said. The words squeezed out around her tongue.

There was noise. Voices. Splashing. She looked up, pinpointed one voice among many. Who? she asked.

"Dr. Gallagher here. John Gallagher. You've made it and it's a few feet to the beach. Would you like a hand?"

Uh-uh. She shook her head. Started to crawl. The water splashed with her. It swept up towards shore. She inched along and didn't stop until her hands touched sand that was dry and then she kept going, a little more she told herself, just a little more, get those legs out of the water too. Her feet. Well she thought she'd lost them long ago. But now they were touching sand too, and the sand was dry. She'd kept goggles on so was effectively blind, but knew it by that touch. It was the sense of touch that distinguished her from fish, that set her apart from the water she'd been in. Had to be separate from something in order to touch it.

"May I?" Hands hovered at her goggle straps. She nodded.

Ilana removed them carefully. The eyes were almost shut. Light shot into them, blinding. Dorey reached to cover her eyes.

"Can you walk?"

She didn't know. She reached for Ilana's hand anyway and then she was standing. She looked awful. She was alternately bleached by salt and rubbed raw by it, swollen with water and nothing but skin and bones. The worn suits hung from her. She looked like some monster baby, crazed eyes half shut. Her tongue swelled out between her lips. She was shaking all over.

Record books would state that Dorey Thomas emerged on the mainland shore just before 8:15 a.m. The crossing had taken 26 hours, 9 minutes, 33 seconds.

A couple of journalists were there taking pictures. There'd be a big story in the local paper. There'd be a one-line mention in the *Times*, and a blurb in *SportsYear*.

Her feet left a couple of uncertain imprints in sand. Then she stopped, everything spinning. She let go of Ilana's hand. Took two steps on her own, then was falling forward. The bodies around her seemed far away, and out of them all she recognized the one she was falling towards.

"Sarge."

"You're one tired baby."

"Am I?" she said, but he didn't understand.

She was overexposed, close to shock, sputtering breath. She looked just about dead. She was dripping water, and alive. Sarge caught her when she crumpled. Sick and proud, her eyes blinked up at his. He held her tight as if it would keep her with him forever, then let go of that impossibility and his touch became gentle. Did it, she said. He lifted her in his arms.